Thomas Percy

Reliques of Ancient English Poetry Consisting of Old Heroic Ballads, Songs, and Other Pieces of Earlier Poets

Volume the Second

Thomas Percy

Reliques of Ancient English Poetry Consisting of Old Heroic Ballads, Songs, and Other Pieces of Earlier Poets
Volume the Second

ISBN/EAN: 9783744793605

Printed in Europe, USA, Canada, Australia, Japan

Cover: Foto ©Andreas Hilbeck / pixelio.de

More available books at **www.hansebooks.com**

RELIQUES

OF

ANCIENT ENGLISH POETRY:

CONSISTING OF

Old Heroic BALLADS, SONGS, and other
PIECES of our earlier POETS,

(Chiefly of the LYRIC kind.)

Together with some few of later Date.

THE SECOND EDITION.

VOLUME THE SECOND.

LONDON:

Printed for J. DODSLEY in Pall-Mall.
MDCCLXVII.

(i)

CONTENTS OF VOLUME THE SECOND.

BOOK THE FIRST.

BOOK THE SECOND.

         6. *Gascoigne's*

CONTENTS.

BOOK THE THIRD.

4. The

CONTENTS. iii

Though

* Lord Thomas and Fair Annet, see in Vol. 3. p. 240.
The Heir of Lynne, and Corydon's doleful Knell, see
above, p. 126. 263.

Though some make slight of Libels, yet you may
see by them how the wind sits : As take a straw and
throw it up into the air, you may see by that which
way the wind is, which you shall not do by casting up
a stone. More solid things do not shew the complexion
of the times so well as Ballads and Libels.

Selden's Table-talk.

Reliques

ANCIENT
SONGS AND BALLADS,
&c.

SERIES THE SECOND.
BOOK I.

I.

RICHARD OF ALMAIGNE,

" *A ballad made by one of the adherents to Simon de*
" *Montfort, earl of Leicester, soon after the battle of Lewes,*
" *which was fought May 14, 1264,*"
—*affords a curious specimen of ancient Satire, and shews*
that the liberty, assumed by the good people of this realm, of

abusing

abusing their kings and princes at pleasure, is a privilege of very long standing.

To render this antique libel intelligible, the reader is to understand that just before the battle of Lewes *which proved so fatal to the interests of Henry* III. *the barons had offered his brother* Richard King *of the* Romans 30,000l. *to procure a peace upon such terms, as would have divested Henry of all his regal power, and therefore the treaty proved abortive.—The consequences of that battle are well known : the king, prince Edward his son, his brother Richard, and many of his friends fell into the hands of their enemies : while two great barons of the king's party, John earl of Warren, and Hugh Bigot the king's Justiciary, had been glad to escape into France.*

In the 1st stanza the aforesaid sum of THIRTY THOUSAND *pounds is alluded to; but with the usual misrepresentation of party malevolence, is asserted to have been the exorbitant demand of the king's brother.*

With regard to the 2d st. the Reader is to note that Richard, along with the earldom of Cornwall, had the honours of WALINGFORD *and* Eyre *confirmed to him on his marriage with* Sanchia *daughter of the Count of Provence, in* 1243.
——WINDSOR *castle was the chief fortress belonging to the king, and had been garrisoned by foreigners : a circumstance, which furnishes out the burthen of each stanza.*

The 3d st. very humorously alludes to some little fact, which history hath not condescended to record. Earl Richard possessed some large WATER-MILLS *near* Istleworth, *which had been plundered and burnt by the Londoners : in these perhaps by way of defence he had lodged a party of soldiers.*

The 4th st. is of obvious interpretation : Richard, who had been elected king of the Romans in 1256, *and had afterwards gone over to take possession of his dignity, was in the year* 1259 *about to return into England, when the barons raised a popular clamour, that he was bringing with him foreigners to over-run the kingdom : upon which he was*

forced

forced to difmifs almoft all his followers, otherwife the barons would have oppofed his landing.

In the 5th ft. the writer regrets the efcape of the Earl of Warren, and in the 6th and 7th fts. infinuates that if he and Sir Hugh Bigot once fell into the hands of their adverfaries, they fhould never more return home. A circumftance, which fixes the date of this ballad; for in the year 1265 both thefe noblemen landed in South Wales, and the royal party foon after gained the afcendant. See Holingfhed, Rapin, &c.

The following is copied from a very ancient MS. in the Britifh Mufeum. [Harl. MSS. 2253. f. 23.] This MS. is judged, from the peculiarities of the writing, to be not later than the time of Richard II; th being every where expreffed by the charaΠer þ; the ẏ is pointed after the Saxon manner, and the î hath an oblique ftroke over it.

Prefixed to this ancient libel on government is a fmall defign, which the engraver intended fhould correfpond with the fubjeΠ. On the one fide a Satyr, (emblem of Petulance and Ridicule) is trampling on the enfigns of Royalty; on the other FaΠion under the mafque of Liberty is exciting Ignorance and Popular Rage to deface the Royal Image; which ftands on a pedeftal infcribed MAGNA CHARTA, *to denote that the rights of the king, as well as thofe of the people, are founded on the laws; and that to attack one, is in effeΠ to demolifh both.*

SITTETH alle ftille, ant herkneth to me;
The kyng of Alemaigne, bi mi leaute,
Thritti thoufent pound afkede he
For te make the pees in the countre,
  Ant fo he dude more.   5
 Richard, thah thou be ever trichard,
 Tricthen fhalt thou never more.

Ver. 2. kyn. MS.

Richard of Alemaigne, whil that he wes kyng,
He ſpende al is treſour opon ſwyvyng,
Haveth he nout of Walingford oferlȳng,   10
Let him habbe, aſe he brew, bale to dryng,
   Maugre Wyndeſore.
  Richard, thah thou be ever, &c.

The kyng of Alemaigne wende do ful wel,
He faiſede the mulne for a caſtel,   15
With hare ſharpe ſwerdes he grounde the ſtel,
He wende that the ſayles were mangonel
   To helpe Wyndeſore.
  Richard, thah thou be ever, &c.

The kyng of Alemaigne gederede ys hoſt,   20
Makede him a caſtel of a mulne poſt,
Wende with is prude, ant is muchele boſt,
Brohte from Alemayne monȳ ſori goſt
   To ſtore Wyndeſore.
  Richard, thah thou be ever, &c.   25

By God, that is aboven ous, he dude muche ſynne,
That lette paſſen over ſee the erl of Warynne :
He hath robbed Engelond, the mores, ant th fenne,
The gold, ant the ſelver, and ȳ-boren henne,
   For love of Wyndeſore.   30
  Richard, thah thou be ever, &c.

Sire

Sire Simond de Mountfort hath fuore bi ẏs chȳn,
Hevede he nou here the erl of Warẏn,
Shuld he never more come to is ẏn,
Ne with fheld, ne with fpere, ne with other gẏn,   35
   To help of Wyndefore.
  Richard, thah thou be ever, &c.

Sire Simond de Montfort hath fuore bi ys 'fot',
Hevede he nou here Sire Hue de Bigot :
Al he fhulde grante here twelfmoneth fcot,   40
Shulde he never more with his fot pot
   To helpe Wyndefore.
  Richard, thah thou be ever trichard,
   Tricthen fhalt thou never more.

Ver. 38. top or cop.
Ver. 40. g'te here. *MS. i. e. grant their. Vid. Glofs.*

*** *The* SERIES OF POEMS *given in this volume will
fhew the gradual changes of the* ENGLISH *Language thro'
a fucceffion of* FIVE HUNDRED *years. This and the following article may be confidered as fpecimens of it in its moft
early ftate, almoft as foon as it ceafed to be* SAXON. *Indeed the annals of this kingdom are written in the Saxon
language almoft down to the end of K. Stephen's reign :
for fo far reaches the* SAXON CHRONICLE ; *within little
more than a century of the date of this poem.*

     II. ON

II.

ON THE DEATH OF K. EDWARD
THE FIRST.

We have here an early attempt at Elegy. EDWARD I.
*died July 7. 1307, in the 3 th year of his reign, and 69th
of his age. This poem appears to have been compofed foon
after his death. According to the modes of thinking peculiar to thofe times, the writer dwells more upon his devotion, than his fkill in government, and pays lefs attention to
the martial and political abilities of this great monarch,
in which he had no equal, than to fome little weaknefses of
fuperftition, which he had in common with all his cotempo-
raries. The king had in the decline of life vowed an expedition to the holy land, but finding his end approach, he dedi-
cated the fum of 32,000l. to the maintenance of a large body
of knights (140 fay hiftorians, 80 fays our poet,) who were
to carry his heart with them into Paleftine. This dying command of the king was never performed. Our poet with the
honeft prejudices of an Englishman, attributes this failure
to the advice of the king of France, whofe daughter Ifabel
our young monarch immediately married. But the truth is,
Edward and his deftructive favourite Piers Gaveston fpent
the money upon their pleafures.—— To do the greater honour
to the memory of his heroe, our poet puts his eloge in the
mouth of the Pope ; with the fome poetic licence, as a more
modern bard would have introduced Britannia, or the Genius of Europe pouring forth his praifes.*

*This antique Elegy is extracted from the fame MS vo-
lume, as the preceding article ; is found with the fame peculiarities of writing and orthography ; and tho' written
at near the diftance of half a century contains little or no*

varia-

variation of idiom: whereas the next following poem by Chaucer, which was probably written not more than 50 or 60 years after this, exhibits almost a new language. This seems to countenance the opinion of some antiquaries, that this great poet made considerable innovations in his mother tongue, and introduced many terms, and new modes of speech from other languages.

ALLE, that beoth of huerte trewe,
　A stounde herkneth to my song
Of duel, that Deth hath diht us newe,
　That maketh me syke, ant sorewe among;
Of a knyht, that wes so strong,　　　　　5
　Of wham God hath don ys wille;
Me-thuncheth that deth hath don us wrong,
　That he so sone shall ligge stille.

Al Englond ahte for te knowe
　Of wham that song is, that y synge;　　10
Of Edward kyng, that lith so lowe,
　Zent al this world is nome con springe:
Treweft mon of alle thinge,
　Ant in werre war ant wys,
For him we ahte oure honden wrynge,　　15
　Of Criftendome he ber the prys.

Byfore that oure kyng wes ded,
　He fpek afe mon that wes in care,
" Clerkes, knyhtes, barons, he fayde,
　" Y charge ou by oure fware,　　　　　20

" That

" That ye to Engelonde be trewe.
    " Y deze, y ne may lyven na more;
" Helpeth mi fone, ant crouneth him newe,
    " For he is neft to buen y-core.

" Ich biqueth myn herte aryht,   25
    " That hit be write at mi devys,
" Oves the fee that Hue * be diht,
    " With fourfcore knyhtes al of prys,
" In werre that buen war ant wys,
    " Azein the hethene for te fyhte,   30
" To wynne the croiz that lowe lys,
    " Myfelf ycholde zef that y myhte."

Kyng of Fraunce, thou hevedeft ' finne,'
    That thou the counfail woldeft fonde,
To latte the wille of ' Edward kyng'   35
    To wende to the holy londe:
That oure kyng hede take on honde
    All Engelond to zeme ant wyffe,
To wenden in to the holy londe
    To wynnen us heveriche bliffe.   40

The meffager to the pope com,
    And feyde that oure kynge wes ded;
Ys oune hond the lettre he nom,
    Ywis his herte wes ful gret:

The

---

* *Thisis probably the name of fome perfon, who was to prefide over this bufinefs.* Ver. 33. funne. *MS.* Ver. 35. kyng Edward. *MS.* Ver. 43. ys is *probably a contraction of* in hys *or* yn his.

The Pope him felf the lettre redde,   45
   Ant fpec a word of gret honour.
" Alas ! he feid, is Edward ded ?
   " Of Criftendome he ber the flour."

The Pope to is chaumbre wende,
   For dol ne mihte he fpeke na more ;   50
Ant after cardinals he fende,
   That muche couthen of Criftes lore,
Bothe the laffe, ant eke the more,
   Bed hem bothe rede ant fynge :
Gret deol me myhte fe thore,   55
   Mony mon is honde wrynge.

The Pope of Peyters ftod at is maffe
   With ful gret folempnetè,
Ther me con the foule bleffe :
   " Kyng Edward honoured thou be :   60
" God love thi fone come after the,
   " Bringe to ende that thou haft bygonne,
" The holy crois y-mad of tre,
   " So fain thou woldeft hit hav y-wonne.

" Jerufalem, thou haft i-lore   65
   " The flour of al chivalrie
" Now kyng Edward liveth na more :
   " Alas ! that he zet fhulde deye !

                " He

Ver. 55. Me, i. e. Men. fo in Robert of Gloucefter paffim.

" He wolde ha rered up ful heyze
    " Oure banners, that bueth broht to grounde ;
" Wel! longe we mowe clepe and crie   70
    " Er we a fuch kyng han y-founde."

Nou is Edward of Carnarvan
    King of Engelond al aplyht,
God lete him ner be worfe man
    Then is fader, ne laffe of myht,   75
To holden is pore men to ryht,
    And underftonde good counfail,
Al Engelong for to wyffe ant dyht;
    Of gode knyhtes darh him nout fail.

Thah mi tonge were mad of ftel,   80
    Ant min herte yzote of bras,
The godnefs myht y never telle,
    That with kyng Edward was :
Kyng, as thou art cleped conquerour,
    In uch bataille thou hadeft prys ;   85
God bringe thi foule to the honour,
    That ever wes, ant ever ys.*

*Here follow in the original three lines more, which,
as apparently fpurious, we chufe to throw to the bottom of the
Page, viz.*

That lafteth ay withouten ende,
    Bidde we God, ant oure Ledy to thilke bliffe
Jefus us fende.   Amen.

III. AN

III.

AN ORIGINAL BALLAD BY CHAUCER.

This little sonnet, which hath escaped all the editors of Chaucer's works, is now printed for the first time from an ancient MS in the Pepysian library, that contains many other poems of its venerable author. The versification is of that species, which the French call RONDEAU, *very naturally englished by our honest countrymen* ROUND O. *Tho' so early adopted by them, our ancestors had not the honour of inventing it: Chaucer picked it up, along with other better things, among the neighbouring nations. A fondness for laborious trifles hath always prevailed in the dawn of literature. The ancient Greek poets had their* WINGS *and* AXES : *the great father of English poesy may therefore be pardoned one poor solitary* RONDEAU.—*Dan Geofrey Chaucer died Oct. 25. 1400. aged 72.*

I. 1.

YOURE two eyn will sle me sodenly,
    I may the beaute of them not sustene,
So wendeth it thorowout my herte kene.

2.

And but your words will helen hastely
My hertis wound, while that it is grene,
Youre two eyn will sle me sodenly.

3.

Upon my trouth I sey yow feithfully,
That ye ben of my liffe and deth the quene ;
For with my deth the trouth shal be sene.
    Youre two eyn, &c.

II. 1.

So hath youre beauty fro your herte chafed
Pitee, that me n' availeth not to pleyn ;
For daunger halt your mercy in his cheyne.

2.

Giltlefs my deth thus have ye purchafed ;
I fey yow foth, me nedeth not to fayn :
So hath your beaute fro your herte chafed.

4.

Alas, that nature hath in yow compafsed
So grete beaute, that no man may atteyn
To mercy, though he fterve for the peyn.
　　　So hath youre beaute, &c.

III. 1.

Syn I fro love efcaped am fo fat,
I nere thinke to ben in his prifon lene ;
Syn I am fre, I counte hym not a bene.

2.

He may anfwere, and fey this and that,
I do no fors, I fpeak ryght as I mene ;
Syn I fro love efcaped am fo fat.

3.

Love hath my name i-ftrike out of his fclat,
And he is ftrike out of my bokes clene :
For ever mo * this is non other mene.
　　　Syn I fro love efcaped, &c.

* Ther.

IV. THE

IV.

THE TURNAMENT OF TOTTENHAM:

" OR, THE WOOEING, WINNING, AND WEDDING
" OF TIBBE, THE REEY'S DAUGHTER THERE."

It does honour to the good sense of this nation, that while all Europe was captivated with the bewitching charms of Chivalry and Romance, two of our writers in the rudest times could see thro' the false glare that surrounded them, and discover whatever was absurd in them both. Chaucer wrote his Rhyme of sir Thopas in ridicule of the latter, and in the following poem we have a humourous burlesque of the former. Without pretending to decide, whether the institution of chivalry was upon the whole useful or pernicious in the rude ages, a question that has lately employed many fine pens, it evidently encouraged a vindictive spirit, and gave such force to the custom of duelling, that it will probably never be worn out. This, together with the fatal consequences which often attended the diversion of the Turnament, was sufficient to render it obnoxious to the graver part of mankind. Accordingly the Church early denounced its censures against it, and the State was often prevailed on to attempt its suppression. But fashion and opinion are superior to authority; and the proclamations against Tilting were as little regarded in those times, as the laws against Duelling are in these. This did not escape the discernment of our poet, who easily perceived that inveterate opinions must be attacked by other weapons, than proclamations and censures; he accordingly made use of the keen one of* RIDICULE. *With this view he has here introduced, with admirable humour, a parcel of clowns, imitating all the solemnities of the Tournay. Here we have the*
regular

---

* See [Mr. Hurd's] Letters on Chivalry, 8vo. 1762. Memoires de la Chevalierie par M. de la Curne des Palais, 1759. 2 tom. 12mo. &c.

regular challenge—the appointed day—the lady for the prize —the formal preparations—the display of armour—the scucheons and devices—the oaths taken on entering the lists—the various accidents of the encounter—the victor leading off the prize,—and, the magnificent feasting,—with all the other solemn fopperies, that usually attended the exercise of the barriers. And how acutely the sharpness of the author's humour must have been felt in those days, we may learn, from what we can perceive of its keenness now, when time has so much blunted the edge of his ridicule.

THE TURNAMENT OF TOTTENHAM *was published from an ancient MS. in* 1631, 4to, *by the rev. Whilhem Bedwell, rector of Tottenham, and one of the translators of the Bible: he tells us it was written by one Gilbert Pilkington, thought to have been some time parson of the same parish, and author of another piece intitled* Paſſio Domini Jeſu Chriſti. *Bedwell, who was eminently skilled in the oriental languages, appears to have been but little conversant with the ancient writers in his own, and he so little entered into the spirit of the poem he was publishing that he contends for its being a serious narrative of a real event, and thinks it must have been written before the time of Edward* III, *because Turnaments were prohibited in that reign.* "I do "verily beleeve, says he, that this Turnament was acted "before this proclamation of K. Edward. For how durst "any to attempt to do that, although in sport, which was "so straightly forbidden, both by the civill and ecclesiasticall "power? For although they fought not with lances, yet, as "our authour sayth, "It was no childrens game." And "what would have become of him, thinke you, which "should have slayne another in this manner of jeasting? "Would he not, trow you, have been HANG'D FOR IT "IN EARNEST? YEA, AND HAVE BENE BURIED LIKE "A DOGGE?" *It is however well known that Turnaments were in use down to the reign of Elizabeth.*

Without pretending to ascertain the date of this Poem, the obsoleteness of the style shews it to be very ancient: It will appear from the sameness of orthography in the above ex-

I

tract

*tract that Bedwell has generally reduced that of the poem to
the standard of his own times; yet, notwithstanding this innovation, the phraseology and idiom shew it to be of an early
date. The poem had in other respects suffered by the ignorance of transcribers, and therefore a few attempts are here
made to restore the text, by amending some corruptions, and
removing some redundancies; but lest this freedom should incur censure, the former readings are retained in the margin.
A farther liberty is also taken, what is here given for the
concluding line of each stanza, stood in the former edition divided as two: e. g.*

> *" Of them that were doughty,*
> *" And hardy indeed :"*

*but they seemed most naturally to run into one, and the fre-
quent neglect of rhyme in the former of them seemed to prove
that the author intended no such division.*

OF all ' the ' kene conquerours to carpe is our kinde;
Of fell fighting folke ' a ' ferly we finde;
The Turnament of Tottenham have I in minde;
It were harme such hardinesse were holden behinde.

> In story as we reade,   5
> Of Hawkin, of Harry,
> Of Timkin, of Terry,
Of them that were doughty, and hardy in deed.

It befell in Tottenham on a deare day,
There was made a shurting by the highway: 10
Thither come all the men of that countray
Of Hiffelton, of High-gate, and of Hakenay,

     And

And all the fweete fwinkers :
There hopped Hawkin,
There daunced Dawkin,   15
There trumped Timkin, and were true drinkers.

'When ' the day was gone, and eve-fong paft,
That they fhould reck'n their fkot, and their counts caft,
Perkin the potter into the preffe paft,
And fay'd, Randill the reve, a daughter thou haft,   20
    Tibbe thy deare,
        Therefore faine weet would I,
        Whether thefe fellowes or I,
        Or which of all this batchelery
Were the beft worthy to wed her his fere.   25

Upftart the gadlings with their lang ftaves,
And fayd, Randill the reve, lo ! the ladde raves,
How proudly among us thy daughter he craves,
And we are richer men then he, and more good haves,
    Of cattell, and of corne.   30
        * Then fayd Perkin, ' I have hight
        ' To Tibbe in my right
' To be ready to fight, and thoughe it were to morne.

                                            Then

Ver. 17. Till. *P. C.*   *Ver.* 25. in his fere. *P. C.*
  * *The latter part of this ftanza feemed embarraffed and redundant, we
have therefore ventured to contract it. It ftood thus ;*
        Then fayd Perkin, to Tibbe I have hight
        That I will bee alwaies ready in my right,
        With a flayle for to fight
    This day feaven-night, and thought it were to morne.
*The two laft lines feem in part to be borrowed from the following ftanza,
where they come in more properly.*

Then fayd Randill the refe, ' Ever' be he waryd
That about this carp'ng lenger would be taryd ; 35
I would not my daughter that fhe were miskaryd,
But at her moft worfhip I would fhe were maryd,
   For the turnament fhall beginne
     This day feav'n-night,
     With a flayle for to fight, 40
And he, that is moft of might, fhall brok her with winne.

He that bear'th him beft in the turnament,
Shall be granted the gree, by the common affent,
For to winne my daughter with doughtineffe of dent,
And Copple my brood-hen, that was brought out of Kent,
   And my dunned cow : 46
     For no fpence will I fpare ;
     For no cattell will I care ;
He fhall have my gray mare, and my fpotted fow.

There was many a bold lad their bodyes to bede ; 50
Then they take their leave, and hamward they hede,
And all the weeke after they gayed her wede,
Till it come to the day, that they fhould do their dede :
   They armed them in mattes ;
     They fet on their nowlls 55
     Good blacke bowlls,
To keep their powlls from battering of battes.
   Vol. II.   C   They

They fewed hem in fheepfkinnes, for they fhould not breft;
And every ilke of hem a black hatte, inftead of a creft,
A bafket or panyer before on their breft,   60
And a flayle in their hande, for to fight`preft,
    Forthe con they fare.
        There was kid mickle force,
        Who·fhould beft fend his corfe ;
He, that had no good horfe, borrowed him a mare. 65

Sich another clothing have I not feene oft,
When all the great company riding to the croft,
Tibbe on a gray-mare was fette up on-loft,
Upon a facke-full of fenvy, for fhe fhould fit foft,
    And led till the gappe :   70
        Forther would fhe not than,
        For the love of no man,
Till Copple her brood-hen wer brought into her lappe.

A gay girdle Tibbe had borrowed for the nonce ;
And a garland on her head full of ruell bones ;   75
And a brouch on her breft full of fapphyre ftones,
The holyroode tokening was written for the nonce ;
    For no fpendings ‘ they had fpar’d :’
        When jolly Jenkin wift her thare,
        He gurd fo faft his gray mare,   80
'That fhe let a fowkin fare at the rere-ward.

                     I make

Ver. 59. ilken. *P. C.*   *Ver.* 65. *Mares were never ufed in Chivalry: It was beneath the dignity of a knight to ride any thing but a
ftallion. V. Memoires de la Chevalerie.*
    Ver. 67. *perhaps*, rid into.   *Ver.* 78. would they fparc. *P. C.*

I make a vowe, quoth ' he, my capul' is comen of kinde
I fhall fall five in the field, and I my flaile finde.
I make a vowe, quoth Hudde, I fhall not leve behinde;
May I meet with lyard or bayard the blinde,   85
        I wote I fhall them grieve.
            I make a vowe, quoth Hawkin,
            May I meete with Dawkin,
For all his rich kin, his flaile I fhall him reve.

I make a vow, quoth Gregge, Tibbe thou fhall fee   90
Which of all the bachelery graunted is the gree :
I fhall fkomfit hem all, for the love of thee,
In what place that I come, they fhall have doubt of mee;
        For I am armd at the full :
            In my armes I beare wele   95
            A dough-trough, and a pele,
A faddle without a pannele, with a fleece of wooll.

Now go downe, quoth Dudman, and beare me bet about,
I make a vow, they fhall abye that I finde out,
Have I twice or thrice ridden thorough the rout,   100
In what place that I come, of me they fhall ha doubt,
        Mine armes bene fo clere;
            I beare a riddle and a rake,
            Powder'd with the brenning drake,
And three cantles of a cake, in ilka cornere.   105
                C 2   I make

Ver. 82. Originally it ftood thus,
    I make a vowe, quoth Tibbe, copple is comen of kinde;
but as this evidently has no connection with the lines that follow, the Editor propofes the above emendation. Ver. 98. Perhaps ' I fhall ' go downe.

I make a vowe, quoth Tirry, and fweare by my crede,
Saw thou never young boy forther his body bede;
For when they fight fafteft, and moft are in drede,
I fhall take Tib by the hand, and away her lede :
  Then bin mine armes beft ;   110
   I beare a pilch of ermin,   '
   Powderd with a cats fkinne,
The cheefe is of perchmine, that ftond'th on the creft.

I make a vow, quoth Dudman, and fweare by the ftra,
While I am moft merry, thou gettſt her not fwa ; 115
For fhe is well fhapen, as light as a rae,
There is no capull in this mile before her will ga :
  Shee will me not beguile ;
   I dare foothly fay,
   Shee will be a Monday   120
Fro Hiffelton to Hacknay, nought other halfe mile.

I make a vow, quoth Perkin, thou carpft of cold roft ;
I will wirke wiflier without any boaft ;
Five of the beft capulls, that are in this hoft,
I will hem lead away by another coft ;   125
  And then laugh Tibbe,
   Wi' loo, boyes, here is hee,
   That will fight and not flee,
For I am in my jollity ; Ioo foorth, Tibbe.
             When

Ver. 113. pechmine. P. C. Ver. 127. We loo. P. C.

When they had their oathes made, forth can they ‘ he’ 130
With flailes, and harniſſe, and trumps made of tre :
There were all the bachelers of that countre ;
They were dight in aray, as themſelves would be :
     Their banner was full bright,
        Of an old rotten fell,   135
        The cheeſe was a plowmell,
And the ſhadow of a bell, quartered with the moone-light.

I wot it was no childrens game, when they togither mette,
When ilka freke in the field on his fellow bette,
And layd on ſtifly, for nothing would they lette,   140
And fought ferly faſt, till ‘ theire’ horſes ſwette ;
     And few wordes were ſpoken :
        There were flailes all to ſlatterd,
        There were ſhields all to clatterd,
Bowles and diſhes all to batterd, and many heads broken.

There was clenking of cart-ſaddles, and clattering of
    cannes,   146
Of fell frekes in the field, broken were their fannes ;
Of ſome were the heads broken, of ſome the braine-pannes,
And evill were they beſene, ere they went thance,
     With ſwipping of ſwipples :   150
        The ladds were ſo weary for fought,
        That they might fight no more on-loft,
But creeped about in the croft, as they were crooked
    cripples.
          C 3   Perkin

Perkin was fo weary, that he beganne to lowte,
Help, Hudde, I am dead in this ilk rowte: 155
An horfe for forty pennys, a good and a ftowte ;
That I may lightly come of mine owne owte ;
    For no coft will I fpare.
      He ftarte up as a fnaile,
       And hent a capull by the taile,   160
And raught of Daukin his flayle, and wanne him a mare.

Perkin wan five, and Hudde wan twa :
Glad and blithe they were, that they ' had ' done fa :
They would have them to Tibbe, and prefent her with tha :
The capuls were fo weary, that they might not ga, 165
    But ftill can they ' ftonde.'
      Alas ! quoth Hudde, my joy I leefe
      Mee had lever then a ftone of cheefe,
That deare Tibbe had all thefe, and wift it were my fonde.

Perkin turned him about in the ilk throng,   170
He fought frefhly, for he had reft him long ;
He was ware of Tirry take Tibbe by the hond,
And would have led her away with a love-fong ;
    And Perkin after ran,
      And off his capull he him drowe,   175
      And gave him of his flayle inowe ;
Then te, he! quoth Tibbe, and lowe, ye are a doughty man.
                   Thus

Ver. 164. would not have. *P. C, Ver.* 166. ftand. *P. C.*

Thus they tugged, and they rugged till it was nigh night:
All the wives of Tottenham come to fee that fight ;
To fetch home their hufbands, that were them trough
    plight, 180
With wifpes and kixes, that was a rich fight ;
    Her hufbands home to fetch.
      And fome they had in armes,
      That were feeble wretches,
And fome on wheel-barrowes, and fome on critches. 185

They gatherd Perkin about on every fide,
And grant him there the gree, the more was his pride :
Tib and hee, with great mirth, hameward can ride,
And were all night togither, till the morrow tide ;
    And to church they went : 190
      So well his needs he has fped,
      That deare Tibbe he fhall wed ;
The cheefemen that her hither lead, were of the turnament.

To the rich feaft come many for the nonce :
Some come hop-halte, and fome tripping thither on the
    ftones ; 195
Some with a ftaffe in his hand, and fome two at once ;
Of fome were the heads broken; of fome the fhoulderbones:
    With forrow come they thither ;
      Wo was Hawkin ; wo was Harry ;
      Wo was Tymkin ; wo was Tirry ; 200
And fo was all the company, but yet they come togither.

C 4

A

At that feaft were they ferved in rich aray ;
Every five and five had a cokeney ;
And fo they fat in jollity all the long day .
Tibbe at night, I trowe, had a fimple aray ;   205
Mickle mirth was them among :
In every corner of the houfe
Was melody delicious,
For to hear precious of fix mens fong.

V.

FOR THE VICTORY AT AGINCOURT.

That our plain and martial anceftors could wield their fwords much better than their pens, will appear from the following homely Rhymes, which were drawn up by fome poet laureat of thofe days to celebrate the immortal victory gained at Agincourt, Oct. 25, 1415. This fong or hymn is given meerly as a curiofity, and is printed from a MS copy in the Pepys collection, vol. I. folio. It is there accompanied with the mufical notes, which are copied in a fmall plate at the end of this volume.

Deo gratias Anglia redde pro victoria !

OWRE kynge went forth to Normandy,
With grace and myzt of chivalry ;
The God for hym wrouzt marveloufly,
Wherefore Englonde may calle, and cry   5
Deo gratias :
Deo gratias Anglia redde pro victoria.

He fette a fege, the fothe for to fay,
To Harflue toune with ryal aray ;
That toune he wan, and made a fray,   10
That Fraunce fhall rywe tyl domes day.
> *Deo gratias, &c.*

Then went owre kynge, with alle his ofte,
Thorowe Fraunce for all the Frenfhe bofte ;
He fpared ' for' drede of lefte, ne moft,   15
Tyl he come to Agincourt cofte.
> *Deo gratias, &c.*

Than for fothe that knyzt comely
In Agincourt feld he fauzt manly,
Thorow grace of God moft myzty   20
He had bothe the felde, and the victory.
> *Deo gratias, &c.*

Ther dukys, and erlys, lorde and barone,
Were take, and flayne, and that wel fone,
And fome were ledde in to Lundone   25
With joye, and merthe, and grete renone.
> *Deo gratias, &c.*

Now gracious God he fave owre kynge,
His peple, and all his wel wyllynge,
Gef him gode lyfe, and gode endynge,   30
That we with merth mowe favely fynge
> *Deo gratias :*
> *Deo gratias Anglia redde pro victoria.*

VI.

THE NOT-BROWNE MAYD.

The sentimental beauties of this ancient ballad have always recommended it to Readers of taste, notwithstanding the rust of antiquity, which obscures the style and expression. Indeed if it had no other merit, than the having afforded the ground-work to Prior's HENRY AND EMMA, *this ought to preserve it from oblivion. That we are able to give it in a more correct manner, than almost any other Poem in these volumes, is owing to the great care and exactness of the accurate Editor of the* PROLUSIONS *8vo. 1760; who has formed the text from two copies found in two different editions of Arnolde's Chronicle, a book supposed to be first printed about 1521. From the correct Copy in the Prolusions the following is printed, with a few additional improvements gathered from another edition of Arnolde's book * preserved in the public Library at Cambridge. All the various readings of this Copy will be found here, either received into the text, or noted in the margin. The references to the* Prolusions *will shew where they occur. It does honour to the critical sagacity of that gentleman, that almost all his conjectural readings are found to be the established ones of this edition. In our ancient folio MS. described in the preface is a very corrupt and defective copy of this ballad, which yet afforded a great improvement in one line that will be found in its due place.*

It has been a much easier task to settle the text of this poem, than to ascertain its date. Mat. Prior published it in the folio edition of his poems, 1718, as then " 300 years old." In making this decision he was probably guided by the learned Wanley, whose judgment in matters of this nature was most consummate. For that whatever related to the reprinting of this old piece was referred to Wanley, appears from two letters

of

---

* This (which a learned friend supposes to be the first Edition) is in folio : the folios are numbered at the bottom of the leaf : the Song begins at folio 75.

of Prior's preserved in the British Museum [Harl. MSS. Nᵒ 3777.] The Editor of the Prolusions thinks it cannot be older than the year 1500, because in Sir Thomas More's tale of THE SERJEANT, *&c. which was written about that time, there appears a sameness of rhythmus and orthography, and a very near affinity of words and phrases with those of this ballad. But this reasoning is not conclusive; for if Sir Thomas More made this ballad his model, as is very likely, that will account for the sameness of measure, and in some respect for that of words and phrases, even tho' this had been written long before: and as for the orthography, it is well known that the old Printers reduced that of most books to the standard of their own times. Indeed it is hardly probable that an antiquarian like Arnolde would have inserted it among his historical Collections, if it had been then a modern piece; at least he would have been apt to have named its author. But to shew how little can be inferred from a resemblance of rhythmus or style, the editor of these volumes has in his ancient folio MS. a poem on the Victory of Floddenfield, written in the same numbers, with the same alliterations, and in orthography, phraseology, and style nearly resembling the Visions of Pierce Plowman, which are yet known to have been composed above 160 years before that battle. As this poem is a great curiosity, we shall give a few of the introductory lines,*

    " Grant gracious God, grant me this time,
    " That I may 'say, or I cease, thy selven to please;
    " And Mary his mother, that maketh this world;
    " And all the seemlie saints, that sitten in heaven;
    " I will carpe of kings, that conquered full wide,
    " That dwelled in this land, that was alyes noble;
    " Henry the seventh, that soveraigne lord, &c.

With regard to the date of the following ballad, we have taken a middle course, neither placed it so high as Wanley and Prior, nor quite so low as the editor of the Prolusions: we should have followed the latter in dividing every other line into two, but that the whole would then have taken up more room, than could be allowed it in this volume.

B E

BE it ryght, or wrong, thefe men among
    On women do complayne ;
Affyrmynge this, how that it is
    A labour fpent in vayne,
To love them wele ; for never a dele   5
    They love a man agayne :
For late a man do what he can,
    Theyr favour to attayne,
Yet, yf a newe do them perfue,
    Theyr firft true lover than   10
Laboureth for nought ; for from her thought
    He is a banyfhed man,

I fay nat, nay, but that all day
    It is bothe writ and fayd
That womans faith is, as who fayth,   15
    All utterly decayd ;
But, nevertheleffe, ryght good wytnèffe
    In this cafe might be layd,
That they love true, and continùe :
    Recorde the not-browne mayde :   20
Which, when her love came, her to prove,
    To her to make his mone,
Wolde nat depart ; for in her hart
    She loved but hym alone.

Than

Ver. 2, Woman. *Prolufions.*   *Ver.* 11. her. *i. e. their.*

Than betwaine us late us dyfcus 25
  What was all the manere
Betwayne them two : we wyll alfo
  Tell all the payne, and fere,
That fhe was in. Nowe I begyn,
  So that ye me anfwère ; 30
Wherfore, all ye, that prefent be
  I pray you, gyve an ere.
" I am the knyght ; I come by nyght,
  As fecret as I can ;
Sayinge, Alas ! thus ftandeth the cafe, 35
  I am a banyfhed man."

SHE:

  And I your wyll for to fulfyll
  In this wyll nat refufe ;
Truftying to fhewe, in wordès fewe,
  That men have an yll ufe 40
(To theyr own fhame) women to blame,
  And caufeleffe them accufe :
Therfore to you I anfwere nowe,
  All women to excufe,—
Myne owne hart dere, with you what chere ? 45
  I pray you, tell anone ;
For, in my mynde, of all mankynde
  I love but you alone.

HE.

HE.

It ſtandeth ſo ; a dede is do
   Wherof grete harme ſhall growe: 50
My deſtiny is for to dy
   A ſhamefull deth, I trowe;
Or elles to fle : the one muſt be;
   None other way I knowe,
But to withdrawe as an outlawe,   55
   And take me to my bowe.
Wherfore, adue, my owne hart true!
   None other rede I can ;
For I muſt to the grene wode go,
   Alone, a banyſhed man.   60

SHE.

O lord, what is this worldys blyſſe,
   That changeth as the mone !
My ſomers day in luſty may
   Is derked before the none.
I here you ſay, farewell ; Nay, nay,   65
   We départ nat ſo ſone :
Why ſay ye ſo ? wheder wyll ye go ?
   Alas ! what have ye done ?
All my welfàre to ſorrowe and care
   Sholde chaunge, yf ye were gone ;   70
For, in my mynde, of all mankynde
   I love but you alone.

IIE.

Ver. 63. The ſomers. *Pɩol.*

HE.

I can beleve, it ſhall you greve,
   And ſomewhat you dyſtrayne ;
But, aftyrwarde, your paynes harde   75
   Within a day or twayne
Shall ſone aſlake ; and ye ſhall take
   Comfort to you agayne.
Why ſholde ye ought ? for, to make thought,
   Your labour were in vayne.   80
And thus I do ; and pray you to,
   As hartely, as I can ;
For I muſt to the grene wode go,
   Alone, a banyſhed man.

SHE.

Now, ſyth that ye have ſhewed to me   85
   The ſecret of your mynde,
I ſhall be playne to you agayne,
   Lyke as ye ſhall me fynde :
Syth it is ſo, that ye wyll go,
   I wolle not leve behynde ;   90
Shall never be ſayd, the not-browne mayd
   Was to her love unkynde :
Make you redy, for ſo am I,
   Allthough it were anone ;
   For, in my mynde, of all mankynde   95
   I love but you alone.

HE.

Ver. 91. Shall it never. *Prol.*   Ver. 94. Although. *Prol.*

HE.

Yet I you rede to take good hede
  What men wyll thynke, and fay:
Of yonge, and olde it fhall be tolde,
  That ye be gone away;   100
Your wanton wyll for to fulfill,
  In grene wode yon to play;
And that ye myght from your delȳght
  No lenger make delay:
Rather than ye fholde thus for me   105
  Be called an yll womàn,
Yet wolde I to the grene wode go,
  Alone, a banyfhed man.

SHE.

Though it be fonge of old and yonge,
  That I fholde be to blame,   110
Theyrs be the charge, that fpeke fo large
  In hurtynge of my name:
For I wyll prove, that faythfulle love
  It is devoy'd of fhame;
In your dyftreffe, and hevyneffe,   115
  To part with you, the fame;
And fure all tho' that do not fo,
  True lovers are they none:
For, in my mynde, of all mankynde
  I love but you alone.   120

HE.

Ver. 117. To fhewe all. *Prot.*

HE.

I counceyle you, remember howe
  It is no maydens lawe,
Nothynge to dout, but to renne out
  To wode with an outlàwe:
For ye muſt there in your hand bere   125
  A bowe, redy to drawe ;
And, as a theſe, thus muſt you lyve,
  Ever in drede and awe ;
Wherby to you grete harme myght growe :
  Yet had I lever than,   130
That I had to the grene wode go,
  Alone, a banyſhed man.

SHE.

I thinke nat, nay, but as ye ſay,
  It is no maydens lore :
But love may make me for your ſake,   135
  As I have ſayd before
To come on fote, to hunt, and ſhote
  To gete us mete in ſtore ;
For ſo that I your company
  May have, I aſke no more :   140
From which to part, it maketh my hart
  As colde as ony ſtone ;
For, in my mynde, of all mankynde
  I love but you alone.

VOL. II.   D   HE.

Ver. 133. I ſay nat, *Prol.* Ver. 138. and ſtore. *Camb. copy.*

He.

For an outlawe this is the lawe,　　145
　　That men hym take and bynde;
Without pytè, hanged to be,
　　And waver with the wynde.
If I had nede, (as God forbede!)
　　What refcous coude ye fynde?　　150
Forfoth, I trowe, ye and your bowe
　　For fere wolde drawe behynde:
And no mervayle: for lytell avayle
　　Were in your counceyle than:
Wherfore I wyll to the grene wode go,　　155
　　Alone, a banyfhed man.

She.

Ryght wele knowe ye, that women be
　　But feble for to fyght;
No womanhede it is indede
　　To be bolde as a knyght:　　160
Yet, in fuch fere yf that ye were
　　With enemyes day or nyght,
I wolde withftande, with bowe in hande,
　　To greve them as I myght,
And you to fave; as woman have　　165
　　From deth 'men' many one:
For, in my mynde, of all mankynde
　　I love but you alone.

He.

Ver. 150. focours. Prol.　　Ver. 162. and night. Camb. Copy.
Ver. 164. to helpe ye with my myght. Prol.

HE.

Yet take good hede ; for ever I drede
　　That ye coude nat fuſtayne　　　　　170
The thornie wayes, the depe valèies,
　　The ſnowe, the froſt, the rayne,
The colde, the hete : for dry, or wete,
　　We muſt lodge on the playne ;
And, us above, none other rofe　　　　175
　　But a brake buſh, or twayne :
Which ſone ſholde greve you, I beleve ;
　　And ye wolde gladly than
That I had to the grene wode go,
　　Alone, a banyſhed man.　　　　　180

SHE.

Syth I have here bene partynère
　　With you of joy and blyſſe,
I muſt alſo parte of your wo
　　Endure, as reſon is :
Yet am I ſure of one pleſùre ;　　　　185
　　And, ſhortely, it is this :
That, where ye be, me ſemeth, pardè,
　　I coude nat fare amyſſe.
Without more ſpeche, I you beſeche
　　That we were ſone agone ;　　　　190
For, in my mynde, of all mankynde
　　I love but you alone.

D 2

HE.

Ver. 174. Ye muſt. Prci.　　Ver. 190. ſhortley gone. Prsi.
I

He.

If ye go thyder, ye muſt conſyder,
    Whan ye have luſt to dyne,
There ſhall no mete be for you gete,   195
    Nor drinke, bere, ale, ne wyne.
Ne ſhetés clene, to lye betwene,
    Maden of threde and twyne;
None other houſe, but leves and bowes,
    To cover your hed and myne.   200
O myne harte ſwete, this evyll dyéte
    Sholde make you pale and wan;
Wherfore I wyll to the grene wode go,
    Alone, a banyſhed man.

She.

Amonge the wylde dere, ſuch a archére,   205
    As men ſay that ye be,
Ne may nat fayle of good vitayle,
    Where is ſo grete plentè:
And water clere of the ryvére
    Shall be full ſwete to me;   210
With which in hele I ſhall ryght wele
    Endure, as ye ſhall ſee:
And, or we go, a bedde or two
    I can provyde anone;
For, in my mynde, of all mankynde   215
    I love but you alone.

He.

Ver. 196. Neyther bere. *Prol.*   *Ver.* 207. May ye nat fayle. *Prol.*

HE.

Lo yet, before, ye muſt do more,
   Yf ye wyll go with me :
As cut your here up by your ere,
   Your kyrtel by the kne ;   220
With bowe in hande, for to withſtande
   Your enemyes, yf nede be :
And this ſame nyght before day-lyght,
   To wode-warde wyll I fle.
Yf that ye wyll all this fulfill,   225
   Do it ſhortely as ye can ;
Els wyll I to the grene wode go,
   Alone, a banyſhed man.

SHE.

I ſhall as nowe do more for you
   Than longeth to womanhede ;   230
To ſhorte my here, a bowe to bere,
   To ſhote in tyme of nede.
O my ſwete mother, before all other
   For you I have moſt drede :
But nowe, adue ! I muſt enſue,   235
   Where fortune doth me lede.
All this make ye : Now let us fle ;
   The day cometh faſt upon ;
For, in my mynde, of all mankynde
   I love but you alone.   240

D 3

HE.

Ver. 219. above your ere. Prol.   Ver. 220. above the kne. Prol.
Ver. 223. the ſame. Prol.

He.

Nay, nay, nat fo; ye fhall nat go,
    And I fhall tell ye why, ——— ,
Your appetyght is to be lyght
    Of love, I wele efpy:
For, lyke as ye have fayed to me,   245
    In lyke wyfe hardely
Ye wolde anfwére whofoever it were,
    In way of company.
It is fayd of olde, Sone hote, fone colde;
    And fo is a womàn.   250
Wherfore I to the wode wyll go,
    Alone, a banyfhed man.

She.

Yf ye take hede, it is no nede
    Such wordes to fay by me;
For oft ye prayed, and longe affayed,   255
    Or I you loved, pardè:
And though that I of aunceftry
    A barons daughter be,
Yet have you proved howe I you loved
    A fquyer of lowe degré;   260
And ever fhall, whatfo befall;
    To dy therfore * anone;
For, in my mynde, of all mankynde
    I love but you alone.

He.

Ver. 251. For I muft to the grene wode go. Prol. Ver. 253. yet
is. Camb. Copy. Perhaps for yt is. Ver. 262. dy with him. Editor's MS,
* i. e. for this caufe; tho' I were to die for having loved you.

HE.

A barons chylde to be begylde !   265
  It were a curſed dede;
To be felàwe with an outlawe !
  Almighty God forbede !
Yet beter were, the pore ſquyère
  Alone to foreſt yede,   270
Than ye ſholde ſay another day,
  That, by my curſed dede,
Ye were betray'd : Wherfore, good mayd,
  The beſt rede that I can,
Is, that I to the grene wode go,   275
  Alone, a banyſhed man.

SHE.

Whatever befall, I never ſhall
  Of this thyng you upbrayd :
But yf ye go, and leve me ſo,
  Than have ye me betrayd.   280
Remember you wele, howe that ye dele ;
  For, yf ye, as ye ſayd,
Be ſo unkynde, to leve behynde,
  Your love, the not-browne mayd,
Truſt me truly', that I ſhall dy   285
  Sone after ye be gone ;
For, in my mynde, of all mankynde
  I love but you alone.

D 4

HE.

Ver. 278. outbrayd. Prol.   Ver. 282. ye be as. Prol.
Ver. 283. Ye were unkynde to leve me behynde. Prol.

HE.

Yf that ye went, ye fholde repent;
 For in the foreft nowe   290
I have purvayed me of a mayd,
 Whom I love more than you;
Another fayrère, than ever ye were,
 I dare it wele avowe;
And of you bothe eche fholde be wrothe 295
 With other, as I trowe:
It were myne efe, to lyve in pefe;
 So wyll I, yf I can;
Wherfore I to the wode wyll go,
 Alone, a banyfhed man.   300

SHE.

Though in the wode I undyrftode
 Ye had a paramour,
All this may nought remove my thought,
 But that I wyll be your:
And fhe fhall fynde me foft, and kynde, 305
 And courteys every hour;
Glad to fulfyll all that fhe wyll
 Commaunde me to my power:
For had ye, lo, an hundred mo,
 ' Of them I wolde be one;' 310
For, in my mynde, of all mankynde
 I love but you alone.

HE.

Ver. 310. *So the Editor's MS. All the printed copies read,*
   Yet wolde I be that one.

HE.

Myne owne dere love, I fe the prove
   That ye be kynde, and true;
Of mayde, and wyfe, in all my lyfe,   315
   The beft that ever I knewe.
Be mery and glad, be no more fad,
   The cafe is chaunged newe;
For it were ruthe, that, for your truthe,
   Ye fholde have caufe to rewe: 320
Be nat difmayed; whatfoever I fayd
   To you, whan I began;
I wyll nat to the grene wode go,
   I am no banyfhed man.

SHE.

Thefe tydings be more gladd to me,   325
   Than to be made a quene,
Yf I were fure they fholde endure:
   But it is often fene,
Whan men wyll breke promyfe, they fpeke
   The wordés on the fplene.   330
Ye fhape fome wyle me to begyle,
   And ftele from me, I wene:
Than, were the cafe worfe than it was,
   And I more wo-begone:
For, in my mynde, of all mankynde   335
   I love but you alone.

HE.

Ver. 315. of all. *Prol.*   *Ver.* 325. gladder. *Prol.*

HE.

Ye fhall nat nede further to drede;
   I wyll nat dyfparàge
You, (God defend!) fyth ye defcend
   Of fo grete a lynàge.   340
Nowe undyrftande; to Weftmarlande,
   Which is myne herytage,
I wyll you brynge; and with a rynge,
   By way of maryage
I wyll you take, and lady make,   345
   As fhortely as I can :
Thus have you won an erlys fon,
   And not a banyfhed man."

AUTHOR.

" Here may ye fe, that women be
   In love, meke, kynde, and ftable :   350
Late never man reprove them than,
   Or call them variable;
But, rather, pray God, that we may
   To them be comfortable;
Which fometyme proveth fuch, as he loveth, 355
   Yf they be charytable.
For fyth men wolde that women fholde
   Be meke to them each one;
Moche more ought they to God obey,
   And ferve but hym alone.   360

VII. A

Ver. 340. grete lynvage. Prol.   Ver. 347. Then have. Prol.
Ver. 348. And no banyfhed. Prol. V. 352. This line wanting in Prol.
V. 355. proved—loved. Prol. Ib. as loveth. Camb. V. 357. Forfoth. Prol.

VII.

A BALET BY THE EARL RIVERS.

The amiable light, in which the character of Anthony Widville the gallant Earl Rivers has been placed by the elegant Author of the Catal. of Noble Writers, interests us in whatever fell from his pen. It is presumed therefore that the insertion of this little Sonnet will be pardoned, tho' it should not be found to have much poetical merit. It is the only original Poem known of that nobleman's; his more voluminous works being only translations. And if we consider that it was written during his cruel confinement in Pomfret castle a short time before his execution in 1483, it gives us a fine picture of the composure and steadiness with which this stout earl beheld his approaching fate.

The verses are preserved by ROUSE *a contemporary historian, who seems to have copied them from the Earl's own hand writing.* In tempore, *says this writer,* incarcerationis apud Pontem-fractum edidit unum BALET in anglicis, ut mihi monstratum est, quod subsequitur sub his verbis : 𝔖𝔲𝔪 𝔴𝔥𝔞𝔱 𝔪𝔲𝔰𝔶𝔫𝔤, &c. " Rossi Hist. 8vo. 2 Edit. p. 213." *The 2d Stanza is, notwithstanding, imperfect, and we have inserted asterisks, to denote the defect.*

This little piece, which perhaps ought rather to have been printed in stanzas of eight short lines, is written in imitation of a poem of Chaucer's, that will be found in Urry's Edit. 1721. pag. 555. beginning thus,

> " *Alone walkyng, In thought plainyng,*
> " *And sore sighying, All desolate.*
> " *Me remembrying Of my livyng*
> " *My death wishyng Bothe erly and late.*

> " *Infortunate Is so my fate*
> " *That wote ye what, Out of mesure*
> " *My life I hate; Thus desperate*
> " *In such pore estate, Doe I endure, &c.*"

SUM-

SUMWHAT mufyng, and more mornyng,
   In remembring the unftydfaftnes;
This world being of fuch whelyng,
   Me contrarieng, what may I geffe?

I fere dowtles, remediles,   5
   Is now to fefe my wofull chaunce.
Lo 'is' this traunce now in fubftaunce,
   * * * * fuch is my dawnce.

Wyllyng to dye, me thynkys truly
   Bowndyn am I, and that gretly, to be content: 10
Seyng playnly, that fortune doth wry
   All contrary from myn entent.

My lyff was lent me to on intent,
   Hytt is ny fpent.   Welcome fortune!
But I ne went thus to be fhent,   15
   But fho hit ment, fuch is hur won.

Ver. 7. in this. Roffi Hift.
Ver. 15. went, i. e. weened.

VIII.

CUPID's ASSAULT: BY LORD VAUX.

The Reader will think that infant Poetry grew apace between the times of RIVERS *and* VAUX, *tho' nearly contemporaries; if the following Song is the composition of that Sir* NICHOLAS *(afterwards Lord)* VAUX, *who was the shining ornament of the court of Henry VII. and died in the year* 1523.

And yet to this Lord it is attributed by Puttenham in his " *Art of Eng. Poesie,* 1589. 4to." *a writer commonly well informed: take the passage at large.* " *In this figure* " *[Counterfait Action] the Lord* NICHOLAS VAUX, *a* " *noble gentleman and much delighted in vulgar making,* " *and a man otherwise of no great learning, but having* " *herein a marvelous facilitie, made a dittie representing the* " *Battayle and Assault of Cupide, so excellently well, as for* " *the gallant and propre application of his fiction in every* " *part, I cannot choose but set downe the greatest part of his* " *ditty, for in truth it cannot be amended.* WHEN CUPID " SCALED, &c." *p.* 200.——*For a farther account of Nicholas Lord Vaux see Mr. Walpole's Noble Authors, Vol.* I.

The following Copy is printed from the first Edit. of Surrey's Poems, 1557, 4to.——*See another Song of Lord Vaux's in the preceding Vol. Book* II. No. II.

WHEN Cupide scaled first the fort,
   Wherin my hart lay wounded sore;
The batry was of such a sort,
   That I must yelde or die therfore.

There sawe I Love upon the wall,   5
   How he is banner did display:
Alarme, alarme, he gan to call:
   And bad his souldiours kepe aray.

The

The armes, the which that Cupide bare,
  Were pearced hartes with teares befprent,   10
In filver and fable to declare
  The ftedfaft love, he alwayes ment.

There might you fe his band all dreft
  In colours like to white and blacke,
With powder and with pelletes preft   15
  To bring the fort to fpoile and facke.

Good-wyll, the maifter of the fhot,
  Stode in the rampire brave and proude,
For fpence of pouder he fpared not
  Affault! affault! to crye aloude.   20

There might you heare the cannons rore;
  Eche pece difcharged a lovers loke;
Which had the power to rent, and tore
  In any place whereas they toke.

And even with the trumpettes fowne   25
  The fcaling ladders were up fet,
And Beautie walked up and downe,
  With bow in hand, and arrowes whet.

Then firft Defire began to fcale,
  And fhrouded him under 'his' targe;   30
As one the worthieft of them all,
  And apteft for to geve the charge.

Then

Ver. 30. fo Fd. 1585. her, Ed. 1557.

Then pushed souldiers with their pikes,
    And halberders with handy strokes ;
The argabushe in fleshe it lightes,   35
    And duns the ayre with misty smokes.

And, as it is the souldiers use
    When shot and powder gins to want,
I hanged up my flagge of truce,
    And pleaded for my livès grant.   40

When Fansy thus had made her breche,
    And Beauty entred with her band,
With bagge and baggage, sely wretch,
    I yelded into Beauties hand.

Then Beautie bad to blow retrete,   45
    And every souldier to retire,
And Mercy wyll'd with spede to fet
    Me captive bound as prisoner.

Madame, quoth I, sith that this day
    Hath served you at all assayes,   50
I yeld to you without delay
    Here of the fortresse all the kayes.

And sith that I have ben the marke,
    At whom you shot at with your eye ;
Nedes must you with your handy warke   55
    Or salve my sore, or let me die.

₊ *SINCE*

*** *SINCE the foregoing Song was first printed off, rea-*
fons have occurred, which incline me to believe that
Lord VAUX *the poet, was not the Lord* NICHOLAS VAUX,
who died in 1523, *but rather a fuccefor of his in the*
title.———For in the firft place it is remarkable that all the
old writers mention Lord Vaux the poet, as contemporary or
rather pofterior to Sir THOMAS WYAT, *and the E. of*
SURREY, *neither of which made any figure till long after*
the death of the firft Lord Nicholas Vaux. Thus Puttenham
in his "Art of Englifh Poefie, 1589." in p. 48. having
named SKELTON, *adds, "In the latter end of the fame*
" kings raigne [Henry VIII.] fprong up a new company of
" courtly Makers, [poets] of whom Sir THOMAS WYAT
" th' elder, and Henry Earl of SURREY *were the two*
" chieftaines, who having travailed into Italie, and there
" tafted the fweet and ftately meafures and ftile of the
" Italian poefie . . greatly polifhed our rude and homely
" manner of vulgar poefie . . . . In the SAME TIME, *or*
" NOT LONG AFTER *was the Lord* NICHOLAS VAUX,
" a man of much facilitie in vulgar makings †." —Webbe
in his Difcourfe of Englifh Poetrie, 1586. ranges them in
the following order, " The E. of Surrey, the Lord VAUX,
Norton, Briftow." And Gafcoigne in the place quoted in the 1ft
vol. of this work, [B. II. No. II.] mentions Lord VAUX
after Surrey.——Again, the ftile and meafure of Lord
VAUX'S *pieces feem too refined and polifhed for the age of*
Henry VII. and rather refemble the fmoothnefs and harmony
of Surrey and Wyat, than the rude metre of Skelton and
Hawes:—But what puts the matter out of all doubt, in the
Britifh Mufeum is a copy of his poem, I lothe that I did
love, *[vid. vol.* 1. *ubi fupra] with this title, " A dyttye or fonet*
" made by the Lord VAUS, *in the time of the noble Queene*
" Marye, reprefenting the image of Death." Harl. MSS.
No. 1703. §. 25.

It is evident then that Lord VAUX *the poet was not he that*
flourifhed in the reign of Henry vij. but either his fon, or
grandfon: and yet according to Dugdale's Baronage, the former
was

---

† *i. e. Compofitions in Englifh.*

was named THOMAS, *and the latter* WILLIAM : *but this difficulty is not great, for none of the old writers mention the chriſtian name of the poetic Lord Vaux*, except Puttenham ; and it is more likely that he might be miſtaken in that Lord's name, than in the time in which he lived, who was ſo nearly his contemporary.*

THOMAS *Lord* VAUX *of Harrowden in Northamptonſhire was ſummoned to parliament in* 1531. *When he died, does not appear ; but he probably lived till the latter end of Queen Mary's reign, ſince his ſon*

WILLIAM *was not ſummoned to parl. till the laſt year of that reign, in* 1558. *This Lord died in* 1595. *See Dugdale, V. 2. p. 304.————Upon the whole I am inclined to believe that Lord* THOMAS *was the* POET.

---

*   * In the Paradiſe of Dainty Deviſes, 1596, he is called ſimply "Lord Vaux the elder."*

IX.

SIR ALDINGAR.

This old fabulous legend is given from the Editor's folio MS, with a few conjectural emendations, and the inſertion of 3 or 4 ſtanzas to ſupply defects in the original copy.

It has been ſuggeſted to the Editor, that the Author of this Poem ſeems to have had in his eye the ſtory of Gunhilda, who is ſometimes called Eleanor, and was married to the Emperor (here called King) Henry.

O U R king he kept a falſe ſtewàrde,
   Sir Aldingar they him call ;
A falſer ſteward than he was one,
   Servde not in bower nor hall.

He wolde have layne by our comelye queene,   5
   Her deere worſhippe to betraye :
Our queene ſhe was a good womàn,
   And evermore ſayd him naye.

Sir Aldingar was wrothe in his mind,
   With her hee was nevér content,   10
Till traiterous meanes he colde devyſe,
   In a fyer to have her brent.

There came a lazar to the kings gate,
   A lazar both blinde and lame :
He took the lazar upon his backe,   15
   And on the queenes bed him layne.

" Lye ſtill, lazàr, wheras thou lyeſt,
   " Looke thou go not hence away ;
" Ile make thee a whole man and a ſound
   " In two howers of the day."   20

Then went him forth ſir Aldingar,
   And hyed him to our king :
" If I might have grace, as I have ſpace,
   " Sad tydings I could bring."

Saye on, ſaye on, ſir Aldingar,   25
   Saye on the ſoothe to mee.
" Our queene hath choſen a new new love,
   " And ſhee will have none of thee.

                          " If

" If fhee had chofen a right good knight,
    " The leffe had beene her fhame ;   30
" But fhe hath chofe her a lazar man,
    " A lazar both blinde and lame."

If this be true, fir Aldingar,
    The tydings thou telleft to me,
Then I will make thee a riche riche knight,   35
    Riche both of golde and fee.

But if it be falfe, fir Aldingar,
    As God nowe grant it bee !
Thy body, I fweare by the holye rood,
    Shall hang on the gallows tree.   40

He brought our king to the queenes chambèr,
    And opend to him the dore.
A lodlye love, king Henrye fayd,
    For our queene dame Elinore !

If thou wert a man, as thou art none,   45
    Here on my fword thouft dye ;
But a payre of new gallowes fhall now be built,
    And there fhalt thou hang on hye.

Forth then hyed our king, I wyfse,
    And an angry man was hee ;   50
And foone he found queene Elinore,
    That bride fo bright of blee.

E 2

Now

Now God you fave, our queene, madame,
  And Chrift you fave and fee;
Heere you have chofen a newe newe love,   55
  And you will have none of mee.

If you had chofen a right good knight,
  The leffe had been your fhame :
But you have chofe you a lazar man,
  A lazar both blinde and lame.   60

Therfore a fyer there fhall be built,
  And brent all fhalt thou bee.——
" Now out alacke ! fayd our comlye queene,
  Sir Aldingar's falfe to mee.

Now out alacke ! fayd our comlye queene,   65
  My heart with griefe will braft.
I had thought fwevens had never beene true ;
  I have proved them true at laft.

I dreamt a fweven on thurfday eve,
  In my bed wheras I laye,   70
I dreamt a grype and a grimlie beaft
  Had carried my crowne awaye ;

My gorget and my kirtle of golde,
  And all my faire head-geere :
And he wolde worrye me with his tufh   75
  And to his neft y-beare :

Saving

Saving there came a litle ' grey' hawke,
    A merlin him they call,
Which untill the grounde did ſtrike the grype,
    That dead he downe did fall.——   80

Giffe I were a man, as now I am none,
    A battell wolde I prove,
To fight with that traitor Aldingar ;
    Att him I caſt my glove.

But ſeeing Ime able noe battell to make,   85
    My liege, grant me a knight
To fight with that traitor Aldingar,
    To maintaine me in my right.".

" Now forty dayes I will give thee
    To ſeeke thee a knight therin :   90
If thou find not a knight in forty dayes
    Thy bodye it muſt brenn."

Then ſhee ſent eaſt, and ſhee ſent weſt,
    By north and ſouth bedeene :
But never a champion colde ſhe find,   95
    Wolde fight with that knight ſoe keene,

Now twenty dayes were ſpent and gone,
    Noe helpe there might be had ;
Many a teare ſhed our comelye queene
    And aye her hart was ſad.   100

E 3

Then

Then came one of the queenes damsèlles,
　And knelt upon her knee,
" Cheare up, cheare up, my gracious dame,
　I truſt yet helpe may be:

And here I will make mine avowe,　　　　105
　And with the ſame me binde ;
That never will I return to thee,
　Till I ſome helpe may finde."

Then forth ſhe rode on a faire palfràye
　Oer hill and dale about:　　　　110
But never a champion colde ſhe finde,
　Wolde fighte with that knight ſo ſtout.

And nowe the daye drewe on a pace,
　When our good queene muſt dye;
All woe-begone was that faire damsèlle,　　115
　When ſhe found no helpe was nye.

All woe-begone was that faire damsèlle,
　And the ſalt teares fell from her eye:
When lo! as ſhe rode by a rivers ſide,
　She met with a tinye boye.　　　　120

A tinye boye ſhe mette, God wot,
　All clad in mantle of golde;
He ſeemed noe more in mans likenèſſe,
　Then a child of four yeere olde.

Why

Why grieve you, damselle faire, he fayd,   125
    And what doth caufe you moane?
The damfell fcant wolde deigne a looke,
    But faft fhe pricked on.

Yet turn againe, thou faire damsèlle,
    And greete thy queene from mee: 130
When bale is att hyeft, boote is nyeft,
    Now helpe enoughe may bee.

Bid her remember what fhe dreamt
    In her bedd, wheras fhee laye;
How when the grype and the grimly beaft   135
    Wolde have carried her crowne awaye,

Even then there came the litle gray hawke,
    And faved her from his clawes:
Then bidd the queene be merry at hart,
    For heaven will fende her caufe.   140

Back then rode that faire damsèlle,
    And her hart it lept for glee:
And when fhe told her gracious dame
    A gladd womàn was fhee.

But when the appointed day was come,   145
    No helpe appeared nye:
Then woeful, woeful was her hart,
    And the teares ftood in her eye.

E 4

And

And nowe a fyer was built of wood ;
   And a ſtake was made of tree ;   150
And now queene Elinore forth was led,
   A ſorrowful ſight to ſee.

Three times the herault he waved his hand,
   And three times ſpake on hye :
Giff any good knight will fende this dame,   155
   Come forth, or ſhee muſt dye.

No knight ſtood forth, no knight there came,
   No helpe appeared nye :
And now the fyer was lighted up,
   Queen Elinore ſhe muſt dye.   160

And now the fyer was lighted up,
   As hot as hot might bee ;
When riding upon a little white ſteed,
   The tinye boy they ſee.

" Away with that ſtake, away with thoſe brands, 165
   And looſe our comelye queene :
I am come to fight with ſir Aldingar,
   And prove him a traitor keene."

Forthe then ſtood ſir Aldingar,
   But when he ſaw the chylde,   170
He laughed, and ſcoffed, and turned his backe,
   And weened he had been beguylde.

Now

Now turne, now turne thee, Aldingar,
  And eyther fighte or flee;
I truft that I fhall avenge the wronge,   175
  Thoughe I am fo fmall to fee.

The boye pulld forth a well good fworde
  So gilt it dazzled the ee;
The firft ftroke ftricken at Aldingar
  Smote off his leggs by the knee.   180

Stand up, ftand up, thou falfe traitòre,
  And fight upon thy feete,
For and thou thriveft, as thou beginneft,
  Of height wee fhal be meete.

A prieft, a prieft, fayes Aldingàr,   185
  While I am a man alive.
A prieft, a prieft, fayes Aldingàr,
  Me for to houzle and fhrive.

I wolde have layne by our comlye queene,
  Bot fhee wolde never confent;   190
Then I thought to betraye her unto our kinge
  In a fyer to have her brent.

There came a lazar to the kings gates,
  A lazar both blinde and lame:
I tooke the lazar upon my backe,   195
  And on her bedd him layne.

Then

Then ranne I to our comlye king,
    Thefe tidings fore to tell.
But ever alacke ! fayes Aldingar,
    Falfing never doth well.   200

Forgive, forgive me, queene, madame,
    The fhort time I muft live.
Nowe Chrift forgive thee, Aldingar,
    As freely I forgive.

Here take thy queene, our king Harry'e,   205
    And love her as thy life,
For never had a king in Chriftentye,
    A truer and fairer wife.

King Henrye ran to clafpe his queene,
    And loofed her full fone :   210
Then turnd to look for the tinye boye ;
    —— The boye was vanifht and gone.

But firft he had touchd the lazar man,
    And ftroakt him with his hand :
The lazar under the gallowes tree   215
    All whole and founde did ftand.

The lazar under the gallowes tree
    Was comelye, ftraight and tall ;
King Henrye made him his head ftewàrde
    To wayte withinn his hall.   *₊*   220

X. THE·

X.

THE GABERLUNZIE MAN.

A Scottish Song.

Tradition assures us that the author of this song was K. James V. of Scotland. This prince (whose character for wit and libertinism bears a great resemblance to that of his gay successor Charles II.) was noted for strolling about his dominions in disguise †, and for his frequent gallantries with country girls. Two adventures of this kind he hath celebrated with his own pen, viz. in this ballad of The Gaberlunzie Man; and in another intitled The Jolly Beggar, beginning thus,

Thair was a jollie beggar, and a begging he was boun,
And he tuik up his quarters into a land'art toun.
Fa, la, la, &c.

It seems to be the latter of these ballads (which was too licentious to be admitted into this collection) that is meant in the Catalogue of Royal and Noble Authors, where the ingenious writer remarks, That there is something very ludicrous in the young woman's distress when she thought her first favour had been thrown away upon a beggar.*

Bp. Tanner has attributed to James V. the celebrated ballad of Christ's Kirk on the Green, which better authorities ascribe to his ancestor James I. and which has all the internal marks of being the production of an earlier age. See the Ever-green, Vol. I.

As for K. James V. he died Dec. 13th, 1542, aged 33.

† *sc. of a tinker, beggar, &c. Thus he used to visit a smith's daughter at Niddry near Edinburgh.* * *Vol. 2. p. 203.*

THE

THE pauky auld Carle came ovir the lee
  Wi' mony good-eens and days to mee,
Saying, Goodwife, for zour courtefie,
  Will ze lodge a filly poor man?
The night was cauld, the carle was wat,
And down azont the ingle he fat;
My dochters fhoulders he gan to clap,
  And cadgily ranted and fang.

O wow! quo he, were I as free,
As firft when I faw this countrie,
How blyth and merry wad I bee!
  And I wad nevir think lang.
He grew canty, and fhe grew fain;
But little did her auld minny ken
What thir flee twa togither were fay'n,
  When wooing they were fa thrang.

And O! quo he, ann ze were as black,
As evir the crown of your dadyes hat,
Tis I wad lay thee by my back,
  And awa wi' me thou fould gang.
And O! quoth fhe, ann I were as white,
As evir the fnaw lay on the dike,
Ild clead me braw, and lady-like,
  And awa with thee Ild gang.

Between the twa was made a plot;
They raife a wee before the cock,
And wyliely they fhot the lock,

And faſt to the bent are they gane.
Up the morn the auld wife raiſe,
And at her leiſure put on her claiths,   30
Syne to the ſervants bed ſhe gaes
   To ſpeir for the ſilly poor man.

She gaed to the bed, whair the beggar lay,
The ſtrae was cauld, he was away,
She clapt her hands, cryd, dulefu' day!   35
   For ſome of our geir will be gane.
Some ran to coffers, and ſome to kiſts,
But nought was ſtown that could be miſt,
She dancid her lane, cryd, praiſe be bleſt,
   I have lodgd a leal poor man.   40

Since naithings awa, as we can learn,
The kirns to kirn, and milk to earn,
Gae butt the houſe, laſs, and waken my bairn,
   And bid her come quickly ben.
The ſervant gaed where the dochter lay,   45
The ſheets was cauld, ſhe was away,
And faſt to her goodwife can ſay,
   Shes aff with the gaberlunzie-man.

O fy gar ride, and fy gar rin,
And haſt ze, find theſe traitors agen;   50
For ſhees be burnt, and hees be ſlein.

The

Ver. 29. The Carline. Other copies.

The wearyfou gaberlunzie man.
Some rade upo horfe, fome ran a fit,
The wife was wood, and out o' her wit;
She could na gang, nor yet could fhe fit,
   But ay did curfe and did ban.

Mean time far hind out owre the lee,
Fou fnug in a glen, where nane could fee,
The twa, with kindlie fport and glee,
   Cut frae a new cheefe a whang.
The priving was gude, it pleas'd them baith,
To lo'e her for ay, he gae her his aith.
Quo fhe, to leave thee, I will be laith,
   My winfome gaberlunzie-man.

O kend my minny I were wi' zou,
Illfardly wad fhe crook her mou,
Sic a poor man fheld nevir trow,
   Aftir the gaberlunzie-mon.
My dear, quo he, zee're zet owre zonge;
And hae na learnt the beggars tonge,
To follow me frae toun to toun,
   And carrie the gaberlunzie on.

Wi' kauk and keel, Ill win zour bread,
And fpindles and whorles for them wha need,
Whilk is a gentil trade indeed

The gaberl unzie to carrie ---- o.
Ill bow my leg and crook my knee,
And draw a black clout owre my ee,
A criple or blind they will cau mee:
While we fall fing and be merrie--o.   80

XI.

ON THOMAS LORD CROMWELL.

*It is ever the fate of a difgraced minifter to be forfaken
by his friends, and infulted by his enemies, always reckoning among the latter the giddy inconftant multitude. We
have here a fpurn at fallen greatnefs from fome angry
partifan of declining popery, who could never forgive the
downfall of their Diana, and lofs of their craft. The
ballad feems to have been compofed between the time of Cromwell's commitment to the tower June 11. 1540, and that
of his being beheaded July 28. following. A fhort inter-
val! but Henry's paffion for Catharine Howard would
admit of no delay. Notwithftanding our libeller, Cromwell
had many excellent qualities; his great fault was too much ob-
fequioufnefs to the arbitrary* WILL of his mafter; but let
it be confidered that this mafter had raifed him from obfcurity,
and that the high-born nobility had fhewn him the way
in every kind of mean and fervile compliance. —— The original copy printed at London in* 1540, is intitled, " A newe
" ballade made of Thomas Crumwel, called* TROLLE ON
" AWAY." To it is prefixed this diftich by way of burthen,*
Trolle on away, trolle on awaye.
Synge heave and howe rombelowe trolle on away.*

BOTH

BOTH man and chylde is glad to here tell
Of that falſe traytoure Thomas Crumwel,
Now that he is ſet to learne to ſpell.

     Synge trolle on away.

When fortune lokyd the in thy face,
Thou haddyſt fayre tyme, but thou lackydyſt grace; 5
Thy cofers with golde thou fyllydſt a pace.

     Synge, &c.

Both plate and chalys came to thy fyſt,
Thou lockydſt them vp where no man wyſt,
Tyll in the kynges treaſoure ſuche thinges were myſt.

     Synge, &c.

Both cruſt and crumme came thorowe thy handes,   10
Thy marchaundyſe ſayled over the ſandes,
Therfore nowe thou art layde faſt in bandes.

     Synge, &c.

Fyrſte when kynge Henry, God ſaue his grace!
Perceyud myſchefe kyndlyd in thy face,
Then it was tyme to purchaſe the a place.   15

     Synge, &c.

Hys grace was euer of gentyll nature,
Mouyd with petye, and made the hys ſeruyture;
But thou, as a wretche, ſuche thinges dyd procure.

     Synge, &c.

       Thou

Thou dyd not remembre, falfe heretyke,
One God, one fayth, and one kynge catholyke,   20
For thou haft bene fo long a fcyfmatyke.
             Synge, &c.

Thou woldyft not learne to knowe thefe thre ;
But euer was full of iniquite :
Wherfore all this lande hathe ben troubled with the.
             Synge, &c.

All they, that were of the new trycke,   25
Agaynft the churche thou baddeft them ftycke ;
Wherfore nowe thou hafte touchyd the quycke.
             Synge, &c.

Bothe facramentes and facramentalles
Thou woldyft not fuffre within thy walles ;
Nor let vs praye for all chryften foules.   30
             Synge, &c.

Of what generacyon thou were no tonge can tell,
Whyther of Chayme, or Syfchemell,
Or elfe fent vs frome the deuyll of hell.
             Synge, &c.

Thou woldeft neuer to vertue applye,
But couetyd euer to clymme to hye,   35
And nowe hafte thou trodden thy fhoo awrye.
             Synge, &c.

Who-fo-euer dyd winne thou wolde not lofe;
Wherfore al Englande doth hate the, as I fuppofe,
Bycaufe thou waft falfe to the redolent rofe.

                              Synge, &c.

Thou myghteft haue learned thy cloth to flocke   40
Upon thy grefy fullers ftocke;
Wherfore lay downe thy heade vpon this blocke.

                              Synge, &c.

Yet faue that foule, that God hath bought,
And for thy carcas care thou nought,
Let it fuffre payne, as it hath wrought.   45

                              Synge, &c.

God faue kyng Henry with all his power,
And prynce Edwarde that goodly flowre,
With all hys lordes of great honoure.

          Synge trolle on awaye, fyng trolle on away.
          Hevye and how rombelowe trolle on awaye.

*** *The foregoing Piece gave rife to a poetic controverfy,
which was carried on thro' a fucceffion of feven or eight
Ballads written for and againft Lord* CROMWELL. *Thefe
are all preferved in the archives of the Antiquarian Society,
in a large folio Collection of Proclamations, &c. made in the
Reigns of K. Hen. VIII. K. Edw. VI. Q. Mary. Q. Eliz.
K. James I. &c.*

                              XII. HAR-

XII.

HARPALUS.

AN ANCIENT ENGLISH PASTORAL.

This beautiful poem, which is perhaps the first attempt at pastoral writing in our language, is preserved among the SONGS AND SONNETTES *of the earl of Surrey, &c. 4to. in that part of the collection, which consists of pieces by* UNCERTAIN AUCTOURS. *These poems were first published in* 1557, *ten years after that accomplished nobleman fell a victim to the tyranny of Henry VIII : but it is presumed most of them were composed before the death of sir Thomas Wyatt in* 1541. *See Surrey's poems, 4to. fol.* 19. 49.

Tho' written perhaps near half a century before the SHEPHERD'S CALENDAR *, this will be found far superior to any of those Eclogues in natural unaffected sentiments, in simplicity of style, in easy flow of versification, and all other beauties of pastoral poetry. Spenser ought to have profited more by so excellent a model.*

PHYLIDA was a faire mayde,
   As fresh, as any flowre;
Whom Harpalus the herdman prayde
   To be his paramour.

Harpalus, and eke Corin,   5
   Were herdmen both yfere :
And Phylida could twist and spinne,
   And thereto sing full clere.

F 2

But

* *First published in* 1579.

But Phylida was all tò coye,
   For Harpalus to winne :   10
For Corin was her ohely joye,
   Who forft her not a pinne.

How often would fhe flowers twine ?
   How often garlandes make
Of couflips and of columbine ?   15.
   And al for Corin's fake.

But Corin, he had haukes to lure,
   And forced more the field :
Of lovers lawe he toke no cure ;
   For once he was begilde.   20

Harpalus prevailed nought,
   His labour all was loft ;
For he was fardeft from her thought,
   And yet he loved her moft.

Therefore waxt he both pale and leane,   25
   And drye as clot of clay :
His flefhe it was confumed cleane ;
   His colour gone away.

His beard it had not long be fhave ;
   His heare hong all unkempt :   30
A man moft fit even for the grave,
   Whom fpitefull love had fhent.

His

His eyes were red, and all 'forewacht';
　　His face befprent with teares :
It femde unhap had him long 'hatcht',   35
　　In mids of his difpaires.

His clothes were blacke, and alfo bare ;
　　As one forlorne was he ;
Upon his head alwayes he ware
　　A wreath of wyllow tree.   40

His beaftes he kept upon the hyll,
　　And he fate in the dale ;
And thus with fighes and forowes fhril,
　　He gan to tell his tale.

Oh Harpalus ! thus would he fay ;   45
　　Unhappieft under funne !
The caufe of thine unhappy day,
　　By love was firft begunne.

For thou wenteft firft by fute to feeke
　　A tigre to make tame,   50
That fettes not by thy love a leeke ;
　　But makes thy griefe her game.

As eafy it were for to convert
　　The froft into 'a' flame ;
As for to turne a frowarde hert,   55
　　Whom thou fo faine wouldft frame.
F 3

Corin

Corin he liveth careleffe :
   He leapes among the leaves :
He eates the frutes of thy redreffe :
   Thou 'reapft', he takes the fheaves.   60

My beaftes, a whyle your foode refraine,
   And harke your herdmans founde :
Whom fpitefull love, alas ! hath flaine,
   Through-girt with many a wounde.

O happy be ye, beaftès wilde,   65
   That here your pafture takes :
I fe that ye be not begilde
   Of thefe your faithfull makes.

The hart he feedeth by the hinde :
   The bucke harde by the doe :   70
The turtle dove is not unkinde
   To him that loves her fo.

The ewe fhe hath by her the ramme :
   The yong cowe hath the bulle :
The calfe with many a lufty lambe   75
   Do fede their hunger full.

But, wel-a-way ! that nature wrought
   Thee, Phylida, fo faire :
For I may fay that I have bought
   Thy beauty all tò deare.   80

What

What reafon is that crueltie
　　With beautie fhould have part ?
Or els that fuch great tyranny
　　Should dwell in womans hart ?

I fee therefore to fhape my death　　　　85
　　She cruelly is preft ;
To th'ende that I may want my breath :
　　My dayes bcen at the beft.

O Cupide, graunt this my requeft,
　　And do not ftoppe thine eares ;　　　90
That fhe may feele within her breft
　　The paines of my difpaires :

Of Corin 'who' is carèleffe,
　　That fhe may crave her fee :
As I have done in great diftreffe,　　　95
　　That loved her faithfully.

But fince that I fhal die her flave ;
　　Her flave, and eke her thrall :
Write you, my frendes, upon my grave
　　This chaunce that is befall.　　　　100

　" Here lieth unhappy Harpalus
　　" By cruell love now flaine :
　" Whom Phylida unjuftly thus,
　　" Hath murdred with difdaine."

F 4　　　　XIII. ROBIN

XIII.

ROBIN AND MAKYNE.

AN ANCIENT SCOTTISH PASTORAL.

The palm of pastoral poesy is here contested by a cotempo-
rary writer with the author of the foregoing. The reader
will decide their respective merits. The author of this poem
has one advantage over his rival, in having his name handed
down to us. Mr. ROBERT HENRYSON *(to whom we are*
indebted for it) appears to so much advantage among the
writers of eclogue, that we are sorry we can give little other
account of him, besides what is contained in the following
eloge, written by W. Dunbar, a Scottish poet, who lived
about the middle of the 16th century :

" *In Dumferling, he [Death] hath tane Broun,*
" *With gude Mr. Robert Henryson."*

Indeed some little farther insight into the history of this
Scottish bard is gained from the title prefixed to some of his
poems preserved in the British Museum ; viz. " The
" *morall Fabillis of Esop compylit be Maister* ROBERT
" HENRISOUN, SCOLMAISTER *of Dumfermling, 1571."*
Harleian MSS. 3865. § 1.

In Ramsay's EVERGREEN, *Vol. I. whence the above distich,*
and the following beautiful poem are extracted, are preserved
two other little Doric pieces by Henryson ; the one intitled
THE LYON AND THE MOUSE; *the other,* THE GARMENT
OF GUDE LADYIS.

R OBIN sat on the gude grene hill,
   Keipand a flock of fie,
Quhen mirry Makyne said him till,
   " O Robin rew on me
" I haif thee luivt baith loud and still,   5
   " Thir towmonds twa or thre :

" My

" My dule in dern but gif thou dill,
    " Doubtlefs bot dreid Ill die.

Robin replied, Now by the rude,
    Naithing of luve I knaw,   10
But keip my fheip undir yon wod:
    Lo quhair they raik on raw.
Quhat can have mart thee in thy mude,
    Thou Makyne to me fchaw ;
Or quhat is luve, or to be lude ?   15
    Fain wald I leir that law.

" The law of luve gin thou wald leir,
    " Tak thair an A, B, C ;
" Be keynd, courtas, and fair of feir,
    " Wyfe, hardy, 'bauld' and frie,   20
" Sae that nae danger do the deir,
    " What dule in dern thou drie ;
" Prefs ay to pleis, and blyth appeir,
    " Be patient and privie."

Robin, he anfwert her again,   25
    I wat not quhat is luve ;
But I half marvel uncertain
    Quhat makes thee thus wanrufe.
The wedder is fair, and I am fain ;
    My fheep gais hail abuve ;   30
And we fould pley us on the plain,
    They wald us baith repruve.
                              " Robin

Ver. 20. kind and frie, MS,

I

" Robin, tak tent unto my tale,
 " And wirk all as I reid;
" And thou fall haif my heart all hale,   35
 " Eik and my maiden-heid:
" Sen God, he fends 'us' bute for bale,
 " And for murning remeid,
" I'dern with thee but give I dale,
 " Doubtlefs I am but deid."   40

Makyne, to-morn be this ilk tyde,
 Gif ye will meit me heir,
Maybe my fheip may gang befyde,
 Quhyle we have liggd full neir;
But maugre haif I, gif I byde,   45
 Frae thay begin to fteir,
Quhat lyes on heart I will nocht hyd,
 Then Makyne mak gude cheir.

" Robin, thou reivs me of my reft;
 " I luve but thee alane."   50
Makyne, adieu! the fun goes weft,
 The day is neir-hand gane.
" Robin, in dule I am fo dreft,
 " That luve will be my bane."
Makyn, gae luve quhair-eir ye lift,   55
 For lemans I luid nane.

          " Robin,

" Robin, I ftand in fic a ftyle,
　" I fich and that full fair."
Makyne, I have bene here this quyle ;
　At hame I wifh I were.　　　　　　　60
" Robin, my hinny, talk and fmyle,
　" Gif thou will do nae mair."
Makyne, fom other man beguyle,
　For hameward I will fare.

Syne Robin on his ways he went,　　　65
　As light as leif on tree ;
But Makyne murnt and made lament,
　Scho trow'd him neir to fee.
Robin he brayd attowre the bent :
　Then Makyne cried on hie,　　　　　70
" Now may thou fing, for I am fhent !
　" Quhat can ail luve at me ?"

Makyne went hame withouten fail,
　And weirylie could weip ;
Then Robin in a full fair dale　　　75
　Affemblit all his fheip :
Be that fome part of Makyne's ail,
　Out-throw his heart could creip,
Hir faft he followt to affail,
　And till her tuke gude keip.　　　　80

Abyd,

Abyd, abyd, thou fair Makyne,
   A word for ony thing ;
For all my luve, it fall be thyne,
   Withouten departing.
All hale thy heart for till have myne,   85
   Is all my coveting ;
My sheip quhyle morn till the hours nyne,
   Will need of nae keiping.

" Robin, thou haft heard fung and fay,
   " In jefts and ftorys auld,   90
  " The man that will not when he may,
   " Sall have nocht when he wald.
" I pray to heaven baith nicht and day,
   " Be eiked their cares fae cauld,
" That preffes firft with thee to play   95
  " Be forreft, firth, or fauld."

Makyne, the nicht is foft and dry,
   The wether warm and fair,
And the grene wod richt neir-hand by,
   To walk attowre all where :   100
There may nae janglers us efpy,
   That is in luve contrair ;
Therin, Makyne, baith you and I
   Unfeen may malk repair.

             " Robin,

" Robin, that warld is now away,   105
  " And quyt brocht till an end.
" And nevir again thereto perfay,
  " Sall it be as thou wend ;
" For of my pain thou made but play,
  " I words in vain did fpend ;   110
" As thou haft done fae fall I fay,
  " Murn on, I think to mend."

Makyne, the hope of all my heil,
  My heart on thee is fet ;
I'll evermair to thee be leil,   115
  Quhyle I may live but lett,
Never to fail as uthers feil,
  Quhat grace fo eir I get.
" Robin, with thee I will not deal ;
  " Adieu, for this we met."   120

Makyne went hameward blyth enough,
  Outowre the holtis hair ;
Pure Robin murnd and Makyne leugh ;
  Scho fang, and he ficht fair :
Scho left him in baith wae and wreuch,   125
  In dolor and in care,
Keipand his herd under a heuch,
  Amang the rufhy gair.

XIV. GENTLE

XIV

GENTLE HERDSMAN, TELL TO ME.

DIALOGUE BETWEEN A PILGRIM AND HERDSMAN.

*The scene of this beautiful old ballad is laid near Walsing-
ham in Norfolk, where was anciently an image of the
Virgin Mary, famous over all Europe for the numerous pilgrimages made to it, and the great riches it possessed. Eras-
mus has given a very exact and humorous description of the
superstitions practised there in his time. See his account of the
VIRGO PARATHALASSIA, in his colloquy, intitled, PERE-
GRINATIO RELIGIONIS ERGO. He tells us, the rich offerings in silver, gold, and precious stones, that were there shewn
him, were incredible, there being scarce a person of any note
in England, but what some time or other paid a visit, or
sent a present to OUR LADY OF WALSINGHAM*. At the
dissolution of the monasteries in 1538, this splendid image,
with another from Ipswich, was carried to Chelsea, and
there burnt in the presence of commissioners ; who, we trust,
did not burn the jewels and the finery.*

*This poem is printed from a copy in the Editor's folio MS.
which had greatly suffered by the hand of time ; but vestiges
of several of the lines remaining, some conjectural supplements
have been attempted, which, for greater exactness, are in this
one ballad distinguished by Italicks.*

G Entle herdſman, tell to me,
   Of curteſy I thee pray,
Unto the towne of Walſingham
   Which is the right and ready way.

" Unto

* *See at the End of this Volume an account of the annual offerings of
the Earls of Northumberland.*

" Unto the towne of Walſingham   5
  " The way is hard for to be gone ;
" And verry crooked are thoſe pathes
  " For you to find out all alone."

Were the miles doubled thriſe,
  And the way never ſoe ill,   10
Itt were not enough for mine offence ;
  Itt is ſoe grievous and ſoe ill.

" Thy yeares are young, thy face is faire,
  " Thy witts are weake, thy thoughts are greene ;
" Time hath not given thee leave, as yett,   15
  " For to committ ſo great a ſinne."

Yes, herdſman, yes, ſoe woldſt thou ſay,
  If thou kneweſt ſoe much as I ;
My witts, and thoughts, and all the reſt,
  Have weil deſerved for to dye.   20

I am not what I ſeeme to bee,
  My clothes, and ſexe doe differ farr:
I am a woman, woe is me !
  Born to greeffe and irkſome care.

For my beloved, and well-beloved,   25
  My wayward cruelty could kill :
And though my teares will nought avail,
  . Moſt dearely I bewail him ſtill.

He was the flower of noble wights,
  None ever more sincere colde bee ;
Of comely mien and shape he was,
  And tenderlye hee loved mee.   30

When thus I saw he loved me well,
  I grewe so proud his paine to see,
That I, who did not know myselfe,   35
  Thought scorne of such a youth as hee.

And grew soe coy and nice to pleafe,
  As womens lookes are often foe,
He might not kiffe, nor hand forfooth,
  Uulefs I willed him foe to doe.   40

Thus being wearyed with delayes
  To fee I pityed not his greeffe,
He gott him to a fecrett place,
  And there hee dyed without releeffe.

·And for his fake thefe weedes I weare,   45
  And facriffice my tender age ;
And every day Ile begg my bread,
  To undergoe this pilgrimage.

Thus every day I faft and praye,
  And ever will doe till I dye ;   50
And gett me to fome fecrett place,
  For foe did hee, and fo will I.

Now,

Now, gentle herdſman, aſke no more,
    But keepe my ſecretts I thee pray ;
Unto the towne of Walſingham   55
    Show me the right and readye way.

" Now goe thy wayes, and God before !
    " For he muſt ever guide thee ſtill :
" Turne downe that dale, the right hand path,
    " And ſoe, faire pilgrim, fare thee well !" 60

XV.

K. EDWARD IV. AND TANNER OF TAMWORTH

*Was a ſtory of great fame among our anceſtors. The au-
thor of the* ART OF ENGLISH POESIE, 1589, 4to, *ſeems
to ſpeak of it, as a real fact.—Deſcribing that vicious mode
of ſpeech, which the Greeks called* ACYRON, *i. e.* " *When
we uſe a dark and obſcure word, utterly repugnant to
that we ſhould expreſs;*" *he adds,* " *Such manner of un-*
" *couth ſpeech did the Tanner of Tamworth uſe to king Ed-*
" *ward the fourth; which Tanner, having a great while*
" *miſtaken him, and uſed very broad talke with him, at*
" *length perceiving by his traine that it was the king,*
" *was afraide he ſhould be puniſhed for it,* [and] *ſaid thus,*
" *with a certaine rude repentance,*

    " *I hope I ſhall be hanged to-morrow,*

" *for* [I feare me] *I ſhall be hanged; whereat the king*
" *laughed a good* *, *not only to ſee the Tanner's vaine*
" *feare, but alſo to heare his illſhapen terme ; and gave*

* *Vid. Gloſſ.*

" *him for recompence of his good sport, the inheritance of*
" *Plumpton-parke.* I AM AFRAID," *concludes this sagaci-*
ous writer, " THE POETS OF OUR TIME, THAT SPEAKE
" MORE FINELY AND CORRECTEDLY, WILL COME
" TOO SHORT OF SUCH A REWARD," *p.* 214.——*The*
phrase, here referred to, is not found in this ballad at pre-
sent, but occurs with some variation in an older poem, in-
titled JOHN THE REEVE, *described in the following vo-*
lume, (see the Preface to THE KING AND THE MILLER),
viz.

 " *Nay, sayd John, by Gods grace,*
" *And Edward wer in this place,*
 " *Hee shold not touch this tonne :*
" *He wold be wroth with John* I HOPE,
" *Thereffore I beshrew the soupe,*
 " *That in his mouth shold come.*" *Pt.* 2. *st.* 24.

 The following text is selected from two copies in black
letter. The one in the Bodleyan library, intitled, " *A mer-*
" *rie, pleasant, and delectable historie betweene K. Edward*
" *the Fourth, and a Tanner of Tamworth, &c. printed*
" *at London, by John Danter,* 1596." *This copy, ancient*
as it now is, appears to have been modernized and altered
at the time it was published; but many vestiges of the more
ancient readings were recovered from another copy, (though
more recently printed,) in one sheet folio, without date, in
the Pepys collection.

IN summer time, when leaves grow greene,
 And blossoms bedecke the tree,
King Edward wolde a hunting ryde,
 Some pastime for to see.

With

With hawke and hounde he made him bowne,   5
    With horne, and eke with bowe ;
To Drayton Baſſet he tooke his waye,
    With all his lordes a rowe.

And he had ridden ore dale and downe
    By eight of clocke in the day,   10
When he was ware of a bold tannèr
    Come ryding along the waye.

A fayre ruſſet coat the tanner had on
    Faſt buttoned under his chin,
And under him a good cow-hide,   15
    And a mare of four ſhilling *.

Nowe ſtand you ſtill, my good lordes all,
    Under the grene wood ſpraye ;
And I will wend to yonder fellowe,
    To weet what he will ſaye.   20

    * *In the reign of Edward IV. Dame Cecill, lady of Tor-boke, in her will dated March* 7. *A. D.* 1466; *among many other bequeſts has this,* " Alſo I will that my ſonne " Thomas of Torboke have 13 s. 4 d. to buy him an " horſe." *Vid. Harleian Catalog.* 2176. 27.——*Now if* 13 s. 4 d. *would purchaſe a ſteed fit for a perſon of quality, a tanner's horſe might reaſonably be valued at four or five ſhillings.*

G 2

God

God fpeede, God fpeede thee, faid our king.
  Thou art welcome, fir, fayd hee.
" The readyeft waye to Drayton Baffet
  I praye thee to fhewe to mee."

" To Drayton Baffet woldft thou goe,   25
  Fro the place where thou doft ftand ?
The next payre of gallowes thou comeft unto,
  Turne in upon thy right hand."

That is an unreadye waye, fayd our king,
  Thou doeft but jeft I fee :   30
Nowe fhewe me out the neareft waye,
  And I pray thee wend with mee.

Awaye with a vengeance! quoth the tanner :
  I hold thee out of thy witt :
All daye have I rydden on Brocke my mare,   35
  And I am fafting yett.

" Go with me downe to Drayton Baffet,
  No daynties we will fpare;
All daye fhalt thou eate and drinke of the beft,
  And I will paye thy fare."   40

Gramercye for nothing, the tanner replyde,
  Thou payeft no fare of mine :
I trowe I've more nobles in my purfe,
  Than thou haft pence in thine.

God

God give thee joy of them, fayd the king,   45
   And fend them well to priefe.
The tanner wolde faine have beene away,
   For he weende he had beene a thiefe.

What art thou, hee fayde, thou fine fellòwe,
   Of thee I am in great feare,   50
For the cloathes, thou weareft upon thy backe,
   Might befeeme a lord to weare.

I never ftole them, quoth our king,
   I tell you, fir, by the roode.
" Then thou playeft, as many an unthrift doth, 55
   And ftandeft in midds of thy goode."

What tydinges heare you, fayd the kynge,
   As you ryde farre and neare ?
" I heare no tydinges, fir, by the maffe,
   But that cowe-hides are deare."   60

" Cowe-hides ! cowe-hides ! what things are thofe ?
   I marvell what they bee ?"
What art thou a foole ? the tanner reply'd ;
   I carry one under mee."

What craftfman art thou, faid the king,   65
   I praye thee tell me trowe.
" I am a barker, fir, by my trade ;
   Nowe tell me what art thou ?"

G 3

I am

I am a poore courtier, fir, quoth he,
  That am forth of fervice worne ;   70
And faine I wolde thy prentife bee,
  Thy cunninge for to learne.

Marrye heaven forfend, the tanner replyde,
  That thou my prentife were:
Thou woldft fpend more good than I fhold winne 75
  By fortye fhilling a yere.

Yet one thinge wolde I, fayd our king,
  If thou wilt not feeme ftrange:
Thoughe my horfe be better than thy mare,
  Yet with thee I faine wold change.   80

" Why if with me thou faine wilt change,
  As change full well maye wee,
By the faith of my bodye, thou proude fellòwe,
  I will have fome boot of thee."

That were againft reafon, fayd the king,   85
  I fweare, fo mote I thee:
My horfe is better than thy mare,
  And that thou well mayft fee.

" Yea, fir, but Brocke is gentle and mild,
  And foftly fhe will fare :   90
Thy horfe is unrulye and wild, I wifs ;
  Aye fkipping here and theare."

What

What boote wilt thou have? our king reply'd;
  Now tell me in this ſtound.
" Noe pence, nor half pence, by my faye,   95
  But a noble in gold ſo round."

" Here's twentye groates of white moneyè,
  Sith thou will have it of mee."
I would have ſworne now, quoth the tanner,
  Thou hadſt not had one penniè.   100

But ſince we two have made a change,
  A change we muſt abide,
Although thou haſt gotten Brocke my mare,
  Thou getteſt not my cowe-hide.

I will not have it, ſayd the kynge,   105
  I ſweare, ſo mote I thee;
Thy foule cowe-hide I wolde not beare,
  If thou woldſt give it to mee.

The tanner hee tooke his good cowe-hide,
  That of the cow was hilt;   110
And threwe it upon the king's ſadèlle,
  That was foe fayrelye gilte.

" Now help me up, thou fine fellòwe,
  'Tis time that I were gone:
When I come home to Gyllian, my wife,   115
  Sheel ſay I am a gentilmon."

G 4

The

The king he tooke him up by the legge;
    The tanner a f * * lett fall.
Nowe marrye, good fellowe, fayd the kyng,
    Thy courtefye is but'fmall.   120

When the tanner he was in the kinges fadèlle,
    And his foote in the ftirrup was ;
He marvelled greatlye in his minde,
    Whether it were golde or brafs.

But when his fteede faw the cows taile wagge,   125
    And eke the blacke cowe-horne ;
He ftamped, and ftared, and awaye he ranne,
    As the devill had him borne.

The tanner he pulld, the tanner he fweat,
    And held by the pummjl faft :   130
At length the tanner came tumbling downe ;
    His necke he had well-nye braft.

Take thy horfe again with avenge ance, he fayd,
    With mee he fhall not byde.
" My horfe wolde have borne thee well enoughe, 135
    But he knewe not of thy cowe-hide.

Yet if againe thou faine woldft change,
    As change full well may wee,
By the faith of my bodye, thou jolly tannèr,
    I will have fome boote of thee."   140

What

What boote wilt thou have, the tanner replyd,
    Nowe tell me in this ftounde ?
,' Noe pence nor halfpence, fir, by my faye,
    But I will have twentye pound."

" Here's twentye groates out of my purfe ;   145
    And twentye I have of thine :
And I have one more, which we will fpend
    Together at the wine,"

The king fet a bugle horne to his mouthe,
    And blewe both loude and fhrille :   150
And foone came lords, and foone came knights,
    Faft ryding over the hille.

Nowe, out alas ! the tanner he cryde,
    That ever I fawe this daye !
Thou art a ftrong thiefe, yon come thy fellowes 155
    Will beare my cowe-hide away.

They are no thieves, the king replyde,
    I fweare, foe mote I thee :
But they are the lords of the north countrèy,
    Here come to hunt with mee.   160

And foone before our king they came,
    And knelt downe on the grounde :
Then might the tanner have beene awaye,
    He had lever than twentye pounde.

A

A coller, a coller*, here: fayd the king,   165
   A coller he loud did crye :
Then woulde he lever then twentye pound,
   He had not beene fo nighe.

A coller, a coller, the tanner he fayd,
   I trowe it will breed forrowe :   170
After a coller comes a halter,
   And I fhall be hanged to-morrowe.

" Awaye with thy feare, thou jolly tannèr,
   For the fport thou haft fhewn to me,
I wote noe halter thou fhalt weare,   175
   But thou fhalt have a knight's fee.

For Plumpton-parke I will give thee,
   With tenements faire befide :
'Tis worth three hundred markes by the yeare,
   To maintaine thy good cowe-hide."   180

Gramercye, my liege, the tanner replyde,
   For the favour thou haft me fhowne ;
If ever thou comeft to merry Tamwòrth,
   Neates leather fhall clout thy fhoen.

***

* *A collar was, I believe, anciently ufed in the ceremony
of conferring knighthood. Or perhaps the King ufed the
French word* Acoller, *fignifying to give the* Acolade, *or
blow that was to dub him a knight. This the Tanner ig-
norantly miftakes for* A collar.

AS

XVI.

AS YE CAME FROM THE HOLY LAND.

DIALOGUE BETWEEN A PILGRIM AND TRAVELLER.

The scene of this song is the same, as in num. XIV. The pilgrimage to Walsingham suggested the plan of many popular pieces. In the Pepys collection, Vol. I. p. 226, is a kind of Interlude in the old ballad style, of which the first stanza alone is worth reprinting,

As I went to Walsingham,
  To the shrine with speede,
Met I with a jolly palmer
  In a pilgrimes weede.
Now God you save, you jolly palmer!
  " Welcome, lady gay,
" Oft have I sued to thee for love."
  —Oft have I said you nay.

The pilgrimages undertaken on pretence of religion, were often productive of affairs of gallantry, and led the votaries to no other shrine than that of Venus.*

The following ballad was once very popular; it is quoted in Fletcher's " Knt. of the burning pestle," Act 2. sc. ult. and in another old play, called, " Hans Beer-pot, his invisible Comedy, &c." 4to, 1618; Act I.—The copy below was communicated to the Editor by the late Mr. Shenstone as corrected by him from an ancient MS, and supplied with a concluding stanza.

We

** Even in the time of Langland, pilgrimages to Walsingham were not unfavourable to the rites of Venus. Thus in his Visions of Pierce Plowman, fo. 1.*

𝕳ermets on a heape, with hoked staves,
Wenten to Walsingham, and her ‡ wenches after.
  ‡ *i. e. their.*

We have placed this, and GENTLE HERDS
thus early in the volume, upon a presumption th.
have been written, if not before the diffolution
nafteries, yet while the remembrance of them u
the minds of the people.

A S ye came from the holy land
  Of ' bleffed ' Walfingham,
O met you not with my true love
  As by the way ye came ?

" How fhould I know your true love,
  " That have met many a one,
" As I came from the holy land,
  " That have both come, and gone ? "

My love is neither white *, nor browne,
  But as the heavens faire ;
There is none hath her form divine,
  Either in earth, or ayre.

" Such an one did I meet, good fir,
  " With an angelicke face ;
" Who like a nymphe, a queene appeard
  " Both in her gait, her grace."

Yes : fhe hath cleane forfaken me,
  And left me all alone;
Who fome time loved me as her life,
  And called me her owne.

* *fc. pale.*

I

"   What is the caufe fhe leaves thee thus,
   " And a new way doth take,
" That fome time loved thee as her life,
   " And thee her joy did make ?"

I that loved her all my youth,   25
   Growe old now as you fee;
Love liketh not the falling fruite,
   Nor yet the withered tree.

For love is like a careleffe childe,
   Forgetting promife paft :   30
He is blind, or deaf, whenere he lift ;
   His faith is never faft.

His 'fond' defire is fickle found,
   And yieldes a truftleffe joye ;
Wonne with a world of toil and care,   35
   And loft ev'n with a toye.

Such is the love of womankinde,
   Or Loves faire name abufde,
Beneathe which many vaine defires,
   And follyes are excufde.   40

' But true love is a lafting fire,
   ' Which viewlefs veftals * tend,
' That burnes for ever in the foule,
   ' And knowes nor change, nor end.'

* fc. Angels.

XVII.

XVII.

H A R D Y K N U T E.

A Scottish Fragment.

As this fine morsel of heroic poetry hath generally past for ancient, it is here thrown to the end of our earliest pieces; that such as doubt of its age, may the better compare it with other pieces of genuine antiquity. For after all, there is more than reason to suspect, that most of its beauties are of modern date; and that these at least (if not its whole exis-tence) have flowed from the pen of a lady, within this pre-sent century. The following particulars may be depended on. One Mrs. Wardlaw, whose maiden name was Halket (aunt to the late Sir Peter Halket of Pitferran in Scotland, who was killed in America along with general Bradock in 1755) pretended she had found this poem, written on shreds of paper, employed for what is called the bottoms of clues. A suspicion arose that it was her own composition. Some able judges asserted it to be modern. The lady did in a manner acknowledge it to be so. Being desired to shew an additional stanza, as a proof of this, she produced the three last beginning with "Loud and schrill," *&c. which were not in the copy that was first printed. The late Lord Pre-sident Forbes, and Sir Gilbert Elliot of Minto (late Lord Justice Clerk for Scotland) who had believed it ancient, contributed to the expence of publishing the first Edition, which came out in folio about the year 1720.—This account is transmitted from Scotland by a gentleman of distinguished rank, learning, and genius, who yet is of opinion, that part of the ballad may be ancient; but retouched and much enlarged by the lady abovementioned. Indeed he hath been informed, that the late William Thompson, the Scottish musician, who*

published

published the ORPHEUS CALEDONIUS, *1733, 2 vols.*
8vo. declared he had heard fragments of it repeated during
his infancy; before ever Mrs. Wardlaw's copy was heard
of.

STately ftept he eaft the wa,
    And ftately ftept he weft,
Full feventy zeirs he now had fene,
    With fkerfs fevin zeirsof reft.
He livit quhen Britons breach of faith   5
    Wroucht Scotland meikle wae:
And ay his fword tauld to their coft,
    He was their deidly fae.

Hie on a hill his caftle ftude,
    With halls and touris a hicht,   10
And guidly chambers fair to fe,
    Quhair he lodgit mony a knicht.
His dame fae peirlefs anes and fair,
    For chaft and bewtie deimt,
Nae marrow had in all the land,   15
    Saif Elenor the quene.

Full thirtein fons to him fcho bare,
    All men of valour ftout ;
In bluidy ficht with fword in hand
    Nyne loft their lives bot doubt :   20
Four zit remain, lang may they live
    To ftand by liege and land ;
Hie was their fame, hie was their micht,
    And hie was their command.

Great

Great luve they bare to Fairly fair,
   Their fifter faft and deir,
Her girdle fhawd her midle gimp,
   And gowden glift her hair.
Quhat waefou wae her bewtie bred ?
   Waefou to zung and auld,   30
Waufou I trow to kyth and kyn,
   As ftory ever tauld.

The king of Norfe in fummer tyde,
   Puft up with powir and micht,
Landed in fair Scotland the yle,   35
   With mony a hardy knicht.
The tydings to our gude Scots king
   Came, as he fat at dyne,
With noble chiefs in braif aray,
   Drinking the blude-reid wine.   40

" To horfe, to horfe, my ryal liege,
   Zours faes ftand on the ftrand,
Full twenty thoufand glittering fpears
   The king of Norfe commands."
Bring me my fteed Mage dapple gray,   45
   Our gude king raife and cryd,
A truftier beaft in all the land
   A Scots king nevir feyd.

Go little page, tell Hardyknute,
   That lives on hill fo hie,   50
To draw his fword, the dreid of faes,
   And hafte and follow me.
The little page flew fwift as dart
   Flung by his mafters arm,
" Cum down, cum down, lord Hardyknute,   55
   And rid zour king frae harm."

Then reid reid grew his dark-brown cheiks,
   Sae did his dark-brown brow;
His luiks grew kene, as they were wont
   In dangers great to do;   60
He hes tane a horn as green as glafs,
   And gien five founds fae fhrill,
That treis in grene wood fchuke thereat,
   Sae loud rang ilka hill.

His fons in manly fport and glie,   65
   Had paft that fummers morn,
Quhen low down in a graffy dale,
   They heard their fatheris horn.
That horn, quod they, neir founds in peace,
   We haif other fport to byde.   70
And fune they heyd themup the hill,
   And fune were at his fyde.

" Late late the zeftrene I weind in peace
   To end my lengthned life,
My age micht weil excufe my arm   75
   Frae manly feats of ftryfe ;
But now that Norfe dois proudly boaft
   Fair Scotland to inthrall,
Its neir be faid of Hardyknute,
   He feard to ficht or fall.   80

" Robin of Rothfay, bend thy bow,
   Thy arrows fchute fae leil,
That mony a comely countenance
   They haif turnd to deidly pale.
Brade Thomas tak ze but zour lance,   85
   Ze neid nae weapons mair,
Gif ze ficht weit as ze did anes
   Gainft Weftmorlands ferfs heir.

" And Malcom, licht of fute as ftag
   That runs in foreft wyld,   90
Get me my thoufands thrie of men
   Well bred to fword and fchield :
Bring me my horfe and harnifine
   My blade of mettal cleir.
If faes kend but the hand it bare,   95
   They fune had fled for feir.

                     " Fareweil

" Fareweil my dame fae peirlefs gude,
  (And tuke her by the hand),
Fairer to me in age zou feim,
  Than maids for bewtie famd: 100
My zoungeft fon fhall here remain
  To guard thefe ftately towirs,
And fhut the filver bolt that keips
  Sae faft zour painted bowirs."

And firft fcho wet her comely cheiks,   105
  And then her boddice grene,
Hir filken cords of twirtle twift,
  Weil plett with filver fchene ;
And apron fett with mony a dice
  Of neidle-wark fae rare,   110
Wove by nae hand, as ze may guefs,
  Saif that of Fairly fair.

And he has ridden owre muir and mofs,
  Owre hills and mony a glen,
Quhen he came to a wounded knicht   115
  Making a heavy mane ;
" Here maun I lye, here maun I dye,
  By treacheries falfe gyles ;
Witlefs I was that eir gaif faith
  To wicked womans fmyles."   120

H 2

" Sir

" Sir knicht, gin ze were in my bowir,
  To lean on filken feat,
My laydis kyndlie care zoud prove,
  Quha neir kend deidly hate :
Hir felf wald watch ze all the day,   125
  Hir maids a deid of nicht;
And Fairly fair zour heart wald cheir,
  As fcho ftands in zour ficht.

" Aryfe young knicht, and mount zour fteid,
  Full lowns the fhynand day :   130.
Cheis frae my menzie quhom ze pleis
  To leid ze on the way."
With fmylefs luke, and vifage wan
  The wounded knicht replyd,
" Kynd chiftain, zour intent purfue,   135
  For heir I maun abyde.

To me nae after day nor nicht
  Can eir be fweit or fair,
But fune beneath fum draping tree,
  Cauld death fhall end my care."   140
With him nae pleiding micht prevail ;
  Brave Hardyknute in to gain,
With faireft words and reafon ftrong,
  Strave courteoufly in vain.

3

Syne

Syne he has gane far hynd attowre   145
    Lord Chattans land fae wyde ;
That lord a worthy wicht was ay,
    Quhen faes his courage feyd :
Of Pictifh race by mothers fyde,
    Quhen Picts ruld Caledon,   150
Lord Chattan claimd the princely maid,
    Quhen he faift Pictifh crown.

Now with his ferfs and ftalwart train,
    He reicht a ryfing heicht,
Quhair braid encampit on the dale,   155
    Norfs menzie lay in ficht.
" Zonder my valiant fons and ferfs,
    Our raging revers wait
On the unconquerit Scottifh fwaird
    To try with us their fate.   160

Make orifons to him that faift
    Our fauls upon the rude ;
Syne braifly fchaw zour veins ar filld
    With Caledonian blude."
Then furth he drew his trufty glaive,   165
    Quhyle thoufands all around
Drawn frae their fheaths glanft in the fun,
    And loud the bougills found.

H 3

To

To join his king adoun the hill
  In haft his merch he made,   170
Quhyle, playand pibrochs, minftralls meit
  Afore him ftatly ftrade.
" Thryfe welcum valziant ftoup of weir,
  Thy nations fcheild and pryde ;
Thy king nae reafon has to feir   175
  Quhen thou art be his fyde."

Then bows were bent and darts were thrawn ;
  For thrang fcarce could they flie ;
The darts clove arrows as they met,
  The arrows dart the trie.   180
Lang did they rage and ficht full ferfs,
  With little fkaith to man,
But bludy bludy was the field,
  Or that lang day was done.

The king of Scots, that findle bruikd   185
  The war that luikt lyke play,
Drew his braid fword, and brake his bow,
  Sen bows feimt but delay.
Quoth noble Rothfay, " Myne i'll keip,
  I wate its bleid a fkore."   190
Haft up my merry men, cryd the king,
  As he rade on before.

The

The king of Norfe he focht to find,
  With him to menfe the faucht,
But on his forehead there did licht   195
  A fharp unfonfie fhaft;
As he his hand put up to find
  The wound, an arrow kene,
O waefou chance! there pinnd his hand
  In midft betweene his ene.   200

" Revenge, revenge, cryd Rothfays heir,
  Your mail-coat fall nocht byde
The ftrength and fharpnefs of my dart:"
  Then fent it thruch his fyde.
Another arrow weil he markd,   205
  It perfit his neck in twa,
His hands then quat the filver reins,
  He law as eard did fa.

" Sair bleids my liege, fair, fair he bleids!"
  Again with micht he drew   210
And gefture dreid his fturdy bow,
  Faft the braid arrow flew:
Wae to the knicht he ettled at;
  Lament now quene Elgreid;
Hie dames to wail zour darlings fall,   215
  His zouth and comely meid.

H 4

" Take

" Take aff, take aff his coftly jupe
    (Of gold weil was it twynd,
Knit lyke the fowlers net, throuch quhilk
    His fteilly harnefs fhynd)   220
Take, Norfe, that gift frae me, and bid
    Him venge the blude it beirs ;
Say, if he face my bended bow,
    He fure nae weapon feirs."

Proud Norfe with giant body tall,   225
    Braid fhoulder and arms ftrong,
Cry'd, " Quhair is Hardyknute fae famd,
    And feird at Britains throne :
Thah Britons tremble at his name,
    I fune fall make him wail,   230
That eir my fword was made fae fharp,
    Sae faft his coat of mail."

That brag his ftout heart could na byde,
    It lent him zouthfou micht :
" I'm Hardyknute ; this day, he cry'd,   235
    To Scotland's king I hecht
To lay thee law, as horfes hufe ;
    My word I mean to keip."
Syne with the firft ftrakeeir he   ftrake,
    He garrd his body bleid.

Norfe

Norſe ene lyke gray goſehawke ſtaird wyld,
    He ſicht with ſhame and ſpyte ;
" Diſgrac'd is now my far-fam'd arm
    That left thee power to ſtryke :"
Then gaif his head a blaw ſae fell,   245
    It made him doun to ſtoup,
As law as he to ladies uſit
    In courtly gyſe to lout.

Full ſune he raisd his bent body,
    His bow he marvelld fair,   250
Sen blaws till then on him but darrd
    As touch of Fairly fair :
Norſe ferliet too as fair as he
    To ſe his ſtately luke ;
Sae ſune as eir he ſtrake a fae,   255
    Sae ſune his lyfe he tuke.

Quhair lyke a fyre to hether ſet,
    Bauld Thomas did advance,
A ſturdy fae with luke enrag'd
    Up towards him did prance ;   260
He ſpurd his ſteid throw thickeſt ranks
    The hardy zouth to quell,
Quha ſtude unmuſit at his approach
    His furie to repell.

                                    " That

" That fchort brown fhaft fae meanly trim'd,   265
    Lukis lyke poor Scotlands geir,
But dreidfull feems the rufty point !"
    And loud he leuch in jeir.
" Aft Britons blude has dimd its fhyne ;
    This poynt cut fhort their vaunt :"   270
Syne pierc'd the boifteris bairded cheik ;
    Nae tyme he tuke to taunt.

Schort quhyle he in his fadill fwang,
    His ftirrup was nae ftay,
Sae feible hang his unbent knee   275
    Sure taken he was fey :
Swith on the hardened clay he fell,
    Richt far was heard the thud :
But Thomas luikt not as he lay
    All waltering in his blude.   280

With cairles gefture, mynd unmuvit,
    On raid he north the plain ;
His feim in thrang of fierceft ftryfe,
    Quhen winner ay the fame :
Nor zit his heart dames dimpelit cheik   285
    Could meife faft love to bruik,
Till vengeful Ann returnd his fcorn,
    Then languid grew his luke.

In

In thrawis of death, with wallowit cheik
   All panting on the plain,   290
The fainting corps of warriours lay,
   Neir to aryse again ;
Neir to return to native land,
   Nae mair with blythsom sounds
To boist the glories of the day,   295
   And schaw their shining wounds.

On Norways coast the widowit dame
   May wash the rocks with teirs,
May lang luke owre the schiples seis
   Befoir hir mate appears.   300
Ceise, Emma, ceise to hope in vain ;
   Thy lord lyis in the clay ;
The valziant Scots nae revers thole
   To carry lyfe away.

There on a lie, quhair stands a crofs   305
   Set up for monument,
Thousands full fierce that summers day
   Filld kene waris black intent.
Let Scots, quhyle Scots, praise Hardyknute,
   Let Norse the name ay dreid,   310
Ay how he faucht, aft how he spaird,
   Sal latest ages reid.

                          Loud

Loud and chill blew the weſtlin wind,
   Sair beat the heavy ſhowir,
Mirk grew the nicht eir Hardyknute   315
   Wan neir his ſtately towir.
His towir that uſd with torches bleiſe
   To ſhyne ſae far at nicht,
Seimd now as black as mourning weid,
   Nae marvel ſair he ſichd.   320

" Thairs nae licht in my ladys bowir,
   Thairs nae licht in my hall ;
Nae blink ſhynes round my Fairly fair,
   Nor ward ſtands on my wall.
" Quhat bodes it ? Robert, Thomas, ſay ;"— 325
   Nae anſwer fits their dreid.
" Stand back, my ſons, I'll be zour gyde :"
   But by they paſt with ſpeid.

" As faſt I haif ſped owre Scotlands faes,"—
   There ceiſt his brag of weir,   330
Sair ſchamit to mynd ocht but his dame,
   And maiden Fairly fair.
Black feir he felt, but quhat to feir
   He wiſt not zit with dreid ;
Sair ſchuke his body, ſair his limbs,   335
   And all the warrior fled.

*　*　*　*　*

*_** Since

** *Since this poem of* HARDYKNUTE *was first printed off, still farther information has been received concerning the original manner of its publication, and the additions made to it afterwards.*

" *The late Dr. John Clerk, a celebrated physician in Edinburgh, one of Lord President Forbes's intimate companions, has left in his own hand writing, an ample account of all the additions and variations made in this celebrated poem, as also two additional stanzas never yet printed.*"

The title of the first edition was, " HARDYKNUTE, A FRAGMENT. EDINBURGH. 1719." *folio.* 12 *pages.*

Stanzas not in the first edition, but added afterwards in the EVERGREEN, 1724, 120. *are the two, beginning at* ver. 129. " *Aryse young knicht,* &c. *to* ver. 144.—*Instead of* ver. 143, 144, *as they stand at present, Dr. Clerk's MS. has*

> With argument, but vainly strave
>
> Lang courteously in vain.

Again, from ver. 153. *Now with his ferss,* &c. *to* 176, *are not in the first edit.*——*In Dr. Clerk's MS.* ver. 170, &c. *runs thus,*

> In haste his strides he bent
>
> While minstrells play and pibrocks fine
>
> Afore him stately went.

Lastly, from ver. 257. *Quhair lyke a fyre,* &c. *to the end of the poem, were not in the* 1st *copy. Variation of line the last (*v. 336.) *is*

> " He feared a' could be feared."

The two additional stanzas come in between ver. 388. *and* v. 389. *and are these,*

> Now darts flew wavering through flaw speed,
>
> Scarce could they reach their aim ;
>
> Or reach'd, scarce blood the round point drew,
>
> 'Twas all but shot in vain :

Right

Right ſtrengthy arms forfeebled grew,
   Sair wreck'd wi' that day's toils ;
E'en fierce-born minds now lang'd for peace,
   And curs'd war's cruel broils.

Yet ſtill wars horns ſounded to charge,
   Swords claſh'd and harneſs rang ;
But ſaftly ſae ilk blaſter blew
   The hills and dales fraemang.
Nae echo heard in double dints,
   Nor the lang-winding horn,
Nae mair ſhe blew out brade as ſhe
   Did eir that ſummers morn.

*This obliging information the Reader owes to David Clerk,
M. D. at Edinburgh, ſon of Dr. John Clerk.*

   *It is perhaps needleſs to obſerve, that theſe two ſtanzas, as
well as moſt of the variations above, are of inferior merit to
the reſt of the poem, and are probably firſt ſketches that were
afterwards rejected.*

THE END OF THE FIRST BOOK.

ANCIENT

SONGS AND BALLADS,

&c.

SERIES THE SECOND.
BOOK II.

I.

A BALLAD OF LUTHER, THE POPE, A CARDINAL, AND A HUSBANDMAN.

In the former Book we brought down this second Series of poems, as low as about the middle of the sixteenth century. We now find the Muses deeply engaged in religious controversy. The sudden revolution, wrought in the opinions of mankind by the Reformation, is one of the most striking events in the history of the human mind. It could not but engross the attention of every individual in that age, and therefore no other writings would have any chance to be read, but such as related to this grand topic. The alterations made in the established religion by Henry VIII, the sudden changes it underwent in the three succeeding reigns with-

in

in so short a space as eleven or twelve years, and the violent
struggles between expiring *Popery*, and growing *Protestan-
tism*, could not but interest all mankind. Accordingly every
pen was engaged in the dispute. The followers of the *Old*
and *New Profession* (as they were called) had their respective
Ballad-makers; and every day produced some popular sonnet
for, or against the *Reformation*. The following ballad, and
that intitled LITTLE JOHN NOBODY, may serve for spe-
cimens of the writings of each party. Both were written
in the reign of *Edward VI*; and are not the worst that
were composed upon the occasion. Controversial divinity is
no friend to poetic flights. Yet this ballad of " *Luther and
the Pope*," is not altogether devoid of spirit; it is of the
dramatic kind, and the characters are tolerably well sustained; especially that of *Luther*, which is made to speak in a
manner not unbecoming the spirit and courage of that vigor-
ous *Reformer*. It is printed from the original black-letter
copy (in the *Pepys collection, vol. I. folio,*) to which is prefixed a large wooden cut, designed and executed by some eminent master. This is copied in miniature in the small En-
graving inserted above.

We are not to wonder that the *Ballad-writers* of that
age should be inspired with the zeal of controversy, when
the very stage teemed with polemic divinity. I have now
before me two very ancient quarto black-letter plays: the
one published in the time of *Henry VIII*, intitled, 𝕰𝖛𝖊𝖗𝖞
𝕸𝖆𝖓; the other called 𝕷𝖚𝖘𝖙𝖞 𝕵𝖚𝖛𝖊𝖓𝖙𝖚𝖘, printed in the
reign of *Edward VI*. In the former of these, occasion
is taken to inculcate great reverence for old mother church
and her superstitions * : in the other, the poet (one R.
WEVER)

---

* Take a specimen from his high encomiums on the priesthood,
" There is no emperour, kyng, duke, ne baron
· That of God hath commissyon,
" As hath the leest preest in the world beynge.
       * * *
" God hath to them more power gyven,
" Than to any aungell, that is in heven:
       " With

WEVER) *with great fuccefs attacks both. So that the Stage in thofe days literally was, what wife men have always wifhed it,—a fupplement to the pulpit :—This was fo much the cafe, that in the play of Lufty Juventus, chapter and verfe are every where quoted as formally, as in a fermon; take an inftance,*

  " *The Lord by his prophet Ezechiel fayeth in this wife*
     playnlye,
  " *As in the xxxiij chapter it doth appere :*
  " *Be converted, O ye children, &c.*"

From this play we learn that moft of the young people were New Gofpellers, or friends to the Reformation ; and that the old were tenacious of the doctrines imbibed in their youth : for thus the Devil is introduced lamenting the downfal of fuperftition,

  " *The olde people would believe ftil in my lawes,*
  " *But the yonger fort leade them a contrary way,*
  " *They wyl not beleve, they playnly fay,*
  " *In olde traditions, and made by men, &c.*"

VOL. II.   I   *And*

" *With v. words he may confecrate*
" *Goddes body in flesfhe and blode to take,*
" *And handeleth his maker bytwene his handes,*
" *The preeft byndeth and unbindeth all bandes,*
" *Bothe in erthe and in heven.*
" *Thou minifters all the facramentes feven.*
" *Though we kyft thy fete thou were worthy ;*
" *Thou art the furgyan that cureth fynne dedly ;*
" *No remedy may we fynde under God,*
" *But alone on preefthode.*
" *Every-man, God gave preeft that dignite,*
" *And letteth them in his ftede amonge us be,*
" *Thus be they above aungels in degre.*"
   * * * * *

            fign. C. j. b.

And in another place Hypocrify urges,

> " *The worlde was never meri*
> " *Since chyldren were fo boulde :*
> " *Now every boy wil be a teacher,*
> " *The father a foole, the chyld a preacher.*"

Of the plays abovementioned, to the firft is fubjoined the following Printer's Colophon, ¶ Thus endeth this moral playe of Every Man. ¶ Imprynted at London in Powles chyrche yarde by me John Skot. +. *In Mr. Garrick's collection is an imperfect copy of the fame play, printed by Richarde Pynfon.*

The other is intitled, An enterlude called Lufty Iuuentus: *and is thus diftinguifhed at the end :* Finis. quod R. Weber. Imprinted at London in Paules churche yeard, by Abraham Dele at the figne of the Lambe. *Of this too Mr. Garrick has an imperfect copy of a different edition.*

Of thefe two Plays the Reader may find fome farther particulars in the former Volume, Book II. fee THE ESSAY ON THE ORIGIN OF THE ENGLISH STAGE.

THE HUSBANDMAN.

LET us lift up our hartes all,
  And prayfe the lordes magnificence,
Which hath given the wolues a fall,
  And is become our ftrong defence :
  For they thorowe a falfe pretens   5
From Chriftes bloude dyd all us leade,

Gettynge

Gettynge from every man his pence,
As satisfactours for the deade.

For what we with our FLAYLES coulde get
   To kepe our houfe, and fervauntes;   10
That did the Freers from us fet,
   And with our foules played the marchauntes:
   And thus they with theyr falfe warrantes
Of our fweate have eafelye lyved,
   That for fatneffe theyr belyes pantes,   15
So greatlye have they us deceaued.

They fpared not the fatherleffe,
   The carefull, nor the pore wydowe;
They wolde have fomewhat more or leffe,
   If it above the ground did growe: 20
   But now we hufbandmen do knowe
Al their fubteltye, and their falfe cafte;
   For the lorde hath them overthrowe
With his fwete word now at the lafte.

DOCTOR MARTIN LUTHER.

Thou antichrift, with thy thre crownes,   25
   Haft ufurped kynges powers,
As having power over realmes and townes,
   Whom thou oughteft to ferve all houres:
   Thou thinkeft by thy jugglyng colours
Thou maift lykewife Gods word oppreffe: 30
I 2

As

As do the deceatful foulers,
When they theyr nettes craftelye dreſſe.

Thou flattereſt every prince, and lord,
  Thretening poore men with fwearde and fyre;
All thofe, that do followe Gods worde,   35
  To make them cleve to thy defire,
  Theyr bokes thou burneſt in flaming fire;
Curfing with boke, bell, and candell,
  Such as to reade them have defyre,
Or with them are wyllynge to meddell.   40

Thy falſe power wyl I bryng down,
  Thou ſhalt not raygne many a yere,
I ſhall dryve the from citye and towne,
  Even with this PEN that thou feyſte here:
  Thou fyghteſt with fwerd, ſhylde, and fpeare,   45
But I wyll fyght with Gods worde;
  Which is now fo open and cleare,
That it ſhall brynge the under the borde.

THE POPE.

Though I brought never fo many to hel,
  And to utter dampnacion,   50
Throughe myne enfample, and confel,
  Or thorow any abhominacion,
  Yet doth our lawe excufe my faſhion.
And thou, Luther, arte accurfed;

For

For blamynge me, and my condicion, 55
The holy decres have the condempned.

Thou ftryveft againft my purgatory,
   Becaufe thou findeft it not in fcripture;
As though I by myne auctorite
   Myght not make one for myne honoure. 60
   Knoweft thou not, that I have power
To make, and mar, in heaven and hell,
   In erth, and every creature?
Whatfoever I do it muft be well.

As for fcripture, I am above it; 65
   Am not I Gods hye vicare?
Shulde I be bounde to folowe it,
   As the carpenter his ruler?
   Nay, nay, heretickes ye are,
That will not obey my auctoritie. 70
   With this SWORDE I wyll declare,
That ye fhal al accurfed be.

THE CARDINAL.

I am a cardinall of Rome,
   Sent from Chriftes hye vicary,
To graunt pardon to more, and fume, 75
   That wil Luther refift ftrongly:
   He is a greate hereticke treuly,
And regardeth to much the fcripture;

I 3

For he thinketh onely thereby
To fubdue the popes high honoure.   80

Receive ye this PARDON devoutely,
    And loke that ye agaynſt him fight;
Plucke up youre herts, and be manlye,
    For the pope fayth ye do but ryght:
    And this be fure, that at one flyghte,   85
Allthough ye be overcome by chaunce,
  Ye ſhall to heaven go with greate myghte;
God can make you no reſiſtaunce.

But thefe heretikes for their medlynge
    Shall go down to hel every one;   90
For they have not the popes bleſſynge,
    Nor regarde his holy pardòn:
    They thinke from all deſtruction
By Chriſtes bloud, to be faved,
    Fearynge not our excommunicacion,   95
Therefore ſhall they al be dampned.

II. JOHN

II.

JOHN ANDERSON MY JO.

A Scottish Song.

While in England verse was made the vehicle of contro-versy, and Popery was attacked in it by logical argument, or stinging satire; we may be sure the zeal of the Scottish Reformers would not suffer their pens to be idle, but many a pasquil was discharged at the Romish priests, and their enormous encroachments on property. Of this kind perhaps is the following, (preserved in an ancient MS. Collection of Scottish poems in the Pepysian library:)

> Tak a Wobſter, that is leill,
> And a Miller, that will not ſteill,
> With ane Prieſt, that is not gredy,
> And lay ane deid corpſe thame by,
> And, throw virtue of thame three,
> That deid corpſe ſall qwyknit be.

Thus far all was fair: but the furious hatred of popery led them to employ their rhymes in a still more licentious man-ner. It is a received tradition in Scotland, that at the time of the Reformation, ridiculous and baudy songs were composed to be sung by the rabble to the tunes of the most favourite hymns in the Latin service Greene sleeves and pudding pies (designed to ridicule the popish clergy) is

I 4

said

ſaid to have been one of theſe metamorphoſed hymns: Maggy
Lauder *was another :* John Anderſon my jo *was a third.
The original muſic of all theſe burleſque ſonnets was very
fine. To give a ſpecimen of their manner, we have inſerted
one of the leaſt offenſive. The Reader will pardon the
meanneſs of the compoſition for the ſake of the anecdote,
which ſtrongly marks the ſpirit of the times.*

*The adaptation of ſolemn church muſic to theſe ludicrous
pieces, and the jumble of ideas, thereby occaſioned, will account for the following fact.—From the Records of the General Aſſembly in Scotland, called, " The Book of the Uni-
verſal Kirk," p. 90. 7th July,* 1568, *it appears, that
Thomas Baſſendyne printer in Edinburgh, printed " a pſalme
" buik, in the end whereof was found printit ane baudy
" ſang, called, " Welcome Fortunes *."*

WOMAN.

JOHN Anderſon my jo, cum in as ze gae bye,
　And ze ſall get a ſheips heid weel baken in a pye;
Weel baken in a pye, and the haggis in a pat :
John Anderſon my jo, cum in, and ze's get that.

MAN.

And how doe ze, Cummer? and how doe ze thrive?
And how mony bairns hae ze? Wom. Cummer, I hae five.
Man. Are they to zour awin gude man? Wom. Na,
　　Cummer, na;
For four of tham were gotten, quhan Wallie was awa'.

---

* *See alſo Biograph. Britan. vol. I. p.* 177.

III.　LITTLE

III.

LITTLE JOHN NOBODY.

*We have here a witty libel on the Reformation under king
Edward VI. written about the year 1550, and preserved in
the Pepys collection, British Museum, and Strype's Mem. of
Cranmer. The author artfully declines entering into the
merits of the cause, and wholly reflects on the lives and actions
of many of the Reformed. It is so easy to find flaws and
imperfections in the conduct of men, even the best of them,
and still easier to make general exclamations about the pro-
fligacy of the present times, that no great point is gained by
arguments of that sort, unless the author could have proved
that the principles of the Reformed Religion had a natural
tendency to produce a corruption of manners: whereas he in-
directly owns, that their* REVEREND FATHER [*archbishop
Cranmer*] *had used the most proper means to stem the tor-
rent, by giving the people access to the scriptures, by teach-
ing them to pray with understanding, and by publishing homilies, and other religious tracts. It must however be acknowledged, that our libeller had at that time sufficient
room for just satire. For under the banners of the Reformed
had inlisted themselves, many concealed papists, who had
private ends to gratify; many that were of no religion;
many greedy courtiers, who thirsted after the possessions of
the church; and many dissolute persons, who wanted to be
exempt from all ecclesiastical censures: And as these men were
loudest of all others in their cries for Reformation, so in
effect none obstructed the regular progress of it so much, or
by their vicious lives brought vexation and shame more on
the truly venerable and pious Reformers.*

The

*The reader will remark the fondness of our Satirist for
alliteration: in this he was guilty of no affectation or singu-
larity; his versification is that of Pierce Plowman's Visions,
in which a recurrence of similar letters is essential: to this
he has only superadded rhyme, which in his time began to be
the general practice. See farther remarks on this kind of
metre in the preface to* BOOK III. BALLAD I.

IN december, when the dayes draw to be short,
    After november, when the nights wax noyfome and
As I paft by a place privily at a port,   [long;
I faw one fit by himfelf making a fong :
His laft * talk of trifles, who told with his tongue
That few were faft i'th' faith. I ' freyned †' that freake,
Whether he wanted wit, or fome had done him wrong.
    He faid, he was little John Nobody, that durft not fpeake.

John Nobody, quoth I, what news ? thou foon note and
What maner men thou meane, that are fo mad.   [tell
He faid, Thefe gay gallants, that wil conftrue the gofpel,
As Solomon the fage, with femblance full fad ;
To difcuffe divinity they nought adread ;
More meet it were for them to milk kye at a fleyke.
Thou lyeft, quoth I, thou lofel, like a leud lad.   [fpeake.
    He faid, he was little John Nobody, that durft not

Its meet for every man on this matter to talk,
And the glorious gofpel ghoftly to have in mind ;
It is fothe faid, that fect but much unfeemly fkalk,
As boyes babble in books, that in fcripture are blind :
                                                    Yet

* *Perhaps* He left talk.   † feyned. *MSS. and P. C.*

Yet to their fancy foon a caufe wil find;
As to live in luft, in lechery to leyke:
Such caitives count to be come of Cains kind;
 But that I little John Nobody durft not fpeake.

For our reverend father hath fet forth an order,
Our fervice to be faid in our feignours tongue;
As Solomon the fage fet forth the fcripture;
Our fuffrages, and fervice, with many a fweet fong,
With homilies, and godly books us among,
That no ftiff, ftubborn ftomacks we fhould freyke:
But wretches nere worfe to do poor men wrong;
 But that I little John Nobody dare not fpeake.

For bribery was never fo great, fince born was our Lord,
And whoredom was never les hated, fith Chrift har-
  rowed hel,
And poor men are fo fore punifhed commonly through
  the world,
That it would grieve any one, that good is, to hear tel:
For al the homilies and good books, yet their hearts be
  fo quel,
That if a man do amiffe, with mifchiefe they wil him
  wreake;
The fafhion of thefe new fellows it is fo vile and fell:
 But that I little John Nobody dare not fpeake.

Thus to live after their luft, that life would they have,
And in lechery to leyke al their long life;

For

Ver. 3. Cain's kind.] So in Pierce the Plowman's creed, the proud friars are faid to be
———— " Of Caymes kind." Vid. Sig. C. ij. b.

For al the preaching of Paul, yet many a proud knave
Wil move mifchiefe in their mind both to maid and wife
To bring them in advoutry, or elfe they wil ftrife,
And in brawling about baudery, Gods commandments
    breake :
But of thefe frantic il fellowes, few of them do thrife ;
    Though I little John Nobody dare not fpeake.

If thou company with them, they wil currifhly carp,
    and not care
According to their foolifh fantacy ; but faft wil they
    naught :
Prayer with them is but prating; therefore they it forbear :
Both almes deeds, and holinefs, they hate it in their
    thought :
Therefore pray we to that prince, that with his bloud
    us bought,
That he wil mend that is amifs : for many a manful freyke
Is forry for thefe fects, though they fay little or nought ;
    And that I little John Nobody dare not once fpeake.

Thus in NO place, this NOBODY, in NO time I met,
Where NO man, ' ne* NOUGHT was, nor NOTHING did
    appear ;
Through the found of a fynagogue for forrow I fwett,
That ' Aeolus †' through the eccho did caufe me to hear.
Then I drew me down into a dale, whereas the dumb deer
Did fhiver for a fhower ; but I fhunted from a freyke :
For I would no wight in this world wift who I were,
    But little John Nobody, that dare not once fpeake.

               IV. Q.

---

* then. *MSS.* *and P. C.*   † Hercules, *MSS. and P. C.*

IV.

Q. ELIZABETH's VERSES, WHILE PRISONER AT WOODSTOCK,

WRIT WITH CHARCOAL ON A SHUTTER,

—are preserved by Hentzner, in that part of his Travels, which has lately been reprinted in so elegant a manner at STRAWBERRY-HILL. In Hentzner's book they were wretchedly corrupted, but are here given as amended by his ingenious Editor. The old orthography, and one or two ancient readings of Hentzner's copy are here restored.

OH, Fortune! how thy restlesse wavering state
   Hath fraught with cares my troubled witt!
Witnes this present prisonn, whither fate
   Could beare me, and the joys I quitt.
Thou causedest the guiltie to be losed   5
From bandes, wherein are innocents inclosed:
   Causing the guiltles to be straite reserved,
   And freeing those that death had well deserved.
But by her envie can be nothing wroughte,
So God send to my foes all they have thoughte.

A.D. MDLV.   ELIZABETHE, PRISONNER.

V. THE

Ver. 4. Could beare, *is an ancient idiom, equivalent to* Did bear *or* Hath borne. *See below the* Beggar of Bednal Green, *ver.* 57. Could say.

V.

THE HEIR OF LINNE.

This old ballad is given from a copy in the editor's folio MS; some breaches and defects in which, rendered the insertion of a few supplemental stanzas necessary. These it is hoped the reader will pardon.

From the Scottish phrases here and there discernable in this poem, it should seem to have been originally composed beyond the Tweed.

The Heir of Linne seems not to have been a Lord of Parliament, but a LAIRD, *whose title went along with his estate.*

PART THE FIRST.

LITHE and listen, gentlemen,
   To sing a song I will beginne :
It is of a lord of faire Scotlànd,
   Which was the unthrifty heire of Linne.

His father was a right good lord,   5
   His mother a lady of high degree ;
But they, alas ! were dead, him froe,
   And he lov'd keeping companie.

To

To spend the daye with merry cheare,
　　To drinke and revell every night,　　　10
To card and dice from eve to morne,
　　It was, I ween, his hearts delighte.

To ride, to runne, to rant, to roare,
　　To alwaye spend and never spare,
I wott, an' it were the king himselfe,　　15
　　Of gold and fee he mote be bare.

Soe fares the unthrifty lord of Linne
　　Till all his gold is gone and spent;
And he mun sell his landes so broad,
　　His house, and landes, and all his rent.　　20

His father had a keen stewàrde,
　　And John o' the Scales was called hee:
But John is become a gentel-man,
　　And John has gott both gold and fee.

Sayes, Welcome, welcome, lord of Linne,　　25
　　Let nought disturb thy merry cheere,
Iff thou wilt sell thy landes soe broad,
　　Good store of gold Ile give thee heere.

My gold is gone, my money is spent;
　　My lande nowe take it unto thee :　　　30
Give me the golde, good John o' the Scales,
　　And thine for aye my lande shall bee.

Then

4

Then John he did him to record draw,
  And John he gave him a gods-pennie * ;
But for every pounde that John agreed,   35
  The lande, I wis, was well worth three.

He told him the gold upon the board,
  He was right glad his land to winne :
The land is mine, the gold is thine,
  And now Ile be the lord of Linne.   40

Thus he hath sold his land soe broad,
  Both hill and holt, and moore and fenne,
All but a poore and lonesome lodge,
  That stood far off in a lonely glenne.

For soe he to his father hight :   45
  My sonne, when I am gonne, sayd hee,
Then thou wilt spend thy lande so broad,
  And thou wilt spend thy gold so free:

But sweare me nowe upon the roode,
  That lonesome lodge thou'lt never spend ;   50
For when all the world doth frown on thee,
  Thou there shalt find a faithful friend.

The heire of Linne is full of golde :
  And come with me, my friends, sayd hee,
Let's drinke, and rant, and merry make,   55
  And he that spares, ne'er mote he thee.

They

* *i. e. earnest-money; from the French 'Denier à Dieu.'*

They ranted, drank, and merry made,
  Till all his gold it waxed thinne;
And then his friendes they flunk away;
  They left the unthrifty heire of Linne.   60

He had never a penny left in his purfe,
  Never a penny left but three,
The tone was brafs, and the tone was lead,
  And tother it was white monèy.

Nowe well-away, fayd the heire of Linne,   65
  Nowe well-away, and woe is mee,
For when I was the lord of Linne,
  I never wanted gold or fee.

But many a truftye friend have I,
  And why fhold I feel dole or care ?   70
Ile borrow of them all by turnes,
  Soe need I not be never bare.

But one, I wis, was not at home,
  Another had payd his gold away;
Another call'd him thriftlefs loone,   75
  And bade him fharpely wend his way.

Now well-away, fayd the heire of Linne,
  Now well-away, and woe is me!
For when I had my landes fo broad,
  On me they liv'd right merrilee.   80
  Vol. II.   K   To

To beg my bread from door to door
  I wis, it were a brenning shame:
To rob and steal it were a sinne:
  To worke my limbs I cannot frame.

Now Ile away to lonesome lodge,
  For there my father bade me wend;
When all the world should frown on mee,
  I there shold find a trusty friend.

PART THE SECOND.

AWAY then hyed the heire of Linne
  O'er hill and holt, and moor and fenne,
Untill he came to lonesome lodge,
  That stood so lowe in a lonely glenne.

He looked up, he looked downe,
  In hope some comfort for to winne,
But bare and lothly were the walles:
  Here's sorry cheare, quo' the heire of Linne.

The little windowe dim and darke
  Was hung with ivy, brere, and yewe;
No shimmering sunn here ever shone;
  No halesome breeze here ever blew.

No chair, ne table he mote fpye,
 No chearful hearth, ne welcome bed,
Nought fave a rope with renning noofe,   15
 That dangling hung up o'er his head.

And over it in broad lettèrs,
 Thefe words were written fo plain to fee:
" Ah! graceleffe wretch, haft fpent thine all,
 " And brought thyfelfe to penurìe?   20

" All this my boding mind mifgave,
 " I therefore left this trufty friend:
" Let it now fheeld thy foule difgracc,
 " And all thy fhame and forrows end."

Sorely fhent wi' this rebuke,   25
 Sorely fhent was the heire of Linne,
His heart, I wis, was near to braft
 With guilt and forrowe, fhame and finne.

Never a word fpake the heire of Linne,
 Never a word he fpake but three: 30
" This is a trufty friend indeed,
 " And is right welcome unto mee."

Then round his necke the corde he drewe,
 And fprang aloft with his bodìe:
When lo! the ceiling burft in twaine,   35
 And to the ground came tumbling hee.

K 2

Aftonyed

Aftonyed lay the heire of Linne,
   Ne knewe if he were live or dead,
At length he looked, and fawe a bille,
   And in it a key of gold fo redd.   40

He took the bill, and lookt it on,
   Strait good comfort found he there:
It told him of a hole in the wall,
   In which there ftood three chefts in fere.

Two were full of the beaten golde,   45
   The third was full of white monèy;
And over them in broad lettèrs
   Thefe words were written fo plaine to fee:

" Once more, my fonne, I fette thee clere;
   " Amend thy life and follies paft;   50
" For but thou amend thee of thy life,
   " That rope muft be thy end at laft."

And let it bee, fayd the heire of Linne;
   And let it bee, but if I amend *:
For here I will make mine avow,   55
   This reade ‡ fhall guide me to the end.

Away then went the heire of Linne;
   Away he went with a merry cheare:

I wis,

---

* i. e. unlefs I amend.   † i. e. advice, counfel.

I wis, he neither ſtint ne ſtayd,
  Till John o' the Scales houſe he came neare.   60

And when he came to John o' the Scales,
  Up at the ſpeere * then looked hee ;
There ſate three lords at the bordes end,
  Were drinking of the wine ſo free.

And then beſpake the heire of Linne   65
  To John o' the Scales then louted hee :
I pray thee now, good John o' the Scales,
  One forty pence for to lend mee.

Away, away, thou thriftleſs loone ;
  Away, away, this may not bee :   70
For Chriſts curſe on my head, he ſayd,
  If ever I truſt thee one pennie.

Then beſpake the heire of Linne,
  To John o' the Scales wife then ſpake he :
Madame, ſome almes on me beſtowe,   75
  I pray for ſweet ſaint Charitìe.

Away, away, thou thriftleſs loone,
  I ſwear thou getteſt no almes of mee ;
For if we ſhold hang any loſel heere,
  The firſt we wold begin with thee.   80

K 3   Then

____

  * _Perhaps the Hole in the door or window, by which it was
ſpeered, i. e. ſparred, faſtened. Query._

Then befpake a good fellowe,
    Which fat at John o' the Scales his bord:
Sayd, Turn againe, thou heire of Linne;
    Some time thou waft a well good lord:

Some time a good fellow thou haft been,   85
    And fparedft not thy gold and fee,
Therefore Ile lend thee forty pence,
    And other forty if need bee.

And ever, I pray thee, John o' the Scales,
    To let him fit in thy companee: 90
For well I wot thou hadft his land,
    And a good bargain it was to thee.

Up then fpake him John o' the Scales,
    All wood he anfwer'd him againe:
Now Chrifts curfe on my head, he fayd,   95
    But I did lofe by that bargaine.

And here I proffer thee, heire of Linne,
    Before thefe lords fo faire and free,
Thou fhalt have it backe again better cheape,
    By a hundred markes, than I had it of thee.   100

I drawe you to record, lords, he faid.
    With that he gave him a gods pennèe:
Now by my fay, fayd the heire of Linne,
    And here, good John, is thy monèy.

And

And he pull'd forth three bagges of gold,   105
    And layd them down upon the bord:
All woe begone was John o' the Scales,
    Soe fhent he cold fay never a word.

He told him forth the good red gold,
    He told it forth with mickle dinne.   110
The gold is thine, the land is mine,
    And now Ime againe the lord of Linne.

Sayes, Have thou here, thou good fellòwe,
    Forty pence thou didft lend mee:
Now I am againe the lord of Linne,   115
    And forty pounds I will give thee.

Now welladay! fayth Joan o' the Scales:
    Now welladay! and woe is my life!
Yefterday I was lady of Linne,
    Now Ime but John o' the Scales his wife.   120

Now fare thee well, fayd the heire of Linne;
    Farewell, good John o' the Scales, faid hee:
When next I want to fell my land,
    Good John o' the Scales, Ile come to thee.

    VI. GAS.

VI.

GASCOIGNE'S PRAISE OF THE FAIR BRIDGES, AFTERWARDS LADY SANDES,

ON HER HAVING A SCAR IN HER FOREHEAD.

George Gascoigne was a celebrated poet in the early part of Q. Elizabeth's reign, and appears to great advantage among the miscellaneous writers of that age. He was author of three or four plays, and of many smaller poems; one of the most remarkable of which is a satire in blank verse, called the STEELE-GLASS, 1576. 4to.

Gascoigne was born in Essex, educated in both universities, whence he removed to Gray's-inn; but, disliking the study of the law, became first a dangler at court, and afterwards a soldier in the wars of the Low Countries. He had no great success in any of these pursuits, as appears from a poem of his, intitled, " Gascoigne's Wodmanship, written " to lord Gray of Wilton." Many of his epistles dedicatory are dated in 1575, 1576, from " his poore house in Wal- " thamstoe:" where he died a middle-aged man in 1578, according to Anth. Wood: or rather in 1577, if he is the person meant in an old tract, intitled, " A remembrance of " the well-employed Life and godly End of GEO. GAS- " COIGNE, Esq; who deceased at Stamford in Lincoln- " shire, Oct. 7. 1577. by Geo. Whetstone, Gent. an eye- " witness of his godly and charitable end in this world," 4to. no date.—[From a MS. of Oldys.]

*A very ingenious critic thinks " Gascoigne has much ex- " ceeded all the poets of his age, in smoothness and harmony " of versification *." But the truth is, scarce any of the earlier poets of Q. Elizabeth's time are found deficient in harmony and smoothness, tho' those qualities appear so rare in the writings of their successors. In the PARADISE OF DAINTY DEVISES†, (the Dodsley's Miscellany of those times)*

will

---

* *Observations on the Faerie Queen, Vol. II. p 168.*
† *Printed in 1578, 1596, and perhaps oftener, in 4to, black let.*

will hardly be found one rough, or inharmonious line * : whereas the numbers of *Jonson*, *Donne*, and most of their contemporaries, frequently offend the ear, like the filing of a saw.——Perhaps this is in some measure to be accounted for from the growing pedantry of that age, and from the writers affecting to run their lines into one another, after the manner of the Latin and Greek poets.

The following poem (which the elegant writer above quoted hath recommended to notice, as possessed of a delicacy rarely to be seen in that early state of our poetry) properly consists of alexandrines of 12 and 14 syllables, and is printed from two quarto black-letter collections of *Gascoigne's* pieces; the first intitled, " *A hundreth sundrie flowres*, " *bounde up in one small posie*, &c. *London*, imprinted for " *Richarde Smith* :" without date, but from a letter of *H. W. (p.* 202.) compared with the Printer's epist. to the Reader, it appears to have been published in 1572, or 3. The other is intitled, " *The Posies of George Gascoigne, Esq*; " *corrected, perfected, and augmented by the authour*; 1575. "——*Printed at Lond. for Richard Smith, &c.*" No year, but the epist. dedicat. is dated 1576.

In the title page of this last (by way of printer's †, or bookseller's device) is an ornamental wooden cut, tolerably well executed, wherein time is represented drawing the figure of Truth out of a pit or cavern, with this legend, OCCULTA VERITAS TEMPORE PATET [R. S.] This is mentioned because it is not improbable but the accidental sight of this or some other title-page containing the same device, suggested to *Rubens* that well-known design of a similar kind, which he has introduced into the Luxemburg gallery §, and which has been so justly censured for the unnatural manner of its execution.——The device abovementioned being not ill adapted to the subject of this volume, is with some small variations copied in a plate, which to gratify the curiosity of the Reader is prefixed to Book III.

IN

---

* The same is true of most of the poems in the Mirrour of Magiſtrates, 1563, 4to, and even of Surrey's Poems, 155⁷.

† *Henrie Binneman.* § LE TEMS DECOUVRE LA VERITE.

IN court whofo demaundes
  What dame doth moft excell;
For my conceit I muft needes fay,
  Faire Bridges beares the bel :

Upon whofe lively cheeke,   5
  To prove my judgment true,
The rofe and lillie feeme to ftrive
  For equall change of hewe :

And therewithall fo well
  Hir graces all agree,   10
No frowning cheere dare once prefume
  In hir fweet face to bee.

Although fome lavifhe lippes,
  Which like fome other beft,
Will fay, the blemifhe on hir browe   15
  Difgraceth all the reft.

Thereto I thus replie,
  God wotte, they little knowe
The hidden caufe of that mifhap,
  Nor how the harm did growe :   20

For when dame Nature firft
  Had framde hir heavenly face,
And thoroughly bedecked it
  With goodly gleames of grace;

                                        It

It lyked hir fo well :   25
  Lo here, quod fhe, a peece
For perfect fhape, that paffeth all
  Appelles' worke in Greece.

This bayt may chaunce to catche
  The greateft God of love,   30
Or mightie thundring Jove himfelf,
  That rules the roaft above.

But out, alas ! thofe wordes
  Were vaunted all in vayne ;
And fome unfeen wer prefent there,   35
  Pore Bridges, to thy pain.

For Cupide, crafty boy,
  Clofe in a corner ftoode,
Not blyndfold then, to gaze on hir :
  I geffe it did him good.   40

Yet when he felte the flame
  Gan kindle in his breft,
And herd dame Nature boaft by hir
  To break him of his reft,

His hot newe-chofen love   45
  He chaunged into hate,
And fodeynly with mightie mace
  Gan rap hir on the pate.

It

It greeved Nature muche
  To fee the cruell deede: 50
Mee feemes I fee hir, how fhe wept
  To fee hir dearling bleede.

Wel yet, quod fhe, this hurt
  Shal have fome helpe I trowe:
And quick with fkin fhe coverd it,   55
  That whiter is than fnowe.

Wherwith Dan Cupide fled,
  For feare of further flame,
When angel-like he faw hir fhine,
  Whome he had fmit with fhame.   60

Lo, thus was Bridges hurt
  In cradel of hir kind:
The coward Cupide brake his browe
  To wreke his wounded mynd.

The fkar ftill there remains;   65
  No force, there let it bee:
There is no cloude that can eclipfe
  So bright a funne, as fhe.

VII. FAIR

Ver. 62. In cradel of her kind: *i. e. in the cradle of her family. Query.—See Warton's obfervations, vol.* 2. *p.* 137.

VII

FAIR ROSAMOND.

Most of the circumstances in this popular story of king Henry II. and the beautiful Rosamond have been taken for fact by our English Historians ; who, unable to account for the unnatural conduct of queen Eleanor in stimulating her sons to rebellion, have attributed it to jealousy, and supposed that Henry's amour with Rosamond was the object of that passion.

Our old English annalists seem, most of them, to have followed Higden the monk of Chester, whose account with some enlargements is thus given by Stow. " Rosamond the fayre " daughter of Walter lord Clifford, concubine to Henry II. " (poisoned by queen Elianor, as some thought) dyed at " Woodstocke [A. D. 1177.] where king Henry had made " for her a house of wonderfull working ; so that no man " or woman might come to her, but he that was instructed " by the king, or such as were right secret with him touch" ing the matter. This house after some was named Laby" rinthus, or Dedalus worke, which was wrought like un" to a knot in a garden, called a Maze ; but it was com" monly said, that lastly the queene came to her by a clue of " thridde, or silke, and so dealt with her, that she lived " not long after : but when she was dead, she was buried " at Godstow in an house of nunnes, beside Oxford, with " these verses upon her tombe,*

" Hic jacet in tumba, Rosa mundi, non Rosa munda:

   " Non redolet, sed olet, quæ redolere solet.

" In

---

* *Consisting of vaults under ground, arched and walled with brick and stone, according to Drayton. See note on his Epistle of Rosamond.*

" *In Engliſh thus :*

" *The roſe of the world, but not the cleane flowre,*
  " *Is now here graven ; to whom beauty was lent :*
" *In this grave full darke nowe is her bowre,*
  " *That by her life was ſweete and redolent :*
  " *But now that ſhe is from this life blent,*
" *Though ſhe were ſweete, now foully doth ſhe ſtinke.*
•• *A mirrour good for all men, that on her thinke.*"

Stowe's Annals, Ed. 1631. p. 154.

How the queen gained admittance into Roſamond's bower
" *is differently related. Hollingſhed ſpeaks of it, as* " *the*
" *common report of the people, that the queene . . . founde*
" *hir out by a ſilken thread, which the king had drawne*
" *after him out of hir chamber with his foot, and dealt*
" *with hir in ſuch ſharpe and cruell wiſe, that ſhe lived*
" *not long after."* Vol. III. p. 115. *On the other hand,*
in Speede's Hiſt. we are told that the jealous queen found
her out " *by a clew of ſilke, fallen from Roſamund's lappe,*
" *as ſhee ſate to take ayre, and ſuddenly fleeing from the*
" *ſight of the ſearcher, the end of her ſilke faſtened to her*
" *foot, and the clew ſtill unwinding, remained behinde :*
" *which the queene followed, till ſhee had found what ſhe*
" *ſought, and upon Roſamund ſo vented her ſpleene, as the*
" *lady lived not long after."* 3d Edit. p. 509. *Our*
ballad-maker with more ingenuity, and probably as much
truth, tells us the clue was gained, by ſurpriſe, from the
knight, who was left to guard her bower.

It is obſervable, that none of the old writers attribute
Roſamond's death to poiſon, (Stow, above, mentions it meerly
as a ſlight conjecture) ; they only give us to underſtand, that
the queen treated her harſhly ; which furious menaces, we
may ſuppoſe, and ſharp expoſtulations, which had ſuch effect
on her ſpirits, that ſhe did not long ſurvive it. Indeed on

her

*her tombstone, as we learn from a person of credit *, among other fine sculptures, was engraven the figure of a* CUP. *This, which perhaps at first was an accidental ornament, might in after times suggest the notion that she was poisoned; at least this construction was put upon it, when the stone came to be demolished after the nunnery was dissolved. The account is, that* " the tombstone of Rosamund Clifford was " taken up at Godstow, and broken in pieces, and that upon " it were interchangeable weavings drawn out and decked " with roses red and green, and the picture of the CUP, out 's of which she drank the poison given her by the queen, " carved in stone."

Rosamond's father having been a great benefactor to the nunnery of Godstow, where she had also resided herself in the innocent part of her life, her body was conveyed there, and buried in the middle of the choir; in which place it remained till the year 1191, *when Hugh bishop of Lincoln caused it to be removed. The fact is recorded by Hoveden, a contemporary writer, whose words are thus translated by Stow.* " Hugh bishop of Lincolne came to the abbey of " nunnes, called Godstow, ... and when he had entred " the church to pray, he saw a tombe in the middle of the " quire, covered with a pall of silke, and set about with " lights of waxe : and demanding whose tombe it was, he " was answered, that it was the tombe of Rosamond, that " was some time lemman to Henry II. . . . . who for the " love of her had done much good to that church. Then " quoth the bishop, take out of this place the harlot, and " bury her without the church, lest christian religion should " grow in contempt, and to the end that, through ex- " ample of her, other women being made afraid may be- " ware, and keepe themselves from unlawfull and advou- " terous company with men." *Annals, p.* 159.

History further informs us, that king John repaired Godstow nunnery, and endowed it with yearly revenues, " that
" these

<hr>

* *Tho. Allen of Gloc. Hall, Oxon. who died in* 1632, *aged* 90. *See Hearne's rambling discourse concerning Rosamond, at the end of Gul. Neubrig Hist. Vol.* 3. *p.* 739.

" *these holy virgins might releeve with their prayers, the*
" *soules of his father king Henrie, and of lady Rosamund*
" *there interred.*" * . . . . *In what situation her remains
were found at the dissolution of the nunnery, we learn from
Leland,* " *Rosamundes tumbe at Godstowe nunnery was*
" *taken up [of] late; it is a stone with this inscription,*
" TUMBA ROSAMUNDÆ. *Her bones were closid in*
" *lede, and withyn that bones were closyd yn lether. When*
" *it was opened a very swete smell came owt of it.*" *See
Hearne's discourse above quoted, written in* 1718; *at
which time, he tells us, were still seen by the pool at Wood-
stock the foundations of a very large building, which were
believed to be the remains of Rosamond's labyrinth.*

*To conclude this (perhaps too prolix) account, Henry had
two sons by Rosamond, from a computation of whose ages, a
modern historian has endeavoured to invalidate the received
story. These were William Longue-espè (or Long-sword)
earl of Salisbury, and Geoffrey bishop of Lincolne* †. *Geoffrey
was the younger of Rosamond's sons, and yet is said to have
been twenty years old at the time of his election to that see in*
1173. *Hence this writer concludes, that king Henry fell in
love with Rosamond in* 1149, *when in king Stephen's reign
he came over to be knighted by the king of Scots; he also
thinks it probable that Henry's commerce with this lady*
" *broke off upon his marriage with Eleanor [in* 1152.] *and*
" *that the young lady, by a natural effect of grief and resent-*
" *ment at the defection of her lover, entered on that occasion*
" *into the nunnery of Godstowe, where she died probably be-*
" *fore the rebellion of Henry's sons in* 1173." [*Carte's hist.
Vol. I. p.* 652.] *But let it be observed, that Henry was but
sixteen years old when he came over to be knighted; that he
staid but eight months in this island,- and was almost all the
time with the king of Scots; that he did not return back to
England till* 1153, *the year after his marriage with Eleanor;
and that no writer drops the least hint of Rosamond's having
ever been abroad with her lover, nor indeed is it probable
that a boy of sixteen should venture to carry over a mistress to*
his

* *Vid. Reign of Henry II. in Speed's Hist. writ by Dr. Barcham,
Dean of Bocking.* † *Afterwards Archbishop of York, temp. Rich. I.*

his mother's court. If all these circumstances are considered, Mr. Carte's account will be found more incoherent and improbable than that of the old ballad; which is also countenanced by most of our old historians.

Indeed the true date of Geoffrey's birth, and consequently of Henry's commerce with Rosamund, seems to be best ascertained from an ancient manuscript in the Cotton library : wherein it is thus registered of Geofferey Plantagenet, " Na- " *tus est 5°. Hen. II. [1159.] Factus est miles 25°. Hen.* " *II. [1179.] Elect. in Episcop. Lincoln. 28°. Hen. II.* " *[1182.]." Vid. Chron. de Kirkstall. (Domitian XII.) Drake's Hist. of York, p. 422.*

The following ballad is printed from four ancient copies in black letter ; two of them in the Pepys library.

W HEN as king Henry rulde this land,
    The second of that name,
Besides the queene, he dearly lovde
    A faire and comely dame.

Most peerlesse was her beautye founde,   . 5
    Her favour, and her face ;
A sweeter creature in this worlde
    Could never prince embrace.

Her crisped lockes like threads of golde
    Appeard to each mans sight ;   10
Her sparkling eyes, like Orient pearles,
    Did cast a heavenlye light.

The blood within her crystal cheekes
    Did such a colour drive,
As though the lillye and the rose   15
    For mastership did strive.

Yea Rofamonde, fair Rofamonde,
   Her name was called fo,
To whom our queene, dame Ellinor,
   Was known a deadlye foe.

The king therefore, for her defence,
   Againft the furious queene,
At Woodftocke builded fuch a bower,
   The like was never feene.

Moft curioufly that bower was built
   Of ftone and timber ftrong,
An hundered and fifty doors
   Did to this bower belong:

And they fo cunninglye contriv'd
   With turnings round about,
That none but with a clue of thread,
   Could enter in or out.

And for his love and ladyes fake,
   That was fo faire and brighte,
The keeping of this bower he gave
   Unto a valiant knighte.

But fortune, that doth often frowne
   Where fhe before did fmile,
The kinges delighte and ladyes joy
   Full foon fhee did beguile:

For why, the kinges ungracious fonne,
  Whom he did high advance,
Againft his father raifed warres
  Within the realme of France.

But yet before our comelye king   45
  The Englifh land forfooke,
Of Rofamond, his lady faire,
  His farewelle thus he tooke:

" My Rofamonde, my only Rofe,
  That pleafeft beft mine eye: 50
The faireft flower in all the worlde
  To feed my fantafye:

The flower of mine affected heart,
  Whofe fweetnefs doth excelle:
My royal Rofe, a thoufand times   55
  I bid thee nowe farewelle!

For I muft leave my faireft flower,
  My fweeteft Rofe, a fpace,
And crofs the feas to famous France,
  Proud rebelles to abafe.   60

But yet, my Rofe, be fure thou fhalt
  My coming fhortlye fee,
And in my heart, when hence I am,
  Ile beare my Rofe with mee."

L 2

When

When Rofamond, that ladye brighte, 65
    Did heare the king faye foe,
The forrowe of her grieved heart
    Her outward lookes did fhowe;

And from her cleare and cryftall eyes
    The teares gufht out apace, 70
Which like the fiver-pearled dewe
    Ranne downe her comely face.

Her lippes, erft like the corall redde,
    Did waxe both wan and pale,
And for the forrow fhe conceivde 75
    Her vitall fpirits faile;

And falling down all in a fwoone
    Before king Henryes face,
Full oft he in his princelye armes
    Her bodye did embrace: 80

And twentye times, with watery eyes,
    He kift her tender cheeke,
Untill he had revivde againe
    Her fenfes milde and meeke.

Why grieves my Rofe, my fweeteft Rofe? 85
    The king did often fay.
Becaufe, quoth fhee, to bloodye warres
    My lord muft part awaye.

But

But fince your grace on forrayne coaftes
   Amonge your foes unkinde   90
Muft goe to hazard life and limbe,
   Why fhould I ftaye behinde ?

Nay rather, let me, like a page,
   Your fworde and target beare ;
That on my breaft the blowes may lighte,   95
   Which would offend you there.

Or lett mee, in your royal tent,
   Prepare your bed at nighte,
And with fweete baths refrefh your grace,
   At your returne from fighte.   100

So I your prefence may enjoye
   No toil I will refufe ;
But wanting you, my life is death ;
   Nay, death Ild rather chufe !

" Content thy felf, my deareft love ;   105
   Thy reft at home fhall bee
In Englandes fweet and pleafant ifle ;
   For travell fits not thee.

Faire ladies brooke not bloodye warres ;
   Soft peace their fexe delightes ;   110
' Not rugged campes, but courtlye bowers ;
   Gay feaftes, not cruell fightes.'

L 3

My

My Rofe fhall fafely here abide,
  With muficke paffe the daye;
Whilft I, amonge the piercing pikes,   115
  My foes feeke far awaye.

My Rofe fhall fhine in pearle, and golde,
  Whilft Ime in armour dighte;
Gay galliards here my love fhall dance,
  Whilft I my foes goe fighte.   120

And you, fir Thomas, whom I trufte
  To bee my loves defence;
Be carefull of my gallant Rofe
  When I am parted hence."

And therewithall he fetcht a figh,   125
  As though his heart would breake:
And Rofamonde, for very griefe,
  Not one plaine word could fpeake.

And at their parting well they mighte
  In heart be grieved fore :   130
After that daye faire Rofamonde
  The king did fee no more.

For when his grace had paft the feas,
  And into France was gone;
With envious heart, queene Ellinor,   135
  To Woodftocke came anone.

And

And forth fhe calles this truftye knighte,
   In an unhappy houre;
Who with his clue of twined thread,
   Came from this famous bower.   140

And when that they had wounded him,
   The queene this thread did gette,
And went where ladye Rofamonde
   Was like an angell fette.

But when the queene with ftedfaft eye   145
   Beheld her beauteous face,
She was amazed in her minde
   At her exceeding grace.

Caft off from thee thofe robes, fhe faid,
   That riche and coftlye bee;   150
And drinke thou up this deadlye draught,
   Which I have brought to thee.

Then prefentlye upon her knees
   Sweet Rofamonde did falle;
And pardon of the queene fhe crav'd   155
   For her offences all.

" Take pitty on my youthfull yeares,
   Faire Rofamonde did crye;
And lett mee not with poifon ftronge
   Enforced bee to dye.   160

L 4

I will

I will renounce my finfull life,
    And in fome cloyfter bide;
Or elfe be banifht, if you pleafe,
    To range the world foe wide.

And for the fault which I have done,   165
    Though I was forc'd theretoe,
Preferve my life, and punifh mee
    As you thinke meet to doe."

And with thefe words, her lillie handes
    She wrunge full often there;   170
And downe along her lovelye face
    Did trickle many a teare.

But nothing could this furious queene
    Therewith appeafed bee;
The cup of deadlye poyfon ftronge,   175
    As fhe knelt on her knee,

Shee gave this comelye dame to drinke;
    Who tooke it in her hand,
And from her bended knee arofe,
    And on her feet did ftand: 180

And cafting up her eyes to heaven,
    Shee did for mercye calle;
And drinking up the poifon ftronge,
    Her life fhe loft withalle.

4

And

And when that death through everye limbe
　　Had showde its greatest spite,　　　　　185
Her chiefest foes did plaine confesse
　　Shee was a glorious wight.

Her body then they did entomb,
　　When life was fled away,
At Godstowe, neare to Oxford towne,
　　As may be seene this day.　　　　　190

VIII.

QUEEN ELEANOR'S CONFESSION.

" *Eleanor, the daughter and heiress of William duke of
Guienne, and count of Poictou, had been married sixteen years
to Louis VII. king of France, and had attended him in a
croisade, which that monarch commanded against the infi-
dels; but having lost the affections of her husband, and
even fallen under some suspicions of gallantry with a handsome
Saracen, Louis, more delicate than politic, procured a divorce
from her, and restored her those rich provinces, which by
her marriage she had annexed to the crown of France. The
young count of Anjou, afterwards Henry II. king of England,
tho' at that time but in his nineteenth year, neither discou-
raged by the disparity of age, nor by the reports of Eleanor's
gallantry, made such successful courtship to that princess,
that he married her six weeks after her divorce, and got
possession of all her dominions as a dowery. A marriage thus
founded upon interest was not likely to be very happy : it*
　　　　　　　　　　　　　　　　　　　happened

happened accordingly. Eleanor, who had disgusted her first husband by her gallantries, was no less offensive to her second by her jealousy: thus carrying to extremity, in the different parts of her life, every circumstance of female weakness. She had several sons by Henry, whom she spirited up to rebel against him; and endeavouring to escape to them disguised in man's apparel in 1173, she was discovered and thrown into a confinement, which seems to have continued till the death of her husband in 1189. She however survived him many years: dying in 1204, in the sixth year of the reign of her youngest son, John." See Hume's Hist. 4to. Vol. 1. p. 260. 307. Speed, Stow, &c.

It is needless to observe, that the following ballad (given from an old printed copy) is altogether fabulous; whatever gallantries Eleanor encouraged in the time of her first husband, none are imputed to her in that of her second.

Q UEENE Elianor was a sicke womàn,
    And afraid that she should dye:
Then she sent for two fryars of France
    To speke with her speedilye.

The king calld downe his nobles all,   5
    By one, by two, by three;
" Earl marshall, Ile goe shrive the queene,
    And thou shalt wend with mee."

A boone, a boone; quoth earl marshàll,
    And fell on his bended knee;   10
That whatsoever queene Elianor saye,
    No harme therof may bee.

The

Ile pawne my landes, the king then cryd,
   My fceptre, crowne, and all,
That whatfoere queen Elianor fayes   15
   No harme thereof fhall fall.

Do thou put on a fryars coat,
   And Ile put on another;
And we will to queen Elianor goe
   Like fryar and his brother.   20

Thus both attired then they goe:
   When they came to Whitehall,
The bells did ring, and the quirifters fing,
   And the torches did lighte them all.

When that they came before the queene   25
   They fell on their bended knee;
A boone, a boone, our gracious queene,
   That you fent fo haftilee.

Are you two fryars of France, fhe fayd,
   As I fuppofe you bee?   30
But if you are two Englifhe fryars,
   You fhall hang on the gallowes tree.

We are two fryars of France, they fayd,
   As you fuppofe we bee,
We have not been at any maffe   35
   Sith we came from the fea.

The

The firft vile thing that ever I did
  I will to you unfolde ;
Earl marfhall had my maidenhed,
  Beneath this cloth of golde.   40

Thats a vile finne, then fayd the king ;
  May God forgive it thee !
Amen, amen, quoth earl marfhall ;
  With a heavye heart fpake hee.

The next vile thing that ever I did,   45
  To you Ile not denye,
I made a boxe of poyfon ftrong,
  To poifon king Henrye.

Thats a vile finne, then fayd the king,
  May God forgive it thee !   50
Amen, amen, quoth earl marfhall ;
  And I wifh it fo may bee.

The next vile thing that ever I did,
  To you I will difcover ;
I poyfoned fair Rofamonde,   55
  All in fair Woodftocke bower.

Thats a vile finne, then fayd the king ;
  May God forgive it thee !
Amen, amen, quoth earl marfhall ;
  And I wifh it fo may bee.   60

Do

Do you fee yonders little boye,
    A toffing of the balle?
That is earl marfhalls eldeft fonne,
    And I love him the beft of all.

Do you fee yonders little boye,   65
    A catching of the balle?
That is king Henryes youngeft fonne,
    And I love him the worft of all.

His head is fafhyond like a bull;
    His nofe is like a boare.   70
No matter for that, king Henrye cryd,
    I love him the better therfore.

The king pulled off his fryars coate,
    And appeared all in redde:
She fhrieked, and cryd, and wrung her hands,   75
    And fayd fhe was betrayde.

The king lookt over his left fhoulder,
    And a grimme look looked hee,
Earl marfhall, he fayd, but for my oathe,
    Or hanged thou fhouldft bee.   80

V. 63, 67. *She means that the eldeft of thefe two was by the earl marfhall, the youngeft by the king.*

IX. THE

IX.

THE STURDY ROCK.

This poem, subscribed M. T. [perhaps invertedly for T. Marshall] is preserved in The Paradise of daintie devises, quoted above in page 136—The two first stanzas may be found accompanied with musical notes in " An howres recreation in musicke, &c. by Richard Alison, Lond. 1606. 4to. :" usually bound up with 3 or 4 sets of " Madrigals set to music by Tho. Weelkes, Lond. 1597. 1600. 1608, 4to." One of these madrigals is so compleat an example of the Bathos, that I cannot forbear presenting it to the reader.*

Thule, the period of cosmographie,
   Doth vaunt of Hecla, whose sulphurious fire
Doth melt the frozen clime, and thaw the skie,
   Trinacrian Ætna's flames ascend not hier :
These things seeme wondrous, yet more wondrous I,
Whose heart with feare doth freeze, with love doth fry.

The Andelusian merchant, that returnes
   Laden with cutchinele and china dishes,
Reports in Spaine, how strangely Fogo burnes
   Amidst an ocean full of flying fishes :
These things seeme wondrous, yet more wondrous I,
Whose heart with feare doth freeze, with love doth fry.

Mr. Weelkes seems to have been of opinion with many of his brethren of later times, that nonsense was best adapted to display the powers of musical composure.

THE

---

* *Vid. Athen. Oxon. p. 152. 316.*

THE sturdy rock for all his strength
    By raging seas is rent in twaine :
The marble stone is pearst at length,
    With little drops of drizling rain :
The oxe doth yeeld unto the yoke,   5
The steele obeyeth the hammer stroke.

The stately stagge, that seemes so stout,
    By yalping hounds at bay is set :
The swiftest bird, that flies about,
    Is caught at length in fowlers net :   10
The greatest fish, in deepest brooke,
Is soone deceived by subtill hooke.

Yea man himselfe, unto whose will
    All things are bounden to obey,
For all his wit and worthie skill,   15
    Doth fade at length, and fall away.
There is nothing but time doeth waste ;
The heavens, the earth consume at last.

But vertue sits triumphing still
    Upon the throne of glorious fame :   20
Though spiteful death mans body kill,
    Yet hurts he not his vertuous name :
By life or death, what so betides,
The state of vertue never slides.

X. THE

X.

THE BEGGAR'S DAUGHTER OF BEDNALL-GREEN.

This popular old ballad was written in the reign of Elizabeth, as appears not only from ver. 23. where the arms of England are called the " Queenes armes ;" but from its tune's being quoted in other old pieces, written in her time. See the ballad on MARY AMBREE *in this volume.—An ingenious gentleman has assured the Editor, that he has formerly seen another old song on the same subject, composed in a different measure from this ; which was truly beautiful, if we may judge from the only stanza he remembered : in this it was said of the old beggar, that " down his neck*

—— his reverend lockes
  In comelye curles did wave;
And on his aged temples grewo
  The bloſſomes of the grave."

The following ballad is chiefly given from the Editor's folio MS. compared with two ancient printed copies : the concluding stanzas, which contain the old Beggar's discovery of himself, are not however given from any of these, being very different from those of the vulgar ballad. They were communicated to the Editor in manuscript ; but he will not answer for their being genuine : he rather thinks them the modern production of some person, who was offended at the absurdities, and inconsistencies, which so remarkably prevailed in this part of the song, as it stood before : whereas by the alteration of a few lines, the story is rendered much more affecting, and is reconciled to probability and true history. For this informs us, that at the decisive battle of
Eveſham,

*Evesham, (fought Aug. 4. 1265.) when Simon de Mont-
fort, the great earl of Leicester, was slain at the head of
the barons, his eldest son Henry fell by his side, and in conse-
quence of that defeat, his whole family sunk for ever, the
king bestowing their great honours and possessions on his second son Edmund earl of Lancaster.*

PART THE FIRST.

ITT was a blind beggar, had long lost his sight,
   He had a faire daughter of bewty most bright;
And many a gallant brave suiter had shee,
For none was soe comelye as pretty Bessee.

And though shee was of favor most faire,   5
Yett seeing shee was but a blinde beggars heyre,
Of ancyent housekeepers despised was shee,
Whose sonnes came as suitors to pretty Bessee.

Wherefore in great sorrow faire Bessy did say,
Good father, and mother, let me goe away   10
To seeke out my fortune, whatever itt bee.
Her suite then they granted to prettye Bessee.

Then Bessy, that was of bewtye soe bright,
All cladd in gray russett, and late in the night
From father and mother alone parted shee;   15
Who sighed and sobbed for prettye Bessee.

Shee went till shee came to Stratford-le-Bowe;
Then knew shee not whither, nor which way to goe:
With teares shee lamented her hard destinie,
So sadd and so heavy was prettye Bessee.   20

She kept on her journey untill it was day,
And went unto Rumford along the hye way;
Where at the Queenes armes entertained was shee:
So faire and wel favoured was prettye Bessee.

Shee had not beene there a month to an end,   25
But master and mistres and all was her friend:
And every brave gallant, that once did her see,
Was strait-way enamourd of prettye Bessee.

Great gifts they did send her of silver and gold,
And in their songs daylye her love was extold;   30
Her beautye was blazed in every degree;
Soe faire and soe comelye was prettye Bessee.

The yong men of Rumford in her had their joy;
Shee shewd herself courteous, and modestlye coye;
And at her commandment still wold they bee;   35
Soe faire and soe comelye was pretty Bessee.

Foure suitors att once unto her did goe;
They craved her favor, but still shee sayd noe;
I wold not wish gentles to marry with mee.
Yett ever they honoured prettye Bessee.   40

The first of them was a gallant yong knight,
And he came unto her disguisde in the night:
The second a gentleman of good degree,
Who wooed and sued for prettye Bessee.

A

A merchant of London, whofe wealth was not fmall, 45
He was the third fuiter, and proper withall:
Her mafters own fonne the fourth man muft bee,
Who fwore he wold dye for prettye Befsee.

And, if thou wilt marry with mee, quoth the knight,
Ile make thee a ladye with joy and delight;   50
My hart's fo inthralled by thy bewtie,
That foone I fhall dye for prettye Befsee.

The gentleman fayd, Come, marry with mee,
As fine as a ladye my Befsy fhal bee:
My life is diftreffed : O heare me, quoth hee ;   55
And grant me thy love, my prettye Befsee.

Let me bee thy hufband, the merchant could fay,
Thou fhalt live in London both gallant and gay
My fhippes fhall bring home rych jewels for thee,
And I will for ever love prettye Befsee.   60

Then Befsy fhee fighed, and thus fhee did fay,
My father and mother I meane to obey ;
Firft gett their good will, and be faithful to mee,
And you fhall enjoye your prettye Befsee.

To every one this anfwer fhee made,   65
Wherfore unto her they joyfullye fayd,
This thing to fulfill wee all doe agree ;
But where dwells thy father, my prettye Befsee ?
M 2

My

My father, fhe fayd, is foone to be feene:
The feely blind beggar of Bednall-greene,   70
That daylye fits begging for charitie,
He is the good father of prettye Befsee.

His markes and his tokens are knowen very well;
He always is led with a dogg and a bell:
A feely olde man God knoweth is hee,   75
Yett hee is the father of prettye Befsee.

Nay then, quoth the merchant, thou art not for mee:
Nor, quoth the innholder, my wiffe fhalt thou bee:
I lothe, fayd the gentle, a beggars degree,
And therefore, adewe, my prettye Befsee!   80

Why then, quoth the knight, hap better or worfe,
I weighe not true love by the weight of the purfse,
And bewtye is bewtye in every degree;
Then welcome unto mee, my prettye Befsee.

With thee to thy father forthwith I will goe.   85
Nay foft, quoth his kinfmen, it muft not be foe;
A poor beggars daughter noe ladye fhal bee,
Then take thy adew of prettye Befsee.

But foone after this, by breake of the day
The knight had from Rumford ftole Befsy away.   90
The yonge men of Rumford, as thicke as might bee,
Rode after to feitch againe prettye Befsee.

As

As fwifte as the winde to ryde they were feene,
Untill they came neare unto Bednall-greene ;
And as the knight lighted moft curteouflie,   95
They all fought againft him for prettye Befsee.

But refcu came fpeedilye over the plaine,
Or elfe the young knight for his love had beene flaine.
This fray being ended, then ftraitway he fee
His kinfmen come rayling at prettye Befsee.   100

Then fpake the blind beggar, Although I be poore,
Yett rayle not againft my child at my owne door :
Though fhee be not decked in velvett and pearle,
Yett I will dropp angells with you for my girle.

And then, if my gold may better her birthe,   105
And equall the gold that you lay on the earth,
Then neyther rayle nor grudge you to fee
The blind beggars daughter a lady to bee.

But firft you fhall promife, and have itt well knowne,
The gold that you drop fhall all be your owne.   110
With that they replyed, Contented bee wee.
Then here's, quoth the beggar, for prettye Befsee.

With that an angell he caft on the ground,
And dropped in angels full three thoufand pound ;
And oftentimes it was proved moft plaine,   115
For the gentlemens one the beggar dropt twayne :

M 3

Soe that the place, wherein they did fitt,
With gold it was covered every whitt,
The gentlemen then having dropt all their ftore,
Sayd, Now, beggar, hold, for we have no more.   120

Thou haft fulfilled thy promife aright.
Then marry my girle, quoth he to the knight;
And heere, added hee, I will now throwe you downe
A hundred pounds more to buy her a gowne.

'The gentlemen all, that this treafure had feene,   125
Admired the beggar of Bednall-greene:
And all thofe, that were her fuitors before,
Their flefhe for very anger they tore.

Thus was faire Beffy a match for the knight,
And then made a ladye in others defpite: 130
A fairer ladye there never was feene,
Than the blind beggars daughter of Bednall-greene.

But of their fumptuous marriage and feaft,
What brave lords and knights thither were preft,
The SECOND FIT* fhall fet forth to your fight   135
With marveilous pleafure, and wifhed delight.

* *The word* FIT, *for* PART, *often occurs in our ancient
ballads and metrical romances; which being divided into
feveral parts for the convenience of finging them at public
entertainments, were in the intervals of the feaft fung by*
FITS,

FITS, *or intermiſſions. So Puttenham in his Art of Engliſh poeſie, 1589, ſays " the Epithalamie was divided by " breaches into three partes to ſerve for three ſeveral* FITS, " *or times to be ſung." p.* 41.——

From the ſame writer we learn ſome curious particulars relative to the ſtate of ballad-ſinging in that age, that will throw light on the preſent ſubject : ſpeaking of the quick returns of one manner of tune in the ſhort meaſures uſed by common rhymers ; theſe, he ſays, " glut the eare, unleſs it be " in ſmall and popular muſickes, ſung by theſe Cantabanqui, " upon benches and barrels heads, where they have none " other audience then boys or countrey fellowes, that paſſe by " them in the ſtreete ; or elſe by *BLIND HARPERS, or ſuch* " like taverne Minſtrels, that give a FIT *of mirth for a* " GROAT, . . . *their matter being for the moſt part ſtories of* " old time, as the tale of Sir Topas, the reportes of Bevis of " Southampton, Guy of Warwicke, Adam Bell and Clymme " of the Clough, and ſuch other old romances or hiſtorical " rimes, made purpoſely for recreation of the common people at " Chriſtmaſſe dinners and brideales, and in tavernes and " alehouſes, and ſuch other places of baſe reſorte." p.* 69.

*This ſpecies of entertainment, which ſeems to have been handed down from the ancient bards, was in the time of Puttenham falling apace into neglect ; but that it was not, even then, wholly excluded more genteel aſſemblies, he gives us room to infer from another paſſage. " We ourſelves, ſays " this courtly * writer, have written for pleaſure a little " brief romance, or hiſtorical ditty in the Engliſh tong of " the Iſle of Great Britaine in ſhort and long meetres, and " by breaches or diviſions [i. e.* FITS,] *to be more com- " modiouſly ſung to the harpe in places of aſſembly, where " the company ſhal be deſirous to heare of old adven- " tures, and valiaunces of noble knights in times paſt, as are*

M 4

"*thoſe*

---

* *He was one of Q. Elizabeth's gent. penſioners, at a time when the whole band conſiſted of men of diſtinguiſhed birth and fortune. Vid. Ath. Ox.*

" *thoſe of king Arthur and his knights of the Round table,*
" *Sir Bevys of Southampton, Guy of Warwicke, and others*
" *like.*" *p.* 33.

In more ancient times no grand ſcene of feſtivity was com-
pleat without one of theſe reciters to entertain the company
with feats of arms, and tales of knighthood, or, as one of
theſe old minſtrels ſays, in the beginning of an ancient ro-
mance in the Editor's folio MS.

 " *When meate and drinke is great plentyè,*
 " *And lords and ladyes ſtill wil bee,*
  " *And ſitt and ſolace * lythe;*   * *Perhaps*
 " *Then itt is time for mee to ſpeake*   " *blythe.*"
 " *Of keene knightes, and kempès great,*
  " *Such carping for to kythe.*"

If we conſider that a GROAT *in the age of Elizabeth*
was more than equivalent to a ſhilling now, we ſhall find
that the old harpers were even then, when their art was on
the decline, upon a far more reputable footing than the ballad-
ſingers of our time. The reciting of one ſuch ballad as this
of the Beggar of Bednal-green, in II parts, was rewarded
with half a crown of our money. And that they made a
very reſpectable appearance, we may learn from the dreſs of
the old beggar, in the following ſtanzas, ver. 34, *where he*
comes into company in the habit and character of one of theſe
minſtrels, being not known to be the bride's father, till after
her ſpeech, ver. 63. *The exordium of his ſong, and his*
claiming a GROAT *for his reward, v.* 76, *are peculiarly*
characteriſtic of that profeſſion.—Moſt of the old ballads be-
gin in a pompous manner, in order to captivate the attention
of the audience, and induce them to purchaſe a recital of the
ſong: and they ſeldom conclude the FIRST *part without large*
promiſes of ſtill greater entertainment in the SECOND. *This*
was a neceſſary piece of art to incline the hearers to be at the
expence of a ſecond groat's-worth—Many of the old romances
extend to eight or nine FITS, *which would afford a conſider-*
able profit to the reciter.

To

To return to the word FIT ; *it seems at first to have peculiarly signified the pause, or breathing-time between the
several parts, (answering to* PASSUS *in the visions of
Pierce Plowman) : thus in the old poem of* JOHN THE
REEVE, *the first part ends with this line,*

   " *The first* FITT *here find wee :"*

i. e. here we come to the first pause or intermission[*].—*By degrees it came to signify the whole part or division preceding
the pause ; and this sense it had obtained so early as the time
of Chaucer : who thus concludes the first part of his rhyme
of Sir Thopas (writ in ridicule of the old ballad romances)*

   " *Lo ! lordis mine, here is a* FITT ;
   " *If ye woll any more of it,*
    " *To tell it woll I fonde."*

* See also above, Vol. I. p. 9.——The reader will find further remarks on the word FIT at the end of this Volume, and in the Glossary to
Vol. I. &c.

PART THE SECOND.

WITHIN a gorgeous palace most brave,
  Adorned with all the cost they colde have,
This wedding was kept most sumptuouslie,
And all for the creditt of prettye Bessee.

All kind of dainties, and delicates sweete   5
Were bought for their banquet, as it was meete ;
Partridge, and plover, and venison most free,
Against the brave wedding of pretty Bessee.

            This

This wedding through England was fpread by report,
So that a great number therto did refort   10
Of nobles and gentles in every degree;
And all for the fame of prettye Beffee.

To church then went this gallant young knight;
His bride followed after, an angell moft bright,
With troopes of ladyes, the like nere was feene   15
That went with fweete Beffy of Bednall-greene.

This marryage being folemnized then,
With muficke performed by the fkilfulleft men,
The nobles and gentles fate downe at that tyde,
Each one admiring the beautifull bryde.   20

Now, after the fumptuous dinner was done,
To talke, and to reafon a number begunn:
They talkt of the blind beggars daughter moft bright,
And what with his daughter he gave to the knight.

Then fpake the nobles, " Much marveil have wee, 25
'This jolly blind beggar we cannot here fee."
My lords, quoth the bride, my father's fo bafe,
He is loth with his prefence thefe ftates to difgrace.

" The prayfe of a woman in queftyon to bringe
Before her own face, were a flattering thinge;   30
But wee thinke thy father's bafenefs, quoth they,
Might by thy bewtye be cleane put awaye."

They

They had no fooner thefe pleafant words fpoke,
But in comes the beggar clad in a filke cloke;
A faire velvet capp, and a fether had hee,　　35
And now a muficyan forfooth he wold bee.

He had a daintye lute under his arme,
He touched the ftrings, which made fuch a charme,
Saies, Pleafe you to heare any muficke of mee,
Ile fing you a fong of prettye Beffee.　　40

With that his lute he twanged ftraightway,
And thereon begann moft fweetlye to play ;
And after that leffons were playd two or three,
He ftrayn'd out this fong moft delicatelie.

" A poore beggars daughter did dwell on a greene, 45
" Who for her faireneffe might well be a queene :
" A blithe bonny laffe, and a dainty was fhee,
" And many one called her prettye Beffee.

" Her father he had noe goods, nor noe land,
" But beggd for a penny all day with his hand ;　　50
" And yett to her marriage he gave thoufands three,
" And ftill he hath fomewhat for prettye Beffee.

" And if any one here her birth doe difdaine,
" Her father is ready, with might and with maine,
" To prove fhee is come of noble degree :　　55
" Therfore never flout at prettye Beffee."

2

With

With that the lords and the company round
With hearty laughter were readye to fwound;
At laft fayd the lords, Full well wee may fee,
The bride and the beggar's beholden to thee.　　60

On this the bride all blufhing did rife,
The pearlie dropps ftanding within her faire eyes,
O pardon my father, grave nobles, quoth fhee,
That throughe blind affection thus doteth on mee.

If this be thy father, the nobles did fay,　　65
Well may he be proud of this happy day;
Yett by his countenance well may we fee,
His birth and his fortune did never agree:

And therfore, blind man, we pray thee bewray,
(And looke that the truth thou to us doe fay)　　70
Thy birth and thy parentage, what it may bee;
For the love that thou beareft to prettye Beffee.

" Then give me leave, nobles and gentles, each one,
" One fong more to fing, and then I have done;
" And if that itt may not winn good report,　　75
" Then do not give me a GROAT for my fport.

" [Sir Simon de Montfort my fubject fhal bee;
" Once chiefe of all the great barons was hee,
" Yet fortune fo cruelle this lorde did abafe,
" Now lofte and forgotten are hee and his race.　　80

" When

" When the barons in armes did king Henrye oppofe,
" Sir Simon de Montfort their leader they chofe ;
" A leader of courage undaunted was hee,
" And oft-times hee made their enemyes flee.

" At length in the battle on Evefhame plaine   85
" The barons were routed, and Montfort was flaine ;
" Mofte fatall that battel did prove unto thee,
" Thoughe thou waft not borne then, my prettye Beffee !

" Along with the nobles, that fell at that tyde,
" His eldeft fon Henrye, who fought by his fide,   90
" Was fellde by a blowe, he receivde in the fight !
" A blowe that deprivde him for ever of fight.

" Among the dead bodyes all lifeleffe he laye,
" Till evening drewe on of the following daye,
" When by a yong ladye difcoverd was hee ;   95
" And this was thy mother, my prettye Beffee !

" A barons faire daughter ftept forth in the nighte.
" To fearch for her father, who fell in the fight,
" And feeing yong Montfort, where gafping he laye,
" Was moved with pitye, and brought him awaye. 100

" In fecrette fhe nurft him, and fwaged his paine,
" While he throughe the realme was beleevd to be flaine:
" At lengthe his faire bride fhe confented to bee,
" And made him glad father of prettye Beffee.

" And

" And nowe left oure foes oure lives fholde betraye, 105
" We clothed ourfelves in beggars arraye;
" Her jewelles fhee folde, and hither came wee:
" All our comfort and care was our prettye Beffee.]

" And here have we lived in fortunes defpite, 109
" Thoughe meane, yet contented with humble delighte:
" Thus many longe winters nowe have I beene
" The fillye blinde beggar of Bednall-greene.

" And here, noble lordes, is ended the fonge
" Of one, that once to your own ranke did belong:
" And thus have you learned a fecrette from mee, 115
" That ne'er had beene knowne, but for prettye Beffee."

Now when the faire companye everye one,
Had heard the ftrange tale in the fong he had fhowne,
They all were amazed, as well they might bee,
Both at the blinde beggar, and prettye Beffee. 120

With that the fweete maiden they all did embrace,
Saying, Sure thou art come of an honourable race,
Thy father likewife is of noble degree,
And thou art right worthy a ladye to bee.

Thus was the feaft ended with joye, and delighte, 125
A bridegroome moft happye then was the yong knighte,
In joye and felicitie long lived hee,
All with his faire ladye, the prettye Beffee.

XI. FANCY

XI.

FANCY AND DESIRE.

BY THE EARL OF OXFORD.

Edward Vere Earl of Oxford was in high fame for his poetical talents in the reign of Elizabeth: perhaps it is no injury to his reputation that few of his compositions are preserved for the inspection of impartial posterity. To gratify curiosity, we have inserted a sonnet of his, which is quoted with great encomiums for its " excellencie and wit," in Puttenham's Arte of Eng. Poesie, and found intire in the Garland of Good-will: A few more of his sonnets (distinguished by the initial letters E. O.) may be seen in the Paradise of Daintie Devises. One of these is intitled, " The Complaint " of a Lover, wearing blacke and tawnie." The only lines in it worth notice are these,*

A crowne of baies shall that man ' beare'
Who triumphs over me ;
For black and tawnie will I weare,
Which mourning colours be.

We find in Hall's Chronicle, that when Q. Catharine of Arragon dyed Jan. 8. 1536 ; " Queen Anne [Bullen] ware " YELLOWE for the mourning." And when this unfortunate princess lost her head May 19. the same year, " on the ascen- " cion day following, the kyng for mourning ware " WHYTE." Fol. 227, 228.

Edward,

---

* *Lond. 1589. p. 172.*

Edward, who was the XVIIth earl of Oxford of the family of Vere, succeeded his father in his title and honours in 1562, and died an aged man in 1604. See Mr. Walpole's Noble Authors. Ath. Ox.

COME hither shepherd's swayne :
    " Sir, what do you require ?"
I praye thee, shewe to me thy name.
    " My name is FOND DESIRE."

When wert thou borne, Desire ?   5
    " In pompe and pryme of may."
By whom, sweet boy, wert thou begot ?
    " By fond Conceit men say."

Tell me, who was thy nurse ?
    " Fresh Youth in sugred joy."   10
What was thy meate and dayly foode ?
    " Sad sighes with great annoy."

What hadst thou then to drinke ?
    " Unsavoury lovers teares."
What cradle wert thou rocked in ?   15
    " In hope devoyde of feares."

What lulld thee then asleepe ?
    " Sweete speech, which likes me best."
Tell me, where is thy dwelling place ?
    " In gentle hartes I rest."   20

What

What thing doth pleafe thee moft ?
   " To gaze on beautye ftille."
Whom doft thou thinke to be thy foe ?
   " Difdayn of my good wille."

Doth companye difpleafe ?   25
   " Yea, furelye, many one."
Where doth Defire delighte to live ?
   " He loves to live alone."

Doth either tyme or age
   Bringe him unto decaye ?   30
" No, no, Defire both lives and dyes
   " Ten thoufand times a daye."

Then, fond Defire, farewelle,
   Thou art no mate for mee ;
I fholde be lothe, methinkes, to dwelle   35
   With fuch a one as thee.

XII.

SIR ANDREW BARTON.

I cannot give a better relation of the fact, which is the subject of the following ballad, than in an extract from a very elegant work lately offered to the public. See Mr. Guthrie's New Peerage, 4to. Vol. I. p. 22.

" *The transaction which did the greatest honour to the earl of Surrey * and his family at this time [A. D. 1511.] was their behaviour in the case of Barton, a Scotch sea-officer. This gentleman's father having suffered by sea from the Portuguese, he had obtained letters of marque for his two sons to make reprisals upon the subjects of Portugal. It is extremely probable, that the court of Scotland granted these letters with no very honest intention. The council board of England, at which the earl of Surrey held the chief place, was daily pestered with complaints from the sailors and merchants, that Barton, who was called Sir Andrew Barton, under pretence of searching for Portuguese goods, interrupted the English navigation. Henry's situation at that time rendered him backward from breaking with Scotland, so that their complaints were but coldly received. The earl of Surrey, however, could not smother his indignation, but gallantly declared at the council board, that while he had an estate that could furnish out a ship, or a son that was capable of commanding one, the narrow seas should not be infested.*

" *Sir Andrew Barton, who commanded the two Scotch ships, had the reputation of being one of the ablest sea-officers of his time.. By his depredations, he had amassed great wealth, and his ships were very richly laden. Henry, notwithstanding his situation, could not refuse the generous offer made by the earl of Surrey. Two ships were immediately fitted out, and put to sea with letters of marque, under his two sons, Sir Thomas † and Sir Edward Howard. After encountering a great deal of foul weather, Sir Thomas came up with the Lion, which was commanded by Sir Andrew Barton in person; and Sir Edward came up with the Union, Barton's other ship, [called by Hall, the bark of Scotland.] The engagement which ensued was extremely obstinate on both sides; but at last the fortune of the Howards prevailed. Sir Andrew was killed fighting bravely, and encouraging his*

men

---

* *Afterwards created Duke of Norfolk.*

† *Called by old historians lord Howard, afterwards created earl of Surrey in his father's life-time.*

1

men with his whiftle, to hold out to the laft ; and the two Scotch ships with their crews, were carried into the river Thames, [Aug. 2. 1511.]

" This exploit had the more merit, as the two Englifh commanders were in a manner volunteers in the fervice, by their father's order. But it feems to have laid the foundation of Sir Edward's fortune ; for on the 7th of April 1512, the king conftituted him (according to Dugdale) admiral of England, Wales, &c,

" King James ' infifted' upon fatisfaction for the death of Barton, and capture of his ship : ' tho' Henry had generoufly difmiffed the crews, and even agreed that the parties accufed might appear in his courts of admiralty by their attornies, to vindicate themfelves." This affair was in a great meafure the caufe of the battle of Flodden, in which James IV. loft his life.

IN the following ballad will be found perhaps fome few deviations from the truth of hiftory : to atone for which it has probably recorded many leffer facts, which hiftory hath not condefcended to relate. I take many of the little circumftances of the ftory to be real, becaufe I find one of the moft unlikely to be not very remote from the truth. In Pt. 2. v. 156. it is faid, that England had before " but two ships of war.' Now the GREAT HARRY *had been built for feven years before, viz. in 1504: which " was properly fpeak-*
" ing the firft ship in the Englifh navy. Before this period,
" when the prince wanted a fleet, he had no other expedient
" but hiring ships from the merchants." Hume.

The following copy (which is given from the Editor's folio MS. and feems to have been written early in the reign of Elizabeth, if not before,) will be found greatly fuperior to the vulgar ballad, which is evidently modernized and abridged from it. Some few deficiences are however fupplied from a black-letter copy of the latter in the Pepys collection.

N 2

THE

THE FIRST PART.

' WHEN Flora with her fragrant flowers
    ' Bedekt the earth ſo trim and gaye,
' And Neptune with his daintye ſhowers
    ' Came to preſent the monthe of Maye; *'
King Henrye rode to take the ayre,   5
    Over the river of Thames paſt hee;
When eighty merchants of London came,
    And downe they knelt upon their knee.

" O yee are welcome, rich merchànts;
    Good ſaylors, welcome unto mee."   10
They ſwore by the rood, they were ſaylors good,
    But rich merchànts they colde not bee:
" To France nor Flanders dare we paſs:
    Nor Bourdeaux voyage dare we fare;
And all for a rover that lyes on the ſeas,   15
    Who robbs us of our merchant ware."

King Henrye frownd, and turned him rounde,
    And ſwore by the Lord, that was mickle of might,
" I thought he had not been in the world,
    Durſt have wrought England ſuch unright."   20
The merchants ſighed, and ſaid, alas!
    And thus they did their anſwer frame,
Hee is a proud Scott, that robbs on the ſeas,
    And Sir Andrewe Barton is his name.

The

---

* *From the* ′r. *copy.*

The king lookt over his left fhouldèr,   25
   And an angrye look then looked hee:
" Have I never a lorde in all my realme,
   Will fetch yon traytor unto mee ?"
Yea, that dare I; lord Howard fayes ;
   Yea, that dare I with heart and hand ;   30
If it pleafe your grace to give me leave,
   Myfelfe wil be the only man.

Thou art but yong ; the king replyed :
   Yond Scott hath numbred manye a yeare.
" Truft me, my liege, Ile make him quail,   35
   Or before my prince I will never appeare."
Then bowemen and gunners thou fhalt have,
   And chufe them over my realme fo free ;
Befides good mariners, and fhipp-boyes,
   To guide the great fhipp on the fea.   40

The firft man, that lord Howard chofe,
   Was the ableft gunner in all the rea'm,
Thoughe he was threefcore yeeres and ten :
   Good Peter Simon was his name.
Peter, fayd he, I muft to the fea,   45
   To bring home a traytor live or dead :
Before all others I have chofen thee ;
   Of a hundred gunners to be head.

      If

If you, my lord, have chofen me
  Of a hundred gunners to be head,   50
Then hang me up on your maine-maft tree,
  If I miffe my marke one fhilling bread†.
My lord then chofe a boweman rare,
  ' Whofe active hands had gained fame,' *
In Yorkfhire he was a gentleman borne,   55
  And William Horfeley was his name.

Horfeley, fayd he, I muft with fpeede
  Go feeke a traytor on the fea,
And now of a hundred bowemen brave
  To be the head I have chofen thee.   60
If you, quoth hee, have chofen mee
  Of a hundred bowemen to be head ;
On your maine-màft lle hanged bee,
  If I mifs twelvefcore one penny bread †.

With pikes and gunnes, and bowemen bold, 65
  The noble Howard is gone to the fea ;
With a valyant heart and a pleafant chèare,
  Out at Thames mouth fayled he.
And days he fcant had fayled three,
  Upon the ' voyage', he tooke in hand,   70
But there he met with a noble fhipp,
  And ftoutly made it ftay and ftand.

Thou

----

† *An old Eng. word for* **Breadth.**

* *Pr. copy.*

' Thou muft tell me, lord Howard fayes,
　　Now who thou art, and what's thy name;
And fhewe me where thy dwelling is:　　　75
　　And whither bound, and whence thou came.
My name is Henry Hunt, quoth hee
　　With a heavye heart, and a carefull mind;
I and my fhipp doe both belong
　　To the Newcaftle, that ftands upon Tyne.　80

Haft thou not heard, nowe, Henrye Hunt,
　　As thou haft fayled by daye and by night,
Of a Scottifh rover on the feas;
　　Men call him fir Andrew Barton, knighte?
Than ever he fighed, and fayd alas!　　　85
　　With a grieved mind, and well away!
But over-well I knowe that wight,
　　I was his prifoner yefterday.

As I was fayling upon the fea,
　　A Burdeaux voyage for to fare;　　　　90
To his arch-borde * he clafped me,
　　And robd me of all my merchant ware:
And mickle debts, God wot, I owe,
　　And every man will have his owne;
And I am nowe to London bounde,　　　95
　　Of our gracious king to beg a boone.

N 4

* _Perhaps_ Hatch-borde.

You shall not need, lord Howard sayes ;
  Lett me but once that robber see,
For every penny tane thee froe
  It shall be doubled shillings three.   100
Nowe God forefend, the merchant sayes,
  That you shold seek soe far amisse !
God keepe you out o' that traitors handes !
  Full litle ye wott what a man he is.

He is brasse within, and steele without.   105
  With beames on his topcastle stronge ;
And thirtye pieces of ordinance
  He carries on each side along :
And he hath a pinnace deerlye dight,
  St. Andrewes crosse itt is his guide ;   110
His pinnace beareth ninescore men,
  And fifteen canons on each side.

Were ye twentye shippes, and he but one ;
  I sweare by kirke, and bower, and hall ;
He wold orecome them every one,   115
  If once his beames they doe downe fall.
This is cold comfort, sayes my lord,
  To welcome a stranger on the sea :
Yet Ile bring him and his shipp to shore,
  Or to Scotland he shall carrye mee,   120

Then

Then a noble gunner you muſt have,
  And he muſt aim well with his ee,
And ſinke his pinnace in the ſea,
  Or elſe he ne'er orecome will be:
And if you chance his ſhipp to borde,   125
  This counſel I muſt give withall,
Let no man to his topcaſtle goe
  To ſtrive to let his beams downe fall.

And ſeven pieces of ordinance,
  I pray your honour lend to mee,   130
On each ſide of my ſhipp along,
  And I will lead you on the ſea.
A glaſſe Ile ſett, that may be ſeene,
  Whether you ſayle by day or night;
And to-morrowe, I ſweare, by nine of the clocke 135
  You ſhall ſee Sir Andrewe Barton knight.

T H E   S E C O N D   P A R T.

T H E merchant ſett my lorde a glaſſe
  Soe well apparent in his ſight,

And

And on the morrowe, by nine of the clocke,
    He fhewed him Sir Andrewe Barton knight.
His hatchborde it was ' gilt' with gold,   5
    Soe deerlye dight it dazzled the ee :
Nowe by my faith, lord Howarde fays,
    This is a gallant fight to fee.

Take in your ancyents, ftandards eke,
    So clofe that no man may them fee ;   10
And put me forth a white willowe wand,
    As merchants ufe that fayle the fea.
But they ftirred neither top, nor maft ;
    Stoutly they paft Sir Andrew by.
What Englifh churles are yonder, he fayd,   15
    That can foe little curtefye ?

Now by the roode, three yeares and more
    I have beene admirall over the fea ;
And never an Englifh nor Portingall
    Without my leave can paffe this way.   20
Then called he forth his ftout pinnace ;
    " Fetch backe yond pedlars nowe to mee :
I fweare by the maffe, yon Englifh churles
    Shall all hang at my maine-maft tree.

With

V. 5. ' hatched with gold.' *MS*.

With that the pinnace itt ſhott off, 25
 Full well lord Howard might it ken ;
For it ſtrake downe his fore-maſt tree,
 And killed fourteen of his men.
Come hither, Simon, ſayes my lord,
 Looke that thy word doe ſtand in ſtead ; 30
For at my maine-maſt thou ſhalt hang,
 If thou miſſe thy marke one ſhilling bread.

Simon was old, but his heart was bolde.
 His ordinance he laid right lowe ;
He put in chaine full nine yardes long, 35
 With other great ſhott leſſe, and moe ;
And he lette goe his great gunnes ſhott ;
 Soe well he ſettled itt with his ee,
The firſt ſight that Sir Andrewe ſawe,
 He ſawe his pinnace ſunke i' the ſea. 40

And when he ſaw his pinnace ſunke,
 Lord, how his heart with rage did ſwell !
 Nowe cutt my ropes, itt is time to be gon ;
 Ile fetch yond pedlars backe myſel."
When my Lord ſawe Sir Andrewe looſe, 45
 Within his heart hee was full faine :
" Nowe ſpread your ancyents, ſtrike up drummes,
 Sound all your trumpetts out amaine."

       Fight

Fight on, my men, Sir Andrewe fayes,
    Weale howfoever this geere will fway;   50
Itt is my lord admirall of Englànd,
    Is come to feeke mee on the fea.
Simon had a fonne, who fhott right well,
    That did Sir Andrewe mickle fcare;
In att his decke he gave a fhott,   55
    Killed threefcore of his men of warre.

Then Henrye Hunt with rigour hott
    Came bravely on the other fide,
Soone he drove downe his fore-maft tree,
    And killed fourfcore men befide.   60
Nowe, out alas! Sir Andrewe cryed,
    What may a man now thinke, or fay?
Yonder merchant theefe, that pierceth mee,
    He was my prifoner yefterday.

Come hither to me, thou Gordon good,   65
    That aye waft readye at my call;
I will give thee three hundred markes,
    If thou wilt let my beames downe fall.
Lord Howard hee then calld in hafte,
    " Horfeley fee thou be true in ftead;   70
For thou fhalt at the maine-maft hang,
    If thou miffe twelvefcore one penny bread.

Then

Then Gordon fwarvd the maine-maft tree,
  He fwarved it with might and maine;
But Horfeley with a bearing arrowe,   75
  Stroke the Gordon through the braine;
And he fell downe to the hatches again,
  And fore his deadlye wounde did bleed:
Then word went through Sir Andrews men,
  How that the Gordon he was dead.   80

Come hither to mee, James Hambilton,
  Thou art my only fifters fonne,
If thou wilt let my beames downe fall,
  Six hundred nobles thou haft wonne.
With that he fwarvd the maine-maft tree,   85
  He fwarved it with nimble art;
But Horfeley with a broad arròwe
  Pierced the Hambilton thorough the heart:

And downe he fell upon the deck,
  That with his blood did ftreame amaine: 90
Then every Scott cryed, Well-away!
  Alas a comelye youth is flaine!
All woe begone was Sir Andrew then,
  With griefe and rage his heart did fwell:
" Go fetch me forth my armour of proofe,   95
  For I will to the topcaftle myfel."

" Goe

" Goe fetch me forth my armour of proofe,
　That gilded is with gold foe cleare :
God be with my brother John of Barton !
　Againſt the Portingals hee it ware ;　　　100
And when he had on this armour of proofe,
　He was a gallant fight to fee :
Ah ! nere didſt thou meet with living wight,
　My deere brothèr, could cope with thee."

Come hither Horſeley, fays my lord,　　　105
　And looke to your ſhaft that it goe right,
Shoot a good ſhoot in time of need,
　And for it thou ſhalt be made a knight.
Ile ſhoot my beſt, quoth Horſeley then,
　Your honour ſhall fee, with might and maine ;　110
But if I were hanged at your maine-maſt tree,
　I have now left but arrowes twaine.

Sir Andrew he did ſwarve the tree,
　With right good will he ſwarved then :
Upon his breaſt did Horſeley hitt,　　　115
　But the arrow bounded back agen.
Then Horſeley ſpyed a privye place
　With a perfeſt eye in a fecrette part ;.
Under the ſpole of his right arme
　He ſmote Sir Andrew to the heart.　　　120

" Fight

" Fight on, my men, Sir Andrew fayes,
    A little Ime hurt, but yett not flaine ;
Ile but lye downe and bleede a while,
    And then Ile rife and fight againe.
" Fight on, my men, Sir Andrew fayes,   125
    And never flinche before the foe ;
And ftand faft by St. Andrewes croffe
    Untill you heare my whiftle blowe."

They never heard his whiftle blow, ——
    Which made their hearts waxe fore adread: 130
Then Horfeley fayd, Aboard, my lord,
    For well I wott Sir Andrew's dead.
They boarded then his noble fhipp,
    They boarded it with might and maine;
Eighteen fcore Scotts alive they found,   135
    The reft were either maimd or flaine.

Lord Howard tooke a fword in hand,
    And off he fmote Sir Andrewes head ;
" I muft ha' left England many a daye,
    If thou wert alive as thou art dead."   140
He caufed his body to be caft
    Over the hatchborde into the fea,
And about his middle three hundred crownes :
    " Wherever thou land this will burye thee."

Thus

Thus from the warres lord Howard came,   145
    And backe he fayled ore the maine,
With mickle joy and triumphìng
    Into Thames mouth he came againe.
Lord Howard then a letter wrote,
    And fealed it with feale and ring ;   150
" Such a noble prize have I brought to your grace,
    As never did fubject to a king.

" Sir Andrewes fhipp I bring with mee ;
    A braver fhipp was never none :
Nowe hath your grace two fhipps of warre,   155
    Before in England was but one."
King Henryes grace with royall cheere
    Welcomed the noble Howard home,
And where, faid he, is this rover ftout,
    That I myfelfe may give the doome ?   160

" The rover, he is fafe, my leige,
    Full many a fadom in the fea ;
If he were alive as he is dead,
    I muft ha' left England many a day :
And your grace may thank four men i'the fhip :65
    For the victory wee have wonne,
Thefe are William Horfeley, Henry Hunt,
    And Peter Simon, and his fonne."

                                        To

To Henry Hunt, the king then fayd,
  In lieu of what was from thee tane,   170
A noble a day now thou fhalt have,
  Sir Andrewes jewels and his chayne."
And Horfeley thou fhalt be a knight,
  And lands and livings fhalt have ftore;
Howard fhall be earle Surrye hight,   175
  As Howards erft have beene before.

Nowe, Peter Simon, thou art old,
  I will maintaine thee and thy fonne:
And the men fhall have five hundred markes
  For the good fervice they have done.   180
Then in came the queene with ladyes fair
  To fee Sir Andrewe Barton knight:
They weend that hee were brought on fhore,
  And thought to have feen a gallant fight.

But when they fee his deadlye face,   185
  And eyes foe hallowe in his head,
I wold give, quoth the king, a thoufand markcs,
  This man were alive as he is dead:
Yet for the manfull part he playd,
  Which fought foe well with heart and hand,   190
His men fhall have twelvepence a day,
  Till they come to my brother kings high land.

XIII.

LADY ANNE BOTHWELL's LAMENT.

A Scottish Song.

*The subject of this pathetic ballad the Editor once thought
might possibly relate to the Earl of Bothwell, and his de-
sertion of his wife Lady Jean Gordon, to make room for
his marriage with the Queen of Scots: But this opinion
he now believes to be groundless; indeed earl Bothwell's
age, who was upwards of 60 at the time of that marriage,
renders it unlikely that he should be the object of so warm a
passion as this elegy supposes. He has been since informed,
that it entirely refers to a private story: A lady of quality
of the name of BOTHWELL, or rather BOSWELL, having
been, together with her child, deserted by her husland or
lover, composed these affecting lines herself; which here are
given from a copy in the Editor's folio MS. compared with
another in Allan Ramsay's Miscellany.*

BALOW, my babe, ly stil and sleipe!
   It grieves me sair to see thee weipe:
If thoust be silent, Ise be glad,
Thy maining maks my heart ful sad.
Balow, my boy, thy mithers joy,   5
Thy father breides me great annoy.
     Balow, my babe, ly stil and sleipe,
     It grieves me sair to see thee weepe.

Whan

Whan he began' to court my luve,
And with his fugred wordes * to muve,   10
His faynings fals, and flattering cheire
To me that time did not appeire:
But now I fee, moft cruell hee
Cares neither for my babe nor mee.
                Balow, &c.   15

Ly ftil, my darling, fleipe a while,
And whan thou wakeft, fweitly fmile:
But fmile not, as thy father did,
To cozen maids: nay God forbid !
Bot yett I feire, thou wilt gae neire   20
Thy fatheris hart, and face to beire.
                Balow, &c.

I cannae chufe, but ever will
Be luving to thy father ftil:
Whair-eir he gae, whair-eir he ryde,   25
My luve with him maun ftil abyde:
In weil or wae, whair-eir he gae,
Mine hart can neire depart him frae.
                Balow, &c.

O 2   Bot

---

* *When* fugar *was firft imported into Europe, it was a very great
dainty; and therefore the epithet* fugred *is ufed by all our old writers
metaphorically to exprefs extreme and delicate fweetnefs. (See above, p.
176.) Sugar at prefent is cheap and common; and therefore fuggefts
now a coarfe and vulgar idea.*

Bot doe not, doe not, prettie mine,   30
To faynings fals thine hart incline;
Be loyal to thy luver trew,
And nevir change hir for a new :
If gude or faire, of hir have care,
For womens banning's wonderous fair.   35
     Balow, &c.

Bairne, fin thy cruel father is gane,
Thy winfome fmiles maun eife my paine ;
My babe and I'll together live,
He'll comfort me whan cares doe grieve :   40
My babe and I right faft will ly,
And quite forgeit man's cruelty.
     Balow, &c.

Fareweil, fareweil, thou falfeft youth,
That evir kift a womans mouth !   45
I wifh all maides be warnd by mee
Nevir to truft mans curtefy ;
For if we doe bot chance to bow,
'They'le ufe us than they care not how.
   Balow, my babe, ly ftil, and fleipe,   50
   It grieves me fair to fee thee weipe.

          XIV. THE

XIV

THE MURDER OF THE KING OF SCOTS.

The cataſtrophe of Henry Stewart, lord Darnley, the unfortunate huſband of Mary Q. of Scots, is the ſubject of this ballad. It is here related in that partial imperfect manner, in which ſuch an event would naturally ſtrike the ſubjects of another kingdom; of which he was a native. Henry appears to have been a vain capricious worthleſs young man, of weak underſtanding, and diſſolute morals. But the beauty of his perſon, and the inexperience of his youth, would diſpoſe mankind to treat him with an indulgence, which the cruelty of his murder would afterwards convert into the moſt tender pity and regret: and then imagination would not fail to adorn his memory with all thoſe virtues, he ought to have poſſeſſed. This will account for the extravagant elogium beſtowed upon him in the firſt ſtanza, &c.

Henry lord Darnley was eldeſt ſon of the earl of Lennox, by the lady Margaret Douglas, niece of Henry VIII. and daughter of Margaret queen of Scotland by the earl of Angus, whom that princeſs married after the death of James IV.—Darnley, who had been born and educated in England, was but in his 21ſt year, when he was murdered, Feb. 9. 1567-8. This crime was perpetrated by the E. of Bothwell, not out of reſpect to the memory of David Riccio, but in order to pave the way for his own marriage with the queen.

This ballad (printed from the Editor's folio MS.) ſeems to have been written ſoon after Mary's eſcape into England in 1568, ſee v. 65.—It will be remembered at v. 5. that this princeſs was Q. dowager of France, having been firſt married to Francis II. who died Dec. 4. 1560.

O 3   WOE

W O E worth, woe worth thee, falfe Scotlànde!
   For thou haft ever wrought by fleighte ;
The worthyeft prince that ever was borne,
   You hanged under a cloud by night.

The queene of France a letter wrote,   5
   And fealed it with harte and ringe ;
And bade him come Scotland within,
   And fhee wold marry and crowne him kinge.

To be a king is a pleafant thing,
   To be a prince unto a peere :   10
But you have heard, and foe have I,
   A man may well buy gold too deare.

There was an Italyan in that place,
   Was as well beloved as ever was hee,
And David Riccio was his name,   15
   Chamberlaine to the queene was hee.

If the king had rifen forth of his place,
   Hee wold have fate him downe i' th' chaire,
Although it befeemed him not fo well,
   And though the kinge were prefent there.   20

. Some lords in Scotlande waxed wroth,
   And quarrelled with him for the nonce ;
And I fhall tell how it befell,
   Twelve daggers were in him att once.

When

When the queene fhee faw her chamberlaine flaine, 25
  For him her faire cheeks fhe did weete,
And made a vowe for a yeare and a day
  The king and fhee wold not come in one fheete.

Then fome of the lords they waxed wroth,
  And made their vow all vehementlye ;   30
That for the death of the chamberlaine,
  How hee, the king himfelfe, fholde dye.

With gun-powder they ftrewed his roome,
  And layd greene rufhes in his waye ;
For the traitors thought that very night   35
  This worthye king for to betraye.

To bedd the king he made him bowne ;
  To take his reft was his defire ;
He was noe fooner caft on fleepe,
  But his chamber was on a blafing fire.   40

Up he lope, and the window brake,
  And hee had thirtye foote to fall ;
Lord Bodwell kept a privy watch,
  All underneath the caftle wall.

Who have we here ? lord Bodwell fayd :   45
  Now anfwer me, that I may know.
" King Henry the eighth my uncle was ;
  For his fweete fake fome pitty fhow."

            Who

Who have we here ? lord Bodwell fayd,
  Now anfwer me when I doe fpeake.   50
" Ah, lord Bodwell, I know thee well ;
  Some pitty on me I pray thee take."

Ile pitty thee as much, he fayd,
  And as much favour fhow to thee,
As thou didft to the queenes chamberlaine,   55
  That day thou deemedft him to die *.

Through halls and towers the king they ledd,
  Through towers and caftles that were nye,
Through an arbor into an orchàrd,
  There on a peare-tree hanged him hye.   60

When the governor of Scotland heard,
  How that the worthye king was flaine ;
He perfued the queen fo bitterlye,
  That in Scotland fhee dare not remaine.

But fhe is fledd into merry England,   65
  And here her refidence hath tane ;
And through the queene of Englands grace,
  In England now fhee doth remaine.

XV. A

* Pronounced after the northern manner &c.

XV.

A SONNET BY Q. ELIZABETH.

*The following lines, if they display no rich vein of poetry,
are yet so strongly characteristic of their great and spirited
authoress, that the insertion of them will be pardoned. They
are preserved in Puttenham's Arte of Eng. Poesie ; a book in
which are many sly addresses to the queen's foible of shining as
a poetess. The extraordinary manner in which these verses
are introduced, shews what kind of homage was exacted from
the courtly writers of those times, viz.*

   " *I find, says this antiquated critic, none example in Eng-*
" *lish metre, so well maintaining this figure* [Exargasia, *or*
" *the Gorgeous, Lat.* Expolitio] *as that dittie of her majes-*
" *ties owne making, passing sweete and harmonicall ; which*
" *figure beyng as his very originall name purporteth the most*
" *bewtifull and gorgious of all others, it asketh in reason to*
" *be reserved for a last complement, and desciphred by a la-*
" *dies penne, herselfe beyng the most bewtifull, or rather bew-*
" *tie of queenes* †. *And this was the occasion : our soveraigne*
" *lady perceiving how the Scottish queenes residence within*
" *this realme at so great libertie and ease (as were skarce*
" *meete for so great and dangerous a prysoner) bred secret*
" *factions among her people, and made many of the nobilitie*
" *incline to favour her partie : some of them desirous of in-*
" *novation in the state : others aspiring to greater fortunes*
" *by her libertie and life. The queene our soveraigne ladie*
" *to declare that she was nothing ignorant of those secret*
" *practizes, though she had long with great wisdome and*
                                             " *pacience*

---

† *She was at this time near three-score.*

" *pacience diſſembled it, writeth this dittie moſt ſweete and*
" *ſententious, not hiding from all ſuch aſpiring minds the*
" *danger of their ambition and diſloyaltie: which after-*
" *wards fell out moſt truly by th' exemplary chaſtiſement of*
" *ſundry perſons, who in favour of the ſaid Scot. Qu. de-*
" *clining from her majeſtie, ſought to interrupt the quiet of the*
" *realme by many evill and undutifull practizes.*"

This ſonnet ſeems to have been compoſed in 1569, *not long
before the D. of Norfolk, the earls of Pembroke and Arundel,
the lord Lumley, Sir Nich. Throcmorton, and others, were
taken into cuſtody. See Hume, Rapin, &c.—It was originally written in long lines or alexandrines, each of which
is here divided into two.*

T H E doubt of future foes
    Exiles my preſent joy;
And wit me warnes to ſhun ſuch ſnares,
    As threaten mine annoy.

For falſhood now doth flow,   5
    And ſubject faith doth ebbe;
Which would not be if reaſon rul'd,
    Or wiſdome wev'd the webbe.

But clowdes of toyes untried
    Do cloake aſpiring mindes;   10
Which turn to raine of late repent,
    By courſe of changed windes.

The

The toppe of hope fuppofed
  The roote of ruthe wil be;
And fruteleffe all their graffed guiles,   15
  As fhortly ye fhall fee.

Then dazeld eyes with pride,
  Which great ambition blindes,
Shal be unfeeld by worthy wights,
  Whofe forefight falfhood finds.   20

The daughter of debate *,
  That eke difcord doth fowe,
Shal reape no gaine where former rule
  Hath taught ftil peace to growe.

No forreine bannifht wight   25
  Shall ancre in this port;
Our realme it brookes no ftrangers force,
  Let them elfewhere refort.

Our rufty fworde with reft
  Shall firft his edge employ,   30
Shall ' quickly' poll their toppes, that feeke
  Such change, and gape for joy.

                                      †‡†

---

* *She evidently means here the Queen of Scots.*

✝✝✝ *I cannot help subjoining to the above sonnet another distich of Elizabeth's preserved by Puttenham (p. 197.)* " *which (says he) our soveraigne lady wrote in defiance* " *of fortune."*

Never thinke you, Fortune can beare the sway,
Where Vertue's force can cause her to obay.

The slightest effusion of such a mind deserves attention.

XVI.

KING OF SCOTS AND ANDREW BROWNE.

This ballad is a proof of the little intercourse that subsisted between the Scots and English, before the accession of James I. to the crown of England. The tale which is here so circumstantially related does not appear to have had the least foundation in history, but was probably built upon some confused hearsay report of the tumults in Scotland during the minority of that prince, and of the conspiracies formed by different factions to get possession of his person. It should seem from ver. 102. to have been written during the regency, or at least before the death, of the earl of Morton, who was condemned and executed June 2. 1581; when James was in his 15th year.

The original copy (preserved in the archives of the Antiquarian Society London) is intitled, "A new Ballad, declar-" ing the great treason conspired against the young king of *" Scots, and how one Andrew Browne an English-man,*" which was the king's chamberlaine, prevented the same. *" To the tune of Milfield, or els to Green-sleeves."* At the *end is subjoined the name of the author* W. ELDERTON.

2

" IN-

" Imprinted at London for Yarathe James, dwelling in New-
" gate Market, over against Ch. Church," in black letter,
folio.

This ELDERTON, *who had been originally an attorney
in the sheriffs courts of London, and afterwards (if we may
believe Oldys) a comedian, was a facetious fuddling companion, whose tippling and his rhymes rendered him famous
among his contemporaries. He was author of many popular
songs and ballads; and probably other pieces in these volumes,
besides the following, are of his composing. He is believed
to have fallen a martyr to his bottle before the year 1592.
His epitaph has been recorded by Camden, and translated
by Oldys.*

Hic situs est sitiens, atque ebrius Eldertonus,
   Quid dico hic situs est? hic potius sitis est.

Dead drunk here Elderton doth lie;
Dead as he is, he still is dry:
So of him it may well be said,
Here he, but not his thirst, is laid.

*See Stow's Lond. [Guild-hall.]—Biogr. Brit. [*DRAYTON,
*by Oldys, Note B.] Ath. Ox.—Camden's Remains.—The
Exale-tation of Ale, among Beaumont's Poems, 8vo. 1653.*

'OUT alas!' what a griefe is this
    That princes subjects cannot be true,
But still the devill hath some of his,
    Will play their parts whatsoever ensue;
Forgetting what a grievous thing   5
It is to offend the anointed king?
    Alas for woe, why should it be so,
    This makes a sorrowful heigh ho.

In

In Scotland is a bonnie kinge,
   As proper a youth as neede to be,   10
Well given to every happy thing,
   That can be in a kinge to fee:
Yet that unluckie country ftill,
Hath people given to craftie will.
   Alas for woe, &c.   15

On Whitfun eve it fo befell,
   A poffet was made to give the king,
Whereof his ladie nurfe hard tell,
   And that it was a poyfoned thing:
She cryed, and called piteouflie ;   20
Now help, or els the king fhall die!
   Alas for woe, &c.

One Browne, that was an Englifh man,
   And hard the ladies piteous crye,
Out with his fword, and beftir'd him than,   25
   Out of the doores in hafte to flie ;
But all the doores were made fo faft,
Out of a window he got at laft.
   Alas for woe, &c.

He met the bifhop coming faft,   30
   Having the poffet in his hande :
The fight of Browne made him aghaft,
   Who bad him ftoutly ftaie and ftand.

With

With him were two that ranne away,
For feare that Browne would make a fray.   35
  Alas for woe, &c.

Bifhop, quoth Browne, what haft thou there ?
  Nothing at all, my friend, fayde he;
But a poffet to make the king good cheere.
  Is it fo ? fayd Browne, that will I fee,   ·40
Firft I will have thyfelf begin,
Before thou go any further in ;
    Be it weale or woe, it fhall be fo,
    This makes a forrowful heigh ho.

The bifhop fayde, Browne I doo know,   45
  Thou art a young man poore and bare;
Livings on thee I will beftowe :
  Let me go on, take thou no care.
No, no, quoth Browne, I will not be
A traitour for all Chriftiantie: 50
    Happe well or woe, it fhall be fo,
    Drink now with a forrowfull, &c.

The bifhop dranke, and by and by
  His belly burft and he fell downe :
A juft rewarde for his traitery.   55
  This was a poffet indeed, quoth Brown !
He ferched the bifhop, and found the keyes,
To come to the kinge when he did pleafe.
    Alas for woe, &c.

3   As

As foon as the king got word of this,   60
  He humbly fell uppon his knee,
And prayfed God that he did mifse
  To taft of that extremity :
For that he did perceive and know,
His clergie would betray him fo :   65
    Alas for woe, &c.

Alas, he faid, unhappie realme,
  My father and grandfather flaine :
My mother banifhed, O extreame !
  Unhappy fate, and bitter bayne !   70
And now like treafon wrought for me,
What more unhappie realme can be !
    Alas for woe, &c.

The king did call his nurfe to his grace,
  And gave her twenty poundes a yeere ;   75
And truftie Browne too in like cafe,
  He knighted him with gallant geere ;
And gave him ' lands and' livings great,
For dooing fuch a manly feat,
  As he did fhowe, to the bifhop's woe,   80
  Which made, &c.

When

V. 67. *His father was Henry Lord Darnley. His grandfather the old Earl of Lenox, regent of Scotland, and father of Lord Darnley was murdered at Stirling, Sept. 5. 1571.*

When all this treafon done and paft,
   Tooke not effect of traytery;
Another treafon at the laft,
   They fought againft his majeftie: 85
How they might make their kinge away,
By a privie banket on a daye.
      Alas for woe, &c.

' Another time' to fell the king
   Beyonde the feas they had decreede: 90
Three noble Earles heard of this thing,
   And did prevent the fame with fpeede.
For a letter came, with fuch a charme,
That they fhould doo their king no harme:
      For further woe, if they did foe,   95
      Would make a forrowful heigh hoe.

The Earle Mourton told the Douglas then,
   Take heede you do not offend the king;
But fhew yourfelves like honeft men
   Obediently in every thing: 100
For his godmother * will not fee
Her noble childe mifus'd to be
      With any woe; for if it be fo,
      She will make, &c.

God graunt all fubjects may be true,   105
   In England, Scotland, every where:

* Q. Elizabeth.

That no such daunger may ensue,
　　To put the prince or state in feare:
That God the highest king may see
Obedience as it ought to be,　　　　　　110
　　In wealth or woe, God graunt it be so
　　To avoide the sorrowful heigh ho.

XVII.

THE BONNY EARL OF MURRAY.

A Scottish Song.

In December 1591, Francis Stewart Earl of Bothwell had made an attempt to seize on the person of his sovereign James VI. but being disappointed, had retired towards the north. The king unadvisedly gave a commission to George Gordon Earl of Huntley, to pursue Bothwell and his followers with fire and sword. Huntley, under cover of executing that commission, took occasion to revenge a private quarrel he had against James Stewart Earl of Murray, a relation of Bothwell's. In the night of Feb. 7. 1592, he beset Murray's house, burnt it to the ground, and slew Murray himself; a young nobleman of the most promising virtues, and the very darling of the people. See Robertson's Hist.

The present Lord Murray hath now in his possession a picture of his ancestor naked and covered with wounds, which had been carried about, according to the custom of that age, in order to inflame the populace to revenge his death. If this picture did not flatter, he well deserved the name of the BONNY EARL, *for he is there represented as a tall and comely personage. It is a tradition in the family, that Gordon of Bucky gave him a wound in the face: Murray half*

expiring,

*expiring, faid, " You hae fpilt a better face than your
awin." Upon this, Bucky pointing his dagger at Huntley's
breaft, fwore, " You fhall be as deep as I ;" and forced
him to pierce the poor defencelefs body.*

*K. James, who took no care to punifh the murtherers, is
faid by fome to have privately countenanced and abetted
them, being ftimulated by jealoufy for fome indifcreet praifes
which his Queen had too lavifhly beftowed on this unfortunate
youth. See the preface to the next ballad. See alfo Mr.
Walpole's Catalogue of Royal Auth. vol. 1. p. 42.*

Y E highlands, and ye lawlands,
   Oh! whair hae ye been ?
They hae flaine the Earl of Murray,
   And hae laid him on the green.

Now wae be to thee, Huntley!   5
   And whairfore did you fae!
I bade you bring him wi' you,
   But forbade you him to flay.

He was a braw gallant,
   And he rid at the ring;   10
And the bonny Earl of Murray,
   Oh! he might hae been a king.

He was a braw gallant,
   And he playd at the ba';
And the bonny Earl of Murray   15
   Was the flower among them a'.

P 2

He

He was a braw gallant,
    And he playd at the gluve;
And the bonny Earl of Murray,
    Oh! he was the Queenes luve.   20

Oh! lang will his lady
    Luke owre the castle downe *,
Ere she see the Earl of Murray
    Cum sounding throw the towne.

* Castle downe *here has been thought to mean the* CASTLE OF DOWNE, *a seat belonging to the family of Murray.*

XVIII.

YOUNG WATERS.

A Sottish Ballad.

It has been suggested to the Editor, that this ballad covertly alludes to the indiscreet partiality, which Q. Anne of Denmark is said to have shewn for the BONNY EARL OF MURRAY; *and which is supposed to have influenced the fate of that unhappy nobleman. Let the Reader judge for himself.*

The following account of the murder is given by a contemporary writer, and a person of credit, Sir James Balfour, Knight, Lyon King of Arms, whose MS. of the Annals of Scotland is in the Advocates library at Edinburgh.

" The seventh of Febry, this zeire, 1592, the Earle of " Murray was cruelly murthered by the Earle of Huntley at "· his house in Dunibrissel in Fysse-shyre, and with him " Dunbar,

" *Dunbar, sheriffe of Murray. It was given out and*
" *publickly talkt, that the Earle of Huntley was only the*
" *instrument of perpetrating this facte, to satisfie the King's*
" *jealousie of Murray, quhum the Queene more raskely than*
" *wisely, some few days before had commendit in the*
" *King's hearing, with too many epithets of a proper*
" *and gallant man. The reasons of these surmises pro-*
" *ceedit from a proclamatione of the Kings, the 13 of*
" *Marche following; inhibiteine the zoung Earle of Mur-*
" *ray to persue the Earle of Huntley, for his father's*
" *slaughter, in respect he being wardeit [imprisoned] in*
" *the castell of Blacknesse for the same murther, was wil-*
" *ling to abide a tryall, averring that he had done nothing*
" *but by the King's majesties commissione; and was neither*
" *airt nor part in the murther †.*"
The following ballad is here given from a copy printed
not long since at Glasgow, in one sheet 8vo. The world
was indebted for its publication to the lady Jean Hume,
sister to the Earle of Hume, who died lately at Gibraltar.

ABOUT Zule, quhen the wind blew cule,
    And the round tables began,
A'! there is cum to our kings court
    Mony a well-favourd man.

The queen luikt owre the castle wa,   5
    Beheld baith dale and down,
And then she saw zoung Waters
    Cum riding to the town.

His footmen they did rin before,
    His horsemen rade behind,   10
And mantel of the burning gowd
    Did keip him frae the wind.

P 3

Gowden

Gowden graith'd his horfe before
    And filler fhod behind,
The horfe zoung Waters rade upon   15
    Was fleeter than the wind.

But than fpake a wylie lord,
    Unto the queen faid he,
O tell me qhua's the faireft face
    Rides in the company.   20

I've fene lord, and I've fene laird,
    And knights of high degree ;
Bot a fairer face than zoung Watèrs
    Mine eyne did never fee.

Out then fpack the jealous king,   25
    (And an angry man was he)
O, if he had been twice as fair,
    Zou micht have excepted me.

Zou're neither laird nor lord, fhe fays,
    Bot the king that wears the crown ;   30
Theris not a knight in fair Scotland
    Bot to thee maun bow down.

For a' that fhe could do or fay,
    Appeasd he wad nae bee ;
Bot for the words which fhe had faid   35
    Zoung Waters he maun dee.

They

They hae taen zoung Waters, and
   Put fetters to his feet ;
They hae taen zoung Waters, and
   Thrown him in dungeon deep.   40

Aft I have ridden thro' Stirling town
   In the wind bot and the weit ;
Bot I neir rade thro' Stirling town
   Wi fetters at my feet.

Aft have I ridden thro' Stirling town   45
   In the wind bot and the rain ;
Bot I neir rade thro' Stirling town
   Neir to return again.

They hae taen to the heiding-hill *
   His zoung fon to his craddle,   50
And they hae taen to the heiding-hill,
   His horfe bot and his faddle.

They hae taen to the heiding-hill
   His lady fair to fee.
And for the words the Queen had fpoke,   55
   Zoung Waters he did dee.

P 4   XIX. MA-

---

* Heiding-hill ; i. e. 'heading [beheading] hill. The place of execution was anciently an artificial hillock.

XIX.

MARY AMBREE.

In the year 1584, *the Spaniards, under the command of
Alexander Farnese prince of Parma, began to gain great
advantages in Flanders and Brabant, by recovering many
strong-holds and cities from the Hollanders, as Ghent, (called
then by the English* GAUNT,) *Antwerp, Mechlin, &c. See
Stow's Annals, p.* 711. *Some attempt made with the assistance
of English volunteers to retrieve the former of those places
probably gave occasion to this ballad. I can find no mention
of our heroine in history, but the following rhymes rendered
her famous among our poets. Ben Johnson often mentions her,
and calls any remarkable virago by her name. See his Epi-
cæne, first acted in* 1609. *Act* 4. *sc.* 2. *His Tale of a Tub,
Act* 1. *sc.* 4. *And his masque intitled the Fortunate Isles,*
1626, *where he quotes the very words of the ballad,*

—— MARY AMBREE,
*(Who marched so free
To the siege of Gaunt,
And death could not daunt,
As the ballad doth vaunt)
Were a braver wight, &c.*

She is also mentioned in Fletcher's Scornful Lady, Act 5.
sub finem.
—— " *My large gentlewoman, my* MARY AMBREE,
" *had I but seen into you, you should have had another bed-*
" *fellow.*" ——

This

This ballad is printed from a black-letter copy in the Pepys Collection, improved from the Editor's folio MS. The full title is, " The valorous acts performed at Gaunt " by the brave bonnie lass Mary Ambree, who in revenge " of her lovers death did play her part most gallantly. The " tune is, The blind beggar, &c."

WHEN captaines couragious, whom death colde
       not daunte,
Did march to the siege of the cittye of Gaunte,
They mustred their souldiers by two and by three,
And formost in battle was Mary Ambree.

When brave Sir John Major* was slaine in her sight, 5
Who was her true lover, her joy, and delight,
Because he was slaine most treacherouslie,
Then vowd to revenge him Mary Ambree.

She clothed herselfe from the top to the toe
In buffe of the bravest, most seemelye to showe; 10
A faire shirt of male † then slipped on shee;
Was not this a brave bonny lass, Mary Ambree ?

A helmett of proofe she strait did provide,
A strong arminge sword shee girt by her side,
On her hand a goodly faire gauntlett had shee; 15
Was not this a brave bonny lass, Mary Ambree ?

Then

* *So MS.* Serjeant Major *in PC.*

† *A common phrase in that age for a Coat of Mail. So Spencer speaks of the Irish Gallowglass or Foot-soldier as " armed in a long Shirt of Mayl." (View of the State of Ireland.)*

Then tooke fhee her fworde and her targett in hand,
Bidding all fuch as wolde, bee of her band,
To wayt on her perfon came thoufand and three :
Was not this a brave bonny lafs, Mary Ambree ?   20

My fouldiers fo valiant and faithfull, fhee fayd,
Nowe followe your captaine, no longer a mayd;
Still formoft in battel myfelfe will I bee :
Was not this a brave bonny laffe, Mary Ambree ?

Then cryed out her fouldiers, and thus they did fay, 25
Soe well thou becomeft this gallant array,
Thy harte and thy weapons foe well do agree,
Noe mayden was ever like Mary Ambree.

Shee cheared her fouldiers, that foughten for life,
With ancyent and ftandard, with drum and with fife, 30
With brave clanging trumpetts, that founded fo free ;
Was not this a brave bonny laffe, Mary Ambree ?

Before I will fee the worft of you all
To come into danger of death, or of thrall,
This hand and this life I will venture fo free :   35
Was not this a brave bonny laffe, Mary Ambree ?

Shee led upp her fouldiers in battel arraye,
Gainft three times theyr number by breake of the daye ;
Seven howers in fkirmifh continued fhee :
Was not this a brave bonny laffe, Mary Ambree ?   40

She

She filled the fkyes with the fmoke of her fhott,
And her enemyes bodyes with bullets foe hott;
For one of her owne men a fcore killed fhee:
Was not this a brave bonny laffe, Mary Ambree?

And when her falfe gunner, to fpoyle her intent,   45
Away all her pellets and powder had fpent,
Straight with her keen weapon fhee flafht him in three:
Was not this a brave bonny laffe, Mary Ambree?

Being falfelye betrayed for lucre of hyre,
At length fhe was forced to make a retyre;   50
Then her fouldiers into a ftrong caftle drew fhee:
Was not this a brave bonny laffe, Mary Ambre?

Her foes they befett her on every fide,
As thinking clofe fiege fhee cold never abide;
To beate down her walles they all did decree;   55
But ftoutlye deffyd them brave Mary Ambree.

Then tooke fhee her fword and her targett in hand,
And mounting the walls all undaunted did ftand,
There daring the captaines to match any three:
O what a brave captaine was Mary Ambree!   60

Now faye, Englifh captaine, what woldeft thou give
To ranfome thy felfe, which elfe muft not live?
Come yield thyfelfe quicklye, or flaine thou muft bee.
Then fmiled fweetlye faire Mary Ambree.

Ye captaines couragious, of valour fo bold,   65
Whom thinke you before you now you doe behold?
A knight, fir, of England, and captaine foe free,
Who fhortelye with us a prifoner muft bee.

No captaine of England; behold in your fight
Two brefts in my bofome, and therfore noe knight: 70
Noe knight, firs, of England, nor captaine you fee,
But a poor fimple mayden, calld Mary Ambree.

But art thou a woman, as thou doft declare,
Whofe valor hath provd fo undaunted in warre?
If England doth yield fuch brave maydens as thee,   75
Full well may they conquer, faire Mary Ambree.

The prince of Great Parma heard of her renowne,
Who long had advanced for Englands faire crowne;
Hee wooed her and fued her his miftrefs to bee,
And offerd rich prefents to Mary Ambree.   80

But this virtuous mayden defpifed them all,
Ile nere fell my honour for purple nor pall:
A mayden of England, fir, never will bee
The whore of a monarcke, quoth Mary Ambree.

Then to her owne country fhee backe did returne,   85
Still holding the foes of faire England in fcorne:
Therfore Englifh captaines of every degree
Sing forth the brave valours of Mary Ambree.

XX.   BRAVE

BRAVE LORD WILLOUGHBY.

Peregrine Bertie lord Willoughby of Eresby had, in the year 1586, distinguished himself at the siege of Zutphen in the Low Countries. He was the year after made general of the English forces in the United Provinces, in room of the earl of Leicester, who was recalled. This gave him an opportunity of signalizing his courage and military skill in several actions against the Spaniards. One of these, greatly exaggerated by popular report, is probably the subject of this old ballad, which, on account of its flattering encomiums on English valour, hath always been a favourite with the people.

" My lord Willoughbie (says a contemporary writer) was " one of the queenes best swordsmen : . . . . he was a great " master of the art military. . . . . . I have heard it spoken, " that had he not slighted the court, but applied himself to " the queene, he might have enjoyed a plentifull portion of " her grace; and it was his saying, and it did him no good, " that he was none of the REPTILIA *; intimating, that he " could not creepe on the ground, and that the court was not " his element ; for indeed, as he was a great souldier; so " he was of suitable magnanimitie, and could not brooke " the obsequiousnesse and assiduitie of the court." (Naunton.)*

Lord Willoughbie died in 1601.—*Both Norris and Turner were famous among the military men of that age.*

The subject of this ballad (which is printed from an old black-letter copy) may possibly receive illustration from what CHAPMAN *says in the Dedicat. to his version of Homer's Frogs and Mice, concerning the brave and memorable Retreat of Sir John Norris, with only* 1000 *men, thro' the whole Spanish army, under the duke of Parma, for three miles together.*

THE

THE fifteenth day of July,
    With gliftering fpear and fhield,
A famous fight in Flanders
    Was foughten in the field :
The moft couragious officers   5
    Were Englifh captains three;
But the braveft man in battel
    Was brave lord Willoughbèy.

The next was captain Norris,
    A valiant man was hee ;   10
The other captain Turner,
    From field would never flee.
With fifteen hundred fighting men,
    Alas ! there were no more,
They fought with fourteen thoufand then   15
    Upon the bloody fhore.

Stand to it noble pikemen,
    And look you round about :
And fhoot you right you bow-men,
    And we will keep them out :   20
You mufquet and callìver men,
    Do you prove true to me,
I'le be the formoft man in fight.
    Says brave lord Willoughbèy.

And

And then the bloody enemy   25
  They fiercely did affail,
And fought it out moft furioufly,
  Not doubting to prevail ;
The wounded men on both fides fell
  Moft pitious for to fee,   30
Yet nothing could the courage quell
  Of brave lord Willoughbèy

For feven hours to all mens view
  This fight endured fore,
Until our men fo feeble grew   35
  That they could fight no more;
And then upon dead horfes
  Full favourly they eat,
And drank the puddle water,
  They could no better get.   40

When they had fed fo freely,
  They kneeled on the ground,
And praifed God devoutly
  For the favour they had found ;
And beating up their colours,   45
  The fight they did renew,
And turning tow'rds the Spaniard,
  A thoufand more they flew.

The

The sharp steel-pointed arrows,
  And bullets thick did fly ;   50
Then did our valiant soldiers
  Charge on most furiously ;
Which made the Spaniards waver,
  They thought it best to flee, ·
They fear'd the stout behaviour   55
  Of brave lord Willoughbèy.

Then quoth the Spanish general,
  Come let us march away,
I fear we shall be spoiled all
  If here we longer stay ;   60
For yonder comes lord Willoughbey
  With courage fierce and fell,
He will not give one inch of way
  For all the devils in hell.

And then the fearful enemy   65
  Was quickly put to flight,
Our men persued couragiously,
  And caught their forces quite ;
But at last they gave a shout,
  Which ecchoed through the sky,   70
God, and St. George for England !
  The conquerers did cry.

This

This news was brought to England
  With all the fpeed might be,
And foon our gracious queen was told   75
 Of this fame victory :
O this is brave lord Willoughbey,
  My love that ever won,
Of all the lords of honour
  'Tis he great deeds hath done.   80

To th' fouldiers that were maimed,
  And wounded in the fray,
The queen allow'd a penfion
  Of fifteen pence a day,
And from all cofts and charges   85
  She quit and fet them free,
And this fhe did all for the fake
  Of brave lord Willoughbèy.

Then courage, noble Englifhmen,   90
  And never be difmaid ;
If that we but one to ten,
  We will not be afraid
To fight with foraign enemies,
  And fet our nation free :
And thus I end the bloody bout   93
  Of brave lord Willoughbèy.

XX.

VICTORIOUS MEN OF EARTH.

This little moral sonnet hath such a pointed application
to the heroes of the foregoing and following ballads, that I
cannot help placing it here, tho' the date of its composition is of
a much later period. It is extracted from " Cupid and
" Death, a masque by J. S. [James Shirley] presented
" Mar. 26. 1653. London printed 1653." 4to.

VICtorious men of earth, no more
  Proclaim how wide your empires are ;
Though you binde in every fhore,
  And your triumphs reach as far
    As night or day,   5
  Yet you proud monarchs muft obey,
And mingle with forgotten afhes, when
Death calls yee to the croud of common men.

Devouring famine, plague, and war,
  Each able to undo mankind,   10
Death's fervile emiffaries are :
  Nor to thefe alone confin'd,
    He hath at will
  More quaint and fubtle wayes to kill ;
A fmile or kifs, as he will ufe the art,   15
Shall have the cunning fkill to break a heart.

XXI. T H E

XXI.

THE WINNING OF CALES.

The subject of this ballad is the taking of the city of Cadiz, (called by our sailors corruptly Cales) *on June 21. 1596, in a descent made on the coast of Spain, under the command of the Lord Howard admiral, and the Earl of Essex general.*

The valour of Essex was not more distinguished on this occasion than his generosity: the town was carried sword in hand, but he stopt the slaughter as soon as possible, and treated his prisoners with the greatest humanity, and even affability and kindness. The English made a rich plunder in the city, but miss'd of a much richer, by the resolution which the Duke of Medina the Spanish admiral took, of setting fire to the ships, in order to prevent their falling into the hands of the enemy. It was computed, that the loss which the Spaniards sustained from this enterprize, amounted to twenty millions of ducats. See Hume's Hist.

The Earl of Essex knighted on this occasion not fewer than sixty persons, which gave rise to the following sarcasm,

A gentleman of Wales, a knight of Cales,
And a laird of the North country;
But a yeoman of Kent with his yearly rent
Will buy them out all three.

The ballad is printed from the Editor's folio MS. and seems to have been composed by some person, who was con-

Q 2

cerned

*cerned in the expedition. Most of the circumstances related
in it will be found supported by history.*

LONG the proud Spaniards had vaunted their con-
        quests,
  Threatning our country with fire and sword;
Often preparing their navy most sumptuous
  With as great plenty as Spain could afford.
    Dub a dub, dub a dub, thus strike their drums;   5
    Tantara, tantara, the Englishman comes.

To the seas hastily went our lord admiral,
  With knights couragious and captains full good;
The brave Earl of Essex, a prosperous general,
  With him prepared to pass the salt flood.   10
    Dub a dub, &c.

At Plymouth speedilye, took they ship valiantlye,
  Braver ships never were seen under sayle,
With their fair colours spread, and streamers o'er their
     head,
  Now bragging Spaniard, take heed of your tayle. 15
    Dub a dub, &c.

Unto Cales cunninglye, came we most speedilye,
  Where the kinges navy securelye did ride;
Being upon their backs, piercing their butts of sacks,
  Ere any Spaniards our coming descry'd.   20
    Dub a dub, &c.

Great

Great was the crying, the running and ryding,
  Which at that feafon was made in that place;
The beacons were fyred, as need then required;
  To hyde their great treafure they had little fpace. 25
    Dub a dub, &c.

There you might fee their fhips, how they were fyred faft,
  And how their men drowned themfelves in the fea;
There might you hear them cry wayle and weep piteoufly,
  When they faw no fhift to fcape thence away.   30
    Dub a dub, &c.

The great St. Phillip, the pryde of the Spaniards,
  Was burnt to the bottom, and funk in the fea;
But the St. Andrew, and eke the St. Matthew,
  Wee took in fight manfullye and brought away. 35
    Dub a dub, &c.

The Earl of Effex moft valiant and hardye,
  With horfemen and footmen march'd up to the town;
The Spanyards, which faw them, were greatly alarmed,
  Did fly for their fafety, and durft not come down. 40
    Dub a dub, &c.

Now, quoth the noble Earl, courage my foldiers all,
  Fight and be valiant, the fpoil you fhall have;
And bè well rewarded all from the great to the fmall;
  But fee the women and children you favе.   45
    Dub a dub, &c.

Q 3

The

The Spaniards at that fight, thinking it vain to fight,
    Hung out flags of truce and yielded the towne;
We marched in prefentlye, decking the walls on high,
    With Englifh colours which purchas'd renowne. 50
      Dub a dub, &c.

Entering the houfes then, of the moft richeft men,
    For gold and treafure we fearched each day;
In fome places we did find, pyès baking left behind,
    Meate at fire rofting, and folk run away.   55
      Dub a dub, &c.

Full of rych merchandize, every fhop catch'd our eyes,
    Damafks and fattens and velvets full fayre; [fwords;
Which foldiers mèafur'd out by' the length òf their
    Of all commodities each had his fhare.   60
      Dub a dub, &c.

Thus Cales was taken, and our brave general
    March'd to the market place, where he did ftand;
There many prifoneres fell to our feveral fhares,
    Many crav'd mercye, and mercye they fonde. 65
      Dub a dub, &c.

When our brave general faw they delayed all,
    And would not ranfome their towne as they faid,
With their fair wanfcots, their preffes and bedfteds,
    Their joint-ftools and tables a fire we made; 70
      And when the town burned all in a flame,
      With tara, tantara, away we all came.

XXII. THE

XXII.

THE SPANISH LADY's LOVE.

This beautiful old ballad moſt probably took its riſe from one of thoſe deſcents made on the Spaniſh coaſts in the time of queen Elizabeth; and in all likelihood from that which is celebrated in the foregoing ballad.

It is printed from an ancient black-letter copy, corrected in part by the Editor's folio MS.

WILL you hear a Spaniſh lady,
  How ſhe wooed an Engliſh man?
Garments gay as rich as may be
  Decked with jewels ſhe had on.
Of a comely countenance and grace was ſhe,   5
And by birth and parentage of high degree.

As his priſoner there he kept her,
  In his hands her life did lye;
Cupid's bands did tye them faſter
  By the liking of an eye.   10
In his courteous company was all her joy,
To favour him in any thing ſhe was not coy.

Q4

But

But at laſt there came commandment
  For to ſet the ladies free,
With their jewels ſtill adorned,   15
  None to do them injury.
Then ſaid this lady mild, Full woe is me,
O let me ſtill ſuſtain this kind captivity!

Gallant captain, ſhew ſome pity
  To a ladye in diſtreſſe;   20
Leave me not within this city,
  For to dye in heavineſſe:
Thou haſt ſet this preſent day my body free,
But my heart in priſon ſtill remains with thee.

" How ſhould'ſt thou, fair lady, love me,   25
  Whom thou knowſt thy countrys foe?
Thy fair wordes make me ſuſpect thee:
  Serpents lie where flowers grow."
All the harm I wiſhe to thee, moſt courteous knight,
God grant the ſame upon my head may fully light. 30

Bleſſed be the time and ſeaſon,
  That you came on Spaniſh ground;
If you may our foes be termed,
  Gentle foes we have you found:
With our city, you have won our hearts each one,   35
Then to your country bear away, that is your own.

" Reſt

" Reſt you ſtill, moſt gallant lady;
    Reſt you ſtill, and weep no more;
Of fair lovers there are plenty,
    Spain doth yield you wonderous ſtore."   40
Spaniards fraught with jealouſy we oft do find,
But Engliſhmen throughout the world are counted kind.

Leave me not unto a Spaniard,
    Thou alone enjoyſt my heart;
I am lovely, young, and tender,   45
    Love is likewiſe my deſert:
Still to ſerve thee day and night my mind is preſt;
The wife of every Engliſhman is counted bleſt.

" It would be a ſhame, fair lady,
    For to bear a woman hence;   50
Engliſh ſoldiers never carry
    Any ſuch without offence."
I'll quickly change myſelf, if it be ſo,
And like a page will follow thee, where'er thou go,

" I have neither gold nor ſilver   55
    To maintain thee in this caſe,
And to travel is great charges,
    As you know in every place."
My chains and jewels every one ſhall be thy own,   59
And eke *tèn thouſand pounds in gold that lies unknown.

                              " On

* ſee. MS.

" On the feas are many dangers,
　　Many ftorms do there arife,
　Which will be to ladies dreadful,
　　And force tears from watery eyes."
Well in troth I fhall endure extremity,　　　　　65
For I could find in heart to lofe my life for thee,

" Courteous ladye, leave this fancy,
　　Here comes all that breeds the ftrife;
　I in England have already
　　A fweet woman to my wife;　　　　　70
I will not falfify my vow for gold nor gain,
Nor yet for all the faireft dames that live in Spain,"

O how happy is that woman
　　That enjoys fo true a friend!
　Many happy days God fend her;　　　　75
　　Of my fuit I make an end :
On my knees I pardon crave for my offence,
Which did from love and true affection firft commence,

Commend me to thy lovely lady,
　　Bear to her this chain of gold;　　　　80
　And thefe bracelets for a token;
　　Grieving that I was fo bold :
All my jewels in like fort bear thou with thee,
For they are fitting for thy wife, but not for me.

2

I will

I will spend my days in prayer,   85
  Love and all his laws defye;
In a nunnery will I shroud mee
  Far from any companye:
But ere my prayers have an end, be sure of this,
To pray for thee and for thy love I will not miss.   90

Thus farewell, most gallant captain!
  Farewell too my heart's content!
Count not Spanish ladies wanton,
  Though to thee my love was bent:
Joy and true prosperity goe still with thee!   95
The like fall ever to thy share, most fair ladie.

XXIII.

ARGENTILE AND CURAN,

— Is extracted from an ancient historical poem in XIII
Books, intitled ALBION'S ENGLAND *by* WILLIAM WAR-
NER: *" An author (says a former editor) only unhappy in*
" the choice of his subject, and measure of his verse. His
" poem is an epitome of the British history, and written
" with great learning, sense, and spirit. In some places fine
" to an extraordinary degree, as I think will eminently appear
" in the ensuing episode [of Argentile and Curan]. A tale
" full of beautiful incidents, in the romantic taste, extremely af-
" fecting, rich in ornament, wonderfully various in style; and
                                                  " in

" *in short, one of the most beautiful pastorals I ever met with.*"
[*Muses library 8vo. 1738.*] *To this elogium nothing can be objected, unless perhaps an affected quaintness in some of his expressions, and an indelicacy in some of his pastoral images.*

WARNER *is said to have been a Warwickshire man, and to have been educated in Oxford at Magdalene Hall* * : *in the latter part of his life he was retained in the service of Henry Cary lord Hunsdon, to whom he dedicates his poem. More of his history is not known. Tho' now his name is so seldom mentioned, his contemporaries ranked him on a level with Spenser, and called them the Homer and Virgil of their age* †. *But Warner rather resembled* OVID, *whose Metamorphosis he seems to have taken for his model, having deduced a perpetual poem from the deluge down to the æra of Elizabeth, full of lively digressions and entertaining episodes. And tho' he is sometimes harsh, affected, and obscure, he often displays a most charming and pathetic simplicity: as where he describes Eleanor's harsh treatment of Rosamond:*

> With that she dasht her on the lippes
> So dyed double red :
> Hard was the heart that gave the blow,
> Soft were those lippes that bled.

The edition of ALBION'S ENGLAND *here followed was printed in 4to, 1602; said in the title-page to have been* " *first penned and published by William Warner, and now* " *revised and newly enlarged by the same author.*" *The story of* ARGENTILE AND CURAN *is I believe the poet's own invention; it is not mentioned in any of our chronicles. It was however so much admired, that not many years after he published it, came out a larger poem on the same subject in stanzas of six lines, intitled,* " *The most pleasant and delightful his-* " *torie of Curan a prince of Danske, and the fayre princesse* " *Argentile,*

* *Athen. Oxon.* † *Ibid.*

" Argentile, daughter and heyre to Adelbright, somtime king
" of Northumberland, &c. by WILLIAM WEBSTER. *Lou-*
" don 1617." in 8 sheets 4to. An indifferent paraphrase of
the following poem.

Tho' here subdivided into stanzas, Warner's metre is the
old-fashioned alexandrine of 14 syllables. The reader there-
fore must not expect to find the close of the stanzas consulted
in the pauses.

THE Brutons 'being' departed hence
    Seaven kingdoms here begonne,
Where diversly in divers broyles
    The Saxons lost and wonne.

King Edel and king Adelbright   5
    In Diria jointly raigne;
In loyal concorde during life
    These kingly friends remaine.

When Adelbright should leave his life,
    To Edel thus he sayes;   10
By those same bondes of happie love,
    That held us friends alwaies;

By our by-parted crowne, of which
    The moyetie is mine;
By God, to whom my soule must passe,   15
    And so in time may thine;

3

I pray

I pray thee, nay I cònjure thee,
    To nourifh, as thine owne,
Thy neece, my daughter Argentile,
    Till fhe to age be growne ;   20
And then, as thou receiveft it,
    Refigne to her my throne.

A promife had for his bequeft,
    The teftatòr he dies ;
But all that Edel undertooke,   25
    He afterwards denies.

Yet well he ' fofters for' a time
    The damfell that was growne
The faireft lady under heaven ;
    Whofe beautie being knowne,   30

A many princes feeke her love ;
    But none might her obtaine ;
For grippell Edel to himfclfe
    Her kingdome fought to gaine ;
And for that caufe from fight of fuch   35
    He did his ward reftraine.

By chance one Curan, fonne unto
    A prince in Danfke, did fee
The maid, with whom he fell in love,
    As much as man might bee.   40

Unhappie

Unhappie youth, what fhould he doe ?
　His faint was kept in mewe ;
Nor he, nor any noble-man
　Admitted to her vewe.

One while in melancholy fits　　　　　　　45
　He pines himfelfe awaye ;
Anon he thought by force of arms
　To win her if he maye :

And ftill againft the kings reftraint
　Did fecretly invay.　　　　　　　　　　50
At length the high controller Love,
　Whom none may difobay,

Imbafed him from lordlines
　Into a kitchen drudge ;
That fo at leaft of life or death　　　　　55
　She might become his judge.

Acceffe fo had to fee and fpeake,
　He did his love bewray,
And tells his birth : her anfwer was,
　She hufbandles would ftay.　　　　　　60

Meane while the king did beate his braines,
　His booty to atchieve,
Nor caring what became of her,

　　　　　　　　　　　　　　　　　　So

So he by her might thrive;
At laſt his reſolution was   65
    Some peſſant ſhould her wive.

And (which was working to his wiſh)
    He did obſerve with joye
How Curan, whom he thought a drudge,
    Scapt many an amo:ous toye.   70

The king, perceiving ſuch his veine,
    Promotes his vaſſal ſtill,
Leſt that the baſeneſſe of the man
    Should lett, perhaps, his will.

Aſſured therefore of his love,   75
    But not ſuſpecting who
The lover was, the king himſelfe
    In his behalf did woe.

The lady reſolute from love,
    Unkindly takes that he   80
Should barre the noble, and unto
    So baſe a match agree :

And therefore ſhifting out of doores,
    Departed thence by ſtealth ;
Preferring povertie before   85
    A dangerous life in wealth.

When

When Curan heard of her efcape,
  The anguifh in his hart
Was more than much, and after her
  From court he did depart ;   90

Forgetfull of himfelfe, his birth,
  His country, friends, and all,
And only minding (whom he mift)
  The foundreffe of his thrall.

Nor meanes he after to frequent   95
  Or court, or ftately townes,
But folitarily to live
  Amongft the country grownes.

A brace of years he lived thus,
  Well pleafed fo to live,   100
And fhepherd-like to feed a flocke
  Himfelfe did wholly give.

So wafting love, by worke, and want,
  Grew almoft to the waine :
But then began a fecond love,   105
  The worfer of the twaine.

A country wench, a neatherds maid,
  Where Curan kept his fheepe,
Did feed her drove : and now on her
  Was all the fhepherds keepe.   110

He borrowed on the working daies
   His holy ruffets oft,
And of the bacon's fat, to make
   His ftartops blacke and foft.

And leaft his tarbox fhould offend,   115
   He left it at the folde :
Sweete growte, or whig, his bottle had,
   As much as it might holde.

A fheeve of bread as browne as nut,
   And cheefe as white as fnow,   120
And wildings, or the feafons fruit
   He did in fcrip beftow.

And whilft his py-bald curre did fleepe,
   And fheep-hooke lay him by,
On hollow quilles of oten ftraw   125
   He piped melody.

But when he fpyed her his faint,
   He wip'd his greafie fhooes,
And clear'd the drivell from his beard,
   And thus the fhepheard wooes.   130

" I have, fweet wench, a peece of cheefe,
  " As good as tooth may chawe,
" And bread and wildings fouling well,
   (And therewithall did drawe

His

Ver. 135. in eating. *Ed.* 1597. 1602. 1612.

His lardrie) and in ' yeaning' fee   135
  " Yon crumpling ewe, quoth he,
" Did twinne this fall, and twin fhouldft thou,
  " If I might tup with thee.

" Thou art too elvifh, faith thou art,
  " Too elvifh and too coy :   140
" Am I, I pray thee, beggarly,
  " That fuch a flocke enjoy ?

" I wis I am not : yet that thou
  " Doeft hold me in difdaine
" Is brimme abroad, and made a gybe   145
  " To all that keepe this plaine.

" There be as quaint (at leaft that thinke
  " Themfelves as quaint) that crave
" The match, that thou, I wot not why,
  " Maift, but miflik'ft to have.   150

" How wouldft thou match ? (for well I wot,
  " Thou art a female) I,
" I know not her that willingly
  " With maiden-head would die.

" The plowmans labour hath no end,   155
  " And he a churle will prove :
" The craftfman hath more worke in hand
  " Then fitteth unto love:

R 2

                                         " The

Ver. 153. *fo Ed.* 1597. Her know I not her that. 1602.

" The merchant, traffiquing abroad,
  " Sufpects his wife at home :   160
" A youth will play the wanton ; and
  " An old man prove a mome.

" Then chufe a fhepheard : with the fun
  " He doth his flocke unfold,
" And all the day on hill or plaine   165
  " He merrie chat can hold ;

" And with the fun doth folde againe ;
  " Then jogging home betime,
" He turnes a crab, or tunes a round,
  " Or fings fome merry ryme.   170

" Nor lacks he gleefull tales, whilft round
  " The nut-brown bowl doth trot ;
" And fitteth finging care-away,
  " Till he to bed be got :

" Theare fleepes he foundly all the night,   175
  " Forgetting morrow-cares ;
" Nor feares he blafting of his corne,
  " Nor uttering of his wares ;

" Or ftormes by feas, or ftirres on land,
  " Or cracke of credit loft :

                             " Not

Ver. 171. to tell, whilft round the bole doth trot.   *Ed.* 1597.

" Not fpending franklier than his flocke
   " Shall ftill defray the coft.

" Well wot I, footh they fay, that fay
   " More quiet nights and daies
" The fhepheard fleeps and wakes, than he   185
   " Whofe cattel he doth graize.

" Beleeve me, laffe, a king is but
   " A man, and fo am I :
" Content is worth a monarchie,
   " And mifchiefs hit the hie ;   190

" As late it did a king and his
   " Not dwelling far from hence,
" Who left a daughter, fave thyfelfe,
   " For fair a matchlefs wench."——
Here did he paufe, as if his tongue   195
   Had done his heart offence.

The neatreffe, longing for the reft,
   Did egge him on to tell
How faire fhe was, and who fhe was.
   " She bore, quoth he, the bell   200

" For beautie : though I clownifh am,
   " I know what beautie is ;
" Or did I not, at feeing thee,
   " I fenceles were to mis,
            *   *   *

R 3

" Her

" Her ftature comely, tall ; her gate   305
  " Well graced ; and her wit
" To marvell at, not meddle with,
  " As matchlefs I omit.

" A globe-like head, a gold-like haire,
  " A forehead fmooth, and hie,   210
" An even nofe ; on either fide
  " Did fhine a grayifh eie :

" Two rofie cheekes, round ruddy lips,
  " White juft-fet teeth within ;
" A mouth in meane ; and underneathe   215
  " A round and dimpled chin.

" Her fnowie necke, with blewifh veines,
  " Stood bolt upright upon
" Her portly fhoulders : beating balles
  " Her veined breafts, anon   220

" Adde more to beautie. Wand-like was
  " Her middle falling ftill,
" And rifing whereas women rife : * * *
  " — Imagine nothing ill.

" And more, her long, and limber armes   225
  " Had white and azure wrifts ;
" And flender fingers aunfwere to
  " Her fmooth and lillie fifts.

2

" A

" A legge in print, a pretie foot ;
 " Conjecture of the reft : 230
" For amorous eies, obferving forme,
 " Think parts obfcured beft.

" With thefe, O raretie ! with thefe
 " Her tong of fpeech was fpare ;
" But fpeaking, Venus feem'd to fpeake, 235
 " The balle from Ide to bear.

" With Phœbe, Juno, and with both
 " Herfelfe contends in face ;
" Wheare equall mixture did not want
 " Of milde and ftately grace. 240

" Her fmiles were fober, and her lookes
 " Were chearefull unto all :
" Even fuch as neither wanton feeme,
 " Nor waiward ; mell, nor gall.

" A quiet minde, a patient moode, 245
 " And not difdaining any ;
" Not gybing, gadding, gawdy, and
 " Sweete faculties had many.

" A nimph, no tong, no heart, no eie,
 " Might praife, might wifh, might fee ; 250
" For life, for love, for forme ; more good,
 " More worth, more faire than fhee.

R 4

" Yea

" Yea such'an one, as such was none,
　" Save only she was such :
" Of Argentile to say the most,　　　　　255
　" Were to be silent much,"

I knew the lady very well,
　But worthles of such praise,
The neatresse said : and muse I do,
　A shepheard thus should blaze　　　　260
The ' coate' of beautie *. Credit me,
　Thy latter speech bewraies

Thy clownish shape a coined shew.
　But wherefore dost thou weepe ?　　　265
The shepheard wept, and she was woe,
　And both doe silence keepe.

" In troth, quoth he, I am not such,
　" As seeming I professe :
" But then for her, and now for thee,
　" I from myselfe digresse.　　　　　270

" Her loved I (wretch that I am
　" A recreant to be)
" I loved her, that hated love,
　" But now I die for thee.

" At Kirkland is my fathers court,　　275
　" And Curan is my name,

　　　　　　　　　　　　　　　　" In

* i. e. emblazon beauty's coat. Ed. 1597. 1602. 1612. Coote.

" In Edels court fometimes in pompe,
　" Till love contrould the fame :

" But now—what now ?—deare heart, how now ?
　" What aileft thou to weepe ?"　　　280
The damfell wept, and he was woe,
　And both did filence keepe.

I graunt, quoth fhe, it was too much
　That you did love fo much :
But whom your former could not move,　　285
　Your fecond love doth touch.

Thy twice-beloved Argentile
　Submitteth her to thee,
And for thy double love prefents
　Herfelf a fingle fee,　　　290
In paffion not in perfon chaung'd,
　And I, my lord, am fhe.

They fweetly furfeiting in joy,
　And filent for a fpace,
When as the extafie had end,　　　295
　Did tenderly imbrace ;
And for their wedding, and their wifh
　Got fitting time and place.

Not England (for of Hengift then
　Was named fo this land)　　　300
Then Curan had an hardier knight ;

His

> His force could none withstand :
> Whose sheep-hooke laid apart, he then
> Had higher things in hand.
>
> First, making knowne his lawfull claime   305
>   In Argentile her right,
> He warr'd in Diria *, and he wonne
>   Bernicia * too in fight :
>
> And so from trecherous Edel tooke
>   At once his life and crowne,   310
> And of Northumberland was king,
>   Long raigning in renowne.

*** During the Saxon heptarchy, the kingdom of Northumberland (consisting of 6 northern counties, besides part of Scotland) was for a long time divided into two lesser sovereignties, viz. Deïra (called here Diria) which contained the southern parts, and Bernicia, comprehending those which lay north.*

XXIV.

CORIN's FATE.

Only the three first stanzas of this song are ancient ; these are extracted from the quarto MS. mentioned in vol. 1. p. 66. As they seemed to want application, this has been attempted by a modern hand.

CORIN,

CORIN, moſt unhappie ſwaine,
   Whither wilt thou drive thy flocke?
Little foode is on the plaine;
   Full of danger is the rocke:

Wolfes and beares doe kepe the woodes;   5
   Foreſts tangled are with brakes:
Meadowes ſubjeƈt are to floodes;
   Moores are full of miry lakes.

Yet to ſhun all plaine, and hill,
   Foreſt, moore, and meadow-ground,   10
Hunger will as ſurely kill:
   How may then reliefe be found?

Such is hapleſs Corins fate:
   Since my waywarde love begunne,
Equall doubts begett debate   15
   What to ſeeke, and what to ſhunne.

Spare to ſpeke, and ſpare to ſpeed;
   Yet to ſpeke will move diſdaine:
If I ſee her not I bleed,
   Yet her ſight augments my paine.   20

What may then poor Corin doe?
   Tell me, ſhepherdes, quicklye tell;
For to linger thus in woe
   Is the lover's ſharpeſt hell.   *.*

XXV. JANE

XXV

JANE SHORE.

Tho' so many vulgar errors have prevailed concerning this celebrated courtezan, no character in history has been more perfectly handed down to us. We have her portrait drawn by two masterly pens ; the one has delineated the features of her person, the other those of her character and story. Sir Thomas More drew from the life, and Drayton has copied an original picture of her. The reader will pardon the length of the quotations, as they serve to correct many popular mistakes relating to her catastrophe. The first is from Sir Thomas MORE'S *history of Rich. III. written in* 1513, *about thirty years after the death of Edw. IV.*

" *Now then by and by, as it wer for anger, not for cove-*
" *tise, the protector sent into the house of Shores wife (for*
" *her husband dwelled not with her) and spoiled her of al that*
" *ever she had, (above the value of 2 or 3 thousand marks)*
" *and sent her body to prison. And when he had a while laide*
" *unto her, for the maner sake, that she went about to bewitch*
" *him, and that she was of counsel with the lord chamberlein*
" *to destroy him : in conclusion when that no colour could fas-*
" *ten upon these matters, then he layd heinously to her charge*
" *the thing that herselfe could not deny, that al the world wist*
" *was true, and that natheles every man laughed at to here*
" *it then so sodainly so highly taken,—that she was naught*
" *of her body.   And for thys cause (as a goodly continent*
" *prince, clene and fautles of himself, sent oute of heaven into*
" *this vicious world for the amendment of mens maners) he*
" *caused the bishop of London to put her to open penaunce, go-*
" *ing before the crosse in procession upon a sonday with a taper*
" *in*

" *in her hand.   In which she went in countenance and pace*
" *demure so womanly ; and albeit she was out of al array*
" *save her kyrtle only, yet went she so fair and lovely, name-*
" *lye, while the wondering of the people caste a comly rud in*
" *her chekes (of which she before had most misse) that her*
" *great shame wan her much praise among those that were*
" *more amorous of her body, then curious of her soule.   And*
" *many good folke also, that hated her living, and glad wer*
" *to se sin corrected, yet pittied thei more her penance then re-*
" *joiced therin, when thei considred that the protector pro-*
" *cured it more of a corrupt intent, then any virtucus affeccion.*
" *This woman was born in London, worshipfully frended,*
" *honestly brought up, and very wel maryed, saving some-*
" *what to soone ; her husbande an honest citizen, yonge, and*
" *goodly, and of good substance.   But forasmuche as they*
" *were coupled ere she wer wel ripe, she not very fervently*
" *loved, for whom she never longed.   Which was happely*
" *the thinge, that the more easily made her encline unto the*
" *king's appetite, when he required her.   Howbeit the respect*
" *of his royaltie, the hope of gay apparel, ease, plesure, and*
" *other wanton welth, was able soone to perse a soft tender*
" *hearte.   But when the king had abused her, anon her*
" *husband (as he was an honest man, and one that could his*
" *good, not presuming to touch a kinges concubine) left her*
" *up to him al together.   When the king died, the lord*
" *chamberlen [Hastings] toke her * : which in the kinges*
" *daies, albeit he was sore enamoured upon her, yet he forbare*
" *her,*

---

* *After the death of Hastings, she was kept by the marquis of Dorset,
son to Edward IV's queen.   In Rymer's Fœdera is a proclamation of
Richard's, dated at Leicester, Oct. 23. 1483. wherein a reward of* 1000
marks in money, or 100 *a year in land is offered for taking* " *Thomas late*
" *marquis of Dorset,*" *who* " *not having the fear of God, nor the sal-*
" *vation of his own soul, before his eyes, has damnably debauched and*
" *defiled many maids, widows, and wives, and* LIVED IN ACTUAL
" ADULTERY WITH THE WIFE OF SHORE." *Buckingham was at
that time in rebellion, but as Dorset was not with him, Richard could not
accuse him of treason, and therefore made a handle of these pretended de-
baucheries to get him apprehended.   Vide Rym. Fœd. tom. xij. pag.* 204.

" *her, either for reverence, or for a certain frendly faithful-*
" *nefs.*

" *Proper fhe was, and faire: nothing in her body that you*
" *wold have changed, but if you would have wifhed her*
" *fomewhat higher. Thus fay thei that knew her in her*
" *youthe. Albeit fome that* NOW SEE HER (FOR YET SHE
" LIVETH) *deme her never to have bene wel vifaged.*
" *Whofe jugement feemeth me fomewhat like, as though men*
" *fhould geffe the bewty of one longe before departed, by her*
" *fcalpe taken out of the charnel-houfe; for now is fhe old,*
" *lene, withered, and dried up, nothing left but ryvilde*
" *fkin, and hard bone. And yet being even fuch, whofo*
" *wel advife her vifage, might geffe and devife which partes*
" *how filled, wold make it a faire face.*

" *Yet delited not men fo much in her bewty, as in her plea-*
" *fant behaviour. For a proper wit had fhe, and could both*
" *rede wel and write; mery in company, redy and quick of*
" *aunfwer, neither mute nor ful of bable; fometime taunting*
" *without displeafure, and not without difport. The king*
" *would fay, That he had three concubines, which in three*
" *divers properties diverfly excelled. One the merieft, an-*
" *other the wilieft, the thirde the holieft harlot in his realme,*
" *as one whom no man could get out of the church lightly to*
" *any place, but it wer to his bed. The other two wer*
" *fomwhat greater perfonages, and natheles of their humilite*
" *content to be nameles, and to forbere the praife of thofe pro-*
" *perties; but the merieft was the Shoris wife, in whom the*
" *king therfore toke fpecial pleafure. For many he had,*
" *but her he loved, whofe favour, to fai the trouth (for*
" *finne it wer to belie the devil) fhe never abufed to any*
" *mans hurt, but to many a mans comfort and relief. Where*
" *the king toke displeafure, fhe would mitigate and appeafe*
" *his mind: where men were out of favour, fhe wold bring*
" *them in his grace: for many, that had highly offended,*
" *fhee obtained pardon: of great forfeitures fhe gate men*
" *remiffion: and finally in many weighty futes fhe ftode many*
" *men in gret ftede, either for none or very fmal rewardes,*

" *and*

" and thofe rather gay than rich : either for that fhe was
" content with the dede felfe well done, or for that fhe de-
" lited to be fued unto, and to fhow what fhe was able to
" do wyth the king, or for that wanton women and welthy
" be not alway covetous.

" I doubt not fome fhal think this woman too fleight a
" thing to be written of, and fet amonge the remembrauncces
" of great matters : which thei fhal fpecially think, that
" happely fhal efteme her only by that thei NOW SEE HER.
" But me femeth the chaunce fo much the more worthy to be
" remembred, in how much fhe is NOW in the more beg-
" gerly condicion, unfrended and worne out of acquaintance,
" after good fubftance, after as grete favour with the
" prince, after as grete fute and feeking to with al thofe,
" that in thofe days had bufynes to fpede, as many other
" men were in their times, which be now famoufe only by
" the infamy of their il dedes. Her doinges were not much
" leffe, albeit thei be muche leffe remembred becaufe thei
" were not fo evil. For men ufe, if they have an evil
" turne, to write it in marble ; and whofo doth us a good
" tourne, we write it in dufte * . Which is not worft
" proved by her ; for AT THIS DAYE fhce beggeth of ma-
" ny at this daye living, that at this day had begged, if
" fhee had not bene." See More's workes, folio, bl. let.
1557. pag. 56. 57.

DRAYTON has written a poetical epiftle from this lady
to her royal lover, in his notes on which he thus draws her
portrait. " Her ftature was meane, her haire of a dark
" yellow, her face round and full, her eye gray, delicate
" harmony being betwixt each part's proportion, and each
" proportion's

" *proportion's colour, her body fat, white and smooth, her*
" *countenance cheerfull and like to her condition. The pic-*
" *ture which I have seen of hers was such as she rose out*
" *of her bed in the morning, having nothing on but a rich*
" *mantle cast under one arme over her shoulder, and sitting*
" *on a chaire, on which her naked arm did lie. What her*
" *father's name was, or where she was borne, is not cer-*
" *tainly knowne : but Shore a young man of right goodly*
" *person, wealth and behaviour, abandoned her bed after*
" *the king had made her his concubine. Richard III.*
" *causing her to do open penance in Paul's church-yard,*
" COMMANDED THAT NO MAN SHOULD RELIEVE
" HER, *which the tyrant did not so much for his hatred to*
" *sinne, but that by making his brother's life odious, he might*
" *cover his horrible treasons the more cunningly."* See
England's Heroical epistles, by Mich. Drayton, Esq; Lond.
1637. 12mo.

*The following ballad is printed from an old black letter
copy in the Pepys collection. Its full title is, " The woefull
" lamentation of Jane Shore, a goldsmith's wife in Lon-
" don, sometime king Edward IV. his concubine. To the
" tune of* LIVE WITH ME, *&c [See the first volume.]
To every stanza is annexed the following burthen :*

Then maids and wives in time amend,
For love and beauty will have end.

IF Rosamonde that was so faire,
   Had cause her sorrowes to declare,
Then let Jane Shore with sorrowe sing,
That was beloved of a king.

In maiden yeares my beautye bright   5
Was loved dear of lord and knight ;
But yet the love that they requir'd,
It was not as my friends defir'd.

My parents they, for thirft of gaine,
A hufband for me did obtaine ;   10
And I, their pleafure to fulfille,
Was forc'd to wedd againft my wille.

To Matthew Shore I was a wife,
Till luft brought ruine to my life ;
And then my life I lewdlye fpent,   15
Which makes my foul for to lament.

In Lombard-ftreet I once did dwelle,
As London yet can witnefs welle ;
Where many gallants did beholde
My beautye in a fhop of golde.   20

I fpred my plumes, as wantons doe,
Some fweet and fecret friende to wooe,
Becaufe chaft love I did not finde
Agreeing to my wanton minde.

At laft my name in court did ring   25
Into the eares of Englandes king,
Who came and lik'd, and love requir'd,
But I made coye what he defir'd :

Vol. II.   S   Yet

Yet Miſtreſs Blague, a neighbour neare,
Whoſe friendſhip I eſteemed deare, 30
Did ſaye, It was a gallant thing
To be beloved of a king.

By her perſuaſions I was led,
For to defile my marriage-bed,
And wronge my wedded huſband Shore, 35
Whom I had married yeares before.

In heart and mind I did rejoyce,
That I had made ſo ſweet a choice ;
And therefore did my ſtate reſigne,
To be king Edward's concubine. 40

From city then to court I went,
To reape the pleaſures of content ;
There had the joyes that love could bring,
And knew the ſecrets of a king.

When I was thus advanc'd on highe 45
Commanding Edward with mine eye,
For Mrs. Blague I in ſhort ſpace
Obtainde a livinge from his grace.

No friende I had but in ſhort time
I made unto promotion climbe ; 50
But yet for all this coſtlye pride,
My huſbande could not mee abide.

His

His bed, though wronged by a king,
His heart with deadlye griefe did ſting ;
From England then he goes away   55
To end his life beyond the ſea.

He could not live to ſee his name
Impaired by my wanton ſhame ;
Although a prince of peerleſſe might
Did reape the pleaſure of his right.   60

Long time I lived in the courte,
With lords and ladies of great ſorte ;
And when I ſmil'd all men were glad,
But when I frown'd my prince grewe ſad.

But yet a gentle minde I bore   65
To helpleſſe people, that were poore ;
I ſtill redreſt the orphans crye,
And ſav'd their lives condemnd to dye.

I ſtill had ruth on widowes tears,
I ſuccour'd babes of tender yeares ;   70
And never look'd for other gaine
But love and thankes for all my paine.

At laſt my royall king did dye,
And then my dayes of woe grew nighe ;
When crock-back Richard got the crowne,   75
King Edwards friends were ſoon put downe.

S 2

I then

I then was punisht for my sin,
That I so long had lived in ;
Yea, every one that was his friend,
This tyrant brought to shamefull end.　　　　80

Then for my lewd and wanton life,
That made a strumpet of a wife,
I penance did in Lombard-street,
In shamefull manner in a sheet.

Where many thousands did me viewe,　　　85
Who late in court my credit knewe;
Which made the teares run down my face,
To thinke upon my foul disgrace.

Not thus content, they took from mee
My goodes, my livings, and my fee,　　　　90
And charg'd that none should me relieve,
Nor any succour to me give.

Then unto Mrs. Blague I went,
To whom my jewels I had sent,
In hope therebye to ease my want,　　　　95
When riches fail'd, and love grew scant :

But she denyed to me the same
When in my need for them I came ;
To recompence my former love,
Out of her doores shee did me shove.　　　100

So love did vanish with my state,
Which now my soul repents too late;
Therefore example take by mee,
For friendship parts in povertie.

But yet one friend among the rest,   105
Whom I before had seen distrest,
And sav'd his life, condemn'd to die,
Did give me food to succour me:

For which, by lawe, it was decreed
That he was hanged for that deed;   110
His death did grieve me so much more,
Than had I dyed myself therefore.

Then those to whom I had done good,
Durst not afford mee any food;
Whereby I begged all the day,   115
And still in streets by night I lay.

My gowns beset with pearl and gold,
Were turn'd to simple garments old;
My chains and gems and golden rings,
To filthy rags and loathsome things.   120

Thus was I scorn'd of maid and wife,
For leading such a wicked life;
Both sucking babes and children small,
Did make their pastime at my fall.

S 3

I could

I could net get one bit of bread,   125
Whereby my hunger might be fed:
Nor drink, but fuch as channels yield,
Or ftinking ditches in the field.

Thus, weary of my life, at lengthe
I yielded up my vital ftrength   130
Within a ditch of loathfome fcent,
Where carrion dogs did much frequent:

The which now fince my dying daye,
Is Shoreditch call'd, as writers faye *,
Which is a witnefs of my finne,   135
For being concubine to a king.

You wanton wives, that fall to luft,
Be you affur'd that God is juft;
Whoredome fhall not efcape his hand,
Nor pride unpunifh'd in this land.   140

If God to me fuch fhame did bring,
That yielded only to a king,
How fhall they fcape that daily run
To practife fin with every one?

You

* *But it had this name long before; being fo called from its being a common SEWER (vulgarly SHORE) or drain. See Stow.*

You husbands, match not but for love,   145
Left some disliking after prove;
Women, be warn'd when you are wives,
What plagues are due to sinful lives:
        Then, maids and wives, in time amend,
        For love and beauty will have end.

XXVI.

CORYDON's DOLEFUL KNELL.

This little simple elegy is given, with some corrections, from two copies, one of which is in "The golden garland of "princely delights."

The burthen of the song, DING DONG, &c. is at present appropriated to burlesque subjects, and therefore may excite only ludicrous ideas in a modern reader; but in the time of our poet it usually accompanied the most solemn and mournful strains. Of this kind is that fine aerial Dirge in Shakespear's Tempest,

> " *Full fadom five thy father lies,*
> " *Of his bones are corrall made;*
> " *Those are pearles that were his eyes;*
> " *Nothing of him, that doth fade,*
> " *But doth suffer a sea-change*
> " *Into something rich and strange:*

S 4

" *Sea-*

" Sea-nymphs hourly ring bis knell,
" Harke now I heare them, Ding dong bell."

[*" Burthen, Ding dong."*]

*I make no doubt but the poet intended to conclude this air in a
manner the most solemn and expressive of melancholy.*

MY Phillida, adieu love!
　　For evermore farewel!
Ay me! I've loft my true love,
　　And thus I ring her knell,
　　　　Ding dong, ding dong, ding dong,　　5
　　　　My Phillida is dead!
　　　I'll ftick a branch of willow
　　　At my fair Phillis' head.

For my fair Phillida
　　Our bridal bed was made:　　　　　　10
But 'ftead of filkes fo gay,
　　She in her fhroud is laid.
　　　　Ding, &c.

Her corpfe fhall be attended
　　By maides in fair array,
Till th' obfequies are ended,　　　　　　15
　　And fhe is wrapt in clay.
　　　　Ding, &c.

Her

Her herse it shall be carried
  By youths, that do excell:
And when that she is buried,
  I thus will ring her knell,   20
    Ding, &c.

A garland shall be framed
  By art and natures skill,
Of sundry-colour'd flowers,
  In token of good-will †:
    Ding, &c.

And sundry-colour'd ribbands   25
  On it I will bestow;
But chiefly black and yellowe *
  With her to grave shall go.
    Ding, &c.

I'll decke her tomb with flowers,
  The rarest ever seen   30
And with my tears, as showers,
  I'll keepe them fresh and green.
    Ding, &c.

Instead

† *It is a custom in many parts of England, to carry a fine garland
before the corpse of a woman who dies unmarried.*

* *See above, page* 175.

Inftead of faireft colours,
   Set forth with curious art *,
Her image fhall be painted   35
   On my diftreffed heart.
     Ding, &c.

' And thereon fhall be graven
   Her epitaph fo faire,
" Here lies the lovelieft maiden,
   " That e'er gave fhepheard care.   40
     Ding, &c.

In fable will I mourne ;
   Blacke fhall be all my weede,
Ay me! I am forlorne,
   Now Phillida is dead.
     Ding dong, ding dong, ding dong, 45
     My Phillida is dead !
     I'll ftick a branch of willow
      At my fair Phillis' head.

*This alludes to the painted effiges of Alabafter, anciently erected upon tombs aad monuments.

THE END OF THE SECOND BOOK.

𝔄𝔫𝔠𝔦𝔢𝔫𝔱
SONGS and BALLADS,
&c.

SERIES the SECOND.
BOOK III.

I.

THE COMPLAINT OF CONSCIENCE.

I shall begin this THIRD BOOK *with an old allegoric Satire: A manner of moralizing, which, if it was not first introduced by the author of* PIERCE PLOWMAN'S VISIONS, *was at least chiefly brought into repute by that ancient satirist. It is not so generally known that the kind of verse used in this ballad hath any affinity with the peculiar metre that writer, for which reason I shall throw together cursory remarks on that very singular species of versific the nature of which has been so little understood.*

On the metre

of

Pierce Plowman's Visions.

We learn from Wormius *(a)*, that the ancient Iſlandic poets uſed a great variety of meaſures : he mentions 136 different kinds, without including RHYME, or a correſpondence of final ſyllables : yet this was occaſionally uſed, as appears from the Ode of Egil, which Wormius hath inſerted in his book.

He hath analyſed the ſtructure of one of theſe kinds of verſe, the harmony of which neither depended on the quantity of the ſyllables, like that of the ancient Greeks and Romans; nor on the rhymes at the end, as in modern poetry; but conſiſted altogether in alliteration, or a certain artful repetition of the ſounds in the middle of the verſes. This was adjuſted according to certain rules of their proſody, one of which was, that every diſtich ſhould contain at leaſt three words beginning with the ſame letter or ſound. Two of theſe correſpondent ſounds might be placed either in the firſt or ſecond line of the diſtich, and one in the other: but all three were not regularly to be crowded into one line. This will be beſt underſtood by the following examples *(b)*.

" *Meire* og *Minne*	" *Gab Ginunga*
Mogu heimdaller."	Enn *Gras* huerge."

There were many other little niceties obſerved by the Iſlandic poets, who as they retained their original language and peculiarities longer than the other nations of

Gothic

(a) Literatura Runica. Hafniæ 1636. 4to.—1651. fol. The ISLANDIC language is of the ſame origin as our ANGLO-SAXON, being both dialects of the ancient GOTHIC or TEUTONIC. Vid. Hickeſii Præfat. in Grammat. Anglo-Saxon. & Moeſſ-Goth. 4to. 1689.

(b) Vid Hickes Antiq. Literatur. Sept-trional. Tom. I. p. 217.

Gothic race, had time to cultivate their native poetry more, and to carry it to a higher pitch of refinement, than any of the reft.

Their brethren the Anglo-faxon poets occafionally ufed the fame kind of alliteration, and it is common to meet in their writings with fimilar examples of the fore-going rules. Take an inftance or two in modern cha-raćters : *(c)*

" *Skeop* tha and *Skyrede*   " *Ham* and *Heahfetl*
    Skyppend ure."   *Heofena* rikes."

I know not however that there is any where extant an entire Saxon poem all in this meafure. But diftichs of this fort perpetually occur in all their poems of any length.

Now, if we examine the verfification of PIERCE PLOW-MAN's VISIONS, we fhall find it conftrućted exaćtly by thefe rules ; and therefore each line, as printed, is in reality a diftich of two verfes, and will, I believe, be found diftinguifhed as fuch, by fome mark or other in all the ancient MSS. viz.

" In a *Somer Seafon*, | when ' hot *(d)* was the *Sunne,*
" I *Shope* me into *Shroubs,* | as I a *Shepe* were ; ·
" In *Habite* as an *Harmet* | un*Holy* of werkes,
" *Went Wyde* in thys world | *Wonders* to heare, &c.

So that the author of this poem will not be found to have invented any new mode of verfification, as fome have fuppofed, but only to have retained that of the old Saxon and Gothic poets; which was probably never wholly laid afide, but occafionally ufed at different intervals ;
tho'

(c) Ibid.
(d) So I would read with Mr. Warton, rather than either ' foft,' as in MS. or ' fet,' as in PCC.

tho' the ravages of time will not fuffer us now to produce a regular feries of poems entirely written in it.

There are fome readers, whom it may gratify to mention, that thefe VISIONS OF PIERCE [i. e. Peter] the
PLOWMAN, are attributed to Robert Langland, a fecular
prieft, born at Mortimer's Cleobury in Shropfhire, and
fellow of Oriel college in Oxford, who flourifhed in the
reigns of Edward III. and Richard II. and publifhed his
poem a few years after 1350. It confifts of xx PASSUS or
Breaks *(e)*, exhibiting a feries of vifions, which he pre-
tends happened to him on Malvern hills in Worcefter-
fhire. The author excells in ftrong allegoric painting,
and has with great humour fpirit and fancy, cenfured
moft of the vices incident to the feveral profeffions of
life; but he particularly inveighs againft the corruptions of the clergy, and the abfurdities of fuperftitiou.
Of this work I have now before me four different editions in black letter quarto. Three of them are printed
in 1550 by Roberte Crowley dwelling in Elye rentes in Hol-
burne. It is remarkable that two of thefe are mentioned
in the title-page as both of the fecond impreffion, tho'
they contain evident variations in every page *(f)*. The
other is faid to be newlye imprynted after the authers olde
copy .... by Owen Rogers, Feb. 21. 1561.

As Langland was not the firft, fo neither was he the
laft that ufed this alliterative fpecies of verfification. To
Rogers's edition of the Vifions is fubjoined a poem,
which

(e) The poem propetly contains xxi parts: the word PASSUS,
adopted by the author, feems only to denote the break or divifion between two parts, tho' by the ignorance of the printer applied to the
parts themfelves. See vol. 3. preface to ballad III. where *Paffus*
feems to fignify *Paufe.*

(f) That which feems the firft of the two, is thus diftinguifhed
in the title-page, nowe the feconde tyme imprinted by Roberte
Crowlye; the other thus, nowe the feconde time imprinted by
Roberte Crowley. In the former the folios are thus erroneoufly
numbered 39, 39. 41. 63. 43. 42. 45. &c. The bookfellers of thofe
days were not oftentatious of multiplying editions.

which was probably writ in imitation of them, intitled
PIERCE THE PLOUGHMAN'S CREDE.   It begins thus,

> " *Cros*, and *Curtcis Chrift*, this beginning fpede
> " For the *Faders Frendfhipe*, that *Fourmed* heaven,
> " And through the *Special Spirit*, that *Sprong* of hem tweyne,
> " And al in one godhed. endles dwelleth."

The author feigns himfelf ignorant of his Creed, to be
inftructed in which he applies to the four religious
orders, viz. the gray friers of St. Francis, the black
friers of St. Dominic, the Carmelites or white friers,
and the Auguftines. This affords him occafion to de-
fcribe in very lively colours the floth, ignorance, and
immorality of thofe reverend drones. At length he
meets with Pierce a poor Ploughman, who refolves
his doubts, and inftructs him in the principles of true
religion. The author was evidently a follower of
Wiccliff, whom he mentions (with honour) as no
longer living *(g)*. Now that reformer died in 1384.
How long after his death this poem was written, does
not appear.

In the Cotton library is a volume of ancient Englifh
poems *(h)*, two of which are written in this alliterative
metre, and have the divifion of the lines into diftichs
diftinctly marked by a point, as is ufual in old poetical MSS. That which ftands firft of the two (tho'
perhaps the lateft written) is intitled THE SEGE OF
ÏERLAM, [i. e. Jerufalem], being an old fabulous
legend compofed by fome monk, and ftuffed with mar-
vellous figments concerning the deftruction of the holy
city and temple. It begins thus,

> " In *Tyberius Tyme* . the *Trewe* emperour
> " *Syr Sefar* hymfelf . befted in Rome

" Whyll

(g) Signature . Ꞇ ii.   *(h)* Caligula A. ig. fol. 1c9. 123.

" Whyll *Pylat* was *Provofte* . under that *Prynce* rych:
" And *Jewes Juftice* alfo . of *Judeas* londe
" *Herode* under empere . as *Herytage* wolde
" *Kyng,* &c.

The other is intitled CHEVELERE ASSIGNE [or De Cigne], that is " The Knight of the Swan," being an ancient Romance, beginning thus,

" All-*Weldynge* God . *Whence* it is his *Wylle*
" *Wele* he *Wereth* his *Werke* . *With* his owene honde
" For ofte *Harmes* were *Hente* . that *Helpe* wene myzte
" Nere the *Hyznes* of *Hym* . that lengeth in *Hevene*
" For this, &c.

Among Mr. Garrick's collection of old plays *(i)* is a profe narrative of the adventures of this fame Knight of the Swan, " newly tranflated out of Frenfhe into Englyfhe " at thinftigacion of the puyffaunt and illuftryous " prynce, lorde Edward duke of Buckynghame." This lord it feems had a peculiar intereft in the book, for in the preface the tranflator tells us, that this " highe " dygne and illuftryous prynce my lorde Edwarde by " the grace of god Duke of Buckyngham, erle of He- " reforde, Stafforde, and Northampton, defyrynge coty- " dyally to encreafe and augment the name and fame " of fuch as were relucent in vertuous feates and tri- " umphaunt actes of chyvalry, and to encourage and " ftyre every lufty and gentell herte by the exemply- " ficacoyn of the fame, havyng a goodli booke of the " highe and miraculous hiftori of a famous and puyf- " faunt kynge, named Oryant, fometime reynynge in " the parties of beyonde the fea, havynge to his wife " a noble lady ; of whome fhe conceyved fixe fonnes " and a daughter, and chylded of them at one only " time ;

" time; " at whofe byrthe echone of them had a
" chayne of-fylver at their neckes, the whiche were
" all tourned by the provydence of god into whyte
" fwannes (fave one) of the whiche this prefent hyftory
" is compyled, named Helyas, the knight of the
" fwanne, OF WHOME LINIALLY IS DYSCENDED MY
" SAYDE LORDE. The whiche ententifly to have the
" fayde hyftory more amply and unyverfally knowen
" in thys hys natif countrie, as it is in other, hath of
" hys hie bountie by fome of his faithful and trufti
" fervauntes cohorted mi mayfter Wynkin de Worde
" (k) to put the faid vertuous hyftori in prynte . . . . . at
" whofe inftigacion and ftiring I (Roberte Copland)
" have me applied, moiening the helpe of god, to re-
" duce and tranflate it into our maternal and vulgare
" englifh tonge after the capacitè and rudeneffe of
" my weke entendement."——A curious picture of
the times ! While in Italy literature and the fine arts
were ready to burft forth with claffical fplendor under
Leo X. the firft peer of this realm was proud to de-
rive his pedigree from a fabulous KNIGHT OF THE
SWAN (l).

To return to the Metre of Pierce Plowman : In the
folio MS. fo often quoted in thefe volumes, are two
poems written in that fpecies of verfification. One
of thefe is an ancient allegorical poem, intitled DEATH
AND LIFFE, (in 2 fitts or parts, containing 458 diftichs)
which, for ought that appears, may have been written
as early, if not before, the time of Langland. The
firft forty lines are broke as they fhould be into diftichs,

(k) W. de Worde's edit. is in 1512. See Ames. p. 92. Mr. G's copy is " ¶ Imprinted at London by me William Copland.

(l) He is faid in the ftory-book to be the grandfather of God-frey of Eoulogne, thro' whom I fuppofe the duke made out his relation to him. This duke was beheaded, May 17. 1521. 13 Hen. VIII.

a diſtinction that is neglected in the remaining part of the poem, in order I ſuppoſe to ſave room. It be-gins,

> " *Chriſt Chriſten king,*
>> that on the *Croſſe* tholed;
> " Hadd *Paines* and *Paſſyons*
>> to defend our ſoules;
> " Give us *Grace* on the *Ground*
>> the *Greatlye* to ſerve,
> " For that *Royall Red* blood
>> that *Rann* from thy ſide."

The ſubject of this piece is a viſion, wherein the poet ſees a conteſt for ſuperiority between " our lady Dame " LIFE," and the " ugly fiend Dame DEATH ;" who with their ſeveral attributes and concomitants are per-ſonified in a fine vein of allegoric painting. Part of the deſcription of Dame LIFE is,

> " Shee was *Brighter* of her *Blec,*
>> then was the *Bright* ſonn :
> " Her *Rudd Redder* then the *Roſe,*
>> that on the *Riſe* hangeth :
> " *Meckely* ſmiling with her *Mouth,*
>> And *Merry* in her lookes ;
> " Ever *Laughing* for *Love,*
>> as ſhee *Like* would.
> " And as ſhee came by the *Bankes,*
>> the *Boughes* eche one
> " They *Lowted* to that *Ladye,*
>> and *Layd* forth their branches ;
> " *Bloſſomes,* and *Burgens*
>> Breathed full ſweete ;

" Flowers

3

    " *Flowers Flourished* in the *Frith*,
        where fhee *Forth* ftepped;
    " And the *Graffe*, that was *Gray*,
        *Gre*ened belive."

DEATH is afterwards fketched out with a no lefs bold and original pencil.

The other poem is that, which is quoted in the 27th page of this volume, and which was probably the laft that was ever written in this kind of metre in its original fimplicity unaccompanied with rhyme. It fhould have been obferved above in pag. 27. that in this poem the lines are throughout divided into diftichs, thus:

    Grant Gracious God,
        Grant me this time, &c.

It is intitled SCOTTISH FEILDE (in 2 FITTS, 420 diftichs,) containing a very circumftantial narrative of the battle of Flodden, fought Sept. 9. 1513: at which the author feems to have been prefent from his fpeaking in the firft perfon plural,

    " Then WE *Tild* downe OUR *Tents*,
        that *Told* were a thoufand."

In the conclufion of the poem he gives this account of himfelf,

    " He was a *Gentleman* by *Jefu*,
        that this *Geft* made:
    " Which *Say* but as he *Sayd (m)*
        for *Sooth* and noe other.

(m) Probebly corrupted for — ' *Says* but as he *Saw*.'

        " At

" At *Bagily* that *Bearne*
    his *Biding* place had;
" And his anceftors of old time
    have yearded *(n)* theire longe,
" Before William Conquerour
    this *Cuntry* did inhabitt.
" Jefus *Bring* ' them *(o)*' to *Bliffe*,
    that *Brought* us forth of BALF,
" That hath *Hearkened* me *Heare*
    or *Heard* my TALE."

The village of Bagily or Baguleigh is in Chefhire, of which county the author appears to have been, from other paffages in the body of the poem, particularly from the pains he takes to wipe off a ftain from the Chefhire-men, who it feems ran away in that battle, and from his encomiums on the Stanleys earls of Derby, who ufually headed that county. He laments the death of James Stanley bifhop of Ely, as what had recently happened when this poem was written : which ferves to afcertain its date, for that prelate died March 22. 1514-5.

Thus have we traced the Alliterative Meafure fo low as the fixteenth century. It is remarkable that all fuch poets as ufed this kind of metre, retained along with it many peculiar Saxon idioms, particularly fuch as were appropriated to poetry : this deferves the attention of thofe, who were defirous to recover the laws of the ancient Saxon Poefy, ufually given up as

in-

(n) Yearded, *i. e. buried, earthed,* earded. It is common to pronounce " Earth," in fome parts of England " Yearth," particularly in the North.——Pitfcottie fpeaking of James III. flain at Bannockbourn, fays, " Nae man wot whar they YEARDED him."
(o) 'us.' MS.

inexplicable: I am of opinion that they will find what they feek in the Metre of Pierce Plowman *(p)*.

About the beginning of the fixteenth century this kind of verfification began to change its form: the author of SCOTTISH FIELD, we fee, concludes his poem with a Couplet of Rhymes: this was an innovation, that did but prepare the way for the general admiffion of that more modifh ornament; till at length the old uncouth verfe of the ancient writers would no longer go down without it. Yet when Rhyme began to be fuperadded, all the niceties of Alliteration were at firft retained along with it; and the fong of LITTLE JOHN NOBODY exhibits this union very clearly. By degrees the correfpondence of final founds engroffing the whole attention of the poet and fully fatisfying the reader, the internal imbellifhment of Alliteration was no longer ftudied, and thus was this kind of metre at length fwallowed up and loft in our common Burlefque Alexandrine, or Anapeftic verfe *(q)*,

LOW

(p) And in that of Robert of Gloucefter. See the next note.

(q) Confifting of four Anapefts (ᴜ ᴜ -) in which the Accent refts upon every third fyllable. This kind of Verfe, which I alfo call the Burlefque Alexandrine (to diftinguifh it from the other Alexandrines of 11 and 14 fyllables, the parents of our lyric meafure: fee examples, p. 138. &c.) was early applied by Robert of Gloucefter to ferious fubjects. That writer's metre, like this of Langland's, is formed on the Saxon models, (each verfe of his containing a Saxon diftich) only inftead of the internal Alliterations adopted by Langland, he rather chofe final Rhymes, as the French poets have done fince. Take a fpecimen.

> " The Saxons tho in ther power, tho thii were fo rive,
>
> " Seve kingdoms made in Engelonde, and futhe but vive:
>
> " The king of Northomberlond, and of Eaftangle alfo,
>
> " Of Kent, and of Weftfex, and of the March, therto."

Robert of Gloucefter wrote in the weftern dialect, and his language differs exceedingly from that of other contemporary Writers,

now never ufed but in ballads and pieces of light humour, as in the following Song of Conscience, and
in that well-known doggrel,
"A cobler there was, and he lived in a ftall."

But although this kind of meafure hath with us been
thus degraded, it ftill retains among the French its
ancient dignity : their grand Heroic Verfe of twelve
fyllables *(r)* is the fame genuine offspring of the old alliterative metre of the ancient Gothic and Francic poets,
ftript like our Anapeftic of its alliteration, and orna-
mented with rhyme : But with this difference, that
whereas this kind of verfe hath been applied by us only
to light and trivial fubjects, to which by its quick
and lively meafure it feemed beft adapted, our Poets
have let it remain in a more lax unconfined ftate, *(s)*
as

who refided in the metropolis or in the midland counties. Had the
Heptarchy continued, our Englifh language would probably have
been as much diftinguifhed for its different dialects as the Greek ;
or at leaft as that of the feveral independent ftates of Italy.

(r) Or of thirteen fyllables, in what they call a feminine verfe.
It is remarkable that the French alone have retained this old Gothic
metre for their ferious poems ; while the Englifh, Spaniards, &c. have
adopted the Italic verfe of ten fyllables : altho' the Spaniards, as well as
we, anciently ufed a fhort lined metre. I believe the fuccefs with which
Petrarch, and perhaps one or two others, firft ufed the heroic
verfe of ten fyllables in Italian Poefy, recommended it to the Spanifh writers ; as it alfo did to our Chaucer, who firft attempted it in
Englifh ; and to his fucceffors Lord Surrey, Sir Thomas Wyat, &c. ;
who afterwards improved it and brought it to perfection. To Ld.
Surrey we alfo owe the firft introduction of Blank Verfe in his
Verfions of the Eneid.

(s) Thus our poets ufe this verfe indifferently with 12, 11, and even
10 fyllables. For though regularly it confifts of 4 Anapefts (◡ ◡ -) or
twelve fyllables, yet they frequently retrench a fyllable from the firft
or third Anapeft ; and fometimes from both : as in thefe inftances
from Prior, and the following Song of Conscience.

Whŏ hăs eēr beĕn ăt Pārĭs, mŭst nēeds knŏw thĕ Grēve,
Thĕ fātăl rĕtrēat ŏf th' ŭnfōrtŭnăte brāve.

Stĕpt tŏ hĭm strāight, ănd dĭd hĭm rĕquīre.

3

as a greater degree of feverity and ftrictnefs would have been inconfiftent with the light and airy fubjects to which they have applied it. On the other hand, the French having retained this Verfe as the vehicle of their Epic and Tragic flights, in order to give it a ftatelinefs and dignity were obliged to confine it to more exact laws of Scanfion; they have therefore limited it to the 'number of twelve Syllables; and by making the Cæfura or Paufe as full and diftinct as poffible; and by other fevere reftrictions, have given it all the folemnity of which it was capable. The harmony of both however depends fo much on the fame flow of cadence and difpofal of the paufe, that they appear plainly to be of the fame original; and every French heroic verfe evidently confifts of the ancient Diftich of their Francic anceftors: which, by the way, will account to us why this verfe of the French fo naturally refolves itfelf into two complete hemiftics. And indeed by making the cæfura or paufe always to reft on the laft fyllable of a word, and by making a kind of paufe in the fenfe, the French poets do in effect reduce their hemiftics to two diftinct and independent verfes: and fome of their old poets have gone fo far as to make the two hemiftics rhyme to each other (t).

After all, the old alliterative and anapeftic metre of the Englifh poets being chiefly ufed in a barbarous age, and in a rude unpolifhed language, abounds with verfes defective in length, proportion, and harmony; and therefore cannot enter into a comparifon with the correct verfification of the beft modern French writers; but making allowances for thefe defects, that fort of metre runs with a cadence fo exactly refembling the French heroic Alexandrine, that I believe no peculiarities of their verfification can be produced, which

T 4

cannot

____

(t) See Inftances in *L'Hift. de la Poefie Françoife par* MASSIEU, &c. In the fame book are alfo fpecimens of alliterative French Verfes.

cannot be exactly matched in the alliterative metre. I shall give by way of example a few lines from the modern French poets confronted with parallels from the ancient poem of Life and Death: in these I shall denote the Cæsura or Pause by a perpendicular line, and the Cadence by the marks of the Latin quantity.

Lĕ sŭccēs fŭt toŭjoŭrs | ŭn ŭnfănt dĕ l' ăudāce;
All shăll drȳe wĭth thĕ dīnts | thăt I dēal wĭth mȳ hīnds.

L' hŏmmĕ prūdĕnt vŏit trōp | l' ĭllūsĭŏn lĕ sūit,
Yōndĕr dāmsĕl ĭs dēath | thăt drēfsĕth hĕr tŏ smīte.

L' ĭntrŭpīdĕ vŏit mĭeux | ĭt lĕ fāntīmĕ fūit*.
Whĕn shĕ dōlefŭllȳ săw | hŏw shĕ dăng dōwne hĭr fōlke.

Mĕme aŭx yeūx dĕ l' ĭnjūste | ŭn ĭnjūste ĕst hŏrrĭblĕ†.
Thĕn shĕ căft ŭp ă crȳe | tŭ thĕ hīgh kĭng ŏf hēavĕn.

Dŭ mĕnsŏngĕ toŭjoŭrs | lĕ vrāi dĕmēurĕ māitrĕ,
Thŏu shălt bīttĕrlyĕ bȳe | ŏr ēlfe thĕ bōokĕ fāilĕth

Poŭr părăitre hŏnnĕte hŏmme | ĕn ŭn mōt, ĭl făut l' ētrĕ‡.
Thŭs I fāred thrōughe ă frȳthe | whĕre thĕ flōwĕrs wĕre mānȳe.

To conclude ; the metre of Pierce Plowman's Visions has no kind of relation with what is commonly called Blank Verse; yet has it a sort of harmony of its own, proceeding not so much from its alliteration, as from the artful disposal of its cadence, and the contrivance of its pause. So that when the ear is a little accustomed to it, it is by no means unpleasing; but claims all the merit of the French heroic numbers, only far less polished ; being sweetened, instead of their final rhymes, with the internal recurrence of similar sounds.

The

---

* Catalina. A. 3.   † Boileau Sat.   ‡ Boil, Sat, 11.

AS I walked of late by an wood side,
   To God for to meditate was mine entent;
Where under an hawthorne I suddenlye spyed
A silly poore creature ragged and rent,
With bloody teares his face was besprent,   5
   His fleshe and his color confumed away,
   And his garments they were all mire, mucke, and clay.

This made me muse, and much ' to' defire
To know what kind of man hee shold bee;
I stept to him straight, and did him require   10
His name and his secretts to shew unto mee.
His head he cast up, and wooful was hee,
   My name, quoth he, is the caufe of my care,
   And makes me fcorned, and left here fo bare.

Then straightway he turnd him, and prayd me sit downe,
And I will, faithe he, declare my whole greefe;   16
My name is called, CONSCIENCE: — wheratt he did
    frowne,
He repined to repeate it, and grinded his teethe,
' Thoughe now, silly wretche, I'm denyed all releef,'

                      ' Yet'

' Yet ' while I was young, and tender of yeeres,   20
I was entertained with kinges, and with peeres.

There was none in the court that lived in fuch fame,
For with the kinges councell I fate in commiffion ;
Dukes, earles, and barons efteem'd of my name ;
And how that I liv'd there, needs no repetition :   25
I was ever holden in honeft condition,
      For how-e'er the lawes went in Weftminfter-hall,
      When fentence was given, for me they wold call.

No incomes at all the landlords wold take,
But one pore peny, that was their fine ;   30
And that they acknowledged to be for my fake.
The poore wold doe nothing without councell mine :
I ruled the world with the right line :
      For nothing ' ere ' paffed betweene foe and friend,
      But Confcience was called to bee at the end.   35

Noe bargaine, nor merchandize merchants wold make
But I was called a witneffe therto :
No ufe for noe money, nor forfett wold take,
But I wold controule them, if that they did foe :
' And ' that makes me live now in great woe,   40
      For then came in Pride, Sathan's difciple,
      That is now entertained with all kind of people.

He broughtwith him three, whofe names ' thus they call '
That is Covetoufnes, Lecherye, Ufury, befide :

They

They never prevail'd, till they wrought my downe-fall; 45
Soe Pride was entertained, but Confcience decried,
And ' now ever fince' abroad have I tryed
  To have had entertainment with fome one or other ;
  But I am rejected, and fcorned of my brother.

Then went I to Court the gallants to winne, · 50
But the porter kept me out of the gate :
To Bartlemew Spittle to pray for my finne,
They bade me goe packe, itt was fit for my ftate ;
Goe, goe, thread-bare Confcience, and feeke thee a mate.
  Good Lord, long preferve my king, prince, and queene,
  With whom I ever efteemed have been. 56

Then went I to London, where once I did ' dwell' :
But they bade away with me, when they knew my name ;
For he will undoe us to bye and to fell !
They bade me goe packe me, and hye me for fhame ; 60
They laught at my raggs, and there had good game ;
  This is old thread-bare Confcience, that dwelt with
      faint Peter :
  But they wold not admitt me to be a chimney-fweeper.

Not one wold receive me, the Lord he doth know ;
I having but one poor pennye in my purfe, 65
On an awle and fome patches I did it beftow ;
For I thought better cobble fhoes than to doe worfe :
Straight then all the coblers began for to curfe,

                                        And

And by ſtatute wold prove me a rogue, and forlorne,
And whipp me out of towne to ſeeke where I was
borne.   70

Then did I remember, and call to my minde,
The Court of Conſcience where once I did ſit,
Not doubting but there I favor ſhold find,
Sith my name and the place agreed ſoe fit;
But ſure of my purpoſe I fayled a whit,   75
   For ' thoughe' the judge us'd my name in every com-
      miſſion,
   The lawyers with their quillets wold get my diſmiſſion.

Then Weſtminſter-hall was no place for me;
Good lord! how the Lawyers began to aſſemble,
And fearfull they were, leſt there I ſhold bee !   80
The ſilly poore clarkes began for to tremble;
I ſhowed them my cauſe, and did not diſſemble;
   Soe they gave me ſome money my charges to beare,
   But ſwore me on a booke I muſt never come there.

Next the Merchants ſaid, Counterfeite, get thee away, 85
Doſt thou remember how we thee fond ?
We baniſht thee the country beyond the ſalt ſea,
And ſett thee on ſhore in the New-found land ;
And there thou and wee moſt friendly ſhook hand,
   And we were right glad when thou didſt refuſe us ; 90
   For when we wold reape here thou woldſt accuſe us.

Then

Then had I noe way, but for to go on
To Gentlemens houfes of an ancyent name ;
Declaring my greeffes, and there I made moane,
Telling how their forefathers held me in fame :   95
And at letting their farmes ' how always I came'.
   They fayd, Fye upon thee ! we may thee curfe :
   Theire leafes continue, and we fare the worfe.

And then I was forced a begging to goe
To hufbandmens houfes, who greeved right fore,   100
And fware that their landlords had plagued them foe,
Thet they were not able to keepe open dore,
Nor nothing had left to give to the poore :
   Therefore to this wood I doe me repayre,
   Where hepps and hawes, it is my beft fare.   105

Yet within this fame defert fome comfort I have
Of Mercye, of Pittye, and of Almes-deeds ;
Who have vowed to company me to my grave.
We are all put to filence, and live upon weeds,
' And hence fuch cold houfe-keeping proceeds' :   110.
   Our banifhment is its utter decay,
   The which the riche glutton will anfwer one day.

Why then, I faid to him, me-thinks it were beft
To goe to the Clergie ; for daylie they preach
Eche man to love you above all the reft ;   115
Of Mercye and Pittye and Almes-deeds they teache.
O. faid he, noe matter a pin what they preache,

For

1

For their wives and their children foe hange them upon,
That whofoever gives alms they will * give none.

Then laid he him down, and turned him away,   120
And prayd me to goe, and leave him to reft.
I told him, I haplie might yet fee the day
For him and his fellowes to live with the beft.
Firft, faid he, banifh Pride, then England were bleft;
  For then thofe wold love us, that now fell their land, 125
  And then good houfe-keeping wold revive out of hand.

** We ought in juftice and truth to read ‘ can’.*

II.

PLAIN TRUTH, AND BLIND IGNORANCE.

*This excellent old ballad is preferved in the little ancient mifcellany intitled, " The Garland of Goodwill."—*IGNO-RANCE *is here made to fpeak in the broad Somerfetfhire dia-lect. The fcene we may fuppofe to be Glaftonbury Abbey.*

TRUTH.

GOD fpeed you, ancient father,
   And give you a good daye ;
What is the caufe, I praye you,
   So fadly here you ftaye ?

And

And that you keep such gazing   5
  On this decayed place,
The which, for superstition,
  Good princes down did raze ?

IGNORANCE.

Chill tell thee, by my vazen,
  That zometimes che have knowne   10
A vair and goodly abbey
  Stand here of bricke and stone ;
And many a holy vrier,
  As ich may say to thee,
Within these goodly cloysters
  Che did full often zee.   15

TRUTH.

Then I must tell thee, father,
  In truthe and veritiè,
A forte of greater hypocrites
  Thou couldst not likely see ;   20
Deceiving of the simple
  With false and feigned lies :
But such an order truly
  Christ never did devise.

IGNORANCE.

Ah ! ah ! che zmell thee now, man ;   25
  Che know well what thou art ;

A vel-

A vellow of mean learning,
　　Thee was not worth a vart :
Vor when we had the old lawe,
　　A merry world was then ;　　　　　30
And every thing was plenty
　　Among all zorts of men.

TRUTH.

Thou giveſt me an anſwer,
　　As did the Jewes ſometimes
Unto the prophet Jeremye,　　　　　35
　　When he accus'd their crimes :
'Twas merry, ſayd the people,
　　And joyfull in our rea'me,
When we did offer ſpice-cakes
　　Unto the queen of heav'n.　　　　40

IGNORANCE.

Chill tell thee what, good vellowe,
　　Before the vriers went hence,
A buſhell of the beſt wheate
　　Was zold vor vourteen pence ;
And vorty egges a penny,　　　　　45
　　That were both good and newe ;
And this che zay my zelf have zeene,
　　And yet ich am no Jewe.

TRUTH.

TRUTH.

Within the facred bible
    We find it written plain,   50
The latter days fhould troublefome
    And dangerous be, certaine;
That we fhould be felf-lovers,
    And charity wax colde;
Then 'tis not true religion   55
    That makes thee grief to holde.

IGNORANCE.

Chill tell thee my opinion plaine,
    And choul'd that well ye knewe,
Ich care not for the bible booke;
    Tis too big to be true.   60
Our bleffed ladyes pfalter
    Zhall for my money goe;
Zuch pretty prayers, as there bee,
    The bible cannot zhowe.

TRUTH.

Nowe haft thou fpoken trulye,   65
    For in that book indeede
No mention of our lady,
    Or Romifh faint we read:
For by the bleffed Spirit
    That book indited was,   70
And not by fimple perfons,
    As was the foolifh maffe.

IGNORANCE.

Cham zure they were not voolifhe
    That made the maffe, che trowe:
Why, man, 'tis all in Latine,   75
    And vools no Latine knowe.
Were not our fathers wife men,
    And they did like it well;
Who very much rejoyced
    To heare the zacring bell?   80

TRUTH.

But many kinges and prophets,
    As I may fay to thee,
Have wifht the light that you have,
    And could it never fee:
For what art thou the better   85
    A Latin fong to heare,
And underftandeft nothing,
    That they fing in the quiere?

IGNORANCE.

O hold thy peace, che pray thee,
    The noife was paffing trim   90
To heare the vriers zinging,
    As we did enter in:
And then to zee the rood-loft
    Zo bravely zet with zaints;—
But now to zee them wandring   95
    My heart with zorrow vaints.

TRUTH.

TRUTH.

The Lord did give commandment,
  No image thou fhouldſt make,
Nor that unto idolatry
  You ſhould your ſelf betake :   100
The golden calf of Iſrael
  Moſes did therefore ſpoile ;
And Baal's prieſts and temple
  Were brought to utter foile.

IGNORANCE.

But our lady of Walfinghame   105
  Was a pure and holy zaint,
And many men in pilgrimage
  Did ſhew to her complaint ;
Yea with zweet Thomas Becket,
  And many other moe ;   110
The holy maid of Kent * likewiſe
  Did many wonders zhowe.

TRUTH.

Such ſaints are well agreeing
  To your profeſſion ſure ;
And to the men that made them   115
  So precious and ſo pure ;
The one for being a traytoure,
  Met an untimely death ;

U 2

The

* By name Eliz. Barton, executed Ap. 21. 1534. Stow, p. 570.

The other eke for treafon
Did end her hateful breath.   120

IGNORANCE.

Yea, yea, it is no matter,
Difpraife them how you wille :
But zure they did much goodneffe ;
Would they were with us ftille !
We had our holy water,   125
And holy bread likewife,
And many holy reliques
We zaw before our eyes.

TRUTH.

And all this while they fed you
With vain and empty fhowe,   130
Which never Chrift commanded,
As learned doctors knowe :
Search then the holy fcriptures,
And thou fhalt plainly fee
That headlong to damnation   135
They alway trained thee.

IGNORANCE.

If it be true, good vellowe,
As thou doft zay to mee,
Unto my heavenly fader
Alone then will I flee :   140

Be-

Believing in the Gospel,
And paſſion of his zon,
And with the zubtil papiſtes
Ich have for ever done.

III.

THE WANDERING JEW.

*The ſtory of the Wandering Jew is of conſiderable anti-
quity : it had obtained full credit in this part of the world
before the year 1228, as we learn from Mat. Paris.   For
in that year, it ſeems, there came an Armenian archbiſhop
into England, to viſit the ſhrines and reliques preſerved in our
churches ; who being entertained at the monaſtery of St. Albans, was aſked ſeveral queſtions relating to his country, &c.
Among the reſt a monk, who ſat near him, inquired " if he
" had ever ſeen or heard of the famous perſon named Joſeph,
" that was ſo much talked of; who was preſent at our Lord's
" crucifixion and converſed with him, and who was ſtill alive
" in confirmation of the Chriſtian faith."   The archbiſhop
anſwered, That the fact was true.   And afterwards one of
his train, who was well known to a ſervant of the abbot's,
interpreting his maſter's words, told them in French, " That
his lord knew the perſon they ſpoke of very well : that he had
dined at his table but a little while before he left the Eaſt :
that he had been Pontius Pilate's porter, by name Cartaphi-
lus ; who, when they were dragging Jeſus out of the door of
the Judgment-hall, ſtruck him with his fiſt on the back, ſay-*
U 3

ing,

ing, " *Go faſter, Jeſus, go faſter ; why doſt thou linger?*"
Upon which Jeſus looked at him with a frown and ſaid,
" *I indeed am going, but thou ſhalt tarry till I come.*" *Soon
after he was converted, and baptized by the name of Joſeph.   He lives for ever, but at the end of every hundred
years falls into an incurable illneſs, and at length into a fit
or ecſtaſy, out of which when he recovers, he returns to the
ſame ſtate of youth he was in when Jeſus ſuffered, being
then about 30 years of age.   He remembers all the circum-
ſtances of the death and reſurrection of Chriſt, the ſaints that
aroſe with him, the compoſing of the apoſtles creed, their
preaching, and diſperſion ; and is himſelf a very grave and
holy perſon.*" *This is the ſubſtance of Matthew Paris's account, who was himſelf a monk of St. Albans, and was
living at the time when this Armenian archbiſhop made the
above relation.*

*Since his time ſeveral impoſtors have appeared at intervals
under the name and character of the* WANDERING JEW ;
*whoſe ſeveral hiſtories may be ſeen in Calmet's dictionary of
the Bible.   See alſo the Turkiſh Spy, Vol. 2. Book 3. Let. 1.
The ſtory that is copied in the following ballad is of one, who
appeared at Hamburgh in* 1547, *and pretended he had been a
Jewiſh ſhoemaker at the time of Chriſt's crucifixion. ——The
ballad however ſeems to be of later date.   It is printed
from a black-letter copy in the Pepys collection.*

WHEN as in faire Jeruſalem
    Our Saviour Chriſt did live,
And for the ſins of all the worlde
    His own deare life did give ;
The wicked Jewes with ſcoffes and ſcornes   5
    Did dailye him moleſt,
That never till he left his life,
    Our Saviour could not reſt.

When

When they had crown'd his head with thornes,
   And scourg'd him to disgrace,   10
In scornfull sort they led him forthe
   Unto his dying place ;
Where thousand thousands in the streete
   Beheld him passe along,
Yet not one gentle heart was there,   15
   That pityed this his wrong.

Both old and young reviled him,
   As in the streete he wente,
And nought he found but churlish tauntes,
   By every ones consente :   20
His owne deare crosse he bore himselfe,
   A burthen far too great,
Which made him in the street to fainte,
   With blood and water sweat.

Being weary thus, he sought for rest,   25
   To ease his burthened soule,
Upon a stone ; the which a wretch
   Did churlishly controule ;
And sayd, Awaye, thou king of Jewes,
   Thou shalt not rest thee here ;   30
Pass on ; thy execution place
   Thou seest nowe draweth neare.

And thereupon he thrust him thence ;
   At which our Saviour sayd,

U 4

I sure

I fure will reft, but thou fhalt walke,   35
    And have no journey ftayed.
With that this curfed fhoemaker,
    For offering Chrift this wrong,
  Left wife and children, houfe and all,
    And went from thence along.   40

Where after he had feene the bloude
    Of Jefus Chrift thus fhed,
And to the croffe his bodye nail'd,
    Awaye with fpeed he fled
Without returning backe againe   45
    Unto his dwelling place,
And wandred up and downe the worlde,
    A runnagate moft bafe.

No refting could he finde at all,
    No eafe, nor hearts content ;   50
No houfe, nor home, nor biding place :
    But wandring forth he went
From towne to towne in foreigne landes,
    With grieved confcience ftill,
Repenting for the heinous guilt   55
    Of his fore-paffed ill.

Thus after fome fewe ages paft
    In wandring up and downe ;
He much again defired to fee
    Jerufalems renowne,   60

But

But finding it all quite deftroyd,
   He wandred thence with woe,
Our Saviours wordes, which he had fpoke,
   To verefie and fhowe.

" I'll reft, fayd hee, but thou fhalt walke,"   65
   So doth this wandring Jew
From place to place, but cannot reft
   For feeing countries newe ;
Declaring ftill the power of him,
   Whereas he comes or goes,   70
And of all things done in the eaft,
   Since Chrift his death, he fhowes.

The world he hath ftill compaft round
   And feene thofe nations ftrange,
That hearing of the name of Chrift,   75
   Their idol gods doe change :
To whom he hath told wondrous thinges
   Of time forepaft, and gone,
And to the princes of the worlde
   Declares his caufe of moane :   80

Defiring ftill to be diffolv'd,
   And yeild his mortal breath ;
But, if the Lord hath thus decreed,
   He fhall not yet fee death.
For neither lookes he old nor young,   85
   But as he did thofe times,

When

When Chrift did fuffer on the croffe
   For mortall finners crimes.

He hath paft through many a foreigne place,
   Arabia, Egypt, Africa,   90
Grecia, Syria, and great Thrace,
   And throughout all Hungaria:
Where Paul and Peter preached Chrift,
   Thofe bleft apoftles deare;
There he hath told our Saviours wordes,   95
   In countries far, and neare.

And lately in Bohemia,
   With many a German towne;
And now in Flanders, as tis thought,
   He wandreth up and downe: 100
Where learned men with him conferre
   Of thofe his lingering dayes,
And wonder much to heare him tell
   His journeyes, and his wayes.

If people give this Jew an almes,   105
   The moft that he will take
Is not above a groat a time;
   Which he, for Jefus' fake,
Will kindlye give unto the poore,
   And thereof make no fpare,   110
Afirming ftill that Jefus Chrift
   Of him hath dailye care.

He

He ne'er was feene to laugh nor fmile,
   But weepe and make great moane;
Lamenting ftill his miferies,   115
   And dayes forepaft and gone:
If he heare any one blafpheme,
   Or take God's name in vaine,
He telles them that they crucifie
   Their Saviour Chrifte againe.   120

If you had feene his death, faith he,
   As thefe mine eyes have done,
Ten thoufand thoufand times would yee
   His torments think upon:
And fuffer for his fake all paine   125
   Of torments, and all woes.
Thefe are his wordes and eke his life
   Whereas he comes or goes.

IV.

THE LYE,

BY SIR WALTER RALEIGH,

— is found in a very fcarce mifcellany intitled " Davifon's
" Poems, or a poeticall Rapfodie divided into fixe books . . . . .
" The

" *The 4th impreſſion newly correċted and augmented, and*
" *put into a forme more pleaſing to the reader. Lond. 1621.*
" *12mo."   This poem is reported to have been written by*
its celebrated author the night before his execution, Oċt. 29.
1618.   But this muſt be a miſtake, for there were at leaſt
two editions of Daviſon's poems before that time, one in
*16c8 *: the other in 1611 †.   So that unleſs this poem*
was an after-inſertion in the 4th edit. it muſt have been
written long before the death of Sir Walter : perhaps it was
compoſed ſoon after his condemnation in 1603.

G O E, ſoule, the bodies gueſt,
　　Upon a thankeleſſe arrant;
Feare not to touche the beſt,
　　The truth ſhall be thy warrant :
　　　Goe, ſince I needs muſt dye,　　　　　　5
　　　And give the world the lye.

Goe tell the court, it glowes
　　And ſhines like rotten wood;
Goe tell the church it ſhowes
　　What's good, and doth no good :　　　　　10
　　　If church and court reply,
　　　Then give them both the lye.

Tell potentates they live
　　Aċting by others aċtions ;
Not lov'd unleſſe they give,　　　　　　　15
　　Not ſtrong but by their faċtions :

　　　　　　　　　　　　　　　　　　　　If

* *Catalog. of T. Rawlinſon 1727.*
* *Cat. of Sion coll. library.   This is either loſt or miſlaid.*

If potentates reply,
Give potentates the lye.

Tell men of high condition,
  That rule affairs of ſtate,   20
Their purpoſe is ambition,
  Their practiſe onely hate ;
    And if they once reply,
    Then give them all the lye.

Tell them that brave it moſt,   25
  They beg for more by ſpending,
Who in their greateſt coſt
  Seek nothing but commending ;
    And if they make reply,
    Spare not to give the lye.   30

Tell zeale, it lacks devotion ;
  Tell love it is but luſt ;
Tell time, it is but motion ;
  Tell fleſh, it is but duſt ;
    And wiſh them not reply,   35
    For thou muſt give the lye.

Tell age, it daily waſteth ;
  Tell honour, how it alters ;
Tell beauty, how ſhe blaſteth ;
  Tell favour, how ſhe falters ;   40

And

And as they shall reply,
Give each of them the lye.

Tell wit, how much it wrangles
    In tickle points of nicenesse;
Tell wisedome, she entangles   45
    Herselfe in over-wisenesse;
        And if they do reply,
        Straight give them both the lye.

Tell physicke of her boldnesse;
    Tell skill, it is pretension;   50
Tell charity of coldnes;
    Tell law, it is contention;
        And as they yield reply,
        So give them still the lye.

Tell fortune of her blindnesse;   55
    Tell nature of decay;
Tell friendship of unkindnesse;
    Tell justice of delay:
        And if they dare reply,
        Then give them all the lye.   60

Tell arts, they have no soundnesse,
    But vary by esteeming;
Tell schooles, they want profoundnesse,
    And stand too much on seeming;

If arts and fchooles reply,   65
     Give arts and fchooles the lye.

Tell faith, it's fled the citie ;
     Tell how the countrey erreth ;
Tell, manhood fhakes off pitie ;
     Tell, vertue leaft preferreth :   70
       And, if they doe reply,
       Spare not to give the lye.

So, when thou haft, as I
     Commanded thee, done blabbing,
Although to give the lye   75
     Deferves no lefs than ftabbing,
       Yet ftab at thee who will,
       No ftab the foule can kill.

V.

VERSES BY KING JAMES I.

*In the former edition of this book were inferted, by way
of fpecimen of his majefty's poetic talents, fome Punning
Verfes made on the difputations at Sterling : but it having
been fuggefted to the editor, that the king only gave the*
                                   quibbling

*quibbling commendations in profe, and that fome obfequious
court-rhymer put them into metre * ; it was thought proper
to exchange them for two SONNETS of K. James's own
compofition. James was a great verfifier, and therefore out
of the multitude of his poems, we have here felected two,
which (to fhew our impartiality) are written in his beft
and his worft manner. The firft would not difhonour any
writer of that time ; the fecond is a moft complete example
of the Bathos.*

A SONNET ADDRESSED BY KING JAMES TO HIS
SON PRINCE HENRY :

*From K. James's works in folio : Where is alfo printed
another called his Majefty's OWN Sonnet ; it would perhaps be too cruel to infer from thence that this was NOT
his Majefty's OWN Sonnet.*

GOD gives not kings the ftile of Gods in vaine,
    For on his throne his fcepter do they fwey :
    And as their fubjects ought them to obey,
So kings fhould feare and ferve their God againe.

If then ye would enjoy a happie reigne,
    Obferve the ftatutes of our heavenly king ;
    And from his law make all your laws to fpring ;
Since his lieutenant here ye fhould remaine.

Rewarde the juft, be ftedfaft, true and plaine ;
    Repreffe the proud, maintayning aye the right ;
    Walke always fo, as ever in HIS fight,
Who guardes the godly, plaguing the prophane.

And

---

* *See a folio intitled " The Mufes welcome to King James."*

And fo ye fhall in princely vertues fhine,
Refembling right your mightie king divine.

A Sonnet occasioned by the bad Weather which hindred the Sports at New-market in January 1616.

This is printed from Drummond of Hawthornden's works, folio : where alfo may be feen fome verfes of Lord Stirling's upon this Sonnet, which concludes with the fineft Anticlimax I remember to have feen.

HOW cruelly thefe catives do confpire ?
    What loathfome love breeds fuch a baleful band
Betwixt the cankred king of Creta land *,
That melancholy old and angry fire,

And him, who wont to quench debate and ire   5
    Among the Romans, when his ports were clos'd †?
    But now his double face is ftill difpos'd,
With Saturn's help, to freeze us at the fire.

The earth ore-covered with a fheet of fnow,
Refufes food to fowl, to bird and beaft :   10
    The chilling cold lets every thing to grow,
And furfeits cattle with a ftarving feaft.
    Curs'd be that love and mought continue fhort,
    Which kills all creatures, and doth fpoil our fport.
Vol. II.   X   VI. K.

* Saturn.   † Janus.

VI

K. JOHN AND THE ABBOT OF CANTERBURY.

The common popular ballad of King John and the Abbot *seem to have been abridged and modernized about the time of James I. from one much older, intitled* King "John and the Bishop of Canterbury." *The Editor's folio MS. contains a copy of this last, but in too corrupt a state to be reprinted; it however afforded many lines worth reviving, which will be found inserted in the ensuing stanzas.*

The archness of the following questions and answers hath been much admired by our old ballad-makers; for besides the two copies above mentioned, there is extant another ballad on the same subject, (but of no great antiquity or merit) intitled, "King Olfrey and the Abbot *." *Lastly, about the time of the civil wars, when the cry ran against the bishops, some Puritan worked up the same story into a very doleful ditty, to a solemn tune, concerning* "King Henry and a Bishop," *with this stinging moral,*

    "*Unlearned men hard matters out can find,*

    "*When learned bishops princes eyes do blind.*"

The

---

* See the collection of Hist. Ballads, 3 vol. 1727. Mr. Wise supposes Olfrey to be a corruption of Alfred, in his pamphlet concerning the White Horse in Berkshire, p. 15.

*The following is chiefly printed from an ancient black-
letter copy, to " The tune of Derry down."*

AN ancient ſtory Ile tell you anon
   Of a notable prince, that was called king John;
And he ruled England with maine and with might,
For he did great wrong, and maintein'd little right.

And Ile tell you a ſtory, a ſtory ſo merrye,   5
Concerning the Abbot of Canterbùrye ;
How for his houſe-keeping, and high renowne,
They rode poſte for him to fair London towne.

An hundred men, the king did heare ſay,
The abbot kept in his houſe every day ;   10
And fifty golde chaynes, without any doubt,
In velvet coates waited the abbot about.

How now, father abbot, I heare it of thee,
Thou keepeſt a farre better houſe than mee,
And for thy houſe-keeping and high renowne,   15
I feare thou work'ſt treaſon againſt my crown.

My liege, quo' the abbot, I would it were knowne,
I never ſpend nothing, but what is my owne ;
And I truſt, your grace will doe me no deere,
For ſpending of my owne true-gotten geere.   20

X 2

Yes,

Yes, yes, father abbot, thy fault it is highe,
And now for the fame thou needeft muft dye;
For except thou canft anfwer me queftions three,
Thy head fhall be fmitten from thy bodìe.

And firft, quo' the king, when I'm in this ftead,   25
With my crowne of golde fo faire on my head,
Among all my liege-men fo noble of birthe
Thou muft tell me to one penny what I am worthe.

Secondlye, tell me, without any doubt,
How foone I may ride the whole world about;   30
And at the third queftion thou muft not fhrink,
But tell me here truly what I do think.

O, thefe are hard queftions for my fhallow witt,
Nor I cannot anfwer your grace as yet;
But if you will give me but three weekes fpace,   35
Ile do my endeavour to anfwer your grace.

Now three weeks fpace to thee will I give,
And that is the longeft time thou haft to live;
For if thou doft not anfwer my queftions three,
Thy lands and thy livings are forfeit to mee.   40

Away rode the abbot all fad at that word,
And he rode to Cambridge, and Oxenford;
But never a doctor there was fo wife,
That could with his learning an anfwer devife.

Then

Then home rode the abbot of comfort fo cold,   45
And he mett his fhepheard a going to fold :
How now, my lord abbot, you are welcome home ;
What newes do you bring us from good king John ?

" Sad newes, fad newes, fhepheard, I muft give ;
That I have but three days more to live :   50
For if I do not anfwer him queftions three,
My head will be fmitten from my bodìe.

The firft is to tell him there in that ftead,
With his crowne of golde fo fair on his head,
Among all his liege men fo noble of birth,   55
To within one penny of what he is worth.

The feconde, to tell him, without any doubt,
How foone he may ride this whole world about :
And at the third queftion I muft not fhrinke,
But tell him there truly what he does thinke."   60

Now cheare up, fire abbot, did you never hear yet,
That a fool he may learn a wife man witt ?
Lend me horfe, and ferving men, and your apparel,
And I'll ride to London to anfwere your quarrel.

Nay frowne not, if it hath bin told unto mee,   65
I am like your lordfhip, as ever may bee :
And if you will but lend me your gowne,
There is none fhall knowe us at fair London towne.

X 3

Now

" Now horſes, and ſerving-men thou ſhalt have,
With ſumptuous array moſt gallant and brave;   70
With crozier, and miter, and rochet, and cope,
Fit to appeare 'fore our fader the pope."

Now welcome, ſire abbot, the king he did ſay,
Tis well thou'rt come back to keepe thy day;
For an if thou canſt anſwer my queſtions three,   75
Thy life and thy living both ſaved ſhall bee.

And firſt, when thou ſeeſt me here in this ſtead,
With my crown of golde ſo fair on my head,
Among all my liege-men ſo noble of birthe,
Tell me to one penny what I am worth.   80

" For thirty pence our Saviour was ſold
Amonge the falſe Jewes, as I have bin told ;
And twenty nine is the worth of thee,
For I thinke, thou art one penny worſer than hee."

The king he laughed, and ſwore by St. Bittel *,   85
I did not think I had been worth ſo littel !
— Now ſecondly tell me, without any doubt,
How ſoone I may ride this whole world about.

" You muſt riſe with the ſun, and ride with the ſame,
Until the next morning he riſeth againe ;   90

And

And then your grace need not make any doubt,
But in twenty-four hours you'll ride it about."

The king he laughed, and fwore by St. Jone,
I did not think, it could be gone fo foone!
—Now from the third queftion thou muft not fhrinke,
But tell me here truly what I do thinke,   96

" Yea, that fhall I do, and make your grace merry :
You thinke I'm the abbot of Canterbùry ;
But I'm his poor fhepheard, as plain you may fee,
That am come to beg pardon for him and for mee."100

The king he laughed, and fwore by the maffe,
Ile make thee lord abbot this day in his place !
" Now naye, my liege, be not in fuch fpeede,
For alacke I can neither write, ne reade."

Four nobles a weeke, then I will give thee,   105
For this merry jeft thou haft fhowne unto mee ;
And tell the old abbot when thou comeft home,
Thou haft brought him a pardon from good king John.

X 4   VII. Y O U

YOU MEANER BEAUTIES.

This little Sonnet was written by Sir HENRY WOTTON Knight, on that amiable Princefs, Elizabeth daughter of James I. and wife of the Elector Palatine, who was chofen King of Bohemia, Sept. 5. 1619. The confequences of this fatal election are well known: Sir Henry Wotton, who in that and the following year was employed in feveral embaffies in Germany on behalf of this unfortunate lady, feems to have had an uncommon attachment to her merit and fortunes, for he gave away a jewel worth a thoufand pounds, that was prefented to him by the Emperor, " becaufe it came from an " enemy to his royal miftrefs the Queen of Bohemia." See Biog. Britan.

This fong is printed from the Reliquiæ Wottonianæ *1651. with fome corrections from an old MS. copy.*

YOU meaner beauties of the night,
   Which poorly fatisfie our eies
More by your number, then your light;
   You common people of the fkies,
   What are you when the Sun fhall rife?   5

Ye violets that firſt appeare,
  By your pure purple mantles known
Like the proud virgins of the yeare,
  As if the Spring were all your own ;
  What are you when the Roſe is blown ?   10

Ye curious chaunters of the wood,
  That warble forth dame Nature's layes,
Thinking your paſſions underſtood
  By your weak accents : what's your praiſe,
  When Philomell her voyce ſhall raiſe ?   15

So when my miſtris ſhal be ſeene
  In ſweetneſſe of her looks and minde ;
By virtue firſt, then choyce a queen ;
  Tell me, if ſhe was not deſign'd
  Th' eclypſe and glory of her kind ?   20

VIII.

THE OLD AND YOUNG COURTIER.

This excellent old ſong, the ſubject of which is a compari-
ſon between the manners of the old gentry, as ſtill ſubſiſting
in the times of Elizabeth, and the modern refinements af-
fected

*fected by their sons in the reigns of her successors, is given
from an ancient black-letter copy in the Pepys collection,
compared with another printed among some miscellaneous
" poems and songs" in a book intituled, " Le Prince d'
" amour." 1660. 8vo.*

A N old song made by an aged old pate,
 Of an old worshipful gentleman, who had a greate
   estate,
That kept a brave old house at a bountiful rate,
And an old porter to relieve the poor at his gate;
  Like an old courtier of the queen's,
  And the queen's old courtier.

With an old lady, whose anger one word asswages;
This every quarter paid their old servants their wage s,
And never knew what belong'd to coachmen, footmen,
   nor pages,
But kept twenty old fellows with blue coats and badges;
  Like an old courtier, &c.

With an old study fill'd full of learned old books,
With an old reverend chaplain, you might know him
   by his looks.
With an old buttery hatch worn quite off the hooks,
And an old kitchen, that maintain'd half a dozen old
   cocks;
  Like an old courtier, &c.

With

With an old hall, hung about with pikes, guns, and bows,
With old fwords, and bucklers, that had born many
  fhrewde blows,
And an old frize coat, to cover his worfhip's trunk hofe,
And a cup of old fherry, to comfort his copper nofe;
   Like an old courtier, &c.

With a good old fafhion, when Chriftmaffe was come,
To call in all his old neighbours with bagpipe, and drum,
With good chear enough to furnifh every old room,
And old liquor able to make a cat fpeak, and man dumb,
   Like an old courtier, &c.

With an old falconer, huntfman, and a kennel of hounds,
That never hawked, nor hunted, but in his own grounds,
Who, like a wife man, kept himfelf within his own
   bounds,
And when he dyed gave every child a thoufand good
   pounds;
   Like an old courtier, &c.

But to his eldeft fon his houfe and land he affign'd,
Charging him in his will to keep the old bountifull mind,
To be good to his old tenants, and to his neighbours be
   kind:
But in the enfuing ditty you fhall hear how he was in-
   clin'd;
    Like a young courtier of the king's,
    And the king's young courtier.

            Like

Like a flourishing young gallant, newly come to his
    land,
Who keeps a brace of painted madams at his command,
And takes up a thousand pound upon his fathers land,
And gets drunk in a tavern, till he can neither go nor
    stand ;
        Like a young courtier, &c.

With a new-fangled lady, that is dainty, nice, and spare,
Who never knew what belong'd to good house-keeping,
    or care,
Who buyes gaudy-color'd fans to play with wanton air,
And seven or eight different dressings of other womens
    hair ;
        Like a young courtier, &c.

With a new-fashion'd hall, built where the old one
    stood,
Hung round with new pictures, that do the poor no
    good,
With a fine marble chimney, wherein burns neither coal
    nor wood,
And a new smooth shovelboard, whereon no victuals
    ne'er stood ;
        Like a young courtier, &c.

With a new study, stuft full of pamphlets, and plays,
And a new chaplain, that swears faster than he prays,

                                    With

With a new buttery hatch, that opens once in four or
      five days,
And a new Frenck cook, to devife fine kickfhaws, and
      toys ;
      Like a young courtier, &c.

With a new fafhion, when Chriftmas is drawing on,
On a new journey to London ftraight we all muft begone,
And leave none to keep houfe, but our new porter John,
Who relieves the poor with a thump on the back with
      a ftone ;
      Like a young courtier, &c.

With a new gentleman-ufher, whofe carriage is com-
      pleat,
With a new coachman, footmen, and pages to carry up
      the meat,
With a waiting-gentlewoman, whofe dreffing is very neat,
Who when her lady has din'd, lets the fervants not eat;
      Like a young courtier, &c.

With new titles of honour bought with his father's old
      gold,
For which fundry of his anceftors old manors are fold ;
And this is the courfe moft of our new gallants hold,
Which makes that good houfe-keeping is now grown fo
      cold,
      Among the young courtiers of the king,
      Or the king's young courtiers.

IX. Sir

IX.

SIR JOHN SUCKLING's CAMPAIGNE.

When the Scottish covenanters rose up in arms, and advanced to the English borders in 1639, many of the courtiers complimented the king by raising forces at their own expence. Among these none were more distinguished than the gallant Sir John Suckling, who raised a troop of horse, so richly accoutred, that it cost him 12,000 l. The like expensive equipment of other parts of the army, made the king remark, that "the Scots would fight stoutly, if it were but "for the Englishmen's fine cloaths." [Lloyd's memoirs.] When they came to action, the rugged Scots proved more than a match for the fine shewy English: many of whom behaved remarkably ill, and among the rest this splendid troop of Sir John Suckling's.

This humorous pasquil has been generally supposed to have been written by Sir John, as a banter upon himself. Some of his contemporaries however attributed it to Sir John Mennis, a wit of those times, among whose poems it is printed in a small poetical miscellany intitled, "Musarum "deliciæ : or the muses recreation, containing several pieces "of poetique wit. 2d edition.—By Sir J. M. [Sir John "Mennis] and Ja. S. [James Smith.] Lond. 1656. "12mo."———[See Wood's Athenæ. II. 397. 418.] In that copy is subjoined an additional stanza, which probably was written by this Sir John Mennis, viz.

" But

" *But now there is peace, he's return'd to increase*
" *His money, which lately he spent-a,*
" *But his lost honour must lye still in the dust;*
" *At Barwick away it went-a.*"

SIR John he got him an ambling nag,
To Scotland for to ride-a,
With a hundred horse more, all his own he swore,
To guard him on every side-a.

No Errant-knight ever went to fight   5
With halfe so gay a bravado,
Had you seen but his look, you'ld have sworn on a book,
Hee'ld have conquer'd a whole armado.

The ladies ran all to the windows to see
So gallant and warlike a sight-a,   10
And as he pass'd by, they said with a sigh,
Sir John, why will you go fight-a?

But he, like a cruel knight, spurr'd on;
His heart would not relent-a,
For, till he came there, what had he to fear?   15
Or why should he repent-a?

The king (God bless him!) had singular hopes
Of him and all his troop-a:
The borderers they, as they met him on the way,
For joy did hollow, and whoop-a.   20

None

None lik'd him fo well, as his own colonell,
   Who took him for John de Wert-a;
But when there were fhows of gunning and blows,
   My gallant was fo nothing pert-a.

For when the Scots army came within fight,   25
   And all prepared to fight-a,
He ran to his tent, they afk'd what he meant,
   He fwore he muft needs goe fh*te-a.

The colonell fent for him back agen,
   To quarter him in the van-a,   30
But Sir John did fwear, he would not come there,
   To be kill'd the very firft man-a.

To cure his fear, he was fent to the reare,
   Some ten miles back, and more-a;
Where Sir John did play at trip and away,   35
   And ne'er faw the enemy more-a.

Ver. 22. JOHN DE WERT *was a German general of great repu-
tation, and the terror of the French in the reign of Louis* XIII.
Hence his name became proverbial in France, where he was called
De Vert. *See Bayle's Dict.*

X.

TO ALTHEA FROM PRISON.

This excellent sonnet, which possessed a high degree of fame among the old Cavaliers, was written by Colonel Richard Lovelace during his confinement in the gate-house Westminster: to which he was committed by the house of Commons, in April 1642, for presenting a petition from the county of Kent, requesting them to restore the king to his rights, and to settle the government. See Wood's Athenæ, Vol. II. p. 228; where may be seen at large the affecting story of this elegant writer, who after having been distinguished for every gallant and polite accomplishment, the pattern of his own sex, and the darling of the ladies, died in the lowest wretchedness, obscurity, and want, in 1658.

This song is printed from a scarce volume of his poems intitled, " Lucasta, 1649. 12mo." collated with a copy in the editor's folio MS.

WHEN love with unconfined wings
   Hovers within my gates,
And my divine Althea brings
   To whisper at my grates ;
When I lye tangled in her haire,   5
   And fetter'd with her eye,
The birds that wanton in the aire,
   Know no such libertye.

When flowing cups run fwiftly round
  With no allaying thames,   10
Our careleffe heads with rofes crown'd,
  Our hearts with loyal flames ;
When thirfty griefe in wine we fteepe,
  When healths and draughts goe free,
Fifhes, that tipple in the deepe,   15
  Know no fuch libertìe.

When, linnet-like, confined I
  With fhriller note fhall fing
The mercye, fweetnefs, majeftye,
  And glories of my king ;   20
When I fhall voyce aloud how good,
  He is, how great fhould be,
Th' enlarged windes, that curle the flood,
  Know no fuch libertìe.

Stone walls doe not a prifon make,   25
  Nor iron barres a cage,
Mindes, innocent, and quiet, take
  That for an hermitage :
If I·have freedom in my love,
  And in my foule am free,   30
Angels alone, that foare above,
  Enjoy fuch libertìe.

XI. THE

Ver. 10. with woe-allaying themes. MS,

XI.

THE DOWNFALL OF CHARING-CROSS.

Charing-cross, as it stood before the civil wars, was one of those beautiful Gothic obelisks erected to conjugal affection by Edward I. who built such a one wherever the herse of his beloved Eleanor rested in its way from Lincolnshire to Westminster. But neither its ornamental situation, the beauty of its structure, nor the noble design of its erection (which did honour to humanity) could preserve it from the merciless zeal of the times: For in 164 . . it was demolished by order of the House of Commons, as popish and superstitious. This occasioned the following not-unhumorous sarcasm, which has been often printed among the popular sonnets of those times.

The plot referred to in ver. 17. was that entered into by Mr. Waller the poet, and others, with a view to reduce the city and tower to the service of the king; for which two of them, Nath. Tomkins, and Rich. Chaloner, suffered death July 5. 1643. Vid. Ath. Ox. II. 24.

UNdone, undone the lawyers are,
   They wander about the towne,
Nor can find the way to Westminster,
   Now Charing-crofs is downe:
At the end of the Strand, they make a stand,   5
   Swearing they are at a lofs,
And chaffing fay, that's not the way,
   They must go by Charing-crofs.

       The

The parliament to vote it down
  Conceived it very fitting,   10
For fear it fhould fall, and kill them all,
  In the houfe, as they were fitting.
They were told god-wot, it had a plot,
  Which made them fo hard-hearted,
To give command, it fhould not ftand,   15
  But be taken down and carted.

Men talk of plots, this might have been worfe
  For any thing I know,
Than that Tomkins, and Chaloner
  Were hang'd for long agoe.   20
Our parliament did that prevent,
  And wifely them defended,
For plots they will difcover ftill,
  Before they were intended.

But neither man, woman, nor child,   25
  Will fay, I'm confident,
They ever heard it fpeak one word
  Againft the parliament.
An informer fwore, it letters bore,
  Or elfe it had been freed ;   30
In troth I'll take my Bible oath,
  It could neither write, nor read.

The committee faid, that verily
    To popery it was bent;
For ought I know, it might be fo,   35
    For to church it never went.
What with excife, and fuch device,
    The kingdom doth begin
To think you'll leave them ne'er a crofs,
    Without doors nor within.   40

Methinks the common-council fhou'd
    Of it have taken pity,
'Caufe, good old crofs, it always ftood
    So firmly to the city.
Since croffes you fo much difdain,   45
    Faith, if I were as you,
For fear the king fhould rule again,
    I'd pull down Tiburn too.

*** *Whitlocke fays, " May* 3. 1643, *Cheapfide crofs and " other croffes were voted down,"* &c. ———— *When this vote was put in execution does not appear, probably not till many months after Tomkins and Chaloner had fuffered. See above ver.* 18.

We had a very curious account of the pulling down of Cheapfide Crofs lately publifhed in one of the numbers of the GENTLEMAN'S MAGAZINE, 1766.

 XII. LOYAL-

XII.

LOYALTY CONFINED.

*This excellent old song is preserved in David Lloyd's
" Memoires of those that suffered in the cause of Charles I."
Lond. 1668. fol. p. 96.   He speaks of it as the composition
of a worthy personage, who suffered deeply in those times,
and was still living with no other reward than the conscience
of having suffered.   The author's name he has not mentioned, but, if tradition may be credited, this song was written by Sir ROGER L'ESTRANGE.—Some mistakes in Lloyd's
copy are corrected by two others, one in MS. the other in
the Westminster Drollery, or a Choice Collection of Songs
and Poems, 1671. 12mo.*

BEAT on, proud billows; Boreas blow;
    Swell, curled waves, high as Jove's roof;
Your incivility doth show,
    That innocence is tempest proof;
Though surly Nereus frown, my thoughts are calm; 5
Then strike, Affliction, for thy wounds are balm.

    That which the world miscalls a jail,
        A private closet is to me:
    Whilst a good conscience is my bail,
        And innocence my liberty: 10

Locks,

Locks, bars, and folitude together met,
Make me no prifoner, but an anchoret.

I, whilft I wifht to be retir'd,
    Into this private room was turn'd ;
As if their wifdoms had confpir'd   15
    The falamander fhould be burn'd ;
Or like thofe fophifts, that would drown a fifh,
I am conftrain'd to fuffer what I wifh.

The cynick loves his poverty ;
    The pelican her wildernefs ;   20
And 'tis the Indian's pride to be
    Naked on frozen Caucafus :
Contentment cannot fmart, Stoicks we fee
Make torments eafie to their apathy.

Thefe manacles upon my arm   25
    I, as my miftrefs' favours, wear ;
And for to keep my ancles warm,
    I have fome iron fhackles there :
Thefe walls are but my garrifon ; this cell,
Which men call jail, doth prove my citadel.   30

I'm in the cabinet lockt up,
    Like fome high-prized margarite,
Or, like the great mogul or pope,
    Am cloyfter'd up from publick fight :

Y 4

Retirement is a piece of majefty,   35
And thus, proud fultan, I'm as great as thee.

Here fin for want of food muft ftarve,
    Where tempting objects are not feen ;
And thefe ftrong walls do only ferve
    To keep vice out, and keep me in :   40
Malice of late's grown charitable fure,
I'm not committed, but am kept fecure.

So he that ftruck at Jafon's life,
    Thinking t' have made his purpofe fure,
By a malicious friendly knife   45
    Did only wound him to a cure :
Malice, I fee, wants wit ; for what is meant
Mifchief, oftimes proves favour by th' event.

When once my prince affliction hath,
    Profperity doth treafon feem ;   50
And to make fmooth fo rough a path,
    I can learn patience from him :
Now not to fuffer fhews no loyal heart,
When kings want eafe fubjects muft bear a part.

What though I cannot fee my king   55
    Neither in perfon or in coin ;
Yet contemplation is a thing,
    That renders what I have not, mine :

My

My king from me what adamant can part,
Whom I do wear engraven on my heart ?   60

Have you not feen the nightingale,
    A prifoner like, coopt in a cage,
How doth fhe chaunt her wonted tale
    In that her narrow hermitage ?
Even then her charming melody doth prove,   65
That all her bars are trees, her cage a grove.

I am that bird, whom they combine
    Thus to deprive of liberty ;
But though they do my corps confine,
    Yet maugre heat, my foul is free :   70
And though immur'd, yet can I chirp, and fing
Difgrace to rebels, glory to my king.

My foul is free, as ambient air,
    Although my bafer part's immew'd,
Whilft loyal thoughts do ftill repair   75
    T' accompany my folitude :
Although rebellion do my body binde,
My king alone can captivate my minde.

XIII. VERSES

XIII.

VERSES BY K. CHARLES I.

*" This prince, like his father, did not confine himself to
" prose : Bishop Burnet has given as a pathetic elegy said
" to be written by Charles in Carisbrook castle [in 1648.]
" The poetry is most uncouth and unharmonious, but there are
" strong thoughts in it, some good sense, and a strain of ma-
" jestic piety." Mr. Walpole's Royal and Noble Authors,
vol. I.*

*It is in his " Memoirs of the Dukes of Hamilton," p. 379.
that Burnet hath preserved this elegy, which he tells us he
had from a gentleman, who waited on the king at the time
when it was written, and copied it out from the original. It
is there intitled " MAJESTY IN MISERY : OR AN
" IMPLORATION TO THE KING OF KINGS."*

*Hume hath remarked of these stanzas, " that the truth of
" the sentiment, rather than the elegance of the expression,
" renders them very pathetic." See his hist. 1763. 4to.
vol. 5. p. 437. 442. which is no bad comment upon them.
—These are almost the only verses known of Charles's composure. Indeed a little Poem ON A QUIET CONSCIENCE,
printed in the Poetical Calendar, 1763. vol. 8th. is attributed
to K. CHARLES I; but I know not upon what authority.*

GReat monarch of the world, from whose power springs
    The potency and power of kings,
Record the royal woe my suffering sings ;

I

And

And teach my tongue, that ever did confine
Its faculties in truth's feraphick line,   5
To track the treafons of thy foes and mine.

Nature and law, by thy divine decree,
(The only root of righteous royaltie)
With this dim diadem invefted me:

With it, the facred fcepter, purple robe,   10
The holy unction, and the royal globe:
Yet am I levell'd with the life of Job.

The fierceft furies, that do daily tread
Upon my grief, my gray difcrowned head,
Are thofe that owe my bounty for their bread.   15

They raife a war, and chriften it THE CAUSE,
While facrilegious hands have beft applaufe,
Plunder and murder are the kingdom's laws;

Tyranny bears the title of taxation,
Revenge and robbery are reformation,   20
Oppreffion gains the name of fequeftration.

My loyal fubjects, who in this bad feafon
Attend me (by the law of God and reafon),
They dare impeach, and punifh for high treafon.

Next

Next at the clergy do their furies frown,   25
Pious epifcopacy muft go down,
They will deftroy the crofier and the crown.

Churchmen are chain'd, and fchifmaticks are freed,
Mechanicks preach, and holy fathers bleed,
The crown is crucified with the creed.   30

The church of England doth all factions fofter,
The pulpit is ufurpt by each impoftor,
Extempore excludes the *Pater-nofter*.

The Prefbyter, and Independent feed
Springs with broad blades. To make the religion bleed 35
Herod and Pontius Pilate are agreed.

The corner ftone's mifplac'd by every pavier:
With fuch a bloody method and behaviour
Their anceftors did crucifie our Saviour.

My royal confort, from whofe fruitful womb   40
So many princes legally have come,
Is forc'd in pilgrimage to feek a tomb.

Great Britain's heir is forced into France,
Whilft on his father's head his foes advance:
Poor child! he weeps out his inheritance.   45

With my own power my majefty they wound,
In the king's name the king himfelf's uncrown'd :
So doth the duft deftroy the diamond.

With propofitions daily they enchant
My people's ears, fuch as do reafon daunt,   50
And the Almighty will not let me grant.

They promife to erect my royal ftem,
To make me great, t' advance my diadem,
If I will firft fall down, and worfhip them !

But for refufal they devour my thrones,   55
Diftrefs my children, and deftroy my bones ;
I fear they'll force me to make bread of ftones.

My life they prize at fuch a flender rate,
That in my abfence they draw bills of hate,
To prove the king a traytor to the ftate.   60

Felons obtain more privilege than I,
They are allow'd to anfwer ere they die ;
'Tis death for me to afk the reafon, why.

But, facred Saviour, with thy words I woo
Thee to forgive, and not be bitter to   65
Such, as thou know'ft do not know what they do.

For

For since they. from their lord are so disjointed,
As to contemn those edicts he appointed,
How can they prize the power of his anointed ?

Augment my patience, nullifie my hate,   70
Preserve my issue, and inspire my mate,
Yet though we perish, BLESS THIS CHURCH and STATE.

XIV.

THE SALE of REBELLIOUS HOUSHOLD-STUFF

*This sarcastic exultation of triumphant loyalty, is printed
from an old black-letter copy in the Pepys collection, corrected by two others, one of which is preserved in " A choice
collection of 120 loyal songs, &c." 1684. 12mo.*—To the
tune of Old Simon the king.

R Ebellion hath broken up house,
    And hath left me old lumber to sell ;
Come hither, and take your choice,
   I'll promise to use you well:
Will you buy the old speaker's chair ?   5
   Which was warm and easie to sit in,
And oft hath been clean'd I declare,
   When as it was fouler than fitting.
     Says old Simon the king, &c.

Will

Will you buy any bacon-flitches,   10
   The fatteft, that ever were fpent ?
They're the fides of the old committees,
   Fed up in the long parliament.
Here's a pair of bellows, and tongs,
   And for a fmall matter I'll fell ye 'um ;   15
They are made of the prefbyters lungs,
   To blow up the coals of rebellion.
      Says old Simon, &c.

I had thought to have given them once
   To fome black-fmith for his forge ,   20
But now I have confidered on't,
   They are confecrate to the church :
So I'll give them unto fome quire,
   They will make the big organs roar,
And the little pipes to fqueeke higher,   25
   Than ever they could before.
      Says old Simon, &c.

Here's a couple of ftools for fale,
   One's fquare, and t'other is round ;
Betwixt them both the tail   30
   Of the RUMP fell down to the ground.
Will you buy the ftates council-table,
   Which was made of the good wain Scot ?
The frame was a tottering Babel
   To uphold the Independent plot.   35
      Says old Simon, &c.

                       Here's

Here's the beeſom of Reformation,
    Which ſhould have made clean the floor,
But it ſwept the wealth out of the nation,
    And left us dirt good ſtore.   40
Will you buy the ſtates ſpinning-wheel,
    Which ſpun for the ropers trade?
But better it had ſtood ſtill,
    For now it has ſpun a fair thread.
           Says old Simon, &c.   45

Here's a glyſter-pipe well try'd,
    Which was made of a butcher's ſtump *,
And has been ſafely apply'd,
    To cure the colds of the rump.
Here's a lump of Pilgrims-Salve,   50
    Which once was a juſtice of peace,
Who Noll and the Devil did ſerve;
    But now it is come to this.
           Says old Simon, &c.

Here's a roll of the ſtates tobacco,   55
    If any good fellow will take it;
No Virginia had e'er ſuch a ſmack-o,
    And I'll tell you how they did make it:

* *Alluding probably to Major-General Harriſon a butcher's ſon, who aſſiſted Cromwell in turning out the long parliament, Ap. 20. 1653.*

'Tis

'Tis th' Engagement, and Covenant cookt
   Up with the Abjuration oath ;   60
And many of them, that have took't,
   Complain it was foul in the mouth.
      Says old Simon, &c.

Yet the afhes may happily ferve
   To cure the fcab of the nation,   65
Whene'er 't has an itch to fwerve
   To Rebellion by Innovation.
A Lanthorn here is to be bought,
   The like was fcarce ever gotten,
For many plots it has found out   70
   Before they ever were thought on.
      Says old Simon, &c.

Will you buy the RUMP's great faddle,
   With which it jocky'd the nation ?
And here is the bitt, and the bridle,   75
   And curb of Diffimulation :
And here's the trunk-hofe of the RUMP,
   And their fair diffembling cloak,
And a Prefbyterian jump,
   With an Independent fmock.   80
      Says old Simon, &c.

Will you buy a Confcience oft turn'd,
   Which ferv'd the high-court of juftice,
And ftretch'd until England it mourn'd :
   But Hell will buy that if the worft is,   85

<table>
<tr><td>VOL. II.</td><td>Z</td><td>Here's</td></tr>
</table>

Here's Joan Cromwell's kitching-ftuff tub,
   Wherein is the fat of the Rumpers,
With which old Noll's horns fhe did rub,
   When fhe was got drunk with falfe bumpers.
     Says old Simon, &c.   90

Here's the purfe of the public faith ;
   Here's the model of the Sequeftration,
When the old wives upon their good troth,
   Lent thimbles to ruine the nation.
Here's Dick Cromwell's Protectorfhip,   95
   And here are Lambert's commiffions,
And here is Hugh Peters his fcrip
   Cramm'd with the tumultuous Petitions.
     Says old Simon, &c.

And here are old Noll's brewing veffels,   100
   And here are his dray, and his flings ;
Here are Hewfon's awl, and his brifles ;
   With diverfe other odd things :
And what is the price doth belong
   To all thefe matters before ye ?   105
I'll fell them all for an old fong,
   And fo I do end my ftory.
     Says old Simon, &c.

XV. THE

Ver. 86. This was a cant name given to Cromwell's wife by the Royalifts, tho' her name was Elizabeth : to the latter part of the verfe hangs fome tale that is now forgotten.

Ver. 94. See Grey's Hudibras, Pt. 1. Cant. 2. ver. 570. &c.

Ver. 100. 102. Cromwell had in his younger years followed the brewing trade at Huntingdon. Col. Hewfon is faid to have been originally a cobler.

XV.

THE BAFFLED KNIGHT, or LADY's POLICY.

Given (with some corrections) from a MS copy, and collated with two printed ones in Roman character in the Pepys collection.

THERE was a knight was drunk with wine,
    A riding along the way, sir;
And there he met with a lady fine,
    Among the cocks of hay, sir.

Shall you and I, O lady faire,   5
    Among the grass lye downe-a:
And I will have a special care
    Of rumpling of your gowne-a.

Upon the grass there is a dewe,
    Will spoil my damask gowne, sir: 10
My gown, and kirtle they are newe,
    And cost me many a crowne, sir.

I have a cloak of scarlet red,
    Upon the ground I'll throwe it;
Then, lady faire, come lay thy head;   15
    We'll play, and none shall knowe it.

Z 2

O yonder

O yonder ſtands my ſteed ſo free
  Among the cocks of hay, ſir ;
And if the pinner ſhould chance to ſee,
  He'll take my ſteed away, ſir.   20

Upon my finger I have a ring,
  Its made of fineſt gold-a ;
And, lady, it thy ſteed ſhall bring
  Out of the pinner's fold-a.

O go with me to my father's hall ;   25
  Fair chambers there are three, ſir :
And you ſhall have the beſt of all,
  And I'll your chamberlaine bee, ſir.

He mounted himſelf on his ſteed ſo tall,
  And her on her dapple gray, ſir :   30
And there they rode to her father's hall,
  Faſt pricking along the way, ſir.

To her father's hall they arrived ſtrait ;
  'Twas moated round about-a ;
She ſlipped herſelf within the gate,   35
  And lockt the knight without-a.

Here is a ſilver penny to ſpend,
  And take it for your pain, ſir ;
And two of my father's men I'll ſend
  To wait on you back again, ſir.   40

                                                    He

He from his fcabbard drew his brand,
    And whet it upon his fleeve-a :
And curfed, he faid, be every man,
    That will a maid believe-a !

She drew a bodkin from her haire,   45
    And whip'd it upon her gown-a ;
And curft be every maiden faire,
    That will with men lye down-a !

A tree there is, that lowly grows,
    And fome do call it rue, fir :   50
The fmalleft dunghill cock that crows,
    Would make a capon of you, fir.

A flower there is, that fhineth bright,
    Some call it mary-gold-a :
He that wold not when he might,   55
    He fhall not when he wold-a.

The knight was riding another day,
    With cloak and hat and feather :
He met again with that lady gay,
    Who was angling in the river.   60

Now, lady faire, I've met with you,
    You fhall no more efcape me ;
Remember, how not long agoe
    You falfely did intrap me.

Z 3

The

The lady blufhed fcarlet red,   65
  And trembled at the ftranger:
How fhall I guard my maidenhed
  From this approaching danger?

He from his faddle down did light,
  In all his riche attyer;   70
And cryed, As I am a noble knight,
  I do thy charms admyer.

He took the lady by the hand,
  Who feemingly confented;
And would no more difputing ftand: 75
  She had a plot invented.

Locke yonder, good fir knight, I pray,
  Methinks I now difcover
A riding upon his dapple gray,
  My former conftant lover.   80

On tip-toe peering ftood the knight,
  Faft by the rivers brink-a;
'The lady pufht with all her might:
  Sir knight, now fwim or fink-a.

O'er head and ears he plunged in,   85
  The bottom faire he founded;
Then rifing up, he cried amain,
  Help, helpe, or elfe I'm drowned!

          Now,

Now, fare-you-well, fir knight, adieu!
    You fee what comes of fooling: 90
That is the fitteft place for you;
    Your courage wanted cooling.

Ere many days, in her fathers park,
    Juft at the clofe of eve-a,
Again fhe met with her angry fparke;   95
    Which made this lady grieve-a.

Falfe lady, here thou'rt in my powre,
    And no one now can hear thee:
And thou fhalt forely rue the hour,
    That e'er thou dar'dft to jeer me.   100

I pray, fir knight, be not fo warm
    With a young filly maid-a:
I vow and fwear I thought no harm,
    'Twas a gentle jeft I playd-a.

A gentle jeft, in foothe! he cry'd,   105
    To tumble me in and leave me:
What if I had in the river dy'd? ——
    That fetch will not deceive me.

Once more I'll pardon thee this day,
    Tho' injur'd out of meafure;   110
But then prepare without delay
    To yield thee to my pleafure.

Z 4

Well

Well then, if I muſt grant your ſuit,
   Yet think of your boots and ſpurs, ſir:
Let me pull off both ſpur and boot,   115
   Or elſe you cannot ſtir, ſir.

He ſet him down upon the graſs,
   And begg'd her kind aſſiſtance:
Now, ſmiling thought this lovely laſs,
   I'll make you keep your diſtance.   120

'Then pulling off his boots half-way;
   Sir knight, now I'm your betters:
You ſhall not make of me your prey;
   Sit there like a knave in fetters.

The knight when ſhe had ſerved ſoe,   125
   He fretted, fum'd, and grumbled:
For he could neither ſtand nor goe,
   But like a cripple tumbled.

Farewell, ſir knight, the clock ſtrikes ten,
   Yet do not move nor ſtir, ſir: 130
I'll ſend you my father's ſerving men,
   To pull off your boots and ſpurs, ſir.

This merry jeſt you muſt excuſe,
   You are but a ſtingleſs nettle:
You'd never have ſtood for boots or ſhoes,   135
   Had you been a man of mettle.

All

All night in grievous rage he lay,
　　Rolling upon the plain-a ;
Next morning a fhepherd paft that way,
　　Who fet him right again-a.   140

Then mounting upon his fteed fo tall,
　　By hill and dale he fwore-a :
I'll ride at once to her father's hall ;
　　She fhall efcape no more-a.

I'll take her father by the beard,   145
　　I'll challenge all her kindred ;
Each daftard foul fhall ftand affeard ;
　　My wrath fhall no more be hindred.

He rode unto her father's houfe,
　　Which every fide was moated :   150
The lady heard his furious vows,
　　And all his vengeance noted.

Thought fhee, fir knight, to quench your rage,
　　Once more I will endeavour ;
This water fhall your fury 'fwage,   155
　　Or elfe it fhall burn for ever.

Then faining penitence and feare,
　　She did invite a parley :
Sir knight, if you'll forgive me heare,
　　Henceforth I'll love you dearly.   160

My

My father he is now from home,
  And I am all alone, fir:
Therefore a-crofs the water come;
  And I am all your own, fir.

Falfe maid, thou canft no more deceive;   165
  I fcorn the treacherous bait-a:
If thou would'ft have me thee believe,
  Now open me the gate-a.

The bridge is drawn, the gate is barr'd,
  My father he has the keys, fir.   170
But I have for my love prepar'd
  A fhorter way and eafier.

Over the moate I've laid a plank
  Full feventeen feet in meafure:
Then ftep a-crofs to the other bank,   175
  And there we'll take our pleafure.

Thefe words fhe had no fooner fpoke,
  But ftrait he came tripping over:
The plank was faw'd, it fnapping broke;
  And fous'd the unhappy lover.   180

⁂

XVI. W H Y

XVI.

WHY SO PALE?

From Sir John Suckling's poems. This sprightly knight was born in 1613, *and cut off by a fever about the* 29th *year of his age. See above, pag.* 318.

WHY so pale and wan, fond lover?
    Prethee, why so pale?
Will, when looking well can't move her,
    Looking ill prevail?
    Prethee why so pale?   5

Why so dull and mute, young sinner?
    Prethee why so mute?
Will, when speaking well can't win her,
    Saying nothing doe't?
    Prethee why so mute?   10

Quit, quit for shame; this will not move,
    This cannot take her;
If of herself she will not love,
    Nothing can make her.
    The devil take her!   15

XVII. OLD

XVII.

OLD TOM OF BEDLAM.

MAD SONG THE FIRST.

*It is worth attention, that the English have more songs
and ballads on the subject of madness, than any of their
neighbours.   Whether it is that we are more liable to this
calamity than other nations, or whether our native gloominess
hath peculiarly recommended subjects of this cast to our writers, the fact is incontestable, as any one may be satisfied,
who will compare the printed collections of French, Italian
Songs, &c. with those in our language.*

*Out of a much larger quantity, we have selected half a
dozen* MAD SONGS *for these volumes.   The three first are
originals in their respective kinds ;   the merit of the three last
is chiefly that of imitation.   They were written at considerable intervals of time ;   but we have here grouped them together, that the reader may the better examine their compa-
rative merits.   He may consider them as so many trials of
skill in a very peculiar subject, as the contest of so many ri-
vals to shoot in the bow of Ulysses.   The two first were probably written about the beginning of the last century ;   the
third about the middle of it ;   the fourth and sixth towards
the end ;   and the fifth within this present century.*

*This is given from the editor's folio MS. compared with
two or three old printed copies.—With regard to the author
of this old rhapsody, in Walton's Compleat Angler, cap.* 3. *is*

a song

a song in praise of angling, which the author says was made at his request " by Mr. WILLIAM BASSE, *one that has " made the choice songs of the* HUNTER IN HIS CAREER, *" and of* TOM OF BEDLAM, *and many others of note."* p. 84. *See Mr.* HAWKINS'*s curious Edition, 8vo. of this excellent old Piece.*

FORTH from my sad and darksome cell,
   Or from the deepe abysse of hell,
Mad Tom is come into the world againe
To see if he can cure his distempered braine.

   Feares and cares oppresse my soule :   5
Harke, howe the angrye Fureys houle !
Pluto laughes, and Proserpine is gladd
To see poore naked Tom of Bedlam madd.

Through the world I wander night and day
   To seeke my straggling senses,   10
In an angrye moode I mett old Time,
   With his pentarchye of tenses :

   When me he spyed,
   Away he hyed,
For time will stay for no man :   15
   In vaine with cryes
   I rent the skyes,
For pity is not common.

   Cold and comfortless I lye :
   Helpe, oh helpe ! or else I dye !   20
             Harke !

Harke! I heare Apollo's teame,
   The carman 'gins to whiſtle;
Chaſt Diana bends her bowe,
   The boare begins to briſtle.

Come, Vulcan, with tools and with tackles,   25
To knocke off my troubleſome ſhackles;
Bid Charles make ready his waine
To fetch me my ſenſes againe.

   Laſt night I heard the dog-ſtar bark;
Mars met Venus in the darke;   30
Limping Vulcan het an iron barr,
And furiouſlye made at the god of war:

   Mars with his weapon laid about,
But Vulcan's temples had the gout,
For his broad horns did ſo hang in his light,   36.
He could not ſee to aim his blowes aright:

Mercurye the nimble poſt of heaven,
   Stood ſtill to ſee the quarrell;
Gorrel-bellyed Bacchus, gyant-like,
   Beſtryd a ſtrong-beere barrell.   40

   To mee he dranke,
   I did him thanke,
But I could get no cyder;

He

He dranke whole butts
  'Till he burſt his gutts,   45
But mine were ne'er the wyder.

Poore naked Tom is very drye:
A little drinke for charitye!

Harke, I hear Acteons horne!
  The huntſmen whoop and hallowe: 50
Ringwood, Royſter, Bowman, Jowler,
  All the chaſe do followe.

The man in the moone drinkes clarret,
Eates powder'd beef, turnip, and carret,
But a cup of old Malaga ſacke   55
Will fire the buſhe at his backe.

XVIII.

THE DISTRACTED PURITAN,

MAD SONG THE SECOND,

—was written about the beginning of the ſeventeenth century by the witty biſhop Corbet, and is printed from the 3d edition of his poems, 12mo. 1672. compared with a more ancient copy in the editor's folio MS.

A M

A M I mad, O noble Feſtus,
    When zeal and godly knowledge
Have put me in hope
To deal with the pope,
As well as the beſt in the college ?   5
    Boldly I preach, hate a croſs, hate a ſurplice,
        Mitres, copes, and rochets ;
    Come hear me pray nine times a day,
        And fill your heads with crochets.

In the houſe of pure Emanuel *   10
I had my education,
    Where my friends ſurmiſe
    I dazel'd my eyes
With the ſight of revelation.
    Boldly I preach, &c.

They bound me like a bedlam,   15
They laſh'd my four poor quarters ;
    Whilſt this I endure,
    Faith makes me ſure
To be one of Foxes martyrs.
    Boldly I preach, &c.

Theſe injuries I ſuffer   20
Through antichriſt's perſwaſion :
                                            Take

* *Emanuel college Cambridge was originally a ſeminary of Puritans.*

Take off this chain,
Neither Rome nor Spain
Can refift my ftrong invafion.
   Boldly I preach, &c.

Of the beafts ten horns (God blefs us!)   25
I have knock'd off three already;
   If they let me alone
   I'll leave none:
But they fay I am too heady.
   Boldly I preach, &c.

When I fack'd the feven-hill'd city,   30
I met the great red dragon;
   I kept him aloof
   With the armour of proof,
Though here I have never a rag on.
   Boldly I preach, &c.

With a fiery fword and target,   35
There fought I with this monfter:
   But the fons of pride
   My zeal deride,
And all my deeds mifconfter.
   Boldly I preach, &c.

I un-hors'd the Whore of Babel,   40
With the lance of Infpiration;

I made her ftink,
And fpill the drink
In her cup of abomination.
   Boldly I preach, &c.

I have feen two in a vifion   45
With a flying book * between them.
   I have been in defpair
   Five times in a year,
And been cur'd by reading Greenham †.
   Boldly I preach, &c.

I obferv'd in Perkins tables ‡   50
The black line of damnation;
   Thofe crooked veins
   So ftuck in my brains,
That I fear'd my reprobation.
   Boldly I preach, &c.

In

---

   * *Alluding to fome vifionary expofition of Zech. ch. v. ver. 1. or, if the date of this fong would permit, one might fuppofe it aimed at one Coppe, a ftrange enthufiaft, whofe life may be feen in Wood's Athen. vol. 2. p. 501. He was author of a book intitled, " The fiery flying Roll:" and afterwards publifhed a Recantation, part of whofe Title is, " The fiery flying Roll's wings clipt," &c.*

   † *See Greenham's works, fol. 1605. particularly the tract intitled, " A fweet comfort for an afflicted confcience."*

   ‡ *See Perkins's works, fol. 1616. vol. 1. p. 11; where is a large half-fheet folded, containing " A furvey, or table declaring the order of " the caufes of falvation, and damnation, &c." the pedigree of damnation being diftinguifhed by a broad black zig-zag line.*

In the holy tongue of Canaan　　　　　55
I plac'd my chiefest pleasure :
　　Till I prick'd my foot
　　With an Hebrew root,
That I bled beyond all measure.
　　　Boldly I preach, &c.

I appear'd before the archbishop *,　　　60
And all the high commission ;
　　I gave him no grace,
　　But told him to his face,
That he favour'd superstition.
　　　Boldly I preach, hate a cross, hate a surplice,
　　Miters, copes, and rotchets :
　　　Come hear me pray nine times a day,
　　And fill your heads with crotchets.

* Laud.

XIX.

THE LUNATIC LOVER,

MAD SONG THE THIRD,

———*is given from an old printed copy in the British Museum,
compared with another in the Pepys collection; both in black
letter.*

GRIM king of the ghosts, make haste,
   And bring hither all your train;
See how the pale moon does waste,
   And just now is in the wane.
Come, you night-hags, with all your charms,   5
   And revelling witches away,
And hug me close in your arms;
   To you my respects I'll pay.

I'll court you, and think you fair,
   Since love does distract my brain: 10
I'll go, I'll wed the night-mare,
   And kiss her, and kiss her again:

But

But if fhe prove peevifh and proud,
  Then, a pife on her love! let her go;
I'll feek me a winding fhroud,   15
  And down to the fhades below.

A lunacy fad I endure,
  Since reafon departs away;
I call to thofe hags for a cure,
  As knowing not what I fay.   20
The beauty, whom I do adore,
  Now flights me with fcorn and difdain;
I never fhall fee her more:
  Ah! how fhall I bear my pain!

I ramble, and range about   25
  To find out my charming faint;
While fhe at my grief does flout,
  And fmiles at my loud complaint.
Diftraction I fee is my doom,
  Of this I am now too fure;   30
A rival is got in my room,
  While torments I do endure.

Strange fancies do fill my head,
  While wandering in defpair,
I am to the defarts lead,   35
  Expecting to find her there.

A a 3   Methinks

Methinks in a fpangled cloud
   I fee her enthroned on high ;
Then to her I crie aloud,
   And labour to reach the fky.

When thus I have raved awhile,
   And wearyed myfelf in vain,
I lye on the barren foil,
   And bitterly do complain.
Till flumber hath quieted me,
   In forrow I figh and weep;
The clouds are my canopy
   To cover me while I fleep.

I dream that my charming fair
   Is then in my rival's bed,
Whofe treffes of golden hair
   Are on the fair pillow befpread.
Then this doth my paffion inflame,
   I ftart, and no longer can lie :
Ah ! Sylvia, art thou not to blame
   To ruin a lover ? I cry.

Grim king of the ghofts, be true,
   And hurry me hence away,
My languifhing life to you
   A tribute I freely pay.

To the elysian shades I post
  In hopes to be freed from care,
Where many a bleeding ghost
  Is hovering in the air.

XX.

THE LADY DISTRACTED WITH LOVE,

MAD SONG THE FOURTH,

————*was originally sung in one of* TOM D'URFEY'S *comedies of Don Quixote acted in* 1694 *and* 1696 ; *and probably composed by himself. In the several stanzas, the author represents his pretty Mad-woman as* 1. *sullenly mad:* 2. *mirthfully mad:* 3. *melancholy mad:* 4. *fantastically mad: and* 5. *stark mad. Both this, and Num. XXII. are printed from D'urfey's " Pills to purge Melancholy."* 1719. *vol. I.*

FROM rosie bowers, where sleeps the god of love,
  Hither, ye little wanton cupids, fly;
Teach me in soft melodious strains to move
  With tender passion my heart's darling joy:
Ah! let the soul of musick tune my voice,   5
To win dear Strephon, who my soul enjoys.

A a 4

Or,

Or, if more influencing
  Is to be brisk and airy,
With a step and a bound,
With a frisk from the ground,   10
  I'll trip like any fairy.

As once on Ida dancing
  Were three celestial bodies :
With an air, and a face,
And a shape, and a grace,   15
  I'll charm, like beauty's goddess.

Ah ! 'tis in vain ! 'tis all, 'tis all in vain !
Death and despair must end the fatal pain :
Cold, cold despair, disguis'd like snow and rain,
Falls on my breast; bleak winds in tempests blow ; 20
My veins all shiver, and my fingers glow ;
My pulse beats a dead march for lost repose,
And to a solid lump of ice my poor fond heart is froze.

Or say, ye powers, my peace to crown,
Shall I thaw myself, and drown   25
  Among the foaming billows ?
Increasing all with tears I shed,
  On beds of ooze, and crystal pillows
Lay down, lay down my lovesick head ?

No, no, I'll strait run mad, mad, mad,   30
  That soon my heart will warm ;

When

When once the fenfe is fled, is fled,
   Love has no power to charm.
Wild thro' the woods I'll fly, I'll fly,
   Robes, locks——fhall thus——be tore !   35
A thoufand, thoufand times I'll dye
Ere thus, thus, in vain,—ere thus in vain adore.

XXI.

THE DISTRACTED LOVER,

MAD SONG THE FIFTH,

——*was written by* HENRY CAREY, *a celebrated compofer
of Mufic at the beginning of this century, and author of feveral little Theatrical Entertainments, which the reader
may find enumerated in the* " Companion to the Play-houfe,"
&c. *The fprightlinefs of this Songfter's fancy could not
preferve him from a very melancholy cataftrophe, which was
effected by his own hand. In his* POEMS, *4to. Lond.* 1729,
may be feen another Mad-Song of this author begining thus,
   " *Gods ! I can never this endure,*
   " *Death alone muft be my cure,* &c.

I Go to the Elyfian fhade,
   Where forrow ne'er fhall wound me ;
Where nothing fhall my reft invade,
   But joy fhall ftill furround me.

I fly

I fly from Celia's cold difdain,　　　　5
　　From her difdain I fly ;
She is the caufe of all my pain,
　　For her alone I die.

Her eyes are brighter than the mid-day fun,
When he but half his radiant courfe has run,　　10
When his meridian glories gaily fhine,
And gild all nature with a warmth divine,

　　See yonder river's flowing tide,
　　　　Which now fo full appears ;
　　Thofe ftreams, that do fo fwiftly glide,　　15
　　　　Are nothing but my tears.

There I have wept till I could weep no more,
And curft mine eyes, when they have wept their ftore,
Then, like the clouds, that rob the azure main,
I've drain'd the flood to weep it back again.　　20

　　　　Pity my pains,
　　　　Ye gentle fwains !
　　Cover me with ice and fnow,
　　I fcorch, I burn, I flame, I glow !

　　　　Furies, tear me,　　　　25
　　　　Quickly bear me
　　To the difmal fhades below !
　　　　Where yelling, and howling

And

And grumbling, and growling
Strike the ear with horrid woe.   30

Hiffing fnakes,
Fiery lakes
Would be a pleafure, and a cure :
Not all the hells,
Where Pluto dwells,   35
Can give fuch pain as I endure.

To fome peaceful plain convey me,
On a moffey carpet lay me,
Fan me with ambrofial breeze,
Let me die, and fo have eafe !   40

XXII.

THE FRANTIC LADY,

MAD SONG THE SIXTH.

*This, like Num. XX, was originally fung in one of
D'URFEY's Comedies of Don Quixote, (firft acted about the
year 1694), and was probably compofed by that popular
Songfter, who died Feb. 26. 1723.*

*This is printed from the " Hive, a Collection of Songs,"
4 vol. 1721. 12mo. where may be found two or three other
MAD Songs not admitted into thefe Volumes.*

I   I Burn,

I Burn, my brain confumes to afhes!
Each eye-ball too like lightning flafhes!
Within my breaft there glows a folid fire,
Which in a thoufand ages can't expire!

Blow, blow, the winds' great ruler! 5
Bring the Po, and the Ganges hither,
'Tis fultry weather,
Pour them all on my foul,
It will hifs like a coal,
But be never the cooler. 10

'Twas pride hot as hell,
That firft made me rebell,
From love's awful throne a curft angel I fell;
And mourn now my fate, 15
Which myfelf did create:
Fool, fool, that confider'd not when I was well!

Adieu! ye vain tranfporting joys!
Off ye vain fantaftic toys!
That drefs this face—this body—to allure!
Bring me daggers, poifon, fire! 20
Since fcorn is turn'd into defire.
All hell feels not the rage, which I, poor I, endure.

XX. LIL`

XXIII.

LILLI BURLERO.

The following rhymes, slight and insignificant as they may now seem, had once a more powerful effect than either the Philippics of Demosthenes, or Cicero; and contributed not a little towards the great revolution in 1688. Let us hear a contemporary writer.

" A foolish ballad was made at that time, treating the
" Papists, and chiefly the Irish, in a very ridiculous manner,
" which had a burden said to be Irish words, " Lero, lero,
" liliburlero," that made an impression on the [king's] army,
" that cannot be imagined by those that saw it not. The
" whole army, and at last the people both in city and country,
" were singing it perpetually. And perhaps never had so
" slight a thing so great an effect." Burnet.

It was written on occasion of the king's nominating to the lieutenancy of Ireland in 1686, general Talbot, newly created earl of Tyrconnel, a furious Papist, who had recommended himself to his bigotted master by his arbitrary treatment of the Protestants in the preceding year, when only lieutenant general; and whose subsequent conduct fully justified his ex-pectations and their fears. The violences of his administra-tion may be seen in any of the histories of those times : parti-cularly in bishop King's " State of the protestants in Ireland." 1691. 4to.

LILLIBURLERO and BULLEN-A-LAH are said to have been the words of distinction used among the Irish Papists in their massacre of the Protestants in 1641.

HO !

HO! broder Teague, doſt hear de decree?
    Lilli burlero bullen a-la.
Dat we ſhall have a new deputie,
    Lilli burlero bullen a-la.
      Lero lero, lilli burlero, lero lero, bullen a-la, 5
       Lero lero, lilli burlero, lero lero, bullen a-la.

Ho! by ſhaint Tyburn, it is de Talbote:
    Lilli, &c.
And he will cut all de Engliſh troate.
    Lilli, &c.   10

Dough by my ſhoul de Engliſh do praat,
    Lilli, &c.
De law's on dare ſide, and Creiſh knows what.
    Lilli, &c.

But if diſpence do come from de pope,   15
    Lilli, &c.
We'll hang Magna Charta, and dem in a rope.
    Lilli, &c.

For de good Talbot is made a lord,
    Lilli, &c.   20
And with brave lads is coming aboard:
    Lilli, &c.

Who all in France have taken a ſware,
    Lilli, &c.

                            Dat

Dat dey will have no proteſtant heir.   25
    Lilli, &c.

Ara! but why does he ſtay behind?
    Lilli, &c.
Ho! by my ſhoul 'tis a proteſtant wind.
    Lilli, &c.   30

But ſee de Tyrconnel is now come aſhore,
    Lilli, &c.
And we ſhall have commiſſions gillore.
    Lilli, &c.

And he dat will not go to de maſs,   35
    Lilli, &c.
Shall be turn out, and look like an aſs.
    Lilli, &c.

Now, now de hereticks all go down,
    Lilii, &c.   40
By Chriſh and ſhaint Patrick, de nation's our own.
    Lilli, &c.

Dare was an old propheſy found in a bog,
    Lilli, &c.
" Ireland ſhall be rul'd by an aſs, and a dog." 45
    Lilli, &c.

And

And now dis prophefy is come to pafs,
    Lilli, &c.
For Talbot's de dog, and Ja**s is de afs.
    Lilli, &c.   50

XXIV.

THE BRAES OF YARROW,

IN IMITATION OF THE ANCIENT SCOTS MANNER,

—*was written by William Hamilton of Bangour, Efq; who died March* 25. 1754. *aged* 50. *It is printed from an elegant edition of his Poems publifhed at Edinburgh,* 1760, 12*mo.*

A. BUSK ye, bufk ye, my bonny bonny bride,
    Bufk ye, bufk ye, my winfome marrow,
Bufk ye, bufk ye, my bonny bonny bride,
    And think nae mair on the Braes of Yarrow.

B. Where gat ye that bonny bonny bride?   5
    Where gat ye that winfome marrow?
A. I gat her where I dare na weil be feen,
    Puing the birks on the Braes of Yarrow.

Weep

Weep not, weep not, my bonny bonny bride,
   Weep not, weep not, my winfome marrow ;   10
Nor let thy heart lament to leive
   Puing the birks on the Braes of Yarrow.

B. Why does fhe weep, thy bonny bonny bride ?
   Why does fhe weep thy winfome marrow ?
And why dare ye nae mair weil be feen   15
   Puing the birks on the Braes of Yarrow ?

A. Lang maun fhe weep, lang maun fhe, maun fhe weep,
   Lang maun fhe weep with dule and forrow ;
And lang maun I nae mair weil be feen
   Puing the birks on the Braes of Yarrow.   20

For fhe has tint her luver, luver dear,
   Her luver dear, the caufe of forrow,
And I hae flain the comlieft fwain
   That eir pu'd birks on the Braes of Yarrow.

Why rins thy ftream, O Yarrow, Yarrow, reid ? 25
   Why on thy braes heard the voice of forrow ?
And why yon melancholious weids
   Hung on the bonny birks of Yarrow ?

What's yonder floats on the rueful rueful flude ?
   What's yonder floats ? O dule and forrow !   30
O 'tis he the comely fwain I flew
   Upon the duleful Braes of Yarrow.

Wafh, O wafh his wounds, his wounds in tears,
  His wounds in tears with dule and forrow;
And wrap his limbs in mourning weids,   35
  And lay him on the Braes of Yarrow.

Then build, then build, ye fifters, fifters fad,
  Ye fifters fad, his tomb with forrow;
And weep around in waeful wife
  His haplefs fate on the Braes of Yarrow.   40

Curfe ye, curfe ye, his ufelefs, ufelefs fhield,
  My arm that wrought the deed of forrow,
The fatal fpear that pierc'd his breaft,
  His comely breaft on the Braes of Yarrow.

Did I not warn thee, not to, not to luve?   45
  And warn from fight? but to my forrow
Too rafhly bauld a ftronger arm
  Thou mett'ft, and fell'ft on the Braes of Yarrow.

Sweet fmells the birk, green grows, green grows the
     grafs,
  Yellow on Yarrow's bank the gowan,   50
Fair hangs the apple frae the rock,
  Sweet the wave of Yarrow flowan.

Flows Yarrow fweet? as fweet, as fweet flows Tweed,
  As green its grafs, its gowan as yellow,

                              As

As fweet fmells on its braes the birk,   55
   The apple frae its rock as mellow.

Fair was thy luve, fair fair indeed thy luve,
   In flow'ry bands thou didſt him fetter;
Tho' he was fair, and weil beluv'd again
   Than me he never luv'd thee better.   60

Buſk ye, then buſk, my bouny bonny bride,
   Buſk ye, buſk ye, my winſome marrow,
Buſk ye, and luve me on the banks of Tweed,
   And think nae mair on the Braes of Yarrow.

C. How can I buſk a bonny bonny bride?   65
   How can I buſk a winſome marrow?
How luve him upon the banks of Tweed,
   That ſlew my luve on the Braes of Yarrow?

O Yarrow fields, may never never rain,
   Now dew thy tender bloſſoms cover,   70
For there was baſely ſlain my luve,
   My luve, as he had not been a lover.

The boy put on his robes, his robes of green,
   His purple veſt, 'twas my awn ſewing:
Ah! wretched me! I little, little kenn'd   75
   He was in theſe to meet his ruin.

B b 2

The

The boy took out his milk-white, milk-white fteed,
   Unheedful of my dule and forrow;
But ere the toofall of the night
   He lay a corps on the Braes of Yarrow.   80

Much I rejoyc'd that waeful waeful day;
   I fang, my voice the woods returning:
But lang ere night the fpear was flown,
   That flew my luve, and left me mourning.

What can my barbarous barbarous father do,   85
   But with his cruel rage purfue me?
My luver's blood is on thy fpear,
   How canft thou, barbarous man, then wooe me?

My happy fifters may be, may be proud
   With cruel, and ungentle fcoffin',   90
May bid me feek on Yarrow's Braes
   My luver nailed in his coffin.

My brother Douglas may upbraid, upbraid,
   And ftrive with threatning words to muve me:
My luver's blood is on thy fpear,   95
   How canft thou ever bid me luve thee?

Yes, yes, prepare the bed, the bed of luve,
   With bridal fheets my body cover,
Unbar, ye bridal maids, the door,
   Let in the expected hufbande lover.   100

But

But who the expected hufband hufband is ?
 His hands, methinks, are bath'd in flaughter :
Ah me ! what ghaftly fpectre's yon
 Comes in his pale fhroud, bleeding after ?

Pale as he is, here lay him, lay him down,   105
 O lay his cold head on my pillow ;
Take aff, take aff thefe bridal weids,
 And crown my careful head with willow.

Pale tho' thou art, yet beft, yet beft beluv'd,
 O could my warmth to life reftore thee !   110
Yet lye all night between my breifts,
 No youth lay ever there before thee.

Pale, pale indeed, O luvely luvely youth,
 Forgive, forgive fo foul a flaughter,
And lye all night between my breifts,   115
 No youth fhall ever lye there after.

A. Return, return, O mournful, mournful bride,
 Return and dry thy ufelefs forrow :
Thy luver heeds nought of thy fighs,
 He lyes a corps in the Braes of Yarrow.   120

XXV.

ADMIRAL HOSIER's GHOST,

———*was written by the ingenious author of* LEONIDAS, *on the taking of Porto Bello from the Spaniards by Admiral Vernon, Nov. 22. 1739.—The case of Hosier, which is here so pathetically represented, was briefly this. In April, 1726, that commander was sent with a strong fleet into the Spanish West-Indies, to block up the galleons in the Ports of that country, or should they presume to come out, to seize and carry them into England: he accordingly arrived at the Bastimentos near Porto Bello, but being restricted by his orders from obeying the dictates of his courage, lay inactive on that station until he became the jest of the Spaniards: he afterwards removed to Carthagena, and continued cruizing in these seas, till far the greater part of his men perished deplorably by the diseases of that unhealthy climate. This brave man, seeing his best officers and men thus daily swept away, his ships exposed to inevitable destruction, and himself made the sport of the enemy, is said to have died of a broken heart. See Smollet's hist.*

The following song is commonly accompanied with a Second Part, or Answer, which being of inferior merit, and apparently written by another hand, hath been rejected.

A S near Porto-Bello lying
    On the gently swelling flood,
At midnight with streamers flying
    Our triumphant navy rode ;

There

There while Vernon fate all-glorious
  From the Spaniards' late defeat:
And his crews, with fhouts victorious,
  Drank fuccefs to England's fleet:

On a fudden fhrilly founding,
  Hideous yells and fhrieks were heard;   10
Then each heart with fear confounding,
  A fad troop of ghofts appear'd,
All in dreary hammocks fhrouded,
  Which for winding-fheets they wore,
And with looks by forrow clouded   15
  Frowning on that hoftile fhore.

On them gleam'd the moon's wan luftre,
  When the fhade of Hofier brave
His pale bands was feen to mufter
  Rifing from their watry grave: 20
O'er the glimmering wave he hy'd him,
  Where the Burford * rear'd her fail,
With three thoufand ghofts befide him,
  And in groans did Vernon hail.

Heed, oh heed our fatal ftory,   25
  I am Hofier's injur'd ghoft,
You, who now have purchas'd glory,
  At this place where I was loft!

B b 4

Tho'

* *The Admiral's fhip.*

Tho' in Porto-Bello's ruin
   You now triumph free from fears,   30
When you think on our undoing,
   You will mix your joy with tears.

See thefe mournful fpectres fweeping
   Ghaftly o'er this hated wave,
Whofe wan cheeks are ftain'd with weeping; 35
   Thefe were Englifh captains brave:
Mark thofe numbers pale and horrid,
   Thofe were once my failors bold,
Lo, each hangs his drooping forehead,
   While his difmal tale is told.   40

I, by twenty fail attended,
   Did this Spanifh town affright;
Nothing then its wealth defended
   But my orders not to fight:
Oh! that in this rolling ocean   45
   I had caft them with difdain,
And obey'd my heart's warm motion
   To have quell'd the pride of Spain!

For refiftance I could fear none,
   But with twenty fhips had done   50
What thou, brave and happy Vernon,
   Haft atchiev'd with fix alone.

Then

Then the baſtimentos never
   Had our foul diſhonour ſeen,
Nor the ſea the ſad receiver   55
   Of this gallant train had been.

Thus, like thee, proud Spain diſmaying,
   And her galleons leading home,
Though condemn'd for diſobeying
   I had met a traitor's doom,   60
To have fallen, my country crying
   He has play'd an Engliſh part,
Had been better far than dying
   Of a griev'd and broken heart.

Unrepining at thy glory,   65
   Thy ſuccefsful arms we hail;
But remember our ſad ſtory,
   And let Hoſier's wrongs prevail.
Sent in this foul clime to languiſh,
   Think what thouſands fell in vain,   70
Waſted with diſeaſe and anguiſh,
   Not in glorious battle ſlain.

Hence with all my train attending
   From their oozy tombs below,
Thro' the hoary foam aſcending,   75
   Here I feed my conſtant woe:

Here

Here the baſtimentos viewing,
   We recal our ſhameful doom,
And our plaintive cries renewing,
   Wander thro' the midnight gloom.   80

O'er theſe waves for ever mourning
   Shall we roam depriv'd of reſt,
If to Britain's ſhores returning
   You neglect my juſt requeſt;
After this proud foe ſubduing,   85
   When your patriot friends you ſee,
Think on vengeance for my ruin,
   And for England ſham'd in me.

XXVI.

JEMMY DAWSON.

JAMES DAWSON *was one of the Mancheſter rebels, who was hanged, drawn, and quartered on Kennington Common in the County of Surrey, July* 30. 1746.—*This ballad is founded on a remarkable fact, which was reported to have happened at his execution. It was written by the late* WILLIAM SHENSTONE, *Eſq; ſoon after the event, and has been printed amongſt his poſthumous works,* 2 *vols.* 8vo. *It is here given from a MS copy, which contained ſome ſmall variations from that lately printed.*

COME

COME liften to my mournful tale,
   Ye tender hearts, and lovers dear;
Nor will you fcorn to heave a figh,
   Nor will you blufh to fhed a tear.

And thou, dear Kitty, peerlefs maid,   5
   Do thou a penfive ear incline;
For thou canft weep at every woe,
   And pity every plaint, but mine.

Young Dawfon was a gallant youth,
   A brighter never trod the plain;   10
And well he lov'd one charming maid,
   And dearly was he lov'd again.

One tender maid fhe lov'd him dear,
   Of gentle blood the damfel came,
And faultlefs was her beauteous form,   15
   And fpotlefs was her virgin fame.

But curfe on party's hateful ftrife,
   That led the faithful youth aftray,
The day the rebel clans appear'd:
   O had he never feen that day!   20

Their colours and their fafh he wore,
   And in the fatal drefs was found;
And now he muft that death endure,
   Which gives the brave the keeneft wound.

How

How pale was then his true love's cheek,   25
    When Jemmy's fentence reach'd her ear?
For never yet did Alpine fnows
    So pale, nor yet fo chill appear.

With faltering voice fhe weeping faid,
    Oh Dawfon, monarch of my heart,   30
Think not thy death fhall end our loves,
    For thou and I will never part.

Yet might fweet mercy find a place,
    And bring relief to Jemmy's woes,
O George, without a prayer for thee   35
    My orifons fhould never clofe.

The gracious prince that gives him life
    Would crown a never-dying flame,
And every tender babe I bore
    Should learn to lifp the giver's name.   40

But though, dear youth, thou fhouldft be dragg'd
    To yonder ignominious tree,
Thou fhalt not want a faithful friend
    To fhare thy bitter fate with thee.

O then her mourning coach was call'd,   45
    The fledge mov'd flowly on before;
Tho' borne in a triumphal car,
    She had not lov'd her favourite more.

She

She followed him, prepar'd to view
  The terrible behefts of law ;   50
And the laft fcene of Jemmy's woes
  With calm and fteadfaft eye fhe faw.

Diftorted was that blooming face,
  Which fhe had fondly lov'd fo long :
And ftifled was that tuneful breath,   55
  Which in her praife had fweetly fung :

And fever'd was that beauteous neck,
  Round which her arms had fondly clos'd :
And mangled was that beauteous breaft,
  On which her love-fick head repos'd :   60

And ravifh'd was that conftant heart,
  She did it every heart prefer ;
For tho' it could his king forget,
  'Twas true and loyal ftill to her.

Amid thofe unrelenting flames   65
  She bore this conftant heart to fee ;
But when 'twas moulder'd into duft,
  Now, now, fhe cried, I'll follow thee.

My death, my death alone can fhow
  The pure and lafting love I bore :   70
Accept, O heaven, of woes like ours,
  And let us, let us weep no more.

The

The difmal fcene was o'er and paft,
    The lover's mournful hearfe retir'd ;
The maid drew back her languid head,   75
    And fighing forth his name, expir'd.

Tho' juftice ever muft prevail,
    The tear my Kitty fheds is due ;
For feldom fhall fhe hear a tale
    So fad, fo tender, and fo true.   80

THE END OF THE THIRD BOOK.

A GLOS-

A GLOSSARY

OF THE OBSOLETE AND SCOTTISH WORDS IN

VOLUME THE SECOND.

Such words, as the reader cannot find here, he is defired to look for in the Gloffaries to the other volumes.

A Deid of nicht. s. *p.* 100. *in dead of night.*
Ahoven ous. *above us.*
Advoutry, advouterous. *adulter, adulterous.*
Aff. s. *off.*
Ahte. *ought.*
Aith. s. *cath.*
Al. *p.* 5. albeit. *although.*
Alemaigne. f. *Germany.*
Alyes. *p.* 27. *probably corrupted for* algates. *always.*
Ancient. *a flag, banner.*
Angel. *a gold coin worth* 10 *s.*
Ant. *and*
Apliht. *p.* 10. al aplyht. *quite complete.*
Argabuflie. *harquebuffe, an old-fafhioned kind of mufket.*
Afe. *as.*
Attowre. s. *out over, over and above.*

Azein, agein. *againft.*
Azont the ingle. s. *beyond the fire. The fire was in the middle of the room* *.

B.

Bairded. s. *bearded.*
Bairn. s. *child.*
Bale. *evil, mifchief, mifery.*
Balow. s. *a nurfery term, bufh! lullaby! &c.*
Ban. *curfe.*
Banning. *curfing.* (*in p.* 196. *it was* baninge *in MS.*)
Battes. *heavy fticks, clubs.*
Bayard. *a noted blind horfe in the old romances. The horfe on which the four fons of Aymon rode, is called* Bayard

* In the weft of Scotland, at this prefent time, in many cottages they pile their peats and turfs upon ftones in the middle of the room. There is a hole above the fire in the ridge of the houfe to let the fmoke out at. In fome places are cottage-houfes, from the front of which a very wide chimney projects like a bow window: the fire is in a grate like a malt-kiln grate, round which the people fit: fometimes they draw this grate into the middle of the room. L.

Mont-

Montalbon, *by Skelton in his* "Philip Sparrow." *p.* 233. Ed. 1736. 12*mo.*

Be. s. *by.* Be that. *by that time.*

Bearn, bairn. s. *child: also, human creature.*

Bed. *p.* 9. *bade.*

Bede. *p.* 17. *offer, engage.*

Befall. *p.* 71. *befallen.*

Befoir. s. *before.*

Belive. *immediately, presently.*

Ben. s. *within, the inner room. p.* 61. ‡

Ben. *p.* 11. *be, are.*

Bene. *p.* 12. *bean, an expression of contempt.*

Beoth. *be, are.*

Ber the prys. *p.* 7. *bare the prize.*

Besprent. *besprinkled.*

Bested. *p.* 271. *abode.*

Bewraies. *discovers, betrays.*

Bet. *better.* Bett. *did beat.*

Bi mi leautè. *by my loyalty, honesty.*

Birk. s. *birch-tree.*

Blent. *p.* 142. *ceased.*

Blink. s. *a glimpse of light: the sudden light of a candle seen in the night at a distance.*

Boist: boisteris. s. *boast: boasters.*

Bonny, s. *handsome, comely.*

Boote. *gain, advantage.*

Bot. s. *but. p.* 215. *besides, moreover.*

Bot. s. *without.* Bot dreid. *without dread, i. e. certainly.*

Bougils. s. *bugle horns.*

Bowne. *ready.*

Braes of Yarrow. s. *the hilly banks of the river Yarrow.*

Brade, braid. s. *broad.*

Braifly. s. *bravely.*

Braw. s. *brave.*

Brayd. s. *arose, hastened.*

Brayd attowre the bent. s. *hasted over the field.*

Brede. *breadth.* So Chauc.

Brenning drake. *p.* 19. *may perhaps be the same as a fire-drake, or fiery serpent, a meteor or fire-work so called: Here it seems to signify* "burning embers or fire-" "brands."

Brimme. *public, universally known.* A. S. bryme. *idem.*

Brok her with winne. *enjoy her with pleasure.* A. S.

Brouch. *an ornamental trinket: a stone buckle for a woman's breast. &c. Vid.* Brooches, *Gloss. vol.* 3.

Buen, bueth. *been, be, are.*

Buik. s. *book.*

Burgens. *buds, young shoots.*

Busk ye. s. *dress ye.*

But. *without.* but let. *without hindrance.*

---

‡ "But o' house" means the outer part of the house, outer-room; viz. that part of the house into which you first enter, suppose, from the street. "Ben o' house," is the inner room, or more retired part of the house.—The daughter did not lie out of doors.—The cottagers often desire their landlords to build them a But, and a Ben. L.

But

But give. s. *p. 74. but if, unless*
Bute. s. *boot, advantage, good.*
Butt. s. *out, the outer room.*

C.

Cadgily. s. *merrily, chearfully.*
Caliver, *a kind of musket.*
Can curtefye, *know, understand good manners.*
Cannes. *p. 21. wooden cups, bowls.*
Cantabanqui. Ital. *ballad-singers, singers on benches.*
Canty. s. *chearful. chatty.*
Cantles. *pieces, corners.*
Capul. *a poor horse.*
Carle. *churl, clown. It is also used in the North, for a strong hale old man.*
Carline. s. *the feminine of Carle.*
Carpe. *to speak, recite : also, to censure.*
Carping. *reciting.*
Chayme. *p. 65. Cain.*
Che. (*Somerset dialect.*) I.
Cheis. s. *chuse.*
Cheese. *p. 20. the upper part of the scutcheon in heraldry.*
Chill. (*Som. dial.*) *I will.*
Chould (*ditto.*) *I would.*
Chylded. *brought forth, was delivered.*
Clattered. *beat so as to rattle.*
Clead. s. *clad, cloath.*
Clenking. *clinking, jingling.*
Clepe. *call.*
Cohorted. *incited, exhorted.*
Cokeney. *p. 24. some dish now*

unknown. *See Chaucer. Perhaps the same as Cockeleky, a dish in the north, being a Cock boiled to rags, with roots, herbs, and barley. The Cock is taken out, and the broth so thickened with the ingredients, that a spoon will stand upright in it. It is then set upon the table.*
Cold roft. (*a phrase*) *nothing to the purpose.*
Com. *p. 8. came.*
Comen of kinde. *p. 19. come of a good breed.*
Con, can. gan. *began. Item,* Con springe (*a phrase*) *sprung.* Con fare. *went, passed.*
Coote. *p. 248. (note) coat*
Coft. *coast, side.*
Cotydyallye. *daily, every day.*
Covetife. *covetousness.*
Could bear. *a phrase for bare.* Could creip. s. *crept.* Could fay. *said.* Could weip. s. *wept.*
Could his good. *p. 253. Knew what was good for him ; Or perhaps, Could live upon his own.*
Couthen. *p. 9. knew.*
Croft. *an inclosure near a house.*
Croiz. *cross.*
Crook my knee. *p. 63. make lame my knee. They say in the north. " The horse is crookit," i. e. lame. " The horse crooks." i. e. goes lame.*
Crouneth. *p. 8. crown ye.*
Crumpling. *crooked ; or perhaps with crooked knotty horns.*

Cul. s. *cool.*

Commer. s. *gossip-friend, fr.*
　Commere, compere.

Cure. *care, heed, regard.*

D.

Dale. s. *deal. p. 74.* but give I
　dale. *unless I deal.*

Dampned. *damned.*

Dan. f. 11. *an ancient title of
　respect.*

Danke. *p. 238. Denmark, query.*

Dareh. *p. 10. perhaps for Thar,
　there.*

Darr'd. s. *bit.*

Dert the trie. s. *hit the tree.*

Daukin. *diminutive of Daniel:
　or perhaps the same as Dob-
　kin.*

Daunger hault. *coyness holdeth.*

Deare day. *charming, pleasant
　day.*

Dede is do. *p. 30. deed is done.*

Deere. *p. 347. hurt, mischief.*

Deerlye dight. *richly fitted out.*

Deimt. s. *deem'd, esteem'd.*

Deir. s. *dear. Item: hurt, trou-
　ble, disturb.*

Dele. *deal.*

Deme, deemed. *judge, doomed.*

Dent. *p. 17. a dint blow.*

Deol. *dole, grief.*

Dere, deere. *dear: also hurt.*

Derked. *darkened.*

Dern. s. *secret. p. 74.* I' dern.
　in secret.

Devyz. *devise, the act of be-
　queathing by will.*

Deze, deye. *die.*

Dight: dicht. s. *decked, dressed,*

prepared, fitted out, done,
　made.

Dyht. *p. 10. to dispose, order.*

Dill. *still, calm, mitigate.*

Dol. *see Deol. Dule.*

Doughtinesse of dent. *sturdiness
　of blows.*

Drake. *See* Brenning Drake.

Drie. s. *suffer.*

Drowe. *drew.*

Dryng. *drink.*

Dude. *did.*

Dule. s. *duel, dol. dole, grief.*

Dyce, s. *dice, chequer work.*

Dyne. s. *p. 96. dinner.*

E.

Eard. e. *earth.*

Earn. s. *to curdle, make cheese.*

Eikd. s. *p. 76. added, enlarged.*

Elvish. *peevish:—fantastical.*

Ene. s. eyn. *eyes.* Ene. s. *even.*

Ensue. *follow.*

Entendement. f. *understanding.*

Ententifly. *to the intent, pur-
　posely.*

Er, ere. *before.* Ere. *ear.*

Ettled. *aimed.*

F.

Fader: Fatheris. s. *father; fa-
　thers.*

Fair of feir. s. *of a fair and
　healthful look (Ramsay) Ra-
　ther, far off (free from) fear.*

Falsing. *dealing in falshood.*

Fannes. *p. 21. instruments for
　winnowing corn.*

Fare. *go, pass, travel.*

Fare.

Fare. *the price of a passage:* p. 84. *abusively; shot, reckoning.*

Fauzt; faucht. s. *fought. Item fight.*

Feil. s. p. 77. *have failed.*

Fell. p. 15. *furious.* p. 21. *skin.*

Fend. *defend.*

Fere. *fear. Item companion, wife.*

Ferliet. s. *wondered.*

Ferly. *wonder; also, wonderful.*

Fey. s. *predestinated to death, or some misfortune: under a fatality.*

Fie. s. *beasts, cattle.*

Firth, Frith. s. p. 76. *a wood. It. an arm of the Sea.* l. fretum.

Fit. s. *foot.*

Fitt. *division, part. See the end of this Glossary.*

Fleyke, p. 122. *a large kind of hurdle: Cows are frequently milked in hovels made of Fleyks.*

Flowan. s. *flowing*

Fond. *contrive: also, endeavour, try.*

Force. p. 140. no force. *no matter.*

Forced. *regarded, heeded.*

Forefend. *avert, hinder.*

For fought. p. 21. *through fighting: or perhaps for fought, over-fought.*

Forwatcht. *over-watched, kept awake.*

Fors. p. 12. I do no fors. *I don't care.*

Forst. p. 68. *heeded, regarded.*

Fowkin. *a cant word for a fart.*

Fox't. *drunk.*

Frae thay begin. p. 74. *from their beginning: from the time they begin.*

Freers, fryars. *friars, monks.*

Freake, freeke, freyke. *man, human creature.*

Freyke. p. 123. *humour, indulge freakishly, capriciously.*

Freyned. *asked.*

Frie. s. fre. *free.*

G.

Ga, gais. s. *go, goes.*

Gaberlunzie. gaberlunyie. s. *a wallet.*

Gaberlunzie-man. s. *a wallet-man,* i. e. *tinker, beggar, &c.*

Gadlings. *gadders, idle fellows.*

Galliard. *a sprightly kind of dance.*

Gar. s. *to make, cause, &c.*

Gayed. *made gay (their cloaths.)*

Gear, geire, geir, gair. s. *goods, effects, stuff.*

Geere will sway. p. 188. *this matter will turn out: affair terminate.*

Gederede ys host. *gathered his host.*

Get, geve. *give.*

Gest. p. 275. *act, feat, story, history. (It is* Jest *in MS.)*

Gie, gien. s. *give, given.*

Gillore. (*Irish.*) *plenty.*

Gimp, jimp. s. *neat, slender.*

Girt. s. *pierced.* Throughgirt. p. 70. *pierced through.*

Give, s. giff. p. 74. *if.*

Glaive.

Glaive. f. *sword.*
Glen. s. *a narrow valley.*
Glie. s. glee. *merriment, joy.*
Glift. s. *gliftered.*
Gode, godnefs. *good, goodnefs.*
God before. *p.* 81. i. e. *God be they guide: a form of blef-fing* *.
Good. *p.* 81. *fc. a good deal.*
Good-e'ens. *good-evenings.*
Gorget. *the drefs of the neck.*
Gowan. s. *the common yellow crowfoot, or goldcup.*
Graithed (gowden). s. *was ca-parifoned with gold.*
Gree. f. *prize, victory.*
Greened. *grew green.*
Gret. *p.* 9. *great.* p. 8. *grieved, forry.*
Grippel. *griping. tenacious, miferly.*
Grownes. grounds. *p.* 241. (*rythmi gratiâ.*(*Vid.* Sowne.)
Growte. *In Northamptonfhire, is a kind of fmall-beer, ex-tracted from the malt, after the ftrength has been drawn off. In Devon, it is a kind of fweet ale medicated with eggs, faid to be a Danifh liquor.*
Grype. *a griffin.*
Gurd. *p.* 18. *girded, lafhed, &c.*

Gybe. *jeft. joke.*
Gyles. s. *guiles.*
Gyn. *engine, contrivance.*
Gyfe, s. *guife, form, fafhion.*

H.

Ha, *have.* ha. s. *hall.*
Habbe, afe he brew. *p.* 4. *have, as he brews.*
Haggis. s. *a fhip's ftomach, ftuffed with a pudding made of mince-meat, &c.*
Hail, hale. s. *whole, altogether.*
Halt. *holdeth.*
Hame, hamward. *home, home-ward.*
Han. *have.* 3. *perf. plur.*
Hare . . fwerdes. p. 4. *their . . fwords.*
Harnifine. *harnefs, armour.*
Harrowed. *haraffed, difturbed.*
Hav. *have.*
Haves (of) *p.* 16. *effects, fub-ftance, riches.*
Hawkin. i. e. *Hobkin, diminu-tive of Robert: unlefs it may rather be thought fynonymous to Halkin, dimin. of Harry.*
He. *p.* 21. *hie, haften.*
Hede. *p.* 17. *hied.* p. 8. *he'd, he would.* p. 35. *heed.*
Hed. *head.*
Heare, here. *p.* 68. *hair.*

---

* So in Shakefpear's K. HENRY V. (A. 3. fc. 8.) the King fays,

"My army's but a weak and fickly guard;
"Yet, GOD BEFORE, tel him we will come on."

PREVENT was ufed in the fame fenfe, as Mr. Johnfon obferves, vol. 4. p. 425.

Heil. s. hele. *health.*

Hecht to lay thee law. s. *promised, engaged to lay thee low.*

Heicht. s. *height.*

Heiding-hill. s. *the 'heading [i. e. beheading] hill. The place of execution was anciently an artificial hillock.*

Helen. *heal.*

Helpeth. *help ye.*

Hem. *them.*

Henne. *hence.*

Hent, hente. *held, laid hold of: also, received.*

Her. *p.* 17. 23. 28. *their.*

Here. *p.* 5. *their. p.* 64. *hear. p.* 37. *hair.*

Herkneth. *hearken ye.*

Hert, hart; heitis. *heart; hearts.*

Hes. s. *has.*

Het. *hot.*

Hether. s. *heath, a low shrub, that grows upon the moors, &c. so luxuriantly, as to choak the grass ; to prevent which the inhabitants set whole acres of it on fire, the rapidity of which gave the poet that apt and noble simile in p.* 105.

Heuch. s. *a rock or steep hill.*

Hevede, hevedeft. *had, hadst.*

Heveriche, hevenriche. *heavenly. p.* 8.

Heyze. *high.* Heyd. s. *hied.*

Hicht, a-hicht. s. *on height.*

Hie dames to wail. s. *p.* 103. *high [or, great] ladies too wail ; Or, hasten ladies to wail, &c.*

Hight. *promised, engaged: also, named.*

Hilt. *taken off, flayed. Sax.* hyl. dan Sax.

Hinch-boys. *pages of honour, men that went on foot attending on persons in office.*

Hind. s. *behind.*

Hinny. s. *honey.*

Hit. *it.* hit be write. *p.* 8. *it be written.*

Holden. *hold.*

Holtis hair. s. *p.* 77. *hoar hills.*

Holy·roode. *holy cross.*

Honden wrynge. *hands wring.*

Hop-halt. *limping ; hopping, and halting.*

Houzle. *give the sacrament.*

Howeres, howers. *hours.*

Huerte. *heart.*

Hye, hyeft. *high, highest.*

Hynd attowre. s. *behind, over, or about.*

Hys. *his ; also, is.*

Hyt, hytt. *it.*

Hyznes. *highness.*

I.

Janglers. *talkative persons, tell-tales.*

I-lore, *lost.* I-strike. *stricken.*

I-trowe. [*I believe,*] *verily.*

I-wiffe. [*I know,*] *verily.*

Ich. *I.* Ich biqueth. *I bequeath.*

Jenkin. *diminutive of John.*

Ilk : *this ilk.* s. *this same.*

Ilke. *p.* 18. every ilke. *every one.*

Illfardly. s. *illfavour'dly, uglily.*

Inowe. *enough.*

    Into.

Into. s. *in.*

Jo. s. *sweet-heart, friend.*

loo, *p.* 20. *should probably be* loo, *i. e. haloo!*

Is. *p.* 4. *his.*

Ise. s. *I shall.*

Its neir. s. *p.* 98. *It shall ne'er.*

Jupe. s. *p.* 104. *an upper garment,* fr. *a petticoat.*

K.

Kauk. s. *chalk.*

Keipand. s. *keeping.*

Keel. s. *raddle.*

Kempes. *soldiers, warriours.*

Kend. s. *knew.*

Kene. *keen.*

Keynd. s. *p.* 73. *kind.*

Kid, kithed. *made known, shown.*

Kind, kinde. *nature. p.* 15. To carpe is our kind. *it is natural for us to talk of.*

Kirm. s. *churn.*

Kists. s. *chests.*

Kith and kin. *acquaintance and kindred.*

Kye. *kine, cows.*

Kirtel, kirtle. *petticoat.*

Kythe. *appear; also, make appear, shew, declare.*

Kythed. s. *appeared.*

L.

Lane, lain. s. *lone.* her lane, *alone, by herself.*

Layd unto her. *p.* 252. *imputed to her.*

Lasse. *less.*

Layne. *lien: also, laid.*

Leek. *p.* 69. *phrase of contempt.*

Leal, leil. s. *loyal, honest, true,* f. loyal.

Leiman, leman. *lover, mistress.*

Leir. s. lere. *learn.*

Lenger. *longer.*

Lengeth in. *p.* 272. *resideth in.*

Lett, latte. *hinder. p.* 21. *slacken, leave off.* late. *let.*

Lever. *rather.*

Leves and bowes. *leaves and boughs.*

Leuch, leugh. s. *laughed.*

Leyke, like. *play. p.* 123. 274.

Lie. s. lee. *p.* 109. *field, plain.*

Liege-men. *vassals, subjects.*

Lightly. *easily.*

Lire. *flesh, complexion.*

Lodlye. *p.* 51. *loathsome.* vid. Gloss. vol. 3. lothly.

Lo'e. s. *love.*

Loo. *haloo!*

Lore. *lesson, doctrine, learning.*

Lore. *lost.*

Lorrel. *a sorry, worthless person.*

Losel. *ditto.*

Loud and still. *phr. at all times.*

Lought; lowe. *laughed.*

Lowns. s. *p.* 100. *blazes.*

Lowte, lout. *bow, stoop.*

Lude, luid, luivt. s. *loved.*

Luiks. s. *looks.*

Lyard. *nimble. p.* 19. *probably the name of some noted horse in the old romances.*

Lys. *lies.*

Lythe. *p.* 168. *easy, gentle.*

Lyven na more. *live no more, no longer.*

Maden.

M.

Maden. *made.*

Making. *p.* 45. *sc. verses: versifying.*

Marrow. s. *equal.*

Mart. s. *marred, hurt, damaged.*

Mane, maining. s. *moan, moaning.*

Mangonel. *an engine used for discharging great stones, arrows, &c. before the invention of gunpowder.*

Margarite. *a pearl.* lat.

Maugre. *p.* 4. *spite of. p.* 74. *ill-will (I incur).*

Me. *p.* 9. *men.* Me con. *men gan.*

Me-thuncheth. *methinks.*

Meane. *moderate, middle sized.*

Meit. s. meet. *fit, proper.*

Meid. s. *p.* 103. *mood.*

Meife. s. *soften, reduce, mitigate. p.* 106.

Mell. *honey.* Lat. Mel.

Menfe the faucht. s. *measure the battel.* To give to the menfe, *is, to give above the measure.* Twelve and one to the menfe, *is common with children in their play. p.* 103.

Menzie. s. meaney. *retinue, company.*

Meffager. f. *meffenger.*

Minny. s. *mother.*

Mirke. s. *dark. black.*

Mirry. s. meri. *merry.*

Mifkaryed. *mifcarried.*

Mifter. s. *to need.*

Mo, moe. *more.*

Moiening. *by means of.* fr.

Mome. *a dull, stupid perfon.*

Mone. *moon.*

More, mure. s. *moor, heath. also marshy ground.*

Mores. *hills. p.* 4. mores ant the fenne. *q. d. hill and dale.*

Morne. *p.* 74. to morn. *tomorrow: in the morning.*

Mornyng. *p.* 44. *mourning.*

Mote I thee, *might I thrive.*

Mowe. *may,* mou. s. *mouth.*

Muchele boft. *mickle boaft, great boaft.*

Mude. s. *mood.*

Mulne. *mill.*

Murne, murnt, murning. s. *mourn, mourned, mourning.*

Myzt; myzty. *might; mighty.*

N.

Natheles. *neverthelefs.*

Neat. *oxen, cows, large cattle.*

Neatherd. *a keeper of cattle.*

Neatreffe. *a female ditto.*

Neir. s. ner, nere. *ne'er, never.*

Nere. *p.* 272. *ne were; were it not for.*

Neft; nyeft. *next; neareft.*

Noble. *a gold coin in value 20 groats, or 6 s. 8 d.*

Nom. *p.* 8. took. Nome. *name.*

Non. *none.* None. *noon.*

Nonce. *purpofe.* for the nonce. *for the occafion.*

Norfe. s. *Norway.*

Nou. *now.*

Nout: nocht. s. *nought: also, not.* Nout. *p.* 10. *feems for* 'ne mought.'

   Nowght.

Nowght. *nought.*
Nowls. *noddles, heads.*

O.

Ocht. s. *ought.*
Oferlyng. *superior, paramount. opposed to* underling. *p. 4.*
On. *p. 44. one, an.*
On-lofte. *p. 18. aloft.*
Or. *ere, before.*
Orisons. s. *prayers.* f. oraisons.
Ou, oure. *p. 7. you, your. ibid. our.*
Out alas! *exclamation of grief.*
Out owre. s. *out over.*
Owene: awen, ain. s. *own.*
Owre. s. *over.*

P.

Pardè, perdie. *verily.* f. par dieu.
Pauky. s. *shrewd, cunning, sly.*
Pece. *p. 16. piece. sc. of cannon.*
Pees, pese. *peace.*
Pele. *a baker's peel.*
Pentarchye of tenses. *five tenses.*
Perchmine. f. *parchment.*
Per fay. s. *verily.* f. par foy.
Perkin. *diminutive of Peter.*
Persit. s. pearced. *pierced.*
Petye. *pity.*
Peyn. *pain.*
Pibrochs. s. *Highland war-tunes.*
Pilch. *p. 20. a vestment made of skins.*
Playand. s. *playing.*

Plett. s. *platted.*
Plowmell. *p. 21. a small wooden hammer occasionally fixed to the plow, still used in the North: in the midland counties in its stead is used a Plow-Hatchet.*
Poll-cat. *a cant word for a whore.*
Powdered. *p. 25. a term in Heraldry, for sprinkled over.*
Powlls. *polls, heads.*
Prest. f. *ready.*
Priefe. *p. 85. prove.*
Priving. s. *proving, tasting.*
Prove. *p. 41. proof.*
Prude. *p. 4. pride.*
Puing. s. *pulling.*
Purchesed. *p. 12. procured.*
Purvayed. *provided.*

Q.

Quat. s. *quitted.*
Quaint. *p. 226. cunning. p. 243. nice. p.　.fantastical.*
Quel. *p. 123. cruel. murderous.*
Quillets. *quibbles.* l. quidlibet.
Quyle. s. *while.*
Quyt. s. *quite.*
Qwyknit. s. *quickened, restored to life.*

R.

Rae. *a roe.*
Raik. s. *to go apace.* Raik on raw. *go fast in a row.*
Ranted. s. *p. 6. were merry. vid. Gl. to Gent. Skepherd.*
Raught. *reached, gained, obtained.*

Rea'me,

Rea'me. *realm.*
Rede, redde. *p.* 9. *read.*
Rede, read. *p.* 30. *advise, advice.*
Redreſſe. *p.* 70. *care, labour.*
Reſe, reve, reeve. *bailiff.*
Reid. s. *advise.*
Remeid. s. *remedy.*
Reſcous. *reſcues.*
Reve. *p.* 19. *bereave, deprive.*
Revers. s. *robbers, pirates, rovers.*
Rew. s. *take pity.*
Rin. s. *run.*
Riſe. *p.* 274. *ſhoot, buſh, ſhrub.*
Rive. *p.* 277. *rife, abounding.*
Rood loft, *the place in the church where the images were ſet up.*
Rudd. *ruddineſs; complexion.*
Rude. s. rood. *croſs.*
Ruell-bones. *p.* 18. *perhaps bones diverſly coloured.* f. riolè.—*or perhaps, ſmall bonerings, from the* Fr. rouelle, *a ſmall ring or hoop.* Cotgrav. Diction.
Rugged. *p.* 23. *pulled with violence.*
Ruſhy. s. *p.* 77. *ſhould be* raſhy gair, *ruſhy ſtuff; ground covered with ruſhes.*
Ruthe. *p.* 41. *pity. p.* 203. *woe.*
Rywe. *rue.*

S.

Saif. s. *ſave.* Savely. *ſafely.*
Saiſede. *ſeized.*
Say. *p.* 27. *aſſay, attempt.*
Scant. *ſcarce.*

Schaw. s. *ſhow.*
Schene. s. *ſheen: ſhining;* It. *brightneſs.*
Schiples. s. *ſhipleſs.*
Scho. s. *ſhe.*
Schuke. s. *ſhook.*
Sclat. *ſlate: p.* 12. *little table-book of ſlates to write upon.*
Scot. *tax, revenue. p.* 5. *a year's tax of the kingdom.*
Se; ſene; ſeying. *ſee; ſeen; ſeeing.*
See, ſees. s. *ſea, ſeas.*
Sely, ſeely. *ſilly, ſimple.*
Selven. *ſelf.*
Selver, ſiller. s. *ſilver.*
Sen. s. *ſince.*
Senvy. *muſtard-ſeed.* f. ſenvie.
Seve. *p.* 277. *ſeven.*
Sey yow. *p.* 11. *ſay to, tell you.*
Seyd. s. *ſaw.*
Shave, *p.* 68. *be ſhave. been ſhaven.*
Sheeve. *a great ſlice or luncheon of bread. p.* 242.
Shirt of male. *coat of mail.*
Sho. s. *ſhe.*
Shope. *p.* 269. *betook me, ſhaped my courſe,*
Shorte. s. *ſhorten.*
Shrive. *confeſs. Item, bear confeſſion.*
Shynand. s. *ſhining.*
Shurting. *recreation, diverſion, paſtime.* Vid. Gaw. Dougl. Gloſſ.
Shunted. *ſhunned.*
Sich, ſic. s. *ſuch.* Sich. s. *ſigh.*
Side. s. *long.*
Sindle. s. *ſeldom.*
Sitteth. *p.* 3. *ſit ye.*

Six-mens fong. *p.* 24. *a fong for fix voices* *.

Skaith, fcath. *harm, mifchief.*

Skalk. *p.* 122. *perhaps from the Germ. Schalck. malicious, perverfe. (Sic Dan. Skalck. Nequitia, malicia, &c. Sheringham de Angl. Orig. p.* 318.)—*Or perhaps from the Germ. Schalchen. to fquint. Hence our Northern word,* Skelly, *to fquint.*

Skinker. *one that ferves drink.*

Skomfit. *difcomfit.*

Skot. *fhot, reckoning.*

Slattered. *flit, broke into fplinters.*

Sle, flea, fley, flo. *flay.*

Slee. s. *fly.*

Sonde. *a prefent.*

Sone. *foon. p.* 9. fon. *p.* . *fun.*

Sonn. *p.* 274. *fun.*

Soth, footh. *truth ; alfo, true.*

Soothly. *truly.*

Sould. s. *fhould.*

Souling, *p.* 242. *victualling.* Sowle is *ftill ufed in the north for any thing eaten with*

bread. A. S. Suple. Suple. *Joh.* 21. 5.

Sowne. *found. p.* 46. (*rhythmi gr.*)

Spec. fpak, fpack. s. *fpake.*

Speere. *p.* 133.

Speered, fparred. *i. e. faftened, fhut. So Bale in his 2d Pt. of Actes of Eng. Votaryes. fo.* " 38. *The Dore therof oft* " *tymes opened and* fpeared *agayne* ||."

Speir. s. fpeer. *fpear.*

Speir. s. (*p.* 61.) fpeer. fpeare. *afk, inquire. Vid. Gloff. vol.* 3.

Spence. *expence.*

Spindles and whorles, *the inftruments ufed for fpinning in Scotland, in the fame manner as fpinning-wheels here* †.

Spilt. s. *fpoilt.*

Spole. *fhoulder.* f. efpaule. *p.* 190. *it feems to mean* " *arm pit.*"

Stalwart. *ftout.*

Startopes. *bufkins worn by ruftics, laced down before.*

Stead, ftede. *place.*

---

* So Shakefpear ufes, THREE MAN SONG-MEN, in his Winter's Tale. A. 3. fc. 3. to denote men that could fing catches compofed for three voices. Of thefe fort are Weelkes's Madrigals mentioned above in p. 158. So again Shakefp. has THREE-MAN BEETLE, i. e. a beetle or rammer worked by three men. 2 Hen. 4. A. 1 fc. 3.

|| So again in an old " Treatyfe agaynft Peftilence, &c. 4to. En-" prynted by Wynkyn de Worde:" we are exhorted to "SPERE " [i. e. fhut, or bar] the wyndowes ayenft the fouth." fol. 5.

† THE ROCK, SPINDLES, and WHORLES are very much ufed in Scotland and the northern parts of Northumberland at this time. The thread for Shoe-makers, and even fome Linen-webs, and all the twine of which the Tweed Salmon-nets are made, are fpun upon SPINDLES. They are faid to make a more even and fmooth thread than Spinning-wheels.

Steir. s. *ftir.*
Stel. *fteel.* fteilly. s. *fteely.*
Stound. *time.* a ftound, *awhile.*
Stown. s. *ftolen.*
Stoup of weir. s. *pillar of war.*
Strike, *p. 12. ftricken.*
Stra, ftrae. s. *ftraw.*
Suthe, fwith. *foon. quickly.*
Suore bi ys chyn. *fworn by his chin.*
Sware. *fwearing, oath.*
Swa, fa. *fo.*
Swarvde, fwarved. *climbed.*
Swaird. *the grafly furface of the ground.*
Swearde, fwerd. *fword.*
Swevens. *dreams.*
Swipping. *p. 21. ftriking faft* ; [*Cimb.* fuipan, *cito agere, or rather ' fcourging,' from volvere, raptare.*] *Scot.* Sweap. *to fcourge. Vid. Gloff. to Gaw. Douglas.*
Swipples, *p. 21.* A Swipple *is that ftaff of the flail, with which the corn is beaten out. vulg.* a Supple : (*called in the midland counties a* Swind gell; *where the other part is termed the* Hand-ftaff.)
Swinkers. *labourers.*
Swyving. *whoring.*
Syke. *figh.*
Syn. *fince.* Syne. s. *then.*
Syfhemell. *p. 65. Ifhmael.*
Syth. *fince.*

T.

Take *p. 25. taken.*
Taken. s. *p. 106. token, fign.*
Targe. *target, fhield.*
Te. *to.* te make, *p. 3. to make.*
Te he! *interjection of laughing.*
Tent. s. *heed.*
Terry. *diminutive of* Thierry. *Theodoricus, Didericus. Lat.*
Tha. *p. 22. them.* Thah. *though.*
Thare, theire, ther, thore. *there.*
The. *thee.*
The God. *p. 24. feems contracted for* The he. *i. e. high God.*
The, thee. *thrive.* So mote I thee. *p. 86. So may I thrive* *.
Thii. *p. 277. they.*
Thi fone. *p. 9. thy fon.*
Thilke. *this.*
Thir. s. *this, thefe.*
Thir towmonds. s. *thefe twelve months.*
Tho. *then. p. 32. thofe.*
Thole; tholed. *fuffer; fuffered.*
Thouft. *thou fhalt, or fhouldeft.*
Thrang. s. *throng: clofe.*
Thrawis. s. *throes.*
Thritti thoufent. *thirty thoufand.*
Thrie. s. thre. *three.*
Thrif. *thrive.*
Thruch, throuch. s. *through.*
Thud. *p. 106. noife of a fall.*
Tibbe. *In Scotland* Tibbe *is the diminutive of* Ifabel.
Tild down. *p. 275. pitched. qu.*
Till. s. *to. p. 16. when. query.*

---

* So in Chaucer, paffim.   See the Sompnour's Tale.
   " What fhulde I fay, God let him never THE."

Urry's Ed. p. 94. ver. 943.
Timkin.

Timkin. *diminutive of Timothy.*
Tint. s. *loft.*
Too fall. s. *p. 372. twilight.*
Traiterye. *treafon.*
Trie. s. tre. *tree.*
Trichard. *treacherous.* f. tricheur.
Trichen. *trick, deceive.*
Trough, trouth. *troth.*
Trow. *think, believe, truft.*
Trumped. *p. 16. boafted, told bragging lies, lying ftories. So in the North they fay,* " *That's a* trump," *i. e. a lie.* " *She goes about* trumping :*"; i. e. telling lies.*
Trumps made of tree. *p. 21. perhaps* " *wooden trumpets:*" *mufical inftruments fit enough for a mock turnament.*
Tuke gude keip. s. *kept a clofe eye upon her.*
Turnes a crab. *fc. at the fire: roafts a crab.*
Twirtle twift. s. *p. 99. thoroughly twifted:* " *twifted,*" *or* " *twirled twift.*" f. tortillè.

V.

Vair. *Somerfetfh. Dialect. fair.*
Valziant. s. *valiant.*
Vazem. *Som. perhaps, faith.*
Uch. *each.*
Vive. *p. 277. Som. five.*
Uncertain. s. *p. 73. doubtful. or perhaps,* on (*i. e.* in) *certain, for certain.*
Unmufit. s. *undifturbed, unconfounded. perh.* unmuvit.
Unfonfie. s. *unlucky, unfortunate.*

Vriers. *Som. friers. p. 288. (it is* Vicars *in* PCC.)
Uthers. s. *others.*

W.

Wa. s. *p. 95. way. p. 213. wall.*
Wad. s. *would.*
Waine. *waggon.*
Wallowit. s. *faded, withered.*
Wame. s. *womb.*
Wan neir. s. *drew near.*
Wanrufe. s. *uneafy.*
War ant wys. *p. 8. wary and wife.*
Ward. s. *watch, fentinel.*
Warke. s. *work.*
Warld. s. *world.*
Waryd. s. *accurfed.*
Wate. s. *weete, wete, wit, witte, wot, wote, wotte. know.*
Weale, weel, weil, wele. s. *well.*
Wearifou'. *wearifome, tirefome, difturbing.*
Wee. s. *little.*
Weet. s. *wet.*
Weid. s. wede, weed. *cloaths, clothing.*
We it. s. *p. 98. with it.*
Weldynge. *ruling.*
Weind. s. wende, went, weende. *weened, thought.*
Wene; weneft. *ween; weeneft.*
Wend, wenden. *go*
Wende. *went. p. 9.* wendeth. *goeth.*
Wer. *were.*
Wereth. *p. 272. defendeth.*
Werre: weir. s. *war.* Waris. s. *war's.*

Wes.

Wes. *was.*

Weftlin. s. *weftern.*

Whang. s. *a large flice.*

Wheder. *p.* 30. *whither.*

Whelyng. *wheeling.*

Whig. *four whey, or butter-milk.*

Whorles. *See* Spindles.

Wildings. *wild apples.*

Winfome. s. *agreeable, engaging.*

Win. s. *get, gain.*

Wirke wiflier. *work more wifely.*

Wifpes and kixes. *p.* 23. *whifpes and kexes.*

Wifs; wift. *know; knew.*

Withouten. *without.*

Wobfter. s. webfter. *weaver.*

Wode-ward. *p.* 37. *towards the wood.*

Woe worth. *woe be to* [*thee.*]

Won. *wont, ufage.*

Wonders. *wonderous.*

Wood. *mad, furious.*

Wote, wot. *know.* I wote. *verily.*

Worfhipfully frended. *p.* 253. *of worfhipful friends.*

Wow. *An exclamation of wonder.*

Wreake. *purfue revengefully.*

Wreuch. s. *wretchednefs.*

Wrouzt. *wrought.*

Wynnen. *win, gain.*

Wiffe. *p.* 8. *direct, govern, take care of.* A. S. pɪʃʃɪan:

Y.

Y. *I.* Y fynge. *I fing.*

Yae. s. *each.*

Y beare; Y-boren. *beare; borne.* fo Y-founde. *found.* Y-mad. *made.* Y-wonne. *won.*

Y-core. *chofen.*

Y-wis. [*I know*] *verily.*

Y-zote. *molten. melted.*

Yalping. s. *yelping.*

Ycholde, yef. *I fhould, if.*

Yearded, *p.* 276. *buried.*

Yede, yede. *went.*

Yfere. *together.*

Yf. *if.*

Yll. *ill.*

Yn. *houfe, home.*

Ys. *p.* 10. *is. p.* 4. *his. p.* 8. *in his.*

Z.

Zacring bell. *Som.* Sacring bell. *a little bell rung to give notice of the elevation of the hoft.* (*It is* Zeering *in* PCC. *p.* 290.)

Zee: zeene. *Som. fee: feen.*

Zef. ycf. *if.*

Zeirs. s. *years.*

Zeme. *take care of.* A. S. ʒeman.

Zent. *through.* A. S. ʒeonð.

Zeftrene. s. *yefter-e'en.*

Zit. s. zct. *yet.*

Zoud. s. *you'd, you would.*

Zule. s. yule. *chriftmas.*

Zung. s. *young.*

POST-SCRIPT.

Since page 166 *was printed off, reafons have offered, which lead us to think that the word* FIT, *originally fignified* " *a po-*
" *etic*

" etic *ſtrain, verſe,*" or " *poem*"; *for in theſe ſenſes it is
uſed by the Anglo-Saxon writers. Thus K. Ælfred in his Bo-
etius, having given a verſion of lib. 3. metr. 5. adds,* Daþe
piþbom tha thaꞃ ꝼitte aꞃunᵹen hæꝼðe, *p. 65. i e. "When
" wiſdom had ſung theſe* [FITTS] *verſes." And in the Proem.
to the ſame book* Foꞃ on ꝼitte, " *Put into* [FITT] *verſe."
So in Cedmon, p. 45.* Feonð cn ꝼitte, *ſeems to mean* " *com-
" poſed a ſong,*" or " *poem.*"

    Spenſer has uſed the ſame word to denote " *a ſtrain of
" muſic:*" *ſee his poem, intitled* COLLIN *Clout's come home again,
where he ſays,* The Shepherd of the ocean [*Sir Walt. Raleigh*]

    Provoked me to play ſome pleaſant FIT,
    And when he heard the muſic which I made
    He found himſelf full greatlye pleas'd at it, &c.

    *From being applied to Muſic, this word was eaſily transferred
to Dancing ; thus in the old play of* Luſty Juventus *(ſee p. 112.)
Juventus ſays,*

    By the maſſe I would fayne go daunce a FITTE.

*And from being uſed as a Part or Diviſion in a Ballad, Poem, &c.
it is applied by* BALE *to a Section or Chapter in a Book, (though I
believe in a ſenſe of ridicule or ſarcaſm) for thus he intitles two
Chapters of his* English Dctarpes, *pt. 2d. viz. ——fol. 49.
" The fyrſt* FYTT *of Anſelme with Kynge Wyllyam Rufus."
——fol. 50. " An other* FYTT *of Anſelme with kynge
Wyllyam Rufus."

    *Other inſtances may be ſeen in the foregoing volume. See
the Gloſſary.*

THE END OE THE GLOSSARY.

✳✳✳✳✳✳✳✳✳✳✳✳✳✳✳✳✳✳✳✳

ADDITIONAL NOTES.

Page 1.

The ſatirical Ballad on RICHARD OF ALMAIGNE *will
riſe in its importance with the curious Reader, when he finds,
that it is even believed to have occaſioned a Law in our Sta-
tute Book, viz.* " *Againſt ſlanderous reports or tales, to
" cauſe diſcord betwixt king and people.*" (WESTM.
PRIMER, c. 34. anno 3. Edw. I.) *And that it had this
effect*

effeEl is the opinion of an eminent Lawyer : See "Observa-
" tions upon the Statutes, chiefly the more Ancient, &c."
4to. 2d Edit. 1766. p. 71.

*If the very learned and ingenious Writer would examine
the Original MS. in the Harl. ColleElion, whence our Ballad was extraEled, he would, I believe, find other fatirical
and defamatory rhymes of the fame age, that might have had
their fhare in contributing to this firft Law againft Libels.*

Page 26.

The Poem of the NUTBROWNE MAYD *was firft revived
in "The Mufes Mercury for June, 1707." 4to. being pre-
faced with a little "Effay on the old Englifh Poets and Po-
" etry:" in which this poem is concluded to be " near 300
": years old," upon reafons, which, though they appear in-
conclufive to us now, were fufficient to determine Prior; who
there firft met with it. However, this opinion had the ap-
probation of the learned* WANLEY, *an excellent judge of ancient books.*

Page 28.

*An ingenious friend propofes to read the firft lines thus, as
a latinifm :*

> Be it right or wrong, 'tis men among,
>
> On women to complayne.

Page 78.

To fhew what conftant tribute was paid to OUR LADY
OF WALSINGHAM, *I fhall give a few extraEls from the
ancient MS. of the " Eftablifhment of the Houfehold of
"* HENRY V. *Earl of Northumberland." (Vid. Vol. I.
p. 367.)*

SeEl. XLIV.

ITEM, *My Lorde ufith yerly to fende afore Michaelmas for
his Lordfhip's Offerynge to our Lady of Walfyngeham.
iiij d.*

ITEM, *My Lorde ufith and accuftomyth to fend yerely for the
upholdynge of the Light of Wax which his Lordfhip fynd-
eth birnyng yerly befor our Lady of Walfyngham, contain-
ynge vj lb. of Wax in it, after vj d. ob. for the fyndynge
of every lb. redy wrought by a covenant maid with the*
Chanon

Chanon by great, for the hole yere, for the findinge of the said Lyght byrnynge, vj s. viij d.

ITEM, *My Lord ufeth and accuftometh to fend yerely to the Chanen that kepith the Light before our Lady of Walfyngham, for his reward for the hole yere, for kepynge of the faid Light, lyghtynge of it at all fervice tymes dayly thorowt the yere, xij d.*

ITEM, *My Lord ufeth and accuftomyth yerely to fende to the Preft that kepith the Light, lyghtynge of it at all ffervice tymes daily thorout the yere, iij s. iiij d.*

Page 256.

An original Picture of JANE SHORE *almoft naked is preferved in the Provoft's Lodgings at Eton ; and another picture of her is in the Provoft's Lodge at King's College Cambridge : to both which foundations fhe is fuppofed to have done friendly offices with* EDWARD IV. *A fmall quarto Mezzotinto Print was taken frcm the former of thefe by* J. FABER.

THE END OF VOLUME THE SECOND.

The Notes referred to Vol. 2.d pag. 24
Deo gratias Anglia redde pro victoria
Owr Kynge went forth to Normandy with grace and
myzt of Chyvalry, the God for hym wrouzt marvelufly
Wherefore Englonde may call and cry, Deo Gratias.
Deo Gratias, Anglia redde pro Victoria.
To come in at the End of Vol. 2.d